D0513909

The Reunion

The Reunion

SUE WALKER

MICHAEL JOSEPH
an imprint of
PENGUIN BOOKS

CORK CITY LIBRARY
4533757
CORK CITY LIBRARY
WITHDRAWN FROM STOCK

MICHAEL JOSEPH

Published by the Penguin Group
Penguin Books Ltd, 80 Strand, London WC2R 0RL, England
Penguin Group (USA) Inc., 375 Hudson Street, New York, New York 10014, USA
Penguin Books Australia Ltd, 250 Camberwell Road,
Camberwell, Victoria 3124, Australia
Penguin Books Canada Ltd, 10 Alcorn Avenue, Toronto, Ontario, Canada M4V 3B2
Penguin Books India (P) Ltd, 11 Community Centre,
Panchsheel Park, New Delhi – 110 017, India
Penguin Group (NZ), cnr Airborne and Rosedale Roads,
Albany, Auckland 1310, New Zealand
Penguin Books (South Africa) (Pty) Ltd, 24 Sturdee Avenue,
Rosebank 2196, South Africa

Penguin Books Ltd, Registered Offices: 80 Strand, London WC2R 0RL, England

TORY TOP ROAD BRANCH

www.penguin.com

First published 2004
1

Copyright © Sue Walker, 2004

The moral right of the author has been asserted

This is a work of fiction, and all the characters
and events described are entirely the product of
the author's imagination. Any resemblance to
persons living or dead is coincidental

All rights reserved
Without limiting the rights under copyright
reserved above, no part of this publication may be
reproduced, stored in or introduced into a retrieval system,
or transmitted, in any form or by any means (electronic, mechanical,
photocopying, recording or otherwise), without the prior
written permission of both the copyright owner and
the above publisher of this book

Set in 13.5/16pt Monotype Garamond
Typeset by Palimpsest Book Production Limited, Polmont, Stirlingshire
Printed in Great Britain by Clays Ltd, St Ives plc

A CIP catalogue record for this book is available from the British Library

HBK ISBN 0–718–14714–6
PBK ISBN 0–718–14775–8

For

Thomas Rennie, Christina Josephine
and Annie

Acknowledgements

The following people made this book possible. My greatest thanks to them all.

Nicolette Bolgar, for her immense intelligence and constant support; Ruthie Smith, for the enlightenment; Lisanne Radice, for all her nurturing – for ever appreciated; Teresa Chris, for her wisdom, judgement and calming influence on me – just the agent I need; Beverley Cousins, for such clever, sympathetic and sensitive editing.

November 8th

Greetings!

Well, here we are again. One more bloody year on. What can I say? Hey, life's great, man! And all that. No doubt our little missives are all crossing in the post.

Yes, I'm still living where I was last year. Yes, with the same person. And yes, in the same job. Thank you very much. Does my life sound boring? 'Tis not, though. Never boring.

I do sometimes wish one of you'd give me some interesting, nay, startling, news one time. But, on second thoughts, that's not such a great idea. Then we'd be forced to meet. No, not such a great idea. We'd be forced to talk. And you know about what! Then some of us would get depressed, some hysterical, some, oh, well, it's not going to happen.

One day we really should wean ourselves off this dreary routine.

Adieu, until (I suppose) next year.

A
XX

Nov. 8

Dear All

I have nothing exceptional to report. I trust you do not either. After all this time I've a good idea what to expect of you. In this – how can I put it – in this strange 'family' of ours there's not much that can't be accurately guessed at, even though we don't actually see each other.

My life is much the same – undeservedly joyful, at times. But when I forget myself and allow myself to be too happy, I just think of this day when I have to write to you and why I have to do so.

That sobers me up.

All contact details remain the same.

Goodbye, for now.

S

All same. You know where I am.

D.

8/11

Greetings!

Well, for someone normally of such few words, you've certainly excelled yourself.

What a bloody turn-up for the books! I shouldn't have tempted fate last year. Saying I wanted something exciting to happen. But we're doing the right thing. Got to keep control, keep things in perspective. There's one hell of a lot at stake.

Remember what I said – let's keep a lid on it.

A

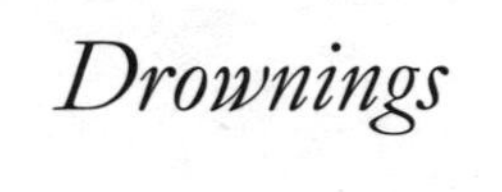

2004 and 1977

File note from Dr Adrian Laurie, Consultant and Medical Director, APU
14 July 1977
RE: Patient, Innes Haldane (d.o.b. 3.4.62)

Yesterday the staff admitted new patient Innes Haldane. At today's case conference all the staff were relieved to see that she had been admitted, since the patient's mother was resisting right up until the last minute, despite our best efforts with Mrs Haldane during family sessions.

Innes is exhibiting classic signs of depression, coupled with the acting out that led to her admission: extensive truancy, shoplifting, a highly disruptive manner when she has attended school and sexually self-destructive behaviour. The final episode, when she picked up two strangers on a bus and took them home to have sex in her parents' bed, was probably the deciding factor for her resistant mother.

It is, of course, Mrs Haldane's own mental problems and her domineering behaviour over her daughter and husband, combined with her jealousy of her own daughter, which have led to Innes's condition. Again, it has classic elements. A loving father who clearly adores his daughter but who is also a weak husband. A frustrated wife and mother who feels life has not dealt her a good hand. Innes's blossoming into an attractive adolescent woman has been the final straw. Mrs Haldane's attempts to undermine her daughter throughout childhood have had their effect on the patient's self-esteem, to a considerable degree. Innes's acting out is a way of saying that she cannot and will not take any more. The sexual episode is undoubtedly her – albeit unconsciously – saying, 'I'm here, I'm young, I'm sexually attractive. You, Mother, are ageing. I have my life ahead of me and a father who loves me. Compete with that!'

I suggest initial work on talking about her relationship with both parents, and work on building up her self-esteem. The latter may be problematic, given the ego issues of some of the other patients in the Unit at present. However, I believe this challenge for Innes will be one that will help her.

That apart, we know Innes to be a tremendously likeable young woman, and that she will probably be popular with many in the Unit, staff and patients alike. I note from the Night Staff Log that last night she spent her first evening with Isabella. If that develops into a friendship, then I think it will be beneficial for both patients. However, Innes's admission and popularity will not go down well with some patients. All staff need to be on the lookout for any friction.

Copy to: Daily Nursing Log
Copy to: patient file, I. Haldane

I

Half seven. Early home for a Monday night. Keys and shopping were dumped at the kitchen door, and she wandered over to open the living-room windows. Let some of the precious, hint-of-spring air from Primrose Hill wash into her home. The answering machine blinked once. She hit the message button and turned up the volume, heading back to the kitchen for a well-earned, ice-cold glass of white from the fridge.

The hesitant, familiarly deep voice boomed throughout the house.

'Innes? Innes, it's Isabella. Isabella Velasco. I . . . I . . . Don't ask me how I got hold of you . . . I . . . we live quite close, you know, would you believe? God, you sound just the same. Just the same! Look . . . please don't be angry . . . I need to talk to you . . . see you. Can you call me as soon as you can? My number is seven fi—'

She smashed a bleeding hand on the stop button and threw herself into the window seat, blind now to the beauty of the evening outside, watching instead the blood dripping its way on to the rug beneath her. She staggered to the kitchen for a tea-towel to act as bandage, ignoring the broken glass on the floor, the overturned wine bottle by the sink.

Back at the phone, she put trembling fingers to the message button. And played the tape back. Six times.

To make sure that she wasn't in a nightmare.

2

She'd always preferred the suited, smart, self-contained, corporate cases to the individual, down-at-heel, outwardly sad ones. Like the man sitting before her this morning.

'So, if you'll just hand over all your credit cards, the cheque books and your debit card, and sign here.'

She watched as he took his great rough paw – a builder's hand and irreplaceable tool of his (former) trade – and signed his financial affairs over to her, for at least the next three years. Not for the first time did she scent the mixture of a Dutch-courage-stiff-whisky and too many cigarettes for eleven in the morning. The man's hand shook slightly. It had to be the worst day of his life. And she wasn't enjoying it much either. It had been some time since she'd had to deal with a 'client' face to face. She eschewed, indeed forbade, in her hearing her junior staff using their preferred 'punter' for those sorry souls who found themselves in this building. It was disrespectful, she told them.

She decided to close the interview with this particular sorry soul. 'All you need to know about your bankruptcy and dealings with the Official Receiver's Office is in this leaflet. We have a lot of staff long-term sick at present, so I'll be handling your affairs for the time being, although that will change when my assistants get back. Any queries in the next few weeks, my number's written at the top there. Next to my name. Innes Haldane.'

She gathered papers and stood up, directing the man

from the interview room towards the lifts, nodding at his mumbled thanks.

Back in the privacy of her office, she poured herself a cup of over-stewed coffee, allowing herself a couple of minutes to glance at the mayhem that was mid-morning Bloomsbury, five floors below. Buses and cars nose-to-tail. Tourist hordes heading for the nearby British Museum, in much the same formation as the traffic. The never-ending hum of pneumatic drills, buzzing up their vibrations from street level. Perfect! She had the beginnings of a killer headache already.

She turned away and sat down heavily at her desk, surveying the lists of tasks for the overworked day ahead. She ran tentative fingertips over the two-week-old scar on her left hand. The wine glass had cut deep. Funny she'd never felt any pain until hours later.

She shoved the memory from her mind – she was good at that – and turned to her diary. She was beginning to heartily despise this job. True, it wasn't to be sniffed at. Dealing with the debtors of the world in the ordered, usually distant way that was incumbent on a senior member of the Official Receiver's Office was structured, clinical and, at her level, very well paid. Though the junior-staff absences meant she'd be having quite a few face-to-face encounters with clients. Too close for comfort perhaps. During this past year or so she'd already forced herself to admit that she was becoming less and less able to cope with the 'people side' of her job. And that was maybe why she enjoyed her seniority. The more paper-pushing and remote decision-making, the better.

Three hours later she allowed herself a stroll to the British Museum courtyard, taking one of the last vacant benches, warmed by the sunshine. She pulled her sushi box and a copy of the latest *Ham & High* from her bag, checking her watch and generously allotting herself precisely twenty-five minutes for lunch.

A scan-read of the local paper was all she usually made time for, but today, for some unknown reason, she found herself lingering on the news section. On the third reading, she was sure there was no mistake.

Swimming-pool death – inquest date set

The body of a woman was found floating in the swimming pool of the Belsize Sports Centre last Tuesday evening. Staff were alerted by a young mother who had attended her regular women-only swimming lessons.

The dead woman has been named as 42-year-old Isabella Velasco, of 12 Belsize Park Square, a Scots-born, leading dental surgeon working in various practices across London and a university departmental head. Both her wrists had been cut and there had been a significant loss of blood. The pool is now closed for the foreseeable future, as police and sports centre staff examine the area.

A police spokeswoman refused to confirm reports of suicide but stated: 'We are not looking for anyone else in relation to this incident.'

An inquest is to be held at St Pancras Coroner's Court on Friday morning.

She was having trouble keeping her breath even and steady, and stood up, only to teeter back down, her head light and dizzy. She pulled out her mobile, punching in the preprogrammed number for her secretary.

'Emma? I . . . I'm going home. I feel . . . I think I'm coming down with something. Cancel all the meetings, will you? No! No calls whatsoever at home for the rest of today.'

She moved cautiously through the museum crowds and headed for the taxi rank by the front gates. Within a minute she was cocooned in a cab and heading home.

To think about the woman she had never called back.

3

Any journey past the arches at King's Cross was guaranteed to be dreary. Those sinister, darkened caverns, immortalized in countless grim TV thrillers were, in reality, as uninviting as they were portrayed. No matter the weather. And today? On foot in London, March rain? Her mood was well in keeping with this gloomy morning of damp chill. She'd had two days to think about coming here since reading the devastating news in the paper. Forty-eight anxiety-filled hours of little sleep and much obsessive thinking. And still she wasn't sure that she had made the right decision.

But curiosity had won out over nervousness and, as quietly as possible, she took a seat at the back of the room, praying no one would take any notice of her late arrival or wonder at her reasons for being there. Verdict: suicide. The usual suspects had given evidence, including an insufferably patronizing GP who had recently prescribed 'the deceased' (never 'my patient') paroxetine for panic attacks – 'It's a member of the Prozac family, you know. Very effective usually' – and suggested that 'the deceased' take time off. A suggestion apparently ignored, since subsequent evidence had made it clear that Isabella Velasco had continued her various practices and lecturing in dentistry. That had made Innes smile. Like herself, Isabella had grown into a workaholic.

She gazed at the sombre suits and faces of the assembled court, her mind numbly trying to take in the proceedings. Forcing herself to concentrate, she momentarily tuned in as an eager young police detective addressed the coroner, referring frequently to his notes. 'Yes, sir, I made extensive inquiries into Professor Velasco's background, both personal and professional . . .' She tuned out again, sparing herself the catalogue of people spoken to, lectures given by Isabella in the past months, etc.

She looked down into her lap, where both hands lay palm upwards. The wine-glass scar was fading now. She dug a fingernail in it. Testing. Just a bit of tenderness left. She moved her fingers to her wrist. Her pulse was racing. Like she'd run a mile. She did her breathing exercises. Breathe in and hold for eight seconds. Exhale for eight seconds. She'd learned how to do this unobtrusively, anywhere. On the bus, in the theatre, even in meetings. Short of openly using a paper bag to breathe and re-breathe into – something she found herself occasionally having to do in the women's toilets at work – she knew that this was the most publicly acceptable way to avoid her hyperventilation panic attacks.

Isabella had suffered from panic attacks too. That haughty, uncaring GP had said as much. Isabella had been on medication for them. As had she herself. Funny, sad parallels. Not surprising, given their shared paths in early life . . . *no*! She'd tried not to think about all that for so long. For much longer than the few weeks since Isabella's wretched phone call. Jesus! How that had just about killed her! She'd never believed it possible. That voice from the past. Or had she really been so surprised? Somehow, hadn't it been just the dreaded outcome that she'd expected? How can you hide from the past for ever? Particularly *that* sort of a past. You can try to hide it from yourself. From your loved ones – if you have any, that is. Then what d'you get? Panic attacks. Failed marriage. Failed relationships, full stop. Failed life. No, that was going too far. Much too far.

She'd lied to her therapist for the best part of the last eight years about *that* part of her past. But it was adolescence, wasn't it? It was a normal, 'off the rails' episode, surely? Why hide it? No, that was self-deluding nonsense. Lies. All lies. To herself. To everyone. And here she was. Sitting in shame. And in fear, fear of discovery. At the inquest into the death of someone she'd . . . she'd what? Shared so much with? Been true friends with? Been ill with . . . She nudged the memory away, drifting back into the young detective's orbit. What he was saying took her breath away.

'Yes indeed, sir. We did find some initially interesting evidence in Professor Velasco's personal life. A new acquaintance. A Mr Danny Rintoul, of Calanais on the Isle of Lewis, in the Western Isles of Scotland. I gleaned evidence from her credit-card records that she had paid numerous and lengthy visits to the Hebrides since last year. I found details of Mr Rintoul in Professor Velasco's address book and in her personal organizer, and there was evidence of frequent telephone communication between them. However, it seems that Mr Rintoul died, drowned off the coast of the Scottish mainland at the beginning of the year. Although an inquest delivered a suicide verdict in his case, I have no reason to believe the events are linked. I also have no evidence to offer as to how Professor Velasco and Mr Rintoul met or knew each other, since no friends or acquaintances of Mr Rintoul ever recall meeting Professor Velasco . . .'

She thanked the gods that she'd chosen to sit on an aisle seat at the back of the court – an unconsciously executed precaution against exactly this sort of eventuality. She followed the ladies' signs and fell into the last cubicle. Although all three were vacant, she always preferred the added security of the end one. Fumbling in her jacket pocket, she pulled out the paper bag, scrunched the neck of it between hooked thumb and index finger, and blew into it. In and out. In and out. Five times. Then relax and repeat. She leaned back, the cistern ice-cold on her neck.

Danny! Danny Rintoul! Isabella had been meeting him! But the witness said he was a 'new' acquaintance. How was that? Had Isabella tried to get in touch with him recently too? Why? Why Danny? Dear Danny Rintoul. Dead too. Drowned too.

She closed her eyes, the paper bag crumpled, forgotten, in her lap, and pictured again that first day. The place lay beyond the comfortable suburbs of the western outskirts of Edinburgh. It was a Sunday. July, 1977. In the middle of that feverishly hot summer . . .

4

The sun was in the way. So searing and bright. She couldn't make it out. Were there four of them? Or five? More perhaps. It was one of those moments that she knew she'd remember for ever. Maybe even a burnt-in memory that would come out in dementia.

She often thought about those special moments, moments that had their own inexplicable atmosphere. Sometimes very pedestrian ones. But ones that would haunt her in later life. Did everyone think that way? About when they were senile? Or just her? Was it a mark of the black depression that had enveloped her for longer than she could remember? Fifteen years old and worrying about when she would be like the sad geriatrics in the ward down the road in the main hospital. It wasn't normal, by any stretch. She'd visited those same geriatrics as part of a school project one term. It was either voluntary service at the Edinburgh Royal Western Hospital (for mad folk – though that wasn't part of its grand title, rather it was known as just the 'Royal Western') or it was duty on the detested hockey field. Hardly a difficult decision.

It had been a wrong one, though. She could still feel the shock of that first-day glimpse. Dozens of wizened, cadaverous bodies, huddled inside themselves. Sitting in rows of high-backed, hellishly uncomfortable-looking chairs. Each summoning up seemingly irrelevant recollections from aeons ago. Another life ago. Youth. She had that now. Physically. Though she felt as ancient inside as the old dears down the road.

She wandered closer. Yes, she could make it out now. The group. Four only. One on a swing. Penduluming away. She was a girl with deep-red hennaed hair, which in the sunlight gave the unsettling impression that her entire head had been dipped in blood.

'Go and say hello. I'll be with you in a minute.' That's what Anna had said ten minutes ago. She'd introduced herself as the Nursing Sister. A tall, good-looking woman who sported hippy clothes. In fact, it looked like a bloody sarong or sari she'd been wearing, though the woman was white-skinned. Oh, well, they were very casual in the Unit. And unusual. 'Unorthodox' was the word Innes remembered her sour-faced mother had pompously used, as she and her husband had reluctantly followed their daughter into those tense, family-therapy meetings. Innes flinched at the memory and dawdled down the path. No way was she going to introduce herself to this lot.

'Innes! Hold on!'

Sister Anna. Cockburn. Yes, that was her last name. She remembered first meeting her weeks ago after family therapy, when still an out-patient. Sister Anna looked out of breath, obviously having sprinted, sari raised above her knees, down the garden of this rather impressive and imposing stone mansion. Well, it would have been lovely if it hadn't been converted into a loony bin. The Adolescent Psychiatric Unit. 'The Unit' for short. In reality she knew exactly what she was entering. A loony bin for teenagers. The Bin. Not 'The Unit'.

Anna had caught up with her. 'Sorry!' Innes put on her best scowl as Anna rattled out her explanation, clearly anxious to get on with things. 'I got tied up on the phone. Let's go and meet some of the others. They've all been home for the weekend. Let's see how they are.'

She deliberately trailed behind the nurse as they approached the cosy little bunch, now huddled around the henna-haired beauty who was lounging on the swing, ensuring that the breeze was making the most of the well-cared-for tresses. Anna beamed a huge smile to them all. 'Hi. Welcome back. Good weekend?'

'Yeah, but Sunday nights are shite!'

Anna waved a dismissive hand. 'Ah, you always moan about Sundays, Danny! Anyway, that's Danny, moaning and smoking himself stupid as ever. Say hello, Dan.'

'Hiya.' The boy Danny spat the greeting out at her with a glob of sodden tobacco from his roll-up, and shrugged into the ancient washed-out Ziggy Stardust t-shirt that hung loosely over his skinny shoulders, slyly giving her a thorough sexual assessment. Innes wondered what his think-bubble about her was. 'Wow! Not bad. Not bad at all . . .' Or, 'Crap, ugly cow . . .' She knew how she saw herself and tried to turn away from him, already feeling a failure.

Sister Anna was keeping the fixed smile, continuing in what Innes thought, and surely everyone else did, was an irritatingly chummy way. 'Listen, this is Innes Haldane. Remember we told you she was joining us?'

'I didn't know we were expecting Nessie! What kind of fuckin' name is *Innes*? It's a fuckin' last name! I had an old boot of a geography teacher called Mrs Innes! Fuckin' hell!' The henna-haired witch smirked at her own witticism and stared. Innes thought it best to look away, making an instant decision on the red-head. She was going to be big trouble. Best give her a wide berth. For now.

Sister Anna was obviously trying to ignore the comment too and the hennaed bitch's sour look. 'Very funny, Caroline. So, that's Caroline, Carrie to us all and th—'

'Only to my friends!' the Carrie girl snapped back.

Innes watched as Anna again ignored Caroline's second plea for attention. 'Yes, okay, it's Carrie to us all, actually. Then . . . here's Simon trying to be invisible as usual.'

Simon had the appearance of a twelve-year-old. Facially at least. But he had to be six foot two if he was an inch. He wore the uniform of the exclusive Edinburgh public school Fettes College, had an unfashionably short haircut and ugly National Health specs. He said nothing but hung his head even lower than it had been, trying to find cover behind Caroline. Innes offered him a curt nod, which he mirrored back to her, his eyes friendly, if timid, behind the thick lenses.

Anna was ploughing on, patience nearly gone. 'And last but not least, this is Lydia.'

'Hello, Innes. Pretty name. Just like you. *You're* very pretty.' Innes felt the redness of her cheeks. *No, I'm not pretty. I feel horrible! Always horrible.* She tried a smile at the Lydia girl. Her voice was posh English. But gentle. She was a big girl. In fact she was huge. Grossly overweight, the rings of fat around her belly and breasts straining at the cotton of her pink summer dress. But she had a friendly face, and, although triple-chinned, she suited the ruby-coloured, velvet Alice-band round her blonde bob. She seemed the friendliest of the lot. And quite normal, if a little on the gushing side. Maybe she was just a bit childish?

She answered the girl with a shy smile and conventional reply. 'Eh, hello, Lydia. Pleased to meet you. Eh . . . actually my name's Gaelic. Gaelic for "island".'

Lydia appeared impressed. 'Ah ha! Well, welcome to the Unit.'

The Caroline girl had started swinging again, flinging her head back until the red hair brushed the grass beneath her as she shouted to the summer sky. 'Yeah. Welcome to the Unit! Welcome to the Mad Hoooooose!'

'There's still a couple of others you need to meet. They'll be at tea now. Come on in.'

She followed Sister Anna. The last two hours had been spent unpacking and in the Nurses' Office, being talked through the routine of the place. Five o'clock was tea-time. She was led into an industrially equipped kitchen with a remarkably bright black-and-white checked lino floor, covered with tables and chairs arranged into a messy circle. The place was scruffy but clean.

She allowed the nurse to direct her to a chair opposite a sulky Caroline, who was playing with a disgustingly greasy fried egg.

There were two new people at the table. Anna made a vague pointing gesture. 'Innes, this is Alex.'

Innes nodded, careful not to stare for too long. Alex was a girl. A girl with a skinhead haircut and revolting, livid, purple scars criss-crossing her forearms. Forearms that she seemed to be brazenly showing off by wearing a skimpy red vest. Her prominent breasts were the only real give-away that she was a girl.

Innes tried a half-smile at Alex, who ignored her and looked over towards Anna. 'What the fuck's this swill meant to be? It tastes like fucking shite! And where the fuck is Sarah?'

There was no attempt to explain to Innes who Sarah was. She watched as Alex dropped a blob of tomato ketchup on to her pile of chips. 'Well?'

Sister Anna seemed calm and sipped at a cup of black tea. 'Sarah's not back on duty till tomorrow.'

Alex dropped her knife. 'How the fuck's that allowed, then?'

Anna gently laid down her cup. 'Cut it out, Alex. It's been arranged. That's all.'

'Like fuck it has!' The crack, as her plate of food hit the far wall, made most of them jump.

Innes flinched and then watched nervously as the other new person scraped her chair back and walked a few steps towards her, hand held out in apparent greeting. 'Don't mind Alex. She always acts up and forgets her manners when someone new arrives. Can't stand anyone else getting the attention. I'm Isabella, by the way. Abby for short. Abby Velasco. Welcome, if that's the right expression, to the Unit.'

5

Swimming-pool death. Verdict: suicide

An inquest returned a verdict of suicide on 42-year-old leading dental surgeon Isabella Velasco, whose body was found floating in the swimming pool of the Belsize Sports Centre ten days ago.

Police say they are satisfied that Professor Velasco slashed her own wrists after a swimming lesson, while suffering from depression. Pathologist's evidence gave the actual cause of death as drowning. Professor Velasco inhaled water after she lost consciousness as a result of catastrophic blood loss and the ingestion of a cocktail of drugs, believed to have been taken from her place of work. Professor Velasco's GP told the inquest that her patient had been suffering from bouts of depression and panic attacks during recent weeks but could not say what factors in Professor Velasco's life had led to this.

Outside the inquest, shocked friends and colleagues said they were 'astonished at such an action' and found it 'incredible' that Professor Velasco would kill herself.

A spokeswoman for the British Dental Association said, 'Professor Velasco was a highly regarded dental surgeon. Isabella will be much missed by her colleagues, students and patients.'

She tossed the newspaper aside, wondering which friends and colleagues had been talking to the press. She hadn't waited around long enough to see or be seen by them. Instead, she'd scuttled away through the rain, feeling troubled and guilty, back home to a bottle or more of wine and greeting the next day's heavy workload with a hangover. That couldn't go on.

'Ms Haldane? Your booth's ready. Number fourteen. Just up those steps. On the left.'

'Oh, right. Thank you.' She waved a vague thanks to the librarian and headed for the microfilm machine.

She'd been at it for half an hour and was practically cross-eyed from rolling through dozens of pages of microfilm. But thanked her lucky stars anyway. The British Newspaper Library had only just received the most recent filmed copies of the *Western Isles Courier*, an online version still being an age away.

The detective at the inquest hadn't pinned down the exact date of Danny Rintoul's death. But 'beginning of the year' was more than enough. She focused weary eyes back on the slowly moving film, running at a slightly skewed angle through the huge screen. And almost missed it.

Man falls to death from island ferry

A man fell to his death yesterday morning from the Stornoway to Ullapool Ferry. He has been named as Danny Rintoul, a 41-year-old crofter from Calanais, Isle of Lewis.

Mr Rintoul's body was found floating about eight miles from the port of Ullapool. A spokesman for Alba Line Ferries said that a full inquiry was being undertaken by their senior staff, police and Health and Safety officials.

Mr Rintoul was unmarried. Originally from Edinburgh, he had kept a croft on the islands for the last fifteen years.

A fatal accident inquiry into the death will be opened in Stornoway next week.

She spooled through the next week's edition. Again the name jumped out at her.

Suicide verdict in ferry-death case

The fatal accident inquiry into Calanais man Danny Rintoul, 41, has returned a verdict of suicide. Mr Rintoul, an unmarried crofter, fell to his death from the Stornoway to Ullapool Ferry last week.

The inquiry heard that Mr Rintoul was largely a loner but on good terms with his neighbours, Mr and Mrs Mackay, of nearby Borasdale Cottage. Mr Murdo Mackay, 53, said that Mr Rintoul had mentioned on several occasions that he could not swim and had a fear of water. The topic had arisen a number of times when Mr Mackay was discussing his daughter, a lifeguard at Stornoway swimming pool.

Mr Rintoul's GP, Dr Archie Fairbairn, said that Mr Rintoul had consulted him during the previous weeks for complaints that he diagnosed as 'psychosomatic'. He considered Mr Rintoul to be suffering from depression and anxiety, but his patient had denied that he had any particular problems.

On the day of his death, the ferry sailing was extremely busy, with both car and foot passengers, and Alba Line staff have no recollection of seeing Mr Rintoul at any stage of his journey. Accidental death was ruled out after the inquest heard evidence that, despite the rough seas on the day in question, the protective barriers on all the public decks were well above recommended safety standards and therefore an accidental fall overboard would not have been possible.

Mr Rintoul leaves no immediate family.

She spooled back and forth again, but that was all she found, except for a brief death notice about the funeral, which was obviously being organized by the neighbouring Mackays. They must have liked him. Who'd have thought he'd end up a crofter in the back of beyond? Yet it wasn't really that surprising. Danny had always been a loner. Despite the sex crime that had brought him into the Unit, he'd been essentially gentle. At moments, heart-rendingly thoughtful. Like the time he'd bought Lydia a new hamster, after the previous one had died because her unthinking parents had gone on holiday without feeding it. He'd kept that one quiet. But Lydia, who had had a mad crush on him right after the incident, had told Innes all about the drama during one of their oft-shared, long, insomniac nights.

And when you heard what his upbringing had been like! Those interminable group sessions with Laurie – Dr Adrian Laurie – Medical Director and 'God' of the Unit staff. Laurie would mercilessly prise the sordid, horrifying details of Danny's abusive childhood out of him. Each strand of personal information ripped red-hot from his being, like a ritual evisceration. How she'd hated Dr Laurie during that period. Later in her treatment she understood why he'd done it. Why he did it to everyone.

She hauled herself back into the present, printing off the two news stories from the microfilm machine, and sat back, her sigh of exhaustion and puzzlement causing irritation from a fellow library user. She fingered the warm photocopies. The similarities. Suicide. Depression. Anxiety. Water. Drownings. And Danny and Isabella had been meeting. Secretly it seemed, since the policeman at the inquest had said no one who knew Danny had ever heard of her. Or vice versa.

But something must have been going on between the two. In some ways it didn't surprise her that they were in touch. But it was the deaths of them *both* that was the shocker. *Both* depressive suicides. In many ways they seemed oddly meant for each other. It had been obvious – to her at least – from the start . . .

6

Anna was 'facilitating'. Innes said the word to herself again. All these technical, psychiatric terms that she was trying to get used to. Anna was being assisted by Sarah. Sarah Melville had been introduced to her as a 'student', but Isabella had told her that she was a fully qualified nurse who wanted to specialize in psychiatric work, especially with adolescents. Innes wondered why. Sarah was attractive in a kind of fit, athletic, games-teacher way. But quite mannish in her bearing. She always wore faded, tight jeans and embroidered cheesecloth shirts. She seemed nice enough. But Innes didn't trust her. Didn't trust anyone right now, come to that. Except maybe Isabella, or 'Abby', as she said she wanted to be called. Yes, Abby seemed fine.

She let herself listen in to the rest of the room. Anna had exchanged her sari for old jeans, tit-hugging t-shirt and a baggy open shirt. Her usual sexually provocative choice for Thursday morning psychodrama, Danny had unsubtly informed Innes in a stage whisper, a rude expression all over his face. She noticed more than *his* pair of eyes sneak a glance at Anna's tall but shapely figure, as she joined them all on the floor. The heat of the already blistering morning had layered a distinctly sensual sheen of light sweat on Anna's face and upper lip, sticking straggling hair to her forehead, which she periodically brushed away with a delicate dab of the wrist. A straw poll would always have put Anna on top of the Unit's sex-symbol league. And she seemed to know it. Though Sarah probably wasn't far behind with some. Boys and girls alike. But Innes thought she'd better keep those observations to herself.

They'd finished the initial relaxation. Innes thought about these opening exercises. They involved lying supine, stretching all muscles from head to toe and lifting as many parts of the body off the floor as possible. The entire performance took about twenty minutes, with Anna, the 'facilitator', wandering around in bare, scarlet-toenail-polished feet, talking gently to each patient. Helping lower a leg here, raising an arm there. Tactile. Calm. Reassuring. Above all, safe. Or that's what it was meant to be. Innes felt both nervous and under scrutiny, since it was her first session.

She felt, rather than saw, Anna scan the darkened room. Innes half opened an eye and took in the view. The floor was littered with patients lying on their backs, spread indiscriminately, like corpses on a battlefield, each one with their eyes shut. Each one with their own thoughts. Some public. Mostly private.

Without a word, Innes heard Anna part the curtains of the large ground-floor lounge, intentionally breaking the impression of serenity that had descended upon the room. It was time to let the light in again. Both physical and emotional.

Anna's voice was raised now. To rouse them. 'Right! In a circle please. Cross-legged. All of you know this one. Except Innes. So if one of you would care to step in, we can show her how it's done.' She cast a slow eye round the ring of faces, stopping at one. 'How 'bout you, Alex? You've not been in the circle for ages.'

Alex scratched her shaven temple, the raised scars on her forearm picked out brightly by the sunlight flowing in from the garden. 'I fucking knew you were going to ask me. Fucking knew it! Well, you can just go and fuck yourself! *I'm not going in.*'

CORK CITY LIBRARY

Innes felt the tension in the room. Everyone was staring at Anna to see how she was going to deal with it. But Anna looked relaxed and quietly continued to observe Alex.

Innes thought about the Alex girl. She had forgotten to drop her *g*'s. Alexandra Baxendale's deep voice always reverted back to her class roots when used in anger. She'd noticed that already. She'd heard that Alex had been a public-school girl who'd joined a skinhead gang when she was thirteen. 'Rebel', 'hard-nut' behaviour. Apparently planned to 'fuck up' Mummy and Daddy's image. Until the gang she'd run with beat the living shit out of an 83-year-old pensioner. The rest of the gang, several years older, got borstal. Alex got the Unit. Lucky, when you considered what else the gang had done. And got away with. Everyone knew she'd had a lucky escape from justice by being in the Unit. Well, the patients did anyway. Abby had told her that she thought the staff didn't know about a lot of the stuff Alex had done when in her 'psycho' mode. You had to watch yourself with that Alex. Never turn your back. Keep out of her way when she was in a mood.

Anna was trying again. 'C'mon, Alex. Everyone else has done the circle recently.'

Alex ignored her. But Innes saw Carrie make a move with her fist. A kind of punching the air. 'Yeah! Get on with it, Alex.' She had caught Alex's eye, and was trying one of her stare-outs.

'Go fuck yourself, Carrie! *You* go in the poncy circle!'

Innes shifted uneasily. Each muscle and sinew in Alex's arms, legs and jaw was tensed. She looked fit to pounce. On Carrie. On anyone. And she was infecting the room with an air of tension. An *excited* air of tension. It felt like some of them at least were enjoying this display. Innes slid her eyes away from Alex. Abby had warned her. Don't get caught in Alex's firing line. Lay low if she's making a scene.

And just as she thought Alex was going to start in on her, Innes watched with relief as Carrie stole the limelight, sneering and spitting her insults into Alex's rigid face.

'I did it last month. Prissy Miss Alexandra's scaaared!'

Danny winked at Innes, as if to say 'watch this'. He reached out a thin but muscled arm and lightly touched Alex. 'It's okay. Ignore her.' He looked like he was readying himself for a Carrie assault.

But Isabella cut in. 'I'll do it. I know I did it just after I came in a couple of months ago. But I don't mind doing it again.'

Silence. All round. Innes watched Anna. She seemed to be letting it ride. Student Sarah was trying to do the same, but she had an almost feverish look in her eyes. Christ! The student really seemed to be getting off on all the gameplay. The nod from Anna to Sarah was subtle, but Innes noticed it. Probably some of the others did too. The student took over. 'Why d'you want to do it again, Abby?'

Abby had uncrossed her legs and pointed her red-socked toes into the centre of the group. 'Well, everyone else has done it more times than me. Except Innes, of course. But she's new, and if Alex doesn't want to do it, I will.'

Anna flashed her eyes at Sarah and retook control. 'Okay, Abby. Come into the centre. All stand.'

Innes took a quick inventory of what everyone else was doing. She stood up and shuffled inwards like the others, until the circle was quite tight around Abby. She watched in wonder as Sarah walked into the centre and put her hands very gently, almost intimately, on Abby's waist, to steady her, and then tied a soft black silk scarf round her eyes. Then, equally gently, she handed Abby to Anna, who, in turn, handed her on to the next in the circle. The pace of Abby's rolling round the circle increased, but she remained limp and trusting in all their arms. She watched as first Danny, followed by Alex, drew Abby's slim body a little too tightly towards their own, before reluctantly, it seemed, passing her on.

The 'game' appeared to end by an invisible sign, as the rolling slowed and Anna held Abby and helped her to the ground, still in the centre of the circle. Anna indicated with both palms downwards that they should all lower themselves on to the floor. Just like the minister in church, telling his congregation to sit after a hymn. Sarah slid forward and gently removed Abby's blindfold, smoothing her dark, slightly tangled hair.

Innes felt a nudge from her neighbour. It was Simon. Sporting a mischievous smirk. 'It's called a trust game. For obvious reasons. It's meant to help us gel as a group, and dilute or defuse any tensions or unsaid hostilities. Get it? It's kindergarten stuff?'

Carrie barked out a laugh. 'Hah! That's right, Si! Simon's going to knock spots off all you psycho staff one day when *he* becomes a psychiatrist. Yeah, Heid Doctor Si!'

Innes watched a slightly dizzy Abby get herself comfortable, still in the circle. Anna reached out and touched her shoulder. 'How d'you feel, Abby?'

Abby smiled. Mainly in Danny's direction. 'I feel . . . *relieved.* Relieved that no one dropped me!'

Danny wasn't taking his eyes off Abby. He laughed with her relief. 'Nae chance of that, Abby! I'd kill anyone who let you down.'

From the look in his eyes, Innes had no doubt that he meant it.

7

It was unusually clear and fine for an early spring day. She'd remained at the stern until the white shoreside buildings of Ullapool were nothing more than toy houses. She couldn't calculate eight miles out, the place where it had happened. But she stood fascinated, watching the frothing waters, where engine and propellers cut the ferry's wake through the glassy waters of the Minch.

'Don't be so glum. It's a rare treat this, you know.'

Innes turned round and saw an elderly man smiling at her. 'I'm sorry?'

His face had the brick-red of the outdoor life. 'The Minch, lass. Like a mill pond. An uncommon thing. Bonnie, though, eh?'

She returned his smile. 'Yes. It's beautiful. But I was thinking about the man who killed himself. Off the ferry? Earlier this year?'

The ruddy face immediately lost its happy look. 'Oh, aye. That man Rintoul. From Calanais way. Poor laddie.'

'You knew him?'

'Nah. But knew *of* him. All islanders know a bit aboot everyone else, lass. He wis a crofter. Had just a small place. Enjoyed a drink. His neighbours liked him. He got oot on to the starboard side up towards the prow and just jumped in. I mean, no one actually saw it. It was far too cold for anyone tae be on deck, and the ferry deck's a noisy place. The wind, the splash o' the waves as they attack the hull. Nae chance o' hearing the poor man falling in. It'd be just one more splash among the many. And I reckon ye'd have tae jump in tae get over the safety rail, see? Anyway, he didnae get pulled under luckily or they'd have had an awfy job identifyin' him.'

'How d'you know all this?'

'Ach, ma second cousin's a deck-hand on this route. Wisnae actually on the boat at the time, but he heard all aboot it. Anyway, that's all in the past. Enjoy the trip, lass. Bye-bye.' He lifted a callused hand in farewell and disappeared down steps into the ship's body.

She sat on one of the empty rows of weather-worn plastic seats facing the stern, wondering at the beauty of the view as the boat cut its way past a host of little islands whose names she neither knew nor would have been able to pronounce – Gaelic, in spite of her first name, was as alien to her as Gujarati.

She zipped up her waterproof tightly around her neck and closed her eyes. The gentle hum of the engines and roll of the swell brought a much needed calm to her. Worry about work had been gnawing away at her. She'd had to lie. Lie to her doctor about some 'virus' that she thought she had. The doctor had found her glands down, her temperature normal, but her pulse high, and had given her the benefit of the doubt. She had a week off. After that, blood tests would be needed and 'further investigations'. She had slunk guiltily from the surgery, convinced that she had been rumbled and would be struck off the doctor's list. An hour later, she had been rational again and realized that an overworked GP just wanted to get her out of his way as soon as possible. If a sick-note would do it, then fine.

Her boss had been exasperated at losing yet another staff member to sickness. But she did consent to Innes being left undisturbed during her convalescence. Meaning no awkward calls at home to discover if she were really in her sick bed. 'Just get better. We'll need you back a.s.a.p. Understand?' More guilt. She'd cancelled a couple of dinner invitations, theatre visits, telling any friends who might be tempted to 'drop round' to cheer her up that she might go somewhere quiet for a few days. And that was that. Deceit accomplished.

As she'd hurriedly and guiltily arranged her double flight from London to Glasgow, and then on to Inverness, she'd been clear in her own mind about her need to get away. Away from London. Away from her normal life. To do *this*! It was only after she'd picked up her hire car at Inverness Airport and was making the drive through the breathtaking scenery on the road to the Ullapool Ferry port, eagles occasionally swooping across her vision, that she began to have doubts.

She viewed her actions with mild astonishment. She'd actually allowed herself to do something on impulse. Of course she'd thought through what she was doing with this Isabella/Danny thing. She could legitimately say to herself that she wanted to know what drove Isabella to kill herself. She could also part-convince herself that she had failed Abby by not returning her call. Though she had had every right and reason not to. A ghost from the past, a past that she, and she presumed many of the others, wanted to bury and let alone. Psychiatric histories had a way of following you in life. Blight and stigma. That hers was an adolescent episode had always seemed to her different. More normal. More expected. She knew it was a self-justifying excuse. The fact was, she had been mentally ill when she was fifteen (and probably for a while before that, if not after) and was put into a psychiatric hospital. No matter how you dressed it up – 'experimental unit', 'innovative programme', the need for everyone inside to have an IQ of above 145, since the brighter the patient the better the response to the treatment, so the story went – it was still a place of sickness. She'd got better, though, hadn't she? And largely forgotten about it all. She'd forged a career . . . been married . . . and divorced . . . had friends . . . sometimes lovers . . . had money . . . had travelled . . . had a life . . . *Stop it!*

She opened her eyes and squinted against the breaking sunshine. She stretched her legs and wandered over to the rail, watching the propellers frothing away. There was no getting away from it. What she was doing was outlandish. So out of character as to be borderline mad. She had left the security of her own home and ordered life to go haring off after what? What did she really care about Isabella? It was sad, shocking even, that the woman had killed herself. And Danny too. But, if she was to be truthful, Abby's and Danny's deaths frightened her because of the vulnerabilities they opened up for herself. Had the Unit somehow preprogrammed both these people to take their own lives in middle age? Or was some weird *folie à deux*, formed all those years ago, now coming to its natural and fatal conclusion? Or was it some form of the then 'new', 'innovative' therapy that had suddenly backfired on these patients in later life? It was terrifying.

She smiled at the thought of Danny. Danny Rintoul. He'd been one of her favourite people in the Unit. A rapist and sexual offender at fourteen. Shocking. To some. But somehow one of the best things about the Unit was that nothing shocked. Everyone saw beyond their own and others' crimes and misdemeanours. Some, invariably soon after admission, had tried to ignore or deny them. But not for long. That was strictly not allowed. Face up and move on, was.

In retrospect, she'd felt rather a lot for Danny. He'd been nothing to write home about. No oil painting. But . . . he'd had a gentleness. He really *did* rehabilitate. And they shared something too. Something that bound them. Something that had led them both to the Unit. Mothers. Special kinds of mothers. Both had been matriarchs. Ruling their dictatorships over frightened only children and weak husbands and unprotecting fathers. The hours she'd spent with him in the record room, playing ghastly 45s of awful seventies glam-rock bands. And those endless evenings down by the swing, talking about their families. His – abusive, dirt-poor. Hers – cold, comfortably-off-thank-you-very-much. Damaging, destructive upbringings, both.

His parents must be dead. The newspaper said he left no family. Dead parents. Like hers. She wondered how he'd felt about that. No parents any more. Triumphant? Relieved? Or, like her, confused and guilty. Matters unresolved.

She wrenched herself out of that line of thought and looked up, seeing again the scenery surrounding her. Danny. Dear, dead Danny. Danny who'd fallen in love. Not with her. But with Isabella. Beautiful, dead Abby.

Abby had been quick to befriend her. Bringing an intimacy and sense of . . . well, almost a sense of security to her first few weeks and days in the Unit . . .

8

'They encourage you to tell everyone *why* you're in. Or why you *think* you're in here. At the end of treatment, they can sometimes be pretty different things. You may come in to confront one thing but then that might open up a can of worms. So I'm told!'

Innes felt almost happy. The sunset was amazing and the night fragrant from the garden. And warm. So warm. She watched Abby rocking gently on the swing, head thrust backwards, taking in the last golden rays. They were getting on fine. And she was settling in. She was steering clear of a few of them. But Abby seemed normal. Though Dr Laurie had made her cry in group therapy that morning. It was horrible. He'd made Abby tell about when her father had locked her in the cellar for a whole day and night. Just because she'd only got a B+ in her history essay. *He* was the one that should have been locked up. But, as Laurie had acknowledged, Abby's dad, a respectable lawyer, had put it all down to his 'disturbed daughter's fantasy'. And her mother? Abby had said that she was a vain, egotistical and fragile woman.

The session had been an eye-opener in more ways than one for Innes. It had been horrible to hear about Abby's bastard of a father, and even more upsetting to see her cry. But Laurie had cooled things down. Started discussing Abby's 'behavioural reactions to what was going on at home', as he put it in his plummy, rather intimidating voice. And Abby's 'behavioural reactions', which Laurie catalogued, had surprised Innes. Looking at her, Abby seemed the most normal, grown-up and pretty, even beautiful girl. But she had a history of running away from home and, like Innes, of not attending school. And she had another, quite peculiar problem but one Dr Laurie said was 'not at all uncommon and very often caused by extreme stress and/or emotional chaos in one's life. Those who suffer from obsessional or compulsive behaviour are seeking control in their lives, lives that they feel are spinning wildly out of control.' He'd talked about Abby being 'over-ordered', of doing things like having to have everything on her bedside table set out exactly in the way she wished, of having to wash and wash her hands. And, when she couldn't do all this organizing behaviour, Laurie said she'd sometimes get frustrated, become withdrawn and generally find the world a very frightening place. Laurie had said most of Abby's 'over-ordered behaviour' happened inside her own head, in her thoughts. Only a bit of it could be seen through her outward behaviour. Somehow, Innes couldn't believe any of this about Abby, but, after she'd stopped crying in the session, Abby seemed quite happy to admit to it. In the few hours since then, Innes had been unable to resist staring at Abby's bedside table, and she saw how unusually neat and carefully positioned everything was.

And even as she watched Abby on the swing in the fading light of the sunset, Innes noticed her fiddling about, checking things in her pocket, ensuring all was as it should be. Nevertheless, she seemed light-hearted now and happy to go through everyone else's reasons for being in. She scraped her feet to stop the swing, chuckling at a private thought.

'Right, you have to be either "highly disturbed and behaviourally out of control", as Dr Laurie would put it. Or just highly disturbed but severely enough to make you unmanageable by parents or others, such as schoolteachers, etc. We certainly all fall into those categories, one way or another!' She paused and smiled at Innes. 'Okay, so Lydia's got an "eating disorder". That's pretty obvious. She's an odd case, actually. She was a late child. Her mum's really old. And she's an only child and very, very spoiled. Laurie's had a few sessions digging things out of Lydia. Looks as if the dad got really jealous after the arrival of Lydia and has been a shit to both mother and child ever since. Lydia's got lots of problems. Manic-depression and her eating thing are just two of them. She's also got a background in arson. Tried, not very successfully, to burn down the family home. And started a fire at her old school. That's all stopped now. But it's a very dodgy side to Lydia. Also, she's very nosy. So look out!

'Now . . . as for Simon. Si's textbook, if you ask me. He was a twin. I say *was* because the twin died. Apparently his cow of a mother blamed Si for the other one's death and has been a complete bitch to him ever since. His dad's away all the time. He's a famous physicist or something. Always abroad. Anyway, Si feels like he's worthless. Shame, 'cos he's really clever. And he notices *everything*! He knows loads of things that the staff don't want us to know. He's even seen the nursing reports. Maybe he'll do that again soon. If we're nice to him. Actually, he's a bit frightened of us girls. Especially Carrie and Alex. He'll be a hopeless husband one day!'

Innes laughed. The first real laugh since she'd come here. 'And what about Carrie? What was all that stuff about drugs this morning?'

'Oh, Anna was just checking Carrie hadn't picked up any dope when she went up to the shops. She's done it before. Carrie's mum's a druggie. There's no dad. Meaning she doesn't know who her dad is. Neither does her mum. Carrie's been beaten up by her mum and her mum's various boyfriends since the year dot. And I think she's been . . . you know?'

Innes raised an eyebrow. 'Been mucked around with?'

She watched Abby give an embarrassed shrug in reply. 'Yeah. Some of her mum's boyfriends fancied Carrie more than they did her mum. I don't necessarily think Carrie asked for it. These . . . these boyfriends were pretty nasty, some of them. *Anyway*, that explains a bit of Carrie's aggression. Best leave well alone. Same with Alex. I really don't get Alex at all. I'm not even sure the staff do, you know? I've seen her mum and dad. Very well-to-do and normal. Alex is *so* different from her older brother and sister. They're really conventional, one's at university, going to be a doctor, the other one's an accountant or something boring like that. Alex . . . Alex's just got something bad in her.'

It looked to Innes as if Abby was really warming to the subject of Alex. Not surprising, really. Alex Baxendale was perhaps the most intriguing – probably because she was the hardest to read and therefore impossible even to begin to understand.

Abby seemed to read her thoughts on that one. 'See, with Alex, there's never, *ever* any "give" with her. You never feel that she can be normal, friendly, nice even. Christ, I've even seen Carrie crying with Simon at the bottom of the garden once or twice. And Simon himself has been near to breaking point in Dr Laurie's sessions. At least you get to see something a bit . . . a bit more . . . *human* with everyone else. But Alex is . . . what does Dr Laurie say? Oh, yeah, he says to Alex in group therapy that she's "shut down". And it's true. You never see a chink in that tough exterior of hers. A good while back, me and Simon overheard the nurses talking about her one night. They were going on about how it was vital to break down her "psychological barriers". They were wittering on, saying stuff like it was the only way to make her better. Cure her . . . her "psychopathy". Si's got a psychology dictionary and we looked it up. It means she's pretty mental. But, as Si pointed out, he reckons that all of us could be described in the same way, depending on how you look at it. Anyway, there's no way the staff have broken through with Alex. Not a chance.'

Innes nodded and broached something that had been on her mind. 'And those scars? On her arms?'

Abby shrugged again and restarted her gentle swinging. 'Oh, those. She did them herself. "Self-mutilation" they call it. Strange stuff. And you'll have noticed she likes looking like a boy. She's like Nurse Sarah in that respect. Know what I mean?'

Innes shied away from pursuing that piece of gossip. The girls and girls, boys and boys, thing was all a bit weird. She quickly moved on to another subject. 'And what about Danny? He raped someone when he was fourteen?'

She felt Abby's change of mood instantly. She was so obviously comfortable with the subject of Alex and the others, but not with this. Innes felt foolish. And worried. Maybe she shouldn't have brought up Danny. It was obvious there was . . . well . . . something between them. But Abby smiled back at her, only her tightening hands on the swing chains giving away that she was tense. 'Yeah, well, there's more to it than that. Apparently the girl led him on. And looked much, much older than she was. It was all a misunderstanding. I don't think Dan should really be in here. Anyway, tell me more about you? You know. Your stuff?'

Innes accepted the clumsy subject-change and moved behind Abby, giving her regular, gentle pushes. 'Well, I didn't go to school for a year. I wrote my own sick-notes and forged my dad's signature. I had sex with men twice my age in my mum and dad's bed. I threw a lab stool at my biology teacher and spat at my maths teacher. And I was expelled. I went up to a Children's Panel and was deemed "out of control".'

Innes stepped back as Abby stopped the swing and turned round to look at her. In astonishment? Admiration? Confusion maybe.

'Wow! That's amazing. But why?'

'Why did I do it? Probably because my mother's a mad, domineering psychotic who truly, and I mean this, *hates* me. Laurie actually accused her of it the other week. Said it right out, in that gentle "killer" way he's got. "Mrs Haldane, I believe that you are jealous of your daughter. Jealous of her and of the life opportunities that lie before her. Opportunities that you never had. Unlike most loving parents who wish the best for their offspring, you do not wish that for Innes. Perhaps you should look at that. Very carefully. And honestly. To hate your own daughter is a strain on all the family. And Mr Haldane? I believe that you are intimidated by your wife. Understandable. But this is having a catastrophic effect on your daughter. Indeed that is why she is here."

'Anyway, she scares Dad. But she doesn't scare me.'

9

'Mind and stop at Scarista. The beach is beyond your dreams. In fact, see them all. It'll take you no time. Then about half a mile inland from the turning point at Scarista you'll see a sign for Scarista Lodge. Ian Gallagher lives there. Good luck, lass.'

She nodded to herself as she replayed in her head the words of Danny's nearest neighbour, a Mrs Rena Mackay. A friendly woman whom Innes had left that morning after a fruitless chat about Danny. According to Rena Mackay, he'd seemed to be a loner, giving little or nothing away about himself.

Innes stopped and stared at the colours. The vistas. The very existence of such things here of all places made her stop the car. She'd been told about these by previous visitors, friends who'd holidayed here, but thought their claims exaggerations, tourist hyperbole.

The journey from seeing Danny's neighbour in Lewis, across the winding isthmus into the territory officially known as the Isle of Harris, had taken her to the beaches. Each and every one had it. Caribbean turquoise sea. Bahamian white sand. Breathtaking. Even the sun stayed out for her. Although the Atlantic Gulf Stream passed through here, the waters that splashed over her paddling feet were icy. She watched in wonder at the sleek, cigar-shaped bodies of the plummeting gannets executing their perfect dives, and resurfacing with their silvery, wriggling prey. Back inland, she scanned beyond the dunes and along the length and breadth of seemingly endless pale shoreline. Not a human soul.

She trudged back to where she'd left her shoes. Time to follow Rena Mackay's second piece of advice.

'You were right to leave it till after four. That's when I finish. But I need to take the dogs out. Down to the beach. You'll have seen it on your way here.'

Innes laughed. 'Oh, yes. Unmissable. I've just been for a paddle.'

'Well, you can have another, if you fancy.'

Déjà vu it was, but this time she didn't go as far as a paddle, preferring to stroll barefoot along the hard-packed white sand. Ian Gallagher was tall, slim, about mid thirties she guessed. Celtic dark colouring. Irish by name. Irish a little by accent, clearly cutting through the well-educated tones as he gave a potted history of his adult life.

'I'm half Irish, half Welsh. My mother was born in Swansea. Anyhow, I did my stint in London. Read art history originally, at Trinity, then left Dublin and gravitated towards London, scraping a living from some highly prized but poorly paid gallery jobs there. Packed that up. Did some very lucrative art dealing for a few years. Then couldn't bear another moment in London.'

He cast a supervisory eye over his two liver-and-white Springers, gambolling their way across the sands, appeared satisfied at what he saw, and went on.

'My sister, Sian, had been coming to the Hebrides for years on and off. She fell in love with them. I did too. So much so that I bought the lodge up there. Still keep my hand in with art deals, toing and froing between London, Edinburgh and Europe now and again. But for the past five years this has been home. I also have a part-time contract with Scottish Heritage as a curator, checking on their monuments. It really is the good life here.'

They walked on in silence. She sensed that he was ready for her to go beyond their initial introduction, when she'd reprised the story given to Rena Mackay, namely, that she was 'an old friend' of Danny.

But she felt the need to add some embellishment. 'I'd been meaning to holiday here for ages actually. Hearing about Danny was a real knock-back, but since I'm here I thought the least I could do was talk to those who knew him. Those who liked him. I suppose suicide is always a bit unbelievable, except in cases like terminal illness or indescribable emotional misery. It's funny, the Danny I knew . . . ah, well, it's silly, really. That was so long ago. But, it depends if you believe in certain aspects of personality staying the same, immutable . . . I'm sorry, I'm waffling. What I'm trying to say, is that it's hard to believe that the Danny I knew would kill himself.'

Without her noticing he'd led her to a gentle dune, where they both sat down, staring out at the endless shore, and the lolloping spaniels, yelping in play. He was picking at a long strand of grass and gouging his thumbnail along its edge. 'I *do* know what you're getting at. I've known two other people in my life who killed themselves, including a former partner of mine who became HIV positive in the days when that meant a certain death sentence. I could understand why he did it. Almost. But in many ways suicide's always going to be a puzzle to the healthy and the relatively happy. The thing about Danny Rintoul was that *he* was a puzzle. I think that's what attracted my sister to him. He wasn't the kind of guy to commit himself about anything, let alone a relationship. That suited Sian. She'd had a messy – I mean very messy – divorce a few years ago. Freedom is what she wanted. That's why she's gone travelling to God knows where now. Yes. Freedom. Danny and she were the same in that respect.'

'She must've been devastated by his death, though.'

He nodded at the strand of grass. 'She was. And surprised. Totally. Though she hadn't been seeing as much of him before his death. They went through these phases of "cooling off", you know. I reckon it's when they thought that emotional dependency was on the way, one or other backed off. They both may have had other lovers during those times. I don't know. Fascinating relationship. Seemed to work, though. I envied it. Good old Danny. I miss him. He was a real mate. Totally accepting too of my sexuality. It just wasn't an issue with him. And he could keep the information to himself. I have a partner on this island, but we have to be careful. It's a beautiful place here but not a liberal one. Yeah, I doubt I'll meet another like Danny as long as I live here. I miss the bugger.'

Innes felt mildly surprised that this man had automatically assumed that she too was trustworthy, and felt touched by what she took to be a compliment. But she sensed something else in Ian Gallagher. A hesitation? A need to go further? She offered him a gentle prod. 'And?'

He looked at her for a moment, and then back to his grass. 'If I'm to be honest, I wasn't completely surprised at what Danny did.'

'Really?' This was unexpected.

He checked on his dogs again. Then went on, his voice measured, almost to a whisper. 'No. You see. I had a habit of dropping in on Danny for a "wee dram" now and again. A few weeks before his death I stopped by his croft. I usually just walked in after a knock. Everyone does that around here. This time his door was locked. But he was in. I heard him. On the phone. He was talking to someone. A man. Well, I think it was a man. He was calling him "pal". They were quarrelling. No . . . that's too strong. The person at the other end was asking him something again and again. Danny just kept saying, "Please, take it easy, everything's all right, honest." Wheedling sort of. It was odd. I left him to it. I was never alone with Danny again. He always avoided going for a drink, or mixing with me, with anybody as far as I know. Became more of a recluse than he normally was.'

'And did you tell anyone about it? About what you heard that time?'

'I told Sian. That's all. She didn't have a clue what it was about. Thought it might've been Danny quarrelling with his landlord. There *had* been a rent hike around that time. But that was so unlikely. Dan always paid in advance. Scrupulous about money, even though he was perpetually broke. Crofting's a bloody hard life up here.'

At her prompting, they stood up and began to stroll back. She smiled as the dogs bounded up to them, the soft hair of their underbellies dripping with sea-soaked fronds. She found herself absent-mindedly petting the overexcited beasts, thinking through what she'd just heard. She wanted to know one more thing. And tried to put it as tactfully as possible.

'Danny's name came up at another suicide inquest, in London. A woman called Isabella. She apparently knew him. Do you know about that?'

He pouted, a puzzled look on his face. 'Yeah. I heard a bit of talk about that, and it's a complete mystery. No one, and I mean *no one*, Sian included, knows anything about her. Maybe there's been some cock-up. Actually, I thought it was that maybe she . . . this Isabella woman, was going to buy a place here. Danny occasionally did some building work on the side. Maybe she got his number from someone else, to ask him to do some work for her? Could be they didn't know each other at all.'

Innes nodded and lied. 'Could be, could well be.' She continued walking up to the road in silence, cursing herself for the lie.

Could be nothing. Danny and Isabella had only known each other since 1977.

10

The swing was there in the moonlight. Moving slowly with the sway of the surrounding trees. A pendulum. Then she was on it. Back and forth. Back and forth. Head up to the stars. Head down to the grass. The wind was warm. Sweet smelling.

La-la-la-dee-da. La-la-la-dee-da. The humming was in her head, but her mouth was closed. How? She stopped the swing. No. The humming was *outside* her head. Coming from behind.

'Hello?'

'La-la-la-dee-da.'

'Who's that?'

'La-la-la-dee-da.'

She twisted round, the straining swing chains grating in her ear. 'Hello?'

He was there. Smoking.

'Danny. What you doing?'

'Nothin'. Thought you wis Abby.'

'C'mon, we'd better get back. It's almost ten.'

'Okay, Innes. But let me give you one more swing.'

She smiled a 'yes' at him. Then he was behind her, gently pushing her shoulders. Then a bit firmer. Then harder. Then too hard. 'Danny? Not so much. Stop it! Stop!'

Then he nudged a final time at her back and she heard him wandering away. She jumped off, stumbling to keep her balance. 'Danny! What's wrong? Danny!'

He turned round. His face had changed. Bloated . . .

rotting . . . hideous. 'I'm dead, Innes. Can't you see? I'm dead. Drowned . . .'

'Wh— Oh, Christ!' She clawed at the phone, desperate to cancel its infernal ringing, falling back on her pillows. Sweaty and sick. She had that momentary 'where-am-I?' feeling, and then, within a second, recognized the comfortable surroundings of the only decent hotel in Lewis.

She dragged the phone to her ear. 'Yes?'

'Ms Haldane, good morning, it's reception here. We've got a package for you.'

She weighed the thing in her hands. Quite heavy. The small white envelope attached to the parcel contained a simple postcard. A delicate watercolour of Scarista Beach.

Herewith, Danny's 'effects' – left to my sister, Sian. She took what she wanted ages ago. Said there's nothing else she wants. Would have told you about them when we met but wanted to think about it for a couple of days. I'm pretty sure you're a true friend of Danny. And, as the cliché goes, I hope you find what you're looking for. In any event, it's obvious that you rated Danny as much as I did. Ciao.

Ian G.

She slumped back, smiling. And feeling guilty again. She'd lied to this kind, gentle man. Secured his trust. Got information out of him. That's what delving into this past of hers meant. Lie after lie. Just like she'd lied to her husband of twelve (and, for her, unsatisfactory) years. Just like she'd lied to friends, lovers, colleagues. She'd rewritten her childhood, her adolescence. She redefined and redesigned herself as an apparently 'together' adult. And they'd bought every bit of it. Her husband had, certainly, if the occasional but passionate letters he wrote to her from his new life in Canada were anything to go by, as he clung on to a love she was now sure she'd never fully reciprocated. And her friends, lovers, colleagues – all seemed satisfied to relate to the two-dimensional version of herself that she put out into the world. That's what lies bought you. Half-relationships. And here she was lying to this man Ian Gallagher. A stranger, but nevertheless a kind man who'd cared about Danny. She had to admit that lies came very easily to her, even if she hadn't been conscious of that fact until now.

Indeed, she had to admit that basic personal ethics were gradually taking a back seat. It was her ghosts from more than half a lifetime ago that were more important, more alive to her than anything else just now. And lying seemed a small price to pay for pursuing them. A month ago it would have been inconceivable for her to have swanned off from her work, her career. But Abby and Danny lived for her *now*, in death, as much as they had when they were all together, alive, in the Unit. She didn't need her therapist, whom she hadn't seen in an age, to explain that one. She didn't believe for one minute that the deaths of these people weren't in some way linked. They had to be. The link was the Unit. And that, whether she liked it or not, involved her.

She turned her attention to the package, ripping off the thick brown paper. What lay inside immediately caught her eye: a mahogany casket, about twelve inches by ten, with a brass hasp and unlocked padlock.

The first glimpse inside immediately struck a chord, hurtling her back through the decades. She remembered the afternoon the photograph had been taken. The last day of the holiday. It was mild for November. And sunny. Lydia had been crying for the best part of two days because she'd grazed her knee on a monkey rope that had refused to take her weight and plunged her to the ground. The big white bandage took pride of place in the middle of the group portrait.

She worked her eyes along the three rows of faces, a soft smile giving way as she reached those she had cared about. And those she hadn't. First the staff. Ranj, Anna and Sarah. They were all okay in their own ways, she supposed, especially Ranj. Although, in retrospect, Anna had been a good professional. Sarah she'd never been sure about. Had never had much to do with. Then the patients. Sour-faced Carrie. Impressionable Simon. Hard-nut, impenetrable Alex. And then she saw them. Side-by-side-by-side. A twenty-six years younger version of herself was standing between them. Isabella and Danny. And, staring at the youthful faces, she noticed something that had never struck her before when she'd last seen this photo, decades ago. It had been a happy day, Lydia's whingeing apart. They were going back home, or at least back to the Unit, after what had been a pretty unsuccessful 'holiday'. So why were so many of them looking . . . depressed? Tense? Uneasy?

She placed the photograph to one side, still mulling over its atmosphere. It was probably just low spirits because the holiday was over. That made sense. They were all a huffy lot, given half the chance. So had she been. With a sigh, she began rummaging through the box. There was a wallet with photos of a lovely woman, whom she took to be Sian Gallagher. She definitely had a look of her brother. There were also other oddments, like the rent book for the croft, paid bills for public utilities, MOT certificate, and suchlike. They were all bundled together by a thick elastic band.

Finally, only a tatty envelope was left. She felt a hard square shape through it. She slipped the computer disk out. Marked in red felt tip on its label was one word, ACCOUNTS.

She looked over at the black case on the floor of the wardrobe. She'd had half a mind to leave the laptop behind. But she was addicted to it. Three minutes later she was opening up the only file on the disk.

The first name to appear was instantly recognizable. And confirmed her deepest suspicions about the ghosts she'd just seen in that photograph . . .

11

After almost four months in this place, she knew by now that any time there was difficult or potentially awkward news to impart, it came from Ranj. His full name was Ranjit or something, but no one ever called him that. Just Ranj. She'd first met him a month after her admission. He'd been away on a course. She liked the fine-featured face under the beard and dark blue turban. He seemed relaxed, approachable.

She noticed that he'd waited until morning therapy was over. He, Anna and Sarah were all sitting in the circle with the rest of them. She heard Simon sigh, and then weigh in. Cut-glass Scottish accent – a male Jean Brodie – the public-school uniform pristine. 'Here we go! What's the big announcement, then? New curfew? Thanks to Lydia, who stayed out late twice last week.'

There was a general murmuring, all eyes in the circle resting on Ranj, cool and relaxed as ever. He gave a polite cough and got stuck in. 'Come on, that's unfair and you know it, Simon. No. I've got good news for us all.' He gave a deliberately over-dramatic pause. Making them wait. 'We're all going on holiday.'

'What the fuck! Are ye off yer skull? It'll be fuckin' November in two minutes, for fuck's sake! Bloody winter!'

'Right! Fuckin' ridiculous!'

Innes flashed a smile at Abby. They were all having a go, led, as ever, by the jeers of Carrie, Danny and Alex. But Ranj was keeping it together. Letting them get it out of their system. Waiting until each last mock groan of pain and mutinous grumble was spent. Anna gave him one of her bossy looks and took over. 'Actually, we're going camping.'

She was holding up both hands to keep their protests down. 'It's a bit flashier than camping, as it happens, though we'll be taking tents in case we fancy moving about a bit and want a night under canvas. But for the main part we'll be staying in huts at an outward-bound centre. *Heated* huts. With hot and cold running water and kitchen facilities. There'll be a chance to do lots of outdoor pursuits. Canoeing, climbing, orienteering. There's also a TV lounge, so you won't miss *Top of the Pops*, okay?'

Innes watched a sulky Carrie let rip. 'Where is this fuckin' place? Do we all have to go, for fuck's sake? An organized, group fucking holiday? Sounds cunting booooring!'

But Anna looked ready for her, ignoring the second-chancer question and attending to the former with a put-on cheerfulness. 'It's up in Argyll. Near Inveraray. Ranj, Dr Laurie and myself have been to see it. It's lovely, no matter what time of year. We've got hold of a long-range weather forecast. Winter hasn't quite kicked in there yet. It'll be cold but fine.'

It was obviously Danny's turn now. 'When we goin'? Can we get time off?'

Ranj answered him quickly, determined not to allow anyone a way out. 'We're going in two weeks. And don't worry, we've organized school breaks. Since you lot only go out of here to school in the afternoons, it's not that difficult. All right? Okay, that's it.'

The meeting was at an end, and everyone was filing out. Innes hovered in the hallway, unseen, and watched as Anna started moving furniture back against the wall.

'Well, Ranj?'

Ranj had grasped one end of the sofa and was pushing

hard. 'Who knows. I think it's just what they need. What we all need. This place feels like a volcano ready to blow.'

Anna stopped what she was doing and stared at him. 'And you don't think we'll be taking the volcano with us?'

Innes headed for the stairs. They were right. The place was beginning to feel tense, edgy. All the time. And she couldn't, for the life of her, work out why.

Twenty-six years later – 2003

Note from Sister Anna Cockburn to Staff Observation File
11 October 1977
RE: Patient, Simon Calder (d.o.b. 23.8.60)

Simon has had a bad day or two. The last family-therapy session with the Calders did not go well. Mrs Calder still insists that she fails to see why there have to be regular sessions including the parents when her son is an in-patient. She maintains that she simply does not have the time to devote one hour every two weeks to her son's welfare, which she makes plain is now the APU staff's sole responsibility. Indeed, Mrs Calder seems increasingly to be in denial about her role in Simon's illness, preferring to disown him while he is in our care. We must address this in future family-therapy sessions and do all we can to ensure that Mrs Calder attends.

Unsurprisingly, Simon's self-esteem issues are more acute than ever. He is spending more and more time alone, which has to be countered. Staff must engage him with them and with the other patients. His relationship with Carrie is, as we know, his key relationship, but she, as we also know, enjoys periodically goading him. When he feels totally unloved he becomes more of a pedant than ever, showing that he is at least good at something. This of course angers others such as Danny, who feels educationally and intellectually inferior (correct on the former but not on the latter), and thus he too acts out.

I suggest close monitoring of Simon for the next few days. He remains an acutely anxious patient.

Copies to: Daily Nursing Log; Night Duty, Special Log

Copy to: patient file, S. Calder

12

Girl abducted – police fears grow

A four-year-old girl from the picturesque fishing village of St Monans, Fife, has been abducted. Katie Calder, who attends the exclusive St Kilda's Nursery School in St Andrews, was waiting at the school gates for her mother in the company of two older friends yesterday afternoon, when she was grabbed by a middle-aged man.

A police spokesman said that they were baffled by the abduction and becoming increasingly concerned for Katie's safety. He insisted that the police search was broadening by the hour, and that extra officers had been drafted in from other forces to help with inquiries. The spokesman said it was 'too early' to link Katie's disappearance with a number of unsolved child abductions that have occurred in the north-east of England and the Scottish Borders over the past two years.

Meanwhile, Katie's two friends are helping police compile an 'E fit' image of the abductor. Katie's parents, Dr Simon Calder, a clinical psychologist, and his wife, Rachel, have another daughter, Lily (6). Neighbours say that the family is 'devastated' and 'desperate for news of Katie'.

'Are you sure she's okay, Simon? It's been practically a fortnight now and you're still keeping her off school. Is that wise? Shouldn't she be mixing again with her friends, trying to take her mind off it?'

Take her mind off it! He cursed the pole-axing insensitivity of his mother. And cursed himself. Dr Simon Calder, clinical psychologist. Physician, heal thyself. That was a bloody laugh. How the hell could he heal anyone in this state? And with *her* around? His was the mother from hell. But so was his situation. It was a quarter to midnight and he'd had enough. He glanced for the umpteenth time at the two-week-old newspaper and threw it across the room, the banner headline seared into his memory, the daily habit of reading and rereading it and others about his daughter now an embedded, settled-in neurosis.

He pressed the phone harder against his ear. 'Mother, Lily's sister has been abducted. She doesn't want to be at school. Besides, she *has* friends in the village *and* she's not the only one still absent from school, believe me. The two girls who were with Katie when she was taken are still being kept away. Listen, my mobile's going. I have to go. If there's any news, I'll let you know straight away.'

He hung up. His mobile lay silent in his pocket, but he felt no guilt whatsoever about the phantom call. His mother was doing what she did best. Interfering. Undermining. Making him feel inadequate. Any normal mother would be pouring out unconditional support to him and his family. But his had never been a normal mother. Well, he couldn't change that. But he was forty-three, not fourteen. He *could* make his own decisions without her sanction. *Could* get through this hell without her.

He left his study and padded up the stairs of his beloved house. Its spectacular aspect, looking out over the mouth of the Firth of Forth, where it met the often angry North Sea, was unmatched. This night, nothing could be seen. Only heard. The swell was quieter than usual. But hypnotically soothing. His first stop on the landing was the double bedroom. Rachel was sound. And not. He could detect rapid-eye movement under the quivering lids. She too was troubled beyond words. Two weeks had passed since the event, and his wife, even in her unconscious, knew that the longer it went on, the worse the expected outcome. He stepped forward to kiss her cheek and left to visit the other occupied bedroom.

For a moment he envied the apparent careless slumber of his daughter. Lily lay on her back, hands flung out in crucifixion, duvet discarded. She looked as at peace as any six-year-old should in sleep. But he didn't need the skills of his professional training to know that the truth was otherwise. He kneeled beside the narrow bed, cartoon characters from the dim night-light grinning their mockery of happiness and reassurance. He kissed his child on the forehead, feeling rather than seeing the imperceptible stirring of her small body. He studiously avoided entering the third – and empty – bedroom, merely giving a single nod of approval as he recognized the glow of Katie's night-light shine out on to the landing.

Back downstairs in his study, he opened a window. He'd do that in most weathers, day and night, until the wind blew his papers away, or the rain and sea-spray mottled his spectacles, obscuring his vision. But it was summer, and the weather fine. He undid the last button of his Polo shirt, and blew air down his hot chest. The stiff whisky sitting undrunk by his elbow eventually aroused his attention. He downed it greedily in one burning gulp and hastily refilled, a few golden drops falling on to the hem of his shorts. Then, bending his head, he unscrewed his fountain pen, ready for that night's attempt at catharsis.

Sunday. Midnight

It is almost two weeks since Katie was abducted. If she is not dead, then we believe she has been raped. We had devastating news today. Katie's socks and skirt have been found. Everyone thinks she's dead. Things are getting worse by the day. The waiting is killing everyone. The police won't confirm it. But I can sense it, see it in their faces, hear it in the changed tones of their voices. They are unofficially linking Katie's disappearance with that of the others – none of which have had a happy outcome. These other little ones may have all been returned. But they were returned . . . damaged.

Why? Of all the children in this part of the world . . . but no, I must not wish this on anyone else. How cruel, how unjust. I know why. I deserve this, but my precious little Katie doesn't. Why couldn't fate have taken its revenge out on me directly? I just can't bear this. Help me. Help us all.

But no one can help. Not even this odd activity can ease my burden. It seems strange that throughout my adult life I have kept a journal. A most unfashionable thing to do. But it has been my salvation many a time. Self-psychoanalysis. A forum for my confused feelings. I used to enjoy the satisfaction of crises survived, when I looked back. But I begin to doubt that this one is survivable.

And worst of all are the memories. Of that time before. Nothing has ever been able to assuage the fearful feelings of that time. Not my work helping and healing others. Not the love of my beautiful wife. Not the births and flourishing of my most precious daughters. That time has always been buried deep but constantly nagging.

I barely sleep now. Because of the dreams. This episode has brought them back after what must be years. Rachel knows nothing of them. She's happy to accept the pills I have given her every night since Katie was taken. My drinking is becoming a problem. I used to be an indifferent drinker. Could take it or leave it. But not now. Rachel knows nothing of that either. I buy secretly – outside of the village – and I dispose of the empties secretly. All is deceit. Lying. Guilt.

Things could have been far worse. The police wanted, practically insisted, that we have an officer here at all times. Unthinkable! I absolutely put my foot down. Thankfully, Rachel was with me on that one. We want no intruders here. We already have enough. All unseen.

As for work? It is fortunate that I have understanding colleagues. My patient workload has been suspended thanks to them. The simple truth is that no one can know why this event has hit me so much harder than anyone else. Rachel cannot know. No one else can. No, that's not quite true. There are others.

I begin to wonder if there is a God after all. If so, He/She/It is having the last laugh now. Savage justice indeed. There it is, plain as plain. Katie's fate is my fault. My punishment. Utterly deserved. Time for bed now. Time for the dreams.

13

The gentlest rat-a-tat. He knew it was her. Irritatingly, she never waited for a reply. Just cracked the door open and then swanned in. He leaned back from his desk, trying a weak smile. He watched as Dr Sheena Logan, Head of Psychological Services, Out-patients, helped herself to a chair opposite.

'Simon, *really*. Are you up to being in? No news, I s'ppose?'

He shook his head, moving his chair a few inches away from the tall, overbearing presence of his boss. She seemed to take up more of the room than he did, and he'd been finding her obvious concern and daily visits to his office oppressive. 'Eh . . . no, Sheena. The police have nothing. And I . . . I *prefer* to be able to come in. Do paperwork, write reports. It's absolutely right that I stay away from my patients just now . . . I agree with you and the department there and . . . and eh, I'm keeping my hours down. So I can be with Lily and Rachel.'

She nodded, seeming satisfied with that, stood up and wandered back to the door. 'That's good, Simon. The family's the most important thing at this time. You should be able to find great comfort together. Okay, I'll be off. Do *not* overwork, though. Got that? Bye for now.'

He pushed his chair forward again, head in hands. Thank God she was gone for another day! He knew only too well why she was being over-solicitous about his well-being. He'd told her. Well, told her some of it, when he was offered the job eighteen months ago. He'd had to tell her about his adolescent psychiatric past. Otherwise he wouldn't have dared take up a post in the very hospital where he'd once been a patient. Even though it had been over a quarter of a century ago. Even though Dr Laurie and the nurses were no longer on the scene. Not to tell would have been too much of a risk to his career. The psychological/psychiatric medicine community was a very small one in Edinburgh.

But Sheena had been fine, breezily saying that he wasn't the only one in the mental-health field who'd had their share of being the 'consumer of services'. She had followed this up with the usual facile observation that it probably made him a better psychologist. *Christ, if she could see into his mind right now.*

He slid open his desk drawer. The photo was getting tatty now. There they were. Staff and patients. All lined up in rows, like a bloody football team. With the glassy waters of Loch Fyne in the background. He ran a finger along the faces. A picture could never tell the whole story. Certainly not this one. Anyone looking at it would see a group of teenagers with a handful of adults, enjoying their outdoor holiday. You had to look closely, *and* know what you were looking for, to even scrape the surface of what was really going on.

Poor Ranj. It had been his state-of-the-art camera, and he'd pre-set it and run to join them at the end of the back row. A week later, back at the Unit, he'd proudly doled out a copy to each of them. Carrie had ceremoniously ripped hers into a million pieces and binned them in front of everyone. Very Carrie. But, as far as he knew, everyone else had kept theirs. Predictable behaviour, from a psychologist's point of view.

He reached back into the drawer. They were neatly in date order. He'd managed to locate and steal them so easily. The records department had abysmal security. He'd more than expected them to have been destroyed. But no. Some administrative oversight had ensured that they'd been squirrelled away, forgotten, collecting dust in an unused basement. The files were incomplete. But there was enough there. Strange, although he'd had the papers for over a year, and the photo for ever, he hadn't been near them for an age. Not until Katie was taken. Then he'd gone to the safe in his study at home and brought them out. They were both talisman and curse to him. A reminder.

Not being a complete fool, he'd often wondered, as he'd applied for and then secured the job here, how much he had been driven to it by the Unit. His choice of career was obviously linked to his past. He wanted to help and, where possible, heal. But to come back to this very same hospital? The ultimate 'working through'? The apotheosis of 'closure'? It wasn't quite that straightforward. The Unit had been situated in the hospital grounds, and had never been part of this, the main building. In actual fact, the Unit building wasn't part of the hospital any more, although the house still stood, neglected. More often than not, he found that he couldn't face going past it, often executing ludicrous detours to avoid even seeing it. But he was slowly developing his own plan for getting over that particular phobia.

He smoothed a yellowing page out before him.

Note from Sister Anna Cockburn to Dr Adrian Laurie, Consultant and Medical Director, APU
15 October 1977
Re: Group Behaviour in APU

There has been a marked change in the Unit's group dynamics of late, and, following consultation with my Charge Nurse and other nursing staff, I judge that we may be in for some difficulties.

The group has undergone a marked sexualization these past weeks, roughly but not exactly coinciding with the admission of Innes Haldane. My opinion is that her admission is the catalyst for some other events, e.g. Lydia Young, to behave in an attention-seeking way, as witnessed by Lydia's threat to 'torch the place' on the very same day that half a can of petrol and a bag of rags were found in the grounds. Although this episode preceded Innes's admission, it coincided with the announcement of her imminent arrival. I believe the events to be related.

However, it is the presence of Isabella Velasco that I believe is leading to the sexualization. Her obvious physical attractiveness has stimulated a number of the patients to notice her, and this has led to a variety of sexual 'games'.

I have already reported to you on the various sexual innuendoes and comments made on a daily basis. There has also been the expected sexual fixation on members of staff as exhibited in the 'sexual psychodrama' game that I surreptitiously witnessed last week, as well as those intimations of violent intent, particularly from Caroline.

The viewing of staff members as sexual objects is of course not unusual and is often an extension of the emotional attachments that patients make to staff. However, the awakening of sexual dynamics within group members at this time is of some concern to me and my nursing team.

In particular, I would urge close monitoring of Danny Rintoul (bearing in mind that it is less than nine months since he raped a fellow school pupil when he was aged only fourteen), Caroline Franks and Lydia Young. We may have to consider extending the use of medication.

Copy to: Daily Nursing Log
Copies to patient files: D. Rintoul; C. Franks;
L. Young

Gently, he placed photo and papers back in the drawer and locked it. All that material needed to be back at the house. He'd only brought it to work . . . to what? Allow himself some time to think, to remember? Well, he was prepared to do just that. Prepared to give the memories free flow. He saw no point in trying to stop them now. That was a loser's game. He allowed his mind to float back to the particular day that Sister Anna had referred to, wondering how she could have known.

He knew it was unusual for them all to be together in one room unless they were in group therapy or psychodrama or a specially called meeting. But it was Thursday night. *Top of the Pops* had ended. The only programme watched by everyone. Except Lydia. He knew, they all did, that if she was on the down-time of her manic depression, she always went to her room, skulking away in search of her secret store of crisps and chocolate bars. Alone. Sullen. Her ability to secrete coveted snacks amazed him, and he knew it irritated everyone, patients and staff alike: patients, because *they* wanted to steal them; staff, because Lydia's eating binges threatened both her body and mind. During those periods, they'd have to watch her stare out from under her curtain of unwashed hair. In a constant battle between her and Them. The staff. The other patients. They all spied on her. But she spied on them too. She was all-seeing, all-knowing. But not as good at it as him. Si-the-spy. He knew more about this place than she ever would.

He felt Carrie prodding him in the belly as he tried to read a book. He knew what she was up to. Time for a bit of Si-baiting. Torment time. She was cackling in his ear. 'Hah-hah! All right, then, swotty. You've finished those boring history and geography essays you've been spending hours on. Not much homework for you for a while now. You going to your school concert? Who you taking? Why don't you ask Isabella?'

Fuck it! He didn't need this right now! He hated it when she was in one of these moods. His plea was almost a whisper. 'Carrie. *Please.*'

He saw Alex's eyes fix on Carrie's and hold them. 'You must be kidding, Carrie! He wouldn't stand a chance. Abby's a bit First Division for you, Si.' Here we go, he thought. Alex enjoyed getting in a dig at him whenever possible. But she was worse than Carrie. There was something out-and-out sadistic about her when she had it in for you. Though, in fairness, anyone and everyone could, and was, in her firing line from time to time. She didn't seem to run any particular vendettas.

But he felt some relief that he was going to be spared an Alex onslaught, as Carrie's perversity started kicking in, making the seamless move from his tormentor to his protector. She would rather have a go at Alex than continue taking the piss with him. He watched with more than a bit of satisfaction as Carrie rasped back at Alex, 'What the fuck d'you mean, skinhead cuntface freak? There's nothing wrong wi' Si. Nothing that a good haircut and decent clothes wouldn't help! He's a fuck of a lot better lookin' than you. You look like a fuckin' boy, *cunt-face freak*!'

He sensed that things were about to go too far, but his plea was being unheeded for a second time. 'Carrie, *please* don't. Leave it.'

Danny was lighting up now: a brown-stained, half-smoked roll-up. He spat out the first lungful of smoke. Always bloody smoking, a roll-up surgically attached to his mouth, day and night. In other places it would have been a mark of defiance, but the staff didn't bother themselves with such trifles. Fair enough. If under-age smoking was all any of them had to worry about, well . . . fat chance.

He watched Danny finish his smoke and knew what was coming next. Yes, Danny was going to have some fun at his expense now. 'Hey, Si? Why don't you ask the lovely Sister Anna? Or maybe she's a bit beyond your league too.' The asinine suggestion brought most of the group out in the usual splutters and giggles.

Carrie flicked both sides of her hair over her shoulders. 'Very smart, Danny. I suppose you think Anna'd have *you*, big boy?'

A voice from the hallway piped up. 'Would you, Danny? *Would you*? *Have* her, I mean?'

Simon glanced from Danny over to the open doorway. Lydia was back and heading for the half-made, well-used, old jigsaw of the Bay City Rollers, laid out on a side table. She'd been bored upstairs obviously. Lonely too. Time to cause trouble for the rest of them. Danny was sauntering over to her, bending down so that his face met hers. 'Oh, grow up, Lydia! Give us all a rest. Go back upstairs and fill yer fat, ugly face.'

He shook his head at Danny. Lydia wouldn't have that. Sure enough, the puzzle pieces were shoved aside and she was practically jumping up and down in her seat. 'Fuck off, Danny!' She was facing each of them in turn, in a weird kind of circular dance, spinning round, making herself dizzy. And her expression had changed to that – familiar to all – manic elation. 'Go on! Go on! Who would everyone like to . . . to . . .' She uttered it as if it was the first time the word had left her lips. 'Which staff would everyone like to *fuck*! And if you don't want to fuck them, what would you like to do with them?'

Not a move. Not a sound. Lydia made a silent plea to him with a plaintive look and wrinkling of the forehead. But Simon let his eyes slew away towards the floor. He felt the others do the same.

'What? What's wrong?' Lydia's cheeks looked hot now. He wished she'd go back upstairs.

He heard Carrie's laugh. Shit! Her voice had that over-excited breathiness in it. 'Yeah! Lydia's right for once! Come on. Let's do it. Our own fuckin' psychodrama! It'll be a bastarding laugh! Come on, ye cunts!'

He joined them as, silently, they all took their shoes off and formed themselves into a ragged circle. He noticed Isabella and Innes hesitate, but then they urged each other on with secretive glances.

'First in? Me!' Bloody Carrie wasn't waiting for any other volunteer and was already settling her long legs across each other, centre-stage, staring down everyone. 'Okay. Start!'

He was surprised that Alex was first off the mark. 'Dr Laurie! What would you do with him?'

He smirked to himself as Carrie held her chin in her hand, eyes heavenward, in a parody of serious contemplation. Making them all wait. Eventually she gave them it. 'Maybe a big snog! But not fuck. He's bald, for fuck's sake!'

Someone else shouted, 'Ranj!'

Carrie hooted. 'French kiss! Maybe fuck.'

Comments were pitching in from all points of the circle. 'But he's got a beard! Horrid!'

'It's soft, though. Nice.'

'Yuck!'

'What about that nurse, Sam, from the main hospital? The one they sometimes have up here?'

'No danger, I'd catch something off him!' Carrie moved out of the circle, pushing him in. 'C'mon, Si, big boy. Your turn next!'

He shoved against her as she tried to push him into the circle. 'No, Carrie. Please. No!'

But Alex was holding up her hand. 'Haven't we forgotten something?'

Carrie scowled back at her. 'Like what?'

'Like Anna and Sarah.'

Carrie had frozen, half in, half out of the group, one hand still gripping his arm. She was tossing her hair back, Miss Nonchalant style. 'Don't be stupid, Alexaaaanderaaaa! They're girls. Idiot!'

He saw Alex's glare at Carrie. It was nothing less than a challenge. 'So what, Carrie? You've still got to say what you'd do to them.'

A twisted grimace had replaced Carrie's usual sneer. 'I'd kick their fuckin' heads in.'

Alex was goading her on, eyes glowing with the excitement. 'I doubt it. They'd have you in a neck-lock and Largactil'd up to your eyeballs before you knew it. Anyway, we were talking about *fucking*, weren't we?'

Simon cringed but knew better than to say a word. Christ! Leave it alone, you bitch! He shook his head, cursing at Alex's wanton and obvious desire to make trouble. She was out to embarrass, unsettle, and God knows what else. He wished she'd shut up. Leave it, leave them all alone. Why did she have to always stir it?

But within a second, he saw that it was Danny who was taking the whole thing up and running with it, enjoying himself now. 'Yeah, Anna and Sarah? Phew! I'll tell you one thing, that Sarah's a goer, and I know just who she'd like to get stuck into.' His eyes slowly roved back and forth around the circle, stopping abruptly at one of them.

He looked away from Danny. There was some real trouble brewing in the place. No doubt about that. Everyone either hated or loved each other. The worst combination possible. A combination that would lead to nothing but hell . . .

Simon shook that memory-path away and, moving sluggishly, packed his briefcase, turned off his desk lamp and headed reluctantly for the misery that was home.

14

He ushered his mother out to her elderly Daimler. Silently, she opened the door, slapping his helping hand away with a sharp 'I can manage!' She clambered in awkwardly, anxious not to crease her skirt, and started the engine.

'Sim—'

'Please, Mother. There's nothing else to say. You've said it all.'

Without a further word, without his usual insincere 'drive carefully', he turned on his heel and strode back into the house, fully aware of Rachel's pale face looming above him as she peered through the upstairs curtains. He checked the vestibule clock. Twenty to midnight. He prayed to God that Lily was asleep. He wandered to his study and did the ritual window opening. A salty gust invited itself in, fluttering the papers on his desk and disappearing so quickly he might have imagined it.

He sat in his chair, staring out to the sea, only yards away. He could see the white horses dashing themselves against the rocks. He could see the whole night clearly. He kept the light off and poured himself a drink, unconsciously rocking to and fro in his chair, reliving the events of an hour ago . . .

She hadn't startled him. He knew she'd been standing there for a while. He'd purposefully ignored her. 'Simon, I'm having an early night. Spend some time with your mother please. She's all alone next door with the TV and the dog for company.'

He'd ignored the barb. He'd felt her move towards him and flinched. His voice had been intentionally icy. 'Why did you say those things to Mother today? And please, just don't . . . don't say "what things". The old cow's just laid into me. She can watch the bloody telly and then fuck off out of here, as far as I'm concerned. I simply cannot believe you'd undermine me to Mother at this of all times. You know what she's like! You know what she's done to me!'

All of this had been said with his back to her, in darkness, facing his sea. Slowly he'd swivelled round and switched on the desk lamp, the yellow glow catching the gauntness of his features. He could see his reflection clearly in the window. A skull's head. Was this how she saw him too? 'Rachel, why the fuck did you say to Mother that I wasn't there for you? Not supporting you? I simply cannot believe that!'

She'd remained in the middle of the floor, silk pyjamas outlining her curvaceous body, in an unconscious transmission of powerful sexuality. That had always been her speciality. Sensual without knowing it. She looked better than she had a right to. But he was impervious to her charms now. He'd sat waiting for her to answer.

She did. 'It's true. It's like you're not really here with me and Lily in this nightmare. You say the right things, do the right things, but your soul's not there. *You're* not there. I've known you a very long time, Simon, and you're not connecting. Our child is missing. I believe she's dead. I'm not frightened to say it, see? It is an agony like no other I've ever known. But I cry. I talk to my friends. I hold Lily. You? You're cold. You're polite. Demonstrative in a false way. I just don't know you now, Simon.'

She'd held herself in check well. He had to give her that.

The corners of her mouth only hinting at the weeping that would follow, alone, upstairs . . .

He imagined that he could hear that weeping now. He threw his head back, staring at the ceiling, as if he could penetrate the layers of plaster and wood and see his wife foetally curled, rocking herself to sleep.

He refilled his glass, nudging the window open an inch further, inviting the breeze in. It was pitiful how far his marriage had descended into this. It was no secret that the parents of abducted children could look forward to their relationships foundering. But usually that was well after the event. The norm was for them to hang together, even become closer than they had been. Just for a while, just until the child was returned or . . . No, he didn't even want to say the words to himself.

And they had been happy, hadn't they? He and Rachel? Until this. He had, certainly. And not telling her about his adolescent past? Well, that was a well-worn deceit. It didn't even register as deceit any more. No, Rachel *had* been happy with him. It was her second marriage. She had been looking for stability, kindness. And children. He had given her all those. And that was what he'd wanted for himself. And it had worked. They fitted well together. By the time they'd met, he in his mid thirties, she a few years younger, he had an established career. He'd done a lot of work on himself, externally and internally. He looked okay, better than okay. Being fit and fashionable had come late to him, but he'd enjoyed the journey and the female attention it had rewarded him with. Though all the encounters with women, even the longer-term ones, had been largely empty. Until Rachel.

And that first meeting! At a mental-health charity dinner in Glasgow, where he'd been working. She'd been there with a psychiatrist friend, who thought she was his date. But *she* didn't think so. The guy had never spoken to him again. And later when she was going home with Simon, she'd said with the loveliest smile, 'You're different. Don't know how but just different.' It could've been a cliché, but she wasn't like that. She was direct, honest, knowing. Yet, not knowing enough. 'You're different.' And she was right. He was different . . .

A sound above roused him. Rachel, padding to and from the bathroom. She was awake. He half rose. He'd go to see her . . . comfort her . . . maybe she would comfort him. But no . . . he sat down again. There was no point. All would be futile, all dishonesty. On his part.

Within a moment, he bent his head forward and began the night's work. On his journal.

15

Girl found – police search for serial abductor

A four-year-old girl, Katie Calder, of St Monans, Fife, is recovering at home after a two-and-a-half-week ordeal during which she was kept captive.

Yesterday, police confirmed that they are linking the abduction to the disappearances of four other girls that have occurred in the north-east of England and Scottish Borders over the past two years. This is the first time the abductor has struck so far north, and Katie's disappearance is the longest to date. Although all the girls have been returned, police confirmed that there was evidence of sexual assault on them all, including Katie. A police spokeswoman said, 'We are deeply anxious that this man should be found. His crimes are escalating and we fear that the next abduction could end in tragedy.' A middle-aged man is being sought in connection with the abductions.

Details are sketchy about the abduction and imprisonment, but it is believed that police were tipped off yesterday afternoon via an anonymous telephone call, thought to have come from the abductor himself. This is the way all the previous abductions have ended. Katie was found, with a puppy she apparently had for company during her ordeal, at a lay-by on the B940 near Baldinnie. The cottage where it is thought Katie was kept prisoner was destroyed by fire before police arrived, in what fire officers are describing as 'an act of arson'.

Last night, Katie's father, Dr Simon Calder, a clinical psychologist, made an emotional plea from the family home in St Monans: 'We are relieved beyond words to have our precious Katie back and all we wish to do now is get her on the long road back to full physical and mental health. My wife, Rachel, and my second daughter, Lily, would like to take this opportunity to thank the community for their kindness during this dreadful time. We also thank the press for publicizing the case. However, we would ask all in the media to leave us in peace as we try to heal our wounds.'

Police say that they will shortly be releasing further details of the man they are seeking.

He crushed the cutting he'd hoarded and obsessively reread for the last three months in his fist and threw it to the winds. He was oblivious to the biting cold. It was the most spectacular graveyard anywhere. He looked up at the black bulk of the Auld Kirk teetering on the very edge of the headland. To some it might seem eerie standing here at the witching hour. But not to him. He relished the wind screaming itself hoarse above the rhythmic whoosh of the waves a few feet below. He wrenched down his hood, shaking his hair free, exposing his face, and marvelling at the soft yet stinging spray kicked up by the breakers as they lashed at the rocks.

He placed a palm on one of the oldest gravestones, the skill of the stonemason's hand long obliterated by the elements. He'd be happy to be buried here. Yes, happy. Happier than now. In this life. Which held no happiness. He moved to the shelter of the kirk porch, a dim outside light offering a gentle welcome to nocturnal visitors. He heaved at the unwieldy, weather-scarred wooden door and entered. As he closed it behind him, battling against a final gush of wind and rain, he found himself in the utter quiet. The storm forgotten, at bay outside.

He opted for a pew halfway down the short aisle. The lighting was low. He was alone. With a smile, he found himself praying yet again to a God he'd never believed in – until three months ago. He added a curse against a devil he'd always believed in.

Katie's back. Thank you. Thank you. He reached inside the layers of wool and waterproofs and took out the delicate auburn curl, tied with pale yellow ribbon. He kissed Katie's hair and held it to his damp cheek. From the same pocket he took the photo. Two symbolic halves of his life. He held one in each hand and stared at them at arm's length. And then closed his eyes against the tears.

The jumble of what the police had reported and surmised from the previous abductions, in addition to what Katie's psychotherapist, Debbie Fry, had got out of his daughter during intensive therapy, was swirling round his head yet again. He'd pieced together something of the mystery of her captivity, but, in the end, it may have been more his fantasy than fact . . .

The man would have heard the yelping of the puppy as he unloaded the shopping from his vehicle. A second-hand, four-wheel drive: second-hand (and bought for cash in a dodgy, late-night deal) because he couldn't possibly use his own vehicle, under the circumstances; four-wheel drive because the place was so deliberately inaccessible. Probably the most remote part of the Fife coast. Perfect. He'd lugged the heavy bags into the kitchen and was greeted by the puppy scratching from inside the girl's locked bedroom door.

He'd turned the key and there she was. A pretty thing in her new summer shorts, allowing the spindly little legs to be browned by the sun, and a brightly striped t-shirt. Clothes the man had supplied her with. Well, she needed some new clothes.

'Hiya, Katie. How's Bobby? Is he behaving himself? Not pee'd in your room or anything?'

'Nah. Bobby's a good dog.'

He'd handed her the ice lolly and watched as she ripped the paper off and started licking frantically at it, immediately smearing red and orange all over her face. But it wasn't going to be enough. He'd known from the frown what was coming.

'Is Mummy and Daddy coming now? And what about Lily? Where is Lily, is she coming too?'

'Lily's just fine, sweetheart. And Mummy and Daddy will be here soon. Very soon, okay? I promise. Now, you and Bobby can play in the back for a while. But don't throw the ball over the high fence. 'Cause we can't get it back. It's just the cliffs and the sea over there. Nothing else. All right?'

She'd nodded and then reluctantly took the ice lolly from her mouth. 'They can all see Bobby. Lily'll like him and we can take him down to the beach at our house, and he can go in the sea with us, because dogs like the sea.'

He'd kept his patience and smiled at her, patting her soft hair. 'Soon, Katie. Soon.'

He'd finished unpacking the shopping and wandered through to her room. The place was in chaos. She and Bobby had obviously been having a field day with the toys, many of which were chewed and split, their stuffing tumbling out on to floor and bed. He had done a quick tidy, and then moved back into the kitchen and pulled out chicken nuggets and oven chips from the freezer.

Five minutes later, he'd sat down in the small living room, coffee by his side, reaching over to the table for the morning paper and for the front-page story: 'Police Concern Grows Over Missing Girl'.

Two weeks later, that final day, he'd kept her and Bobby out in the back garden for as long as possible. The stench of petrol must have been overpowering. The man would have cast a final, regretful glance at her bedroom, the toys, the books. Then he'd poked his head out of the back door. She and Bobby would have been sitting in a heap on the grass, in the sunshine.

'Okay, you two. It's time.'

He would have had a clear vantage point. The fire would have taken a grip, and the cottage become a ruin before the emergency services were anywhere near it. He'd have walked over to the telephone box, gloved hands making him unworried about anything of himself being left behind.

The 999 call would have been answered immediately. 'Yes, I need the police please. It's about that missing girl. Katie Calder.'

A screaming gust that managed to penetrate the sanctum roused him. With trembling delicacy he placed the items back into the warmth of his breast pocket. Closest to his heart. Reluctantly he paced back down the aisle and into the maelstrom outside. He glanced over towards his house, only yards away. A solitary lamp beaconed out into the Firth. The one in his study. The only part of his home he could bear to be in right now. It had been another evening of hell . . .

The rumble of family noises. Girls squealing, Rachel shooing them upstairs to get ready for bed. Followed by the wagging-tailed backside of his elderly golden Labrador, the puppy scampering behind it. He'd ignored Rachel as she wandered back into the kitchen, where he was throwing the dried remains of a roast chicken into the bin. 'How come you're back so late with the girls? Dinner's inedible.'

She was staring at him, waiting for him to look at her. Instead, he'd turned his back and began washing the roasting tin, over-vigorously rubbing and scraping.

Her voice was glacial. 'We've eaten. I took the girls to a movie and then we went for a pizza, after the session. Your mother met us with the dogs.' Then, a bitter staccato laugh. 'Hah-hah! Ironic, isn't it? Those dogs've been so good for your mother. Keeping her company while we're in France.

And Katie adores them too. Absolutely ironic. So, Simon? Why didn't you turn up for the session? Dr Fry said you'd rung her twenty minutes before we were due to start. Said you had a work emergency. I wasn't aware that you were on call this weekend. That's the whole reason Dr Fry agreed to offer us a Saturday appointment. At considerable inconvenience to herself, since she doesn't normally consult on Saturdays.'

He'd swivelled round, roughly drying his hands on the tea-towel. 'Really? I know a number of child psychotherapists who consult on Saturdays, simply because they don't want their patients dragged out of the routine of school. Evidently Debbie Fry is different.'

He'd followed her in silence out of the kitchen, catching her words as she headed for the stairs. 'I'm going to put the girls to bed. By the way, Dr Fry says that Katie's lack of progress these past three months is a direct result of your failing to attend the family-therapy sessions. I hope you can live with that. Goodnight . . .'

He walked unhurriedly through the sea-mist and icy rain, back to the house, unzipped his waterproof and left it dripping on the coat-stand. Unconsciously, he took a right turn into his study and closed the door, sliding the newly installed bolt across. He still needed air. The window was flung open, the wind catching his papers and performing its usual whirlpool of chaos. He sat down and began the ritual twisting of his fountain pen, screwing and unscrewing the top. Then he laid it down and headed for his safe.

The letter was only a few months old but his repeated handling had left it torn and grubby.

Dear Simon

I want to say how very sorry I am about your little girl. I read the dreadful news about your daughter in the paper last night. I really could not believe what I was reading. It seemed unreal. But I know that it is. Of all the places for something like this to happen. I'd never have imagined it happening in your part of the world.

I'll never forget the day we all had that reunion picnic in St Monans. You chose the place and you said that one day you were going to own the old manse up by the church. And you said you were going to be a psychologist. You were in your second year at university and studying psychology, I think. You said both things with such a serious face that I believed you. It's funny what things stick in your mind, isn't it?

I also know that I should not be contacting you but I have. I think it is obvious why. (Although there has always been provision for emergencies like this, hasn't there, outside the normal contact arrangement? Surely?) Otherwise – anyway, I hope you know what I mean. Please, if you want to contact me, that's totally fine with me. I might be the best person to talk to, if you see what I mean. If not, that's okay.

As you know, I live a long way away, on the Isle of Lewis. I lead a quiet life. One that has caused me to think a great deal. Maybe I can help.

Anyway Simon, I hope all goes well.

Danny R
018513 0055787

Tonight had convinced him. Not from some dramatic spiritual revelation assailing him in the church. More a slow-burn realization. It was time to answer the letter. But first, he had to mark the evening with an entry in his journal. The formal daily record of his dismal life.

Mine is a double guilt. It is now confirmed that Katie is not getting better because I will not, cannot, attend the sessions with her psychotherapist. So, now it's not just me blaming myself for Katie but Rachel too, and Dr Fry. How dare Debbie Fry say as much to Rachel? Bloody cheek. I have a good mind to – but no. I don't suppose she actually put it literally like that. Rachel will have exaggerated. Taken enjoyment in seeing me hurt.

But what can I tell her? What can I do? How can I sit through those family-therapy sessions? It'd be a mockery! Like some diabolically cruel joke! Yes indeed, Nemesis – or God – or the devil – or them all – sits prettily by my side all the time now – for eternity? My little darling's abduction and return was the sign. The sign that it's time for me to do that infamous thing.

The Right Thing.

16

Morningside. He reckoned there must be nearly as many psychotherapists per square inch in this part of Edinburgh as Manhattan. It was a sign of the city's affluence that it could support so many. Some, of course, were better than others. Debbie Fry was, by all accounts, one of the best child psychotherapists around. He'd done his homework on her. After studying psychology to Ph.D. level, she'd switched to psychotherapy, training at the Tavistock in London, initially specializing in treating adolescents. She'd then become involved in child therapy, particularly victims of child abuse and other serious crimes. She was an acknowledged expert witness, and the police used her a lot.

Sheena, his boss, had offered the entrée, for which he was grateful. And not. That Katie was being seen by the best had to be a force for good. That he hadn't attended any of the sessions and been politely but effectively summoned to her practice to explain himself was tricky. He had the distinct feeling that Dr Fry and his wife had been having quite a few conversations about him, behind his back. The thought added to his feeling of dread as he tugged at the old-fashioned bell pull.

He checked the clock on her mantelpiece. They'd been pussy-footing around for ten minutes. She'd outlined Katie's progress and prognosis. Both favourable, despite Rachel's claims to the contrary. However, there was a 'but'. He sat back and waited for Debbie Fry to expand, though he knew what was coming. He took another look around the beautifully appointed therapy room. High ceilinged, with two long sash windows giving out to the garden. And what a garden. It had a wild look. Grasses, rowan trees, a couple of rockeries where two blue point Siamese cats were slinking about. Focusing back on the interior, he wondered where the usual tools of a child therapist's trade were. The anatomically correct dolls and suchlike. Maybe this wasn't her working room after all.

He met her eye again. He guessed her to be mid to late forties. Extremely attractive, much of that attractiveness stemming from the fact that she looked so fit and bursting with health. To add to that impression, she obviously spent a fair bit of time in sunnier parts of the world, judging by the tanned face and arms. And what else was coming through? Yes, she had a definite air of self-confidence. Sexual self-confidence. Clad unseasonably for an Edinburgh autumn in tight t-shirt, Levis and sandals, she had an athletic body and didn't mind showing it off. And she was happy to let her dark cropped hair show its grey streaks. A good decision, he thought.

'The thing is, Simon, as I've said to Rachel, I do feel that Katie's progress, which will in any case be slow and long term, would be bettered if the *whole* family was involved. I know that you, of all people, understand the vital importance to a traumatized patient of having those who love her highly visible during the healing process. Would it help if I changed the session times to accommodate you? Are you back to full clinical duties now? I know that's a heavy workload.'

And just how did she know about his resuming work duties and its implication that he'd reduced them in the first place? Educated guesswork? Rachel? He hoped Sheena

Logan wasn't discussing him with Debbie Fry. That would be entirely unethical. Furthermore, his refusal to attend Katie's sessions might indicate to Sheena that he wasn't up to resuming work. No, Debbie Fry had better not be discussing anything with his boss. He decided it was time.

'I'm sorry, Debbie. Let me clarify a few things, which of course will remain entirely confidential, like the rest of this conversation. I have my own reasons for feeling that it would be best to proceed with Katie's treatment *without* my input. Personal, deeply held reasons. It's not that I can't make the time to attend. I just do not wish to.'

She uncrossed her legs and leaned forward in her armchair, the look penetrating. 'Can I ask, is it that Katie's experience has echoes for you, perhaps in your own past?'

The accuracy of the question floored him. Sheena Logan had told her. It had to be. Had told her that he'd had treatment in the past, even though it was more than a quarter of a century ago. Outrageous! And what if Debbie Fry tells Rachel? It was a nightmare! He'd have to confront Sheena about this. She didn't know the details, but probably when Sheena and Debbie Fry had discussed him, they'd assumed, quite wrongly, that his adolescent illness was linked to that holy grail of child therapy – sexual abuse. He had been abused, all right. But in a more invisible way, psychologically bludgeoned and undermined by a bullying mother.

He had to close this conversation down. 'You're perfectly entitled to make an assumption of that sort, but I'm really not prepared to expand on what I've said. Whatever my issues are, I'm dealing with them elsewhere.'

He knew it sounded near to a rebuke, but she seemed far from offended. Instead, she gave him a warm smile and stood up. 'That's absolutely fine, Simon. Katie will be okay anyway. Be assured of that. We'll work on, and please, feel free to ring me any time you want an update.'

He was relieved beyond words at her reaction. Of course, as a therapist, it was the right thing to do. She had no other leverage. If he was saying he didn't want to attend his daughter's sessions because of overwhelming personal reasons, there was bugger all she could do. And she had to keep him on side, as part of the therapy. The last thing she needed, in an already fractured family, was to open up another crack.

As they reached the wide hallway, he heard the clink of keys.

'Oh God, sorry, Deb. I didn't think you were going to be working this afternoon.'

He looked at the smiling woman who'd come in. She appeared remarkably similar to Debbie Fry. Fit, tanned, casually dressed. A sister?

Debbie Fry was smiling back at the woman. 'No, no problem. I'm not working. Eh . . . sorry, Simon. This is my partner. Sarah . . . Sarah Melville.'

The barman was beginning to look at him anxiously. It was his third double in less than twenty minutes. He took himself and his drink to the back of the pub, and sat in the darkest corner. The nearest pub to Debbie Fry's house was the Hermitage, one he'd known well, and it brought back fleeting snatches of his courtship with Rachel. They'd had a Saturday-afternoon ritual of going to the art-house cinema up the road and then walking down here for a pint or few. Happy days. Past days.

He analysed his feelings. He'd tried to be rational about what had just happened. The world of psychological medicine was pretty small and tight-knit in the central belt of

Scotland. The world of psychotherapy, operating around the axis of Edinburgh and Glasgow, at elite level anyway, had to be minute. Debbie Fry was renowned. He didn't know about Sarah Melville, but she'd said something about lecturing in the discipline, so she was probably pretty well thought of. No, it wasn't really surprising at all.

God, he was reeling! But he'd dealt with the encounter in a quick-thinking way and, he hoped, with aplomb. He'd been completely up front . . .

'Good grief! Sarah Melville? Yes, it *is* you. You won't remember but I was your patient once. Nineteen seventy-seven? The APU?'

And after a few exclamations and hand-shakings and slightly tense laughs from both women, she'd rallied. 'Simon, don't be so modest. You were one of our star patients. We watched and admired your progress into clinical psychology. Actually, we might well have bumped into one another if I'd stayed nursing, but I got the call to psychotherapy and haven't looked back.'

There was the briefest of hiatuses. He knew all three of them had to think this one of the bizarrest situations possible. He'd handled it well, was holding his own. And then suddenly he'd run out of steam. Had to get out . . .

And within four minutes he was here, ordering brandies by the barrelful. She'd been a pretty cool customer too. He'd no doubt that she was right about the Unit staff being pleased at his progress, long after discharge. They probably had kept tabs on, or at least taken some kind of active interest in, high-achieving ex-patients. His entrance into a branch of medicine allied to their own would have been significant to them. They probably did feel a sense of achievement themselves. Especially given the aspirations of the Unit itself. No, that all had the ring of truth. And she also seemed completely relaxed about her relationship with Debbie Fry. They were clearly open about it and why not, in this day and age, in comfortable, professional, middle-class Edinburgh? The only thing was that it confirmed what he had thought about Sarah Melville then, back in the Unit. That she was interested in women. Though it hadn't really been that significant at the time. Not to any of the patients, to any great extent. Not even to Alex, who, in retrospect, he didn't think even knew her sexuality then. No, gay culture and its social acceptance were essentially unknown quantities in those days. If Sarah Melville had been an active gay woman at that time, she would, he was sure, have kept it from everyone. It would have been just too risky.

The surprise meeting had set off a host of questions and worries in him. And it was those that had him sitting in the pub in the middle of the day. She and her partner were bound to discuss him. He already had a gnawing anxiety about indiscretions between Debbie Fry and Sheena, as well as with his wife. How much would Sarah Melville tell her partner? She had said something about the Unit days being so long ago and a very faint memory. That was probably true, and anyway she'd worked on at the Unit for a while – she'd have had a host of other patients far more interesting than him. No, an ex-patient was bound to attach more significance to their time in the Unit, indeed, to their time in any psychiatric institution, than would the staff. And as for the staff? They were doing a job and couldn't be expected to remember everyone and what went on during their time there.

He stopped his line of thinking. Of course he wanted, *needed* to think that this was true. And yes, in his own practice some patients were more memorable than others. But, what it came down to was, were he and his fellow Unit patients uniquely different from others, in the separate or collective memories of the Unit's staff? He truly hoped not. No, he felt satisfied that Sarah would recall very little detail about him from that time. But he *would* be a conversation piece between her and Fry. How could he not be? And there was a more horrifying possibility. What if Sarah had seen the press reports about Katie? If so, it was worryingly likely that she'd given chapter and verse about him to her partner. Fry, in her turn, would be off, saying that she was treating Katie! True, he saw no hint that Sarah was anything other than completely taken by surprise at seeing him. And Fry made formal introductions, giving no hint that she knew of any connection between them.

He needed to calm down. There was no rational evidence that Sarah knew anything about his reasons for being there. Strictly speaking, Fry shouldn't say *anything* to her partner about why he was at her house. But he knew she would. That led to further worries about what might pass between Fry and his wife and also his boss.

On balance, he thought she'd tread carefully with Rachel. But what he was worried about was what might be said to Sheena. As a trusted and respected member of her department, he had assured her that things were going along okay and that he was ready for work. He didn't want her asking any searching questions about his decision to absent himself from Katie's treatment that might, in turn, affect his professional standing in her eyes. Maybe he was getting things out of proportion, though, and it wouldn't come to anything like that. He'd made the confidential nature of his conversation with Fry crystal clear. She couldn't have missed it, despite what happened in her hallway half an hour ago. Though the additional problem of Sheena meeting Sarah

Melville raised its head. God, that would be a nightmare! But Sheena hadn't given the impression of being so chummy with Fry that she was meeting her partner.

He finished his drink. The rapid hits of alcohol in the middle of the day were having their effect on him now. Despite feeling more than a bit gone, there was something else nagging away at him about Sarah Melville. There was something . . . something else about her . . . something subtle. He thought about the encounter as if it had been a consultation with a new patient. The meeting and greeting so important. Her demeanour, what she said, how she said it, the body language, the tone of her voice, her facial expressions, her eyes. And then he had it. Her eyes. Shining, healthy, bright, aware. And a flicker of something else. Anxiety? Alarm? No, he knew what it was, and he didn't know why it was there. But he was now convinced that what he'd seen had been deep worry, even fear. Why?

He shrugged to himself and got ready to go. Beyond all these worries, uppermost in his mind was the *significance* of meeting someone from those days *now*. It was yet another symbol. Like Katie's being taken. Most clearly, most urgently of all, was that it reinforced his need to do something about his past. Reinforced his decision to answer Danny's letter. Maybe it was all just meant to be. And God knows where it would lead.

'Accidents'

Six months later – 2004, and 1977

Handover note, Sister Anna Cockburn to Nurse Sarah Melville
2 November 1977
RE: Staffing for holiday in Argyll

I'm leaving early tonight before you get on night duty, so won't have time for verbal handover.

I've consulted with Adrian and Ranjit and we all agree that you should accompany me and Ranjit as the third staff member on the holiday. Granted, there are main-hospital staff who are experienced in taking patient groups on holiday, but Adrian stressed that what we don't want is any further rupturing of the group, given the recent atmosphere in the Unit. A new and temporary staff member just for the holiday may cause severe disruption among the patients.

Also, Ranjit pointed out, and I agree with him, that your work with Alex is going really well, and she has shown some positive behaviour of late. We don't want that to be interrupted. You're doing really well with that.

Who knows, we may even enjoy ourselves!

Copy to: Handover File only

17

The room was a bomb-site. Every photo, scrap of paper, scribbled note seemed to be glaring up at her. She clumsily sloshed the remnants of a second bottle of wine into her glass. Quietly pissed. Solitarily pissed. A good feeling. A feeling she needed. Cut off from the outside world in this upmarket yet comforting hotel. No visitors welcomed or expected. No calls answered. Innes Haldane was out. Out of it.

She fingered the ageing photograph. It had once been stuck up somewhere in Danny's life. The back had the telltale, dirty, grey marks of Blu-Tack. Who'd taken the photo of that last afternoon of their camping holiday? That's right . . . it was Ranj's fancy camera. He'd set it and run back to take his position with the rest of them. She remembered now. He'd given them all a copy. She'd burned her copy soon after her release. No doubt in an attempt at denial and obliteration of her past. Denial and obliteration she'd carried with her until these recent weeks. She shook her head at the photo.

God, that bloody camping holiday! Not really camping, though, except for one disastrous night that she'd cried off from, exaggerating the beginnings of a flu that, in reality, was nothing more than a heavy cold. The outward-bound centre itself had been comfortable. Little roughing-it involved. She slugged back her drink, a trickle running down her chin and drip, drip, dripping on to the photo. Along with the beginnings of tears. What the hell was she doing getting maudlin with all this drink, for God's sake! Get a grip!

She ran her palm across Danny's effects. And the printout from his computer disk. There'd been no household accounts on it, despite its label to that effect. Was Danny anxious to hide its contents? After all, it was a special file. Very special. Of names that shot her back into adolescence.

CAROLINE FRANKS. Deceased. Drugs overdose, Edinburgh, 1984.

ALEXANDRA BAXENDALE. Married (second time) but retains maiden name. Internet entrepreneur (formerly City of London trader). Home: 112 Gamekeeper's Gardens, Edinburgh. Second residence in Sussex – rarely used.

DANNY RINTOUL. Unmarried, crofter on Isle of Lewis. Moved there in eighties. Home: 'Sula', Calanais, Isle of Lewis.

*INNES HALDANE. Trained as lawyer, specializing in civil/commercial law. Now Senior Manager, Official Receiver's Office. Divorced. Childless. Home: 29 Primrose Hill Gardens, London NW3.

*LYDIA YOUNG. Married (name 'Shaw'). Three children. Home: 'Craigleith', Dunes Road, Yellowcraigs, East Lothian, Scotland.

??ISABELLA VELASCO. Dental surgeon. Divorced. Childless. Home: 12 Belsize Park Square, London NW3.

DR SIMON CALDER. Clinical psychologist in Edinburgh. Married with two daughters. Home: 'The Old Manse', Fillan's Lane, St Monans, Fife. Second home in France.

ANNA COCKBURN. Deceased. Road traffic accident, 1989.

DR ADRIAN LAURIE. Since 1996, Professor of Adolescent Psychiatry, University of Chicago, USA.

RANJIT SINGH. Former Charge Nurse. Whereabouts unknown. Ceased working at the Unit late 1978. No longer on Nursing Register.

SARAH MELVILLE. Former student nurse. Left nursing late eighties. Retrained as psychoanalytic psychotherapist, with practice in Glasgow.

She'd spent the entire ferry journey back to the mainland poring over the list, emotions bobbing to and fro with the sea swell. That seemed like a lifetime away from the warm familiarity of the fashionable Edinburgh hotel that she found herself in now. Given what she'd been looking at, there was no way she was ready to go back to London.

Staring back down at the list, she felt just the same as when she'd first read it. Puzzlement at what Danny was doing with it. The second page had further details on it: full postal addresses, some landline and mobile numbers, including her own. It couldn't be his own work, since there was no reason to have his own details on it, though on checking when it was last accessed and edited, she could see that it was sometime before his death.

She shook her head again in amazement that she'd been living in such close proximity to Isabella but had never seen her. Or had they passed each other on the street, in a shop, café, bar? The thought was too strange and sad to mull over any longer. Another part of her looked at the list in wonder at the paths people's lives had taken. Hardly a surprise that Simon was indeed now a 'heid doctor' as he, backed up by Carrie, had always promised. And Alex? Again no surprises. Her ingrained aggression would have made her a great City trader, and no doubt now she was a rip-roaring success as an internet entrepreneur. How fitting. Innes paused a moment over the sad inevitability of Caroline's fate. Hardly a surprise. And then the other feelings seeped through. Shock at Anna's death. Confusion at the significance of the various asterisks and question marks, including the asterisk against her own name.

But all that paled beside the real shocker. She'd found the two clippings stuffed inside a recent gas bill. They were dated only weeks before Danny's death. With disbelief she read them again.

Father and three children die in Christmas-fire tragedy – mother 'critical'

A father and his three children died last night in a fire that destroyed their house. The mother survived but is on the critical list at East Lothian General Hospital. Firemen were unable to save Robin Shaw (44), an officer in the Royal Navy, or his three children, Angus (12), Harriet (9) and Hamish (5), as flames engulfed the family home, 'Craigleith', a detached house on the exclusive Dunes Road, overlooking the spectacular beach of Yellowcraigs.

Mr Shaw's wife, Lydia (42), was spotted trapped under fallen roof timbers and cut free by firemen.

Local fire-investigation officers have yet to confirm the cause of the blaze but a spokeswoman said, 'We are not at this stage ruling out the possibility that the fire may have been started deliberately.'

Inquiry finds family-death fire 'may have been started deliberately'

A fatal-accident inquiry has issued an open verdict on the deaths of a father and his three children, stating that the fire in which they died 'may have been started deliberately'. Naval officer Robin Shaw (44) and his three children, Angus (12), Harriet (9) and Hamish (5), may have been the victims of arson at their exclusive beach-front home in Dunes Road, Yellowcraigs. Their mother, Lydia Shaw (42), remains critically ill with serious head injuries in East Lothian General Hospital, after being pulled alive from underneath the collapsed roof of the house.

Police and fire-investigation experts gave evidence that traces of 'an accelerant, thought probably to be petrol' were found at the scene and may have been used to start the fire in the cellar of the six-bedroomed mansion.

Lieutenant Shaw was a keen amateur racing enthusiast and had several cars and motorbikes garaged at the home, along with oil and petrol supplies that may have led to the fire being started accidentally.

Police have indicated that, if the blaze was started deliberately, then they are 'baffled' as to why the 'quiet but well-liked' family of five would have been targeted. However, neighbours and the family's GP have offered some clues that may be relevant if arson was involved. They told the inquiry that Mrs Shaw had seemed depressed and anxious in recent weeks. Local GP Dr Richard Buchanan said that Mrs Shaw had consulted him recently with severe symptoms of anxiety and depression, and he had prescribed appropriate medication for her. It is thought that police are pursuing, among several lines of inquiry, the theory that Mrs Shaw may have been aware of some threat to her family. She remains unconscious and unable to talk to police.

Anyone who was in the vicinity of Dunes Road on the evening of Saturday, 12 December, is being asked to contact their local police station.

The surprising fact that Lydia had married well, given birth to three children and presumably found some form of domestic happiness was obliterated in Innes's mind by the imagined horror of the event. The inescapable knowledge that Lydia had a background in fire-starting left a chilling and overwhelming question mark in her mind. Could Lydia really be responsible for killing her husband and three little ones? She hauled herself back into the present. What in God's name was happening? Three fatal incidents within a few months. Only one an 'accident'. Maybe.

She shook her head at the shocking news of Lydia. A strange and petulant girl, always attention-seeking, always putting everyone's back up . . .

18

'Ach! Fir Christ's sake! Whit's she done now? Innes? D'you know what the fuck she's moaning about now?' Innes shrugged her reply as Caroline tugged painfully at tangled wet hair with a brush and headed over towards the source of the noise. Innes decided to follow, more out of boredom than curiosity. She had a bad cold and was not going to be able to take part in the day's orienteering challenge or stay in tents overnight at a planned bivouac a few miles north. She was very happy with that and began, for the umpteenth time, ostentatiously blowing her running nose. She hated camping and hated roughing it. The screaming and yelling was reaching banshee proportions. She saw Ranj and Anna clustered around a now well-nigh hysterical Lydia, who was rolling on her side, clutching her left knee.

'The monkey rope broke! My knee! It's bleeding! Waaaaaaa!'

Caroline had stuffed the brush into a back pocket of her jeans and rubbed at the frayed end of rope hanging from the stout oak. She quipped, 'Aye. It wasnae designed wi' elephants in mind. Yer too fat! That's how it broke. Silly coo.'

But Anna rounded on her. 'Cut it out, Carrie. Be useful for once. Go and get Sarah and tell her to bring the first-aid box! Go on! Now!'

Innes watched Caroline saunter off, insolence in every casual step. 'Aye, aye. Keep yer knickers on, Sis.'

Half an hour later Innes joined a few of them sitting around a blazing fire, slurping lunchtime soup. Lydia had been persisting in her claims, claims that had replaced the weeping and wailing. 'I'm telling you, someone cut that rope. They wanted me to break my neck!' And then she'd limped off to skulk in her bunk.

Alex was hunched forward, anorak hood covering her shaven head. She'd disappeared for most of the morning into the dorm hut, refusing to talk to anyone. But now she seemed, to Innes, strangely and unexpectedly animated. She was nodding vigorously and talking to no one in particular. 'Well? We couldn't have bloody Lydia trailing along with us today. She'd be fucking hopeless.'

Innes listened to the general murmur of agreement from Danny, Simon and Carrie. She raised an eyebrow at Isabella, who asked the obvious.

'What? So you *did* tamper with the rope? That's a bit iffy. Lydia could've been really hurt.'

'Rubbish!' Carrie tossed a bread crust into the fire and watched it incinerate. 'It wasn't very far to fall, for fuck's sake. Listen, this orienteering, camping thing today and tonight is about our only chance for a bit of fun before we go back. That fat cow would just hold us back. I'm with Alex. It'll be better with just us lot, except for you, Innes. How's "the flu" anyway? Skiver!'

Innes felt the rush of red to her face, annoyed and surprised at her plan being flushed out so easily. But she tried a nonchalant shrug. 'I'm really feeling crap, Carrie, whatever you think. You'll be better off without me. Anyway, have fun. I'm off to bed.' She stood up, flashing a conspiratorial smile at Abby. Yeah, she hoped at least Abby would have a good time.

The shouting and banging woke her up with a start, heart hammering away from being shocked out of such a deep and badly needed sleep. It was pitch black. Hurriedly, she scrambled out of her bunk and switched a side light on. Her watch said ten twenty-five. She'd been asleep for hours! Outside, she could make out Sarah battering against the door of the female staff's hut.

'Anna! Anna! C'mon!'

Lydia had sidled up beside Innes, swathed in a huge bath towel, her hair dripping. 'What the . . .'

Innes left her standing in the doorway and headed across the grass towards Sarah, just as Anna wrenched the hut door open. 'Oh, God, Anna!'

Innes could see Sarah's face clearly now in the yellow light pouring from Anna's hut. She was pale, drawn, frightened.

Anna looked sleepy. 'What you doing here? You and Ranj are meant to be with the kids. What's goi—'

But Sarah was grabbing her by both shoulders. 'They've gone, Anna. Gone! We've lost them! Ranj is up on the high road in the Land Rover.'

Anna stepped out of the hut and was roughly pulling Sarah's hands away. 'Fucking hell, Sarah! How'd that happen? Jesus! A'right. C'mon! Round up Lydia and Innes. We can't leave them here on their own. And let's get the other Land Rover and get looking. They can't be far.'

Innes retreated into her own hut and closed the door, leaning her back against it. She should have known something like this would happen. As she dragged on jeans and a warm jumper, she thanked her lucky stars that she'd stayed here. God only knew what had happened to that lot in their current weird mood. A flicker of concern for Abby ran through her mind, but she shook it off. Danny was out there and he would never, *ever* let harm come to her.

With that sense of relief, she took a deep breath and headed outside.

19

She shouldn't have done it. It had been a long time since she'd got herself in that state. Innes dragged herself through the torture of a deliberately lukewarm shower, desperate to wake herself up. Then watched as the two tablets fizzed their way up the tumbler. The room was a sty. The empty wine bottles glinted searing sunlight back at her. Accusing. No need. Her head and stomach were punishment enough. She wondered at being here again. A home city she'd given the cold shoulder to since the death of her parents. Nothing much to visit for. Until now.

The hangover was hellish. Agonizing. She could barely shuffle downstairs to get to the hire car. Probably still well over the limit too. Had to get going, though. Within twenty minutes she'd arrived. There it was. She could feel her heart quicken, her throat constrict, she laid a cold hand on her pocket, satisfied at the crinkling sound of the paper bag, ready to hand. The detached stone mansion lay at the end of an exclusive cul-de-sac. Her house. Except it had never been that. Mercifully, mother had gone first, followed by a broken and also cancer-ridden father a mere seven months later. She'd had the house cleared in a week. Paced its empty hallways for three days and nights. Then put it on the market, never setting foot inside again.

It was a house with children now. Two toddlers' bicycles leaned crookedly against the ivied front wall, and she could hear whoops of laughter from the open side door. It was a happy house. More than it had ever been during her occupation . . .

'You're a nasty, ugly little girl. I'm ashamed that you're my daughter. I wish you'd never been born to me. Now get away. To your room. Just you wait. I'll be speaking to your father.'

'. . . now come on, Innes. What's this your mother's been telling me about? You've got to understand that your mother . . . well . . . your mother can . . . can be . . . be . . . *difficult*. It's much better if you just be careful around her . . . be careful . . .'

Careful! It had become so clear in adulthood. Mother had been mentally ill *and* malevolent: a sickening combination. Innes always thought it a miracle that neither she nor Dad had taken an iron bar to her skull. There had been enough provocation, for God's sake. She was still working it out in therapy. Families. A naturally dysfunctional unit in almost every case. Not bitterness. Not cynicism. Just an empirically provable truth.

The rain had started up, picking away at the windscreen and kicking up spray in front of her headlights. The March evening had turned as dark and cold as any winter's night. But it mattered little to her. There was no stopping now. She pondered the seeming irrationality of what she was doing. It made perfect sense to her. Of course, she hadn't a clue if the building would still be standing. She half smiled as she thought about a previous nocturnal visit years earlier, after a particularly fraught stay with her parents. The circumstances, the emotional ones at least, had been reasonably similar. Her mother had been getting at her for never holding down a 'successful relationship', only too aware that her daughter's marriage was faltering. Innes had stormed out, driving her car recklessly in fog to this place, in an act of both penance and pilgrimage. Back then, it still was alive, lit up, a large sign with ADOLESCENT PSYCHIATRIC UNIT (APU) clearly visible.

The road the house stood on wasn't private as such. But it was little used. Its chief function was as a cut-through to the main hospital and its various outlying clinics. She rolled the car to a stop and put out the lights. The house was still there. But it was in darkness. The old APU sign was half torn down, the wooden stake supporting it pointing at a crooked angle.

She got out of the car, all four indicators giving a simultaneous orange blink as she activated the remote-locking system. She stood at the main entrance. No evidence of life or recent occupation. She walked a few yards down the road and looked back, straining to see through the ground-floor windows of the old morning-meetings/psychodrama room. It looked like the wooden shutters were firmly shut against inquisitive intruders like her. Whatever was going on, the place wasn't being used any more. It had the sad air of the forgotten and neglected. A blot on the night's landscape.

She looked down the length of the garden. The night was clear enough to make it out. The swing was still there. Incredible! She'd hopped over the short wall and was halfway across the lawn before she thought about what she was doing. Christ. It was dark. She was a woman on her own. This was madness. But the swing was so near now. Just a few more yards. When she reached it, she tugged tentatively on both chains, using her sleeve to wipe the excess moisture from the faded, wooden seat, and sat down.

The familiar creaking started up as she gently allowed her feet to leave the security of the muddy ground beneath her. Slowly, slowly, she tilted her head back, looking through the overhanging trees to the sky above. A few stars, wispy clouds and half a moon. Calm. All calm . . .

That summer. Summer of '77. Everyone had a 'summer of', didn't they? Funny hers should be one spent in a mental hospital. The summer to remember. And not. What could she remember of it? Hot. Rainy too. Everything verdant. Obscenely lush. Over-green. Yeah, yeah, but what else? What about *here*? This very place? The place she'd first set eyes on them. Carrie, Simon, Danny, Lydia. They'd all spent countless golden, sunny evenings together here. Lydia liked the swing too. At tea-time – when she repeatedly had to be called in. Attention. All she craved. And who else loved the swing? Abby visited it when she could be alone. And alone with Danny. Yes, that had caused some jealousy. Danny and Abby. She swinging. He occasionally pushing. Carrie and Simon too. Heads bent. In intimacy? In conspiracy?

She blanked out the memory. Eyes still closed, she was enjoying the cradling motion when another noise, a distinct rustling, joined the creaking of the metal chain links. Her head shot up and she stamped her muddy feet firmly down to halt the swing.

Pushing herself out of the seat, she started a brisk walk up the garden that soon broke into a slippery and sliding sprint, as she headed for the relative security of the car and nearby street lamps. She allowed herself one backward glance, and watched as the little bit of moonlight caught the metal on the swing chains, as it toed and froed its empty way to a halt.

Back at the car, she leaned over the bonnet, keys at the ready, heavy breathing turning to falsely jolly, self-convincing laughter.

'Idiot. There's nothing there. Just old, harmless ghosts!'

Sitting in the warmth and safety of her locked car, she

felt reluctant to leave. Something about being in such close proximity to the Unit building allowed her mind to travel the memory paths she had for so many years successfully blocked off.

She glanced towards the swing. Thinking back, there was more conspiracy going on than she had known at the time. Or that she'd paid attention to. Especially around that Christmas . . .

20

Seven inches! So much of the stuff! Every tree branch, grass blade and pathway of the garden, obliterated.

Innes was at the top of the hilly lawn watching Carrie hurl an enormous snowball at Danny. 'Come on, fuck arse!' But Danny was quick and had ducked, swiftly returning fire. 'Bull's-eye!' And suddenly he stopped, tuning in to a repeated grunting noise a few feet behind them. 'Alex! What ye doin'?' He dusted ice fragments from his two sodden, woollen gloves, and shrugged his puzzled amusement at Innes, as he watched the coated and scarfed figure of Alex, shaven head red-raw with cold, chopping the limbs off one of three snowmen with a broom handle.

Innes heard Lydia scuttling up to join them. She let out a childish and manic giggle as she prodded Innes's arm. 'Oh-oh. She's got it in for Anna. Bet you Sarah's next. This'll be fun!'

Innes knew the others had sensed that something more interesting than a snowball fight was going on. Isabella and Simon were moving up the lawn as well, shaking their heads at a demented Alex, making short work of the next snow sculpture. Innes reckoned it had taken Alex just under two and a half hours to build three snow nurses. All clearly identifiable: Ranj, with tea-towel turban; Anna, complete in a turquoise sari, made from an old curtain; Sarah . . . well, hadn't Alex been clever? God only knew where she'd got it. Stuck in the mouth of the student nurse's snowman statue was a baby bottle. They'd all heard Lydia taunt Sarah with the term 'baby nurse', in attempts to provoke. Attempts that Sarah unfailingly refused to react to. Now Alex had taken the taunt a dramatic step further.

Carrie was rubbing her frozen hands together. 'Alex's fuckin' lost her marbles now. Shall we get someone?'

Danny shook his head. 'Nah. Let her get on with it.'

Innes stepped forward to peer upwards. She thought there had been a movement in an upper window. 'They know anyway. There's Ranj upstairs. Sarah too. Wonder what she thinks of it?'

Abby was at her side now. 'Goodness knows. Strange behaviour, though. Creation and destruction. One for the nursing log, I think.'

Innes more than agreed with her but kept her opinion to herself. The past few weeks had been regularly marred by violent outbursts from Alex. She'd become increasingly moody and uncommunicative, and every time she was in the group, there was a general uneasiness. Why, Innes had no idea. But it wasn't all just down to Alex. Carrie had been aggressive and tetchy too. Danny had been unusually sullen, hardly ever joking. Not like he used to be. Simon? Hard to tell. Here he was.

Simon was clapping his hands in delight, smiling with glee at her and Abby. 'Absolutely *is* one for the nursing log! The staff'll make a real meal out of this. Betcha Laurie raises it at tomorrow's therapy? "Now, Alexandra, tell us. Why did you make snowmen that resembled the staff and why did you ruin your creation with such apparent pleasure?" Yeah. He'll have a field day. Actually, I'm impressed. Alex's obviously got an artistic streak that we all missed. She can carve snow sculptures better than she carves up her arms.'

Two feet away, Innes joined in the laughter at the uncannily accurate aping of Dr Laurie's pompous voice, but hoped to hell that Alex hadn't heard Simon's cruel comment about her self-mutilation. She needn't have worried. She saw how engrossed Alex was in viciously swiping at the heads and torsos of the three snow nurses.

Simon kept up the light air of banter, but his face told another story, and Innes heard him whisper to Carrie, 'Alex is at her worst now! Well, almost worst. What the fuck are we going to do with her?'

Carrie was slapping him on the back reassuringly. 'Dinnae worry. I've been talkin' tae Danny. Alex'll need watching. Warning. Teachin' a lesson, maybe. See, Alex isnae as tough as she makes out. You know that fine well. She's got her . . . how shall we say . . . her *weak* points. I think we just need tae remind her, in a way that she'll understand, that she needs tae watch hersel'. For all our sakes.'

Danny brushed past them both, heading towards the kitchen entrance, pulling off gloves and unwinding his scarf, mumbling to himself as much as to the rest of them. 'Fuck it! Alex is a born nutter. I'm going in. Remember, as if any of us could forget, it's the Christmas party tonight. Fun and fucking games!'

'Right, time for the raffle I reckon. Agreed, Anna?'

She'd never seen Anna so jolly as she nodded her agreement to Ranj, speech being useless above the raucous din. Innes stood behind her and surveyed the scene. The group-therapy/psychodrama room seemed bigger than ever. All unwanted furniture and the TV had been moved out of the way. The new Christmas tree was at least a foot taller than the previous one, which had been torched two days before. There had been an 'inquiry' about that, but no proof. Apparently Ranj and Anna had had a stand-up row, Ranj convinced that Lydia was up to her fire-starting tricks, Anna that it was the faulty electrics causing a blow-out of the fairy lights, which in turn ignited the tree. But Innes had overheard scraps of conversation about the incident. Enough to know that it involved Simon and Carrie and maybe others. Simon's words to Carrie had stayed with her: 'And that's what everyone's meant to think. That it was loony Lydia. It's called distracting attention, dear Carrie. Got it? The fact is, our dear nursing staff are very sensitive. Very aware of the atmospheres and nuances in this bloody place. It's why they're here and not wiping the arses of some geriatrics down the road. I know that they had an emergency case-conference on Tuesday. Just before the fire. They know something's amiss. So, we needed to give them something to worry about, didn't we? Let them put out the wrong fires, as it were . . .'

What it was all about, Innes didn't have a clue. But it was just another example of this place running askew.

She shook off the recent memory and gazed at the rainbow-coloured fairy lights twinkling away. The four long and elegant bay windows offered a magnificent view on to the lawn, now coated with the freshest of snow shimmering in the moonlight. Inside, the walls were predictably bedecked with tinsel, shiny Father Christmases and spangly, glitter-strewn snowmen decorations.

The decorating of the room had been a pleasant experience. Everyone had chipped in; even God, aka Dr Laurie, had gone up a stepladder! And the fire incident had, it seemed, been set aside for the festive season. Sister Anna had had one last try at prising something out of them at that morning's group meeting. But she, and the rest of the staff, knew they were wasting their time. Apart from Lydia's regular bleats of innocence, no one was talking about it any more. To Innes's disappointment, even Abby had refused to be drawn on the subject. And Innes had, with some shame, kept her knowledge of what Simon had said to Carrie strictly to herself.

'Anna – dance?' Innes had found a comfortable niche at the back of the room, in shadow. She watched, smiling, as Adrian Laurie whisked the nurse away before Anna had time to reply. They disappeared into a throng of patients, their friends, their siblings. No parents. By order. At least that was a good decision. But she wasn't so sure about this party. Things had been so . . . so . . . *off* recently. It seemed really false to have some jolly party as if everything was fine. She wasn't even sure if any of them, herself included, were 'getting better'. Their individual and collective heads were a bit more of a challenge than a bloody common cold, and she was beginning to doubt whether the Unit or its staff were up to the job.

She spied student Sarah a few feet in front of her, having a furtive look around. After a few seconds, she slipped a quarter bottle of vodka out of her pocket and poured a more than generous measure into her Coke, taking a long pull, unaware of Innes's scrutiny. And then Anna was standing beside the student, slightly breathless from her energetic dance with Dr Laurie. Without turning her head from the crowd, Sarah asked, 'Going pretty well, Anna, don't you think?'

Anna was tilting her head as if the question was a hard one. 'Seems to be. Never know for sure what's going on in their bloody sick minds, though!'

Innes watched as Sarah blinked her astonishment. The student must have been as shocked as she was at Anna's outburst, even though it probably chimed with Sarah's own thoughts. And then the student gave her boss a comradely nudge. 'Ach, they're going home tomorrow. Give us all a proper holiday. Not like the bloody fiasco in Argyll last month. Sod it, things'll be different next year.'

Anna started to disagree. 'Think so? I tell y—'

Her words were drowned out by Ranj, who was standing on a makeshift stage where a three-man combo had just finished grinding out festive tunes. 'All right, quieten down, everyone! Quie . . . t! Time for the wonderful . . . fabulous . . . superb . . . Unit Christmas raffle! Proceeds as you know going to the Maybury Wing, for those with head injuries. A good cause, I'm sure you'll agree.' The remaining murmurs died down, and Ranj held up a small red Santa sack. 'Get a move on, Danny. You drew the short straw last week to hand out the prizes. Number one!'

Innes smiled as Danny, complete in red bobble hat and silver tinsel scarf, stepped up beside Ranj, sucked a last draw from his roll-up and ground it out underfoot. 'Okay. There's three runner-up prizes. *Numero uno* is . . .' He dug his hand into the sack held out for him by Ranj. He unwrapped the square of paper and shouted out the number. 'Number zero one five!' Innes joined in the scuffle to check counterfoils. Nothing. Danny tried again. 'Number zero one five!'

'I'm zero one six! I think my auntie's got the one before that. But she's not here.' Everyone was craning to see Lydia, more rotund than ever in a billowing scarlet and white abomination posing as an evening gown.

Ranj stepped forward, the look of forced patience on his gentle face that Innes had come to recognize as the one he used when the Unit was at its most stressed-out. He held up a hand to quiet the crowd. 'Okay, let's leave that one. We'll put that prize aside, Lydia, and you can check with your aunt later.' A few complaining grumbles were ignored as Ranj urged Danny to continue. 'Okay. Next?'

Danny plunged his hand in again. 'Righto. Second runner-up. Number zero twenty-three! Zero two three!'

'Yes! Me!' Innes watched as a giggling Sarah pushed her way to the front and joined the other two on the tiny stage. She teetered precariously on the edge as Ranj handed her the prize. She ripped off the green crêpe paper and laughed, holding a pound box of Black Magic and a book token aloft. 'Thanks, everyone! When you next see me in two weeks' time, I'll be the size of a house and cross-eyed! Merry Christmas!'

There was some half-hearted clapping and then Danny was digging in for the second-to-last time. 'Zero three one. Zero thirty-one!'

A little boy of about ten elbowed his way forward, raffle ticket waving above his head. Dr Matt Benson, an American psychiatrist from the main hospital, scooped him up into his arms, shouting in his Southern drawl: 'For those of you who haven't met him yet, this is Dale. My nephew. He lives in London with my sister, Lee-Anne, whom I saw a minute ago. Lee-Anne, you there?'

'She's in the bog!' someone shouted. Innes joined in the general laughter.

Matt Benson was lifting the little boy on to the stage. Ranj bent down, holding out the long, fat, cracker-shaped parcel. It was far too heavy for the child, and Innes stayed back as the crowd unconsciously made a semicircle around him while his uncle lay the gift on the floor. Within two minutes all was revealed: a bright orange tent.

'Wow!' Matt Benson hoisted the boy on to his shoulders. 'Say a big thank you, Dale. Dale loves camping. Anyone mind if we set up in the garden right now? Only joking!'

Innes noticed Anna, standing on the outside of the circle, meeting Adrian Laurie's eye. They'd picked it up immediately.

The atmosphere had turned – subdued, edgy. She felt, rather than saw, the darting looks passing between some of the others. It was too dark to make much out. But Ranj was charging on, unaware. 'Right! Star-prize time! Danny, do the honours please!'

Innes stood on tip-toe as Danny, like an expert illusionist, ostentatiously pulled his shirtsleeve back and dipped his hand slowly in. 'Zero zero seven! Double o seven. Lucky for more than James Bond, it seems!'

'*Yes*! Mine's ya bass!' Alex was right at the front and was hauling herself up beside Danny and Ranj. Ranj handed her the lavishly beribboned box, stopped a moment and frowned as he seemed to weigh it in his hands. Then continued smiling and congratulating. 'Well done, Alex. I know you'll enjoy this. Have a great Christmas!'

All eyes were on her, straining to see what she'd won. Innes was reminded of the snowmen frenzy in the garden a few hours earlier as Alex ripped at the paper, offering a running commentary to all. 'Ah . . . right, I see. It's one of these trick presents. Paper on paper, boxes in boxes. Like bloody Russian dolls! Sneaky buggers! Here we go.' She'd already shed three layers of wrapping and emptied two boxes. Ripping at the lid she pulled back the last of the red tissue and stared at what was nestling among it. With a yelp, she dropped everything, leaped off the stage, and kicked and punched her way through the crowd, howling.

'*No! No! Nooo!*'

Each watched as she fled from the room. Innes inched forward, anxious to see the upturned box. Ranj was there, kneeling down. Carefully he lifted the box and scowled. Still entwined in the crumpled tissue was Alex's prize.

Climbing rope and a hunting knife.

21

Innes had slept like the dead. No dreaming. That surprised her after her visit to the Unit building. She'd got very jittery there. Stupid, really. And so many memories came flooding back. Things she hadn't thought about for years. But this morning she'd allowed herself to consider what she was doing. And why.

Three, *three*, out of the six people she'd spent the best part of a year with in a psychiatric hospital had recently been involved in fatal incidents. Lydia might well be alive, but, by the sound of things, the quality of that life was compromised beyond repair.

She mused on their lives in the Unit. Of all the crazy games they'd played to amuse themselves, annoy each other, goad staff, they'd never played who'll-be-dead-in-a-quarter-of-a-century. Not surprising. Like all youth, they had times when they had seen themselves as immortal. However, unlike most other teenagers, they had all suffered their share of pole-axing morbidity, when intrusive, depressing thoughts were on the agenda day and night. But she would never in a million years have predicted that, counting Carrie as well, three of them would be dead. Another half dead. All by their own hands.

And that was why she was doing this. At six thirty that morning, meaningful, *rational* – to her at least – resolve had set in. Three former patients' lives had been effectively obliterated in a handful of months. The only known link between these people was the Unit. Coincidence was totally inadequate as an explanation. For God's sake, what the hell had been happening at that bloody place to lead to this? For the hundredth time that morning she lay back on the bed, notepad on knees, her scribbled jottings beginning to hurt her eyes.

She'd written *drugs/drugs therapy?* It was an obvious one. And yet not. The simple fact was that very few of the patients were given any medication. That was part of the new-fangled regime. Keep away from the more conventional treatments. Only use them if all else has failed, if absolutely necessary and for short periods of time. Certainly, a few of them had been given medication but very sparingly. The 'chemical cosh', so reviled now but in constant use then in psychiatric hospitals, was never a built-in feature of the go-ahead Unit.

As the morning wore on, she'd resisted giving too much credence to a slowly forming 'sci-fi' theory that maybe experimental drugs had been used in that most experimental of places. Maybe there was some kind of horrendous neuropsychological backlash that manifested itself in middle age in the patients? Christ, maybe they'd all been given it in the food, drink or something. Or maybe they'd all been subject to hypnotherapy and couldn't remember anything. She'd smiled to herself and scored a line through these more outlandish ideas. Too *X-Files*!

But it didn't stop the other, more nebulous worry: that maybe something in them all, either in their treatments or in their various illnesses, had unwittingly created psychological time-bombs. Time-bombs that ended in agonizing, reckless, unnecessary deaths . . .

An hour later, she pulled out of the hotel car park, skirted the city and headed south. She was relieved to be doing something and leaving her unhealthy, brooding mood far behind in the hotel room. Traffic and weather went her way, and she was pulling into the beach-side car park by midday. Yellowcraigs was windy. She clambered up to the top of a dune. A lot of people out for a weekday. Various mothers with children. Old ladies and men with dogs. Hoods up and heads down against the sand-blasting gale.

She turned inland and made the five-minute walk to Dunes Road. A carved wooden sign at the entrance to the short drive told her she was at 'Craigleith'. She studied the blackened mass that had once been a fine family house. And, ultimately, the crematorium for a father and his three children.

'Can I help you?'

She spun round to see the smiling face of an elderly woman, who was clutching the tartan lead of a soaking wet West Highland Terrier.

'Oh, I, I, eh, I'm sorry.'

The woman nodded to the remnants of 'Craigleith'. 'What a mess. And an awful tragedy. I'm Jean Lamont. I live next door. In "Kittiwake". Are you visiting or . . . ?'

The small, neat woman let the question trail off. Innes knew she wasn't suspicious of her. She clearly looked too respectable to be a burglar. Nevertheless, the woman wanted to know why a stranger was in her private road.

Innes crouched to pet the small dog, blowing kisses at the beast, making it overexcited and causing it to bark shrilly. She stood up again and looked at 'Craigleith'. 'Actually I knew someone who lived there.'

'My goodness! Not dear Lydia? Robin?'

Innes offered a suitably doleful smile in reply, not wanting to invite too many unanswerable questions about her interest in the place. 'Yes. Lydia. What actually happened? I just heard something about a fire.'

The old woman sat down on the brick wall, inviting Innes to do the same, and she talked on, staring into the mid-distance towards the sea. On closer inspection Innes could see that the woman really was getting on. Eighty if she was a day. Her hair was white and thinning. But her complexion was good. Tanned. Lined. Healthy. A strong face. She had a refined, lilting accent. The north-east, Caithness or Sutherland, she reckoned, as she listened to the woman's story of her former neighbour.

'Lydia was a lovely girl. Had a lot to cope with, what with her man being an officer in the Navy and everything, and being away from home for long periods. The children were all at private school down the road. I think Angus was about to go to boarding school. Wee Hamish was the youngest and had just started at school. Lydia was a good mother. Always telling me she wanted the best for them. I get the impression that maybe she hadn't had a very happy childhood. I didn't even know, until I read it in the papers, that she had any parents still living. She never mentioned them and they never visited. And they just live in Edinburgh. So near. Ach, well. You never know what goes on in other people's families, do you?'

Innes couldn't have agreed more, and leaned forward to pat the dog, attempting to seem casual in her next inquiry. 'Uh-huh. And this fire? I've only read a couple of reports. There's a suggestion that it was started deliberately?'

Jean Lamont paused, head shaking in bewilderment and pity. 'It was well covered in the local paper and at the inquiry into their deaths. My granddaughter works there at the paper, so I've got a bit of the "inside track", as they say. Anyway, there's no absolute proof about that. If it was arson, no one knows who did it or why. They think Lydia was under some sort of stress before it happened. May have known of some threat. You see, she'd been awfy depressed. But she told no one, not even her husband. And no one noticed.

Myself included. It only came out when her GP gave evidence at the inquiry. When he suggested that she share things with her family and friends, you know, take the load off, apparently Lydia became very agitated. Was adamant that no one should know there was anything wrong. But, in terms of the tragedy, that was all a bit circumstantial. It may just have been pure coincidence that Lydia was having a hard time and this happened. On the other hand, there was gossip about her husband's job in the Navy. Something "top secret", perhaps. But he didn't do secret things, like captain a nuclear submarine. He was just a career officer on a ship, for goodness sake. And of course there was his racing stuff. All those cars and motorcycles and petrol and oil on the premises. A bit dangerous, I would have thought. But, who knows?'

Innes waited as the old woman paused for a wistful moment and then went on. 'Lydia's doing well apparently. Physically that is. But she's . . . they're not sure, really. They thought she had brain damage at first and it seems that there *is* some loss there, but it also looks like she's got rather serious . . . serious *psychiatric* problems now. They say it might be . . . what do they call it? Yes, some sort of *post-traumatic* problem. She's in a specialist place not far from here. The Broughton Clinic. A few miles down the coast in North Berwick. I visit her regularly. I'm not sure she knows me, to be honest. It's been terrible, terrible.'

Jean Lamont edged herself closer to Innes. 'There *was* one funny thing. It's been on my mind. About two weeks before the fire, Lydia had some visitors. Two. A man and a woman. Not together. The man I didn't see very well. It was at night. But the other one, that one I got a good look at. It was very unusual. You see, they never had visitors other than tradesmen and his, Robin's family.'

Innes shrugged, unsure of where this was going. 'So? Why should that matter? These visitors, I mean?'

'I think it matters. Because she was never the same after that. Every time I saw her she was nervy. Odd. You see, I saw her at her front door with the man. The one I didn't get a good look at. You could see that she didn't really want him there. But it was a couple of days later when I saw her with a woman. Youngish. Attractive. Smartly dressed. They were talking out on the drive. I couldn't hear what was being said. But I'm telling you, Lydia looked scared. Terrified out of her wits! I can't explain it any more clearly. She just looked ill. Dreadful. Like she'd seen a ghost.'

She met up with Jean Lamont again after a couple of hours' break. Innes had spent the time down at the harbour of the seaside town of North Berwick, picking away at an unappetizing sandwich, worrying about the ethics of her next step. Her mood had changed again: back to one of mild dread. Maybe it was time to return to London. Stop this now. But that wasn't going to be the answer. She'd embarked on this most surprising of personal journeys. She felt utterly alone in it. Although how could it be any other way? This was *her* past she was excavating. Only she could do it. And it was high time she did. It was still there – the underlying nag of fcar that had stayed stubbornly in her gut since Isabella's phone message. *That* had been the catalyst for all this. And she wouldn't, *couldn't*, ignore it.

The old lady was rattling on as they stepped out of the car at the visitors' parking area. 'You're not allowed any further by car unless you're passing through. Still, the walk's a nice one on a day like this. The Broughton Clinic's in a separate building from the main hospital. It actually has quite a few functions, including two locked wards for some real poor souls.'

The long semi-rural walk down a tree-lined private road to the clinic was more of a reminder of the Unit than Innes needed. She slowed her pace, the urge to turn on her heel and run almost irresistible. But, as they rounded the corner, the mirage was broken. The Broughton Clinic bore no resemblance whatsoever to the old Unit mansion. Here was a modern two-storey ugly box of a building.

They approached a reception area that had more glass and hot-house plants in its atrium than Innes's own overpriced health club back in London. A quick glance to her left and she knew why. An unobtrusive but clear sign PRIVATE WING THIS WAY answered her questions about the expensive architecture. She wondered how on earth they'd managed to put the locked wards, with presumably the most seriously mentally ill, cheek-by-jowl with those who wanted to be pampered.

She checked out of Jean Lamont's well-meaning but inane babbling to the receptionist and paid attention to herself. She was nervous. It was an important moment. This was the first time she'd met a Unit patient since she'd left the damn place.

And what of Lydia? Innes's view of her twenty-six years ago had been of a basically nice girl who could sometimes have the devil in her. A manic depressive. If she was 'up', life was great and Lydia loved everyone, well, almost everyone. But her 'downs' had cast a dark and sour pall over the Unit, staff included. During those episodes, Lydia would withdraw into herself, monosyllabic at best, creepily mute at worst. But Innes had known the girl was an acute observer during those periods. Lydia spied on people. She hadn't been the only one. But Innes had often seen her doing it. Eavesdropping. Watching. Perhaps even plotting, paranoia conjoining with the black despair in her sick mind.

'Lydia Shaw is no longer in Ward 17. She was moved to what we call the Annexe last week.' The receptionist was smiling helpfully at them both.

Jean Lamont took a step forward. 'The Annexe?'

'It's a kind of halfway house. Locked at night but open during the day. It means she's doing well. You'll be pleased, Mrs Lamont. Just a moment, I'll call one of the nurses to come and see you.'

Moments later, a pretty-faced, obviously gay male nurse was standing in front of Innes, smiling a welcome to both. Muscular, shaven-headed and called Charge Nurse Johnny Wallace.

'Hi, Jean, lovely to see you again.' Innes shook his hand as Jean Lamont made the introductions. 'And welcome to you, Innes. It's good to see Lydia having new visitors. She doesn't get enough of them.'

'But what about her parents?' Innes asked.

She caught an eye-to-eye exchange between Jean and Nurse Johnny before he answered. He kept the smile as he delivered the sad truth. 'They don't visit. Lydia has no other blood relatives. That's why we encourage friends and the like to come.'

That was hardly surprising. How could the bitter divisions, present in Lydia's family twenty-six years ago, have led to anything other than estrangement?

'And her husband's family?'

The awkward Jean/Johnny exchange happened again. He just shook his head at Innes.

'Oh, I see.' She followed the other two down a long airy corridor. So, Lydia's in-laws thought she'd killed their son and grandchildren. What other reason could they have for staying away?

Johnny was keeping up a running commentary about

Lydia's condition. 'It's still very early days. We thought there'd been *some* neurological damage. It's just very difficult to know exactly what. The senior medical staff here are a bit puzzled by Lydia's case actually. She performs well in various tests which involve tasks both physical and mental but she seems to have blocks of some kind in communication. She can also get very aggressive. The main problem seems to be behavioural, which of course can have a physical cause, in terms of brain damage, *or* a psychological one. By that I mean the shock and trauma of the event itself.

'Lydia is very difficult to deal with. I know that you, Jean, have found her to be a different person from the one you used to know. Personality change is not uncommon in such cases. After the fire she was in a coma for three weeks. Then just came out of it. *Anyway*, I can't promise she'll know either of you today, but it's worth a try. Sometimes she responds to Jean. Sometimes not, eh? We'll see. It's certainly better for her to be here, seeing visitors and being able to get outside. Lydia's obviously no longer the severe worry she was when she first came in. It's just we don't really know what's going on with her. We can only hope for the best and keep her stimulated and occupied.'

They were led around the side of the ugly building, and the world suddenly changed. The garden was sloped and landscaped. Trees, shrubbery, lawns and the sound of a fountain somewhere. It reminded her of a Swiss sanatorium from the turn of the century – except, instead of consumptive convalescents in bath-chairs and tartan knee rugs, there were various, disparate huddles of people in twos and threes. Despite the chilly March air, all the patients wore some form of night attire. Some had brightly coloured fashionable dressing gowns on, in silky reds and blues. Others were more conventionally dressed in dull towelling affairs. Every patient she could see looked very ill, some chuntering away to nobody in particular, some bent over, withdrawn into their own universes. Johnny chattered on.

'All the patients are aged between twenty-five and forty-five. All have a history of brain injury and psychological disturbance. *But* the good news is that they're doing well. Lydia has made remarkably fast progress, remember. Just the very fact that she's in the Annexe means that. You know, this is one of the best places in the UK. And all on the good old NHS. It was originally funded by a generous bequest, and some trust money helps out. And we get rent from the private wing. Anyway, Lydia's round here, I think.' He squinted against the sun. 'Yes, there she is. Down by the swing. D'you want me to come to introduce you?'

She barely heard his offer. She could scarcely believe her eyes. It was the hair-style that she recognized first. The same blonde bob with an Alice-band framing a far less chubby face than of old. The swing was an over-stylized copy of a Victorian contraption. An attempt had been made to train climbing plants around the rope hangings, but it hadn't worked. The seat was a huge, wooden board painted bright vermilion. Lydia was swinging slowly, legs held straight out in front of her and locked at the knees. Her head hung down, strands of hair covering each cheek. Her choice of dressing gown was a long, satiny, pink confection. Perfectly respectable, since she had on brushed cotton pyjamas that were clearly visible underneath, the trousers strangely rolled above the knees, exposing pale, flabby calves.

Jean Lamont touched Innes's arm. 'Shall we try, then, my dear?'

Innes nodded, and they approached slowly. With each step she had to force the unwelcome images of the Unit's garden swing from her mind.

Jean Lamont's voice was soft. 'Lydia? Lydia dear?'

Five feet from them, Lydia remained oblivious, head hanging down towards the ground. Penduluming to and fro.

Innes heard the old lady trying again, a bit louder this time. 'Lydia? Lydia, hello? Lydia!'

The face that looked up had only one memorable feature for Innes. The striking blue eyes still held their colour, though most of the life in them had gone elsewhere. Innes's shock at the vacant look of Lydia's face made her step back. The Lydia of twenty-six years ago had been lively, intelligent, fresh-faced. What was left still had a good complexion, full lips. But the lifeless eyes had the effect of disfiguring the face. Lydia had lost a considerable amount of weight since her binge-eating days in the Unit. She was still big, though not obese. And she looked at least a decade older than she really was, especially around those eyes. The skin there was jaundiced and wrinkled. Only the hair had held on to its original promise, though on closer examination all it had was bottled colour. Still, someone had been trying to look after Lydia's appearance. That apart, the exceptional shine and gloss had gone with the loss of youth. And health. And care.

Innes offered Lydia a smile as she silently admonished herself for such a reaction. What the hell did losing your entire family do to you if not ruin your looks as well as everything else? Whether or not Lydia had brought this all on herself, Innes felt the strangling emotion of pity as she stared on.

'Who you?' It was little more than a throaty, Neanderthal grunt, and they both strained to work out what Lydia was saying.

'Who you, cunt?' The second utterance was marginally clearer. The expletive seemed to leave Jean Lamont unruffled, as she was just about to answer, when Lydia started up again.

'Fag? Fag? Got fag? Fag?' The staccato grunting was unsettling. For the first time in God knows how long, Innes cursed herself for being a non-smoker.

Jean Lamont whispered, 'It's okay, she always starts like this. Hello, Lydia! It's Jean here. Your neighbour from "Kittiwake". I'm the lady with the Westie. Remember, you liked to walk him with me. You remember Scampi, don't you?' She turned back to Innes. 'I should've brought the dog. I did once before and she loved it. Never mind.'

'Fag! Fag! Got fag! Fag!' Slowly, in an almost obscenely sensuous gesture, Lydia reached under her dressing gown and brought out a ten-pack of extra long cigarettes. The plastic lighter, with 'Welcome to Blackpool' incongruously etched into it, followed. She sucked at the first draw. The grimace that accompanied exhalation showing exceptionally well-cared-for teeth.

Jean patted Innes on the arm again. 'Tell you what. I'll go up to the café and get us some coffees and biccies. That'll settle her down. You'll be okay here, won't you, dear?'

Innes was relieved at the old woman's departure. It would give her a chance to talk to Lydia on her own. She stepped forward to the swing.

'Hello, Lydia. I'm Innes. I've come to visit you. Nurse Johnny says you don't get many visitors.'

'Nurse Johnny poof! Nurse Johnny poof cunt!'

The sun was shining directly into the blank face, and Lydia turned her head to one side, eyes swivelled to keep the visitor in her sights. Innes walked round in front of her, casting a protective shadow. She couldn't work out if Lydia had had something like a stroke. Her way of talking was garbled, mumbling – gone was the perfect diction of her youth – but her face was symmetrical and mobile. Lydia's one-word sentences punctuated by Tourette's-style obscenities had her wondering exactly what damage she had suffered. Innes tried again on the visitor tack.

'So, who visited you last time, Lydia? Was it Jean?'

The suck on the cigarette came first. Then, 'Cunt!'

Innes was unclear if this was directed against Jean or was just a general outburst. She decided to leave the visitor issue alone. The problem was, she didn't know if Lydia's child-like behaviour reflected her actual take on the world now. How the hell could she possibly raise the issue of the Unit with this, this shell of a once intelligent, at times exuberant girl? It was cruel. And wrong.

'Push, cunt. Please.'

The request and the 'please' had to be some kind of breakthrough. Innes moved slowly behind and gently began to push the swing, the action bringing a shudder as she reached her guilt-ridden decision.

'Lydia? I used to know you before.'

Silence.

'Yes. I knew you as Lydia Young. In the Unit. Remember? I'm Innes? Innes Haldane.'

Nothing.

She checked up towards the main building, anxious that Jean Lamont shouldn't return too soon. She pushed Lydia again. 'There was Carrie? Simon? Alex?' She paused before the last two, her hands giving a final firm shove. Then she walked round to face Lydia again. 'And remember Isabella? And Danny?'

She slipped the group photograph of them all at the camping holiday out of her pocket and held it in front of Lydia's eyes. 'See, here we all are.'

Lydia was fiddling with her cigarette packet again, pulling out one cigarette after another and then pushing them back in. Her pretence of not looking at the photo was poor and Innes could see her eyes slewing towards it.

Then, 'D'nny. D'nny cunt!'

'Danny, that's right. Danny Rintoul?'

Lydia planted her trainered feet on the ground, bringing the swinging to an abrupt halt. Her entire concentration was now on the cigarette packet's lid, which she tore at, eventually wrenching it off and hurling it to the ground.

Innes bent down, trying to force Lydia to meet her eye while simultaneously pointing her finger at Danny's image in the photograph. 'Danny? You remember Danny? Do you, Lydia? Look, remember this day at the holiday in Argyll? The day you hurt your leg falling from the monkey rope? Remember? We had a lovely holiday a—'

At this Lydia shot her head up. 'No! No, cunt!'

Something had clearly disturbed her. Innes held out her hand and put it on Lydia's cold knee. 'It's okay, Lydia. That's all right. Here.' She gently uncurled the short, fat, babyish fingers and lit Lydia's second cigarette for her.

'Innes, thanks. Nessie thanks.'

'You're welcome, Lydia.' So, she remembered Carrie Franks's old nickname for her.

'Innes. Nessie Abby. Nessie Abby cunt.'

Innes's now accustomed ear picked out Lydia's reference to Isabella. She pushed. 'Abby, yes. Isabella, you remember Abby?'

For no obvious reason, Lydia suddenly put out her cigarette, the ember flicked off in a lightning-quick twist of finger and thumb.

'Abby dead. Abby cunt dead.'

Unthinkingly, the shock at what she had heard blinding her, Innes grabbed a beefy arm. 'What did you say, Lydia? How d'you know Abby's dead? How d'you know?'

Lydia pulled away from the grip that was hurting her.

'No touch, cunt! Abby cunt dead. Danny cunt dead. Danny dead cunt! Cunt! Cunt!'

Innes felt Lydia's agitation but couldn't stop herself. She tightened her grip, shaking the heavy body. '*Lydia, tell me. How d'you know they're dead? Tell me. Please.*'

'Nooo No cuuunt! Hurty hurty hurty cunt!'

Within seconds, two nurses were at Lydia's side, talking soothingly to her, and Innes couldn't help but notice them exchanging worried looks. Jean Lamont hurried up, the tray of refreshments wobbling in her hands. 'What's going on? What happened?'

Innes wanted to make a run for it. She fumbled quickly for a plausible lie. 'Eh, I don't know. I said something about her family. Her father. It upset her.'

Nurse Johnny had arrived and nodded his head slowly. 'I see. Shame. She's not had any outbursts in weeks.' He shouted over to the other two nurses by Lydia's side. 'Better take her in now. Go on now, Lydia, love.'

She stood up from the creaking swing seat, gazing blankly, straight ahead. Then, with no warning, Innes saw her shuffle sideways to within a foot of where she was standing. Lydia had cocked her head and was looking directly into her eyes, cigarette-sour breath warm on Innes's cheek.

'*Abby dead! Danny dead! Everyone dead!*'

Lydia's parting utterance had left her reeling. How on earth could she know about the deaths? Lydia had been in this place when Danny and Abby died. Innes felt chilled and sick. And real fear was settling in now. As she tried to gather herself together, the recurring question chiselled its way back into her thoughts.

What on earth had been going on these past months to lead to this?

Reunions

Six months earlier – late 2003

File note from Charge Nurse Ranjit Singh to Sister Anna Cockburn
18 November 1977
RE: Morning group session

Given that more than one patient will be given their dates for discharge in coming weeks, I decided to run the morning's group session on that theme. I had discussed the idea yesterday with Adrian, who approved.

What happened, I can only say, is odd. There was a distinctly strained atmosphere throughout the session, with several patients unwilling to contribute. Abby, Innes and Lydia were active participants. Innes showing real affection for Abby, expressing how much she would miss her when she goes, and also expressing her desire to get better and be given a leaving date, though she recognized that this would be some months away. All this I took to be very positive. Abby too said that she was looking forward to leaving, though she admitted to being a bit scared. All expected and understandable. (Adrian has warned her that she can expect to be given a leaving date in the next few weeks.)

Lydia, predictably, became rather overexcited by all the talk of leaving. It was somewhat of a challenge to get her to see that she was quite a bit away from being given her own leaving date. But she took that in good spirits today, thankfully.

However, it is the behaviour of the rest of the group that is worthy of note. When the topic was initially raised, Carrie labelled it 'boring' and tried to enforce a subject change, with some help from a particularly supercilious Simon. Alex wouldn't say a word, and Danny was monosyllabic and aggressive in equal measure.

When Lydia raised the subject of them all keeping in touch, as she put it, 'for ever' and 'all being the best of friends for ever' once they left, the atmosphere became very dark. There were odd looks among Carrie, Alex and Simon, while Danny repeatedly told Lydia to shut up, even getting out of his chair to threaten her, until I intervened.

I haven't the slightest clue as to what this is about, but we'll need to monitor those four very closely for a while. I feel something's brewing. The holiday seems to have made things worse rather than better. Pity.

Copy to: Daily Nursing Log
Copies to: patient files, D. Rintoul; C. Franks; L. Young; S. Calder; A. Baxendale

22

The bar was seedy but quiet. In a shitty part of Edinburgh, off the Easter Road. It had been Danny's choice: conveniently near the mate's flat that he was staying at for a couple of nights. Simon nodded his thanks to the barman and took his double whisky to a corner table. For the hundredth time he checked his watch. Not yet eight. He was early. He sat back, trying to look relaxed, and picked up a stained and torn copy of the *Edinburgh Evening News*. Seeking shelter from the curious eyes of locals behind the newspaper, he felt worry pick away at him. He doubted he would recognize Danny, though he at least knew what he'd be wearing. 'I'll have on my usual tatty biker's jacket, pal. What aboot you?' And he'd replied that he'd be wearing a dark blue overcoat and a red scarf. Unmissably smart in this dump of a place.

Reluctantly, he let his mind rove back to the events of the day. What timing! The very day he was going to meet Danny Rintoul. That afternoon there'd been an uncomfortable return to the house by Rachel and the girls. Katie looked well. She would survive her ordeal after all. France had been good for her – for all three, by the looks of them. He'd had hopes of life getting back to normal again. Being a family once more. Should he cancel seeing Dan? But it had all lasted precisely three hours, as Rachel packed more clothes for her and the girls.

His anger and shock at seeing Mother and that bloody golden Labrador, once his faithful companion – the dog's changing allegiances symbolic of all that had gone wrong with his family – turning up to collect *his* family, *his family*, to take them back to her house still curdled within him. Rachel had made it plain. She was taking the girls back to France in a few days. For a lengthier stay. A 'healing stay' – undoubtedly a quote straight from the mouth of Debbie Fry. Oh, and he needn't worry about driving them to the airport for their return flight to France. His mother would do that. His mother, for fuck's sake! It was a nasty betrayal by her. And Rachel. Though predictable, if only he'd thought about it, since Rachel consistently refused to see the truth about her mother-in-law. Not surprising. The old bitch was a chameleon. She wanted to keep on Rachel's side because she wanted access to the grandchildren. *Her* grandchildren! Proprietorial cow!

So, he had to face it. He'd lost everything. Rachel had made mollifying noises, like 'It's just for a while, until you get yourself back to normal.' But he'd never get back to normal until he faced a few things. He'd had some sessions with a colleague as part of his assessment for starting clinical work again. The time was spent looking only at the immediate effects of Katie's abduction. It was a waste of time. He, Dr Simon Calder, knew all the psychological tricks of the game. There was no chance he was going to go down those other dark, mind-game and mind-fuck roads.

He sank half the burning whisky in a oner. Careful – he was driving. His eyes returned to the headlines on the paper's sports pages and then blurred out again as he replayed the phone conversation of a week earlier, Danny's now much deeper voice still sounding improbably familiar . . .

'. . . I just felt I had tae write to you, pal. It seemed incredible. Unbelievable! But yer wee one's okay now, eh?'

He didn't want to get into it all yet. 'Eh . . . yeah. Look,

Danny. I need to see you. I have to talk to someone. Someone from that time. You're the one, Dan. The only one I feel I can talk to. Please. I need to see you . . .'

The shadow cast over the newspaper he wasn't reading roused him.

'Simon?'

He looked up at the man he'd not set eyes on for a lifetime. The transformation was hard to credit. Danny Rintoul looked the outdoors type now. Weather-beaten. Strong as an ox. Seemingly a good foot taller than he'd been before. Ruggedly handsome too. Simon could scarcely believe that the nondescript, skinny whippersnapper of old had turned into this. But he immediately detected a more profound inner change too. Given away by the relaxed body language, the lazy smile. Danny was much stiller at his centre. Calmer. At ease with himself. Simon envied him the quality.

He stood up, hand outstretched. 'Jesus, man! Look at you! Good to see you . . . and . . . and thanks for coming. I really mean that. Now, first things first. Let me get a drink in.' He laid a tentative hand on Danny's shoulder and led him to the bar.

There'd been little small talk during the past half-hour. Just enough to confirm what Simon already knew about Danny. And what of him? Well, thankfully Danny wasn't, never had been, a man to talk about himself. He'd quickly, if a bit clumsily, got on to the most important matter of all.

'I'm glad your wee girl's back now. But . . . but how is she? What happened . . . what did he . . . I mean, sorry, Simon, if you don't want to talk about it, that's fine. You know, the papers don't say much, quite rightly and I just wondered . . .'

He let Danny's unfinished and crudely put question fade.

Truth be known, he was glad to be able to articulate what had now become off-limits with the person he most needed to share it with. Rachel had set her face against any discussion with him of Katie's ordeal, instead emphasizing that she preferred to talk to Debbie Fry. 'Someone sympathetic and knowledgeable' as she tersely put it, who'd been available to her 'day and night' to talk things through on the phone, in person, any time. 'Absolutely invaluable.' The message was clear. He was surplus to requirements.

He shook his head slowly at Danny. 'It may seem . . . *difficult* to understand this but . . . the physical . . . sexual assault side of it . . . well, frankly, it could've been worse. It was limited to occasional touching, exposure, and . . . but . . . look, I thought it would be easier to talk about this. Y' know with someone a bit removed? But . . . I really don't want to go into it now, okay?' He paused to look at Danny, who had dropped his eyes, and was sitting stiffly hunched in his chair, clearly not daring to move. 'There's something else. Evidence that he might have taken some photos. Katie's talked about him saying he took some "holiday pictures". Apparently the others were photographed. Christ! As for everything that went on . . . we haven't got to the bottom of it yet. Katie's therapist is doing that sort of work with her. My big worry is about her long-term psychological and emotional health.

'These . . . these abominations can be got over. I mean, clinical research shows that, given the right treatment . . . but Jesus! Listen to me! I hate talking about my little girl as if she were some case . . . it's, it's just that I want her to be all right again. The man who took her managed to convince her that he was . . . well, a friend of mine and of Rachel. I mean, Jesus! The fucking manipulation. And of course what I'm worried about is the trust issue with her. She seems to be okay with Rachel but . . . I don't know how she's seeing me at the moment. It's very . . . *uncomfortable*. And her sister too. I can't help feeling that in some way Lily blames me. Y'know, "why-did-Daddy-let-this-happen" sort of thing. It's a nightmare, Dan. A nightmare.

'I've thought and thought and thought about it. Trying to make sense of it. We were convinced she was dead. Her clothes were found, and we thought the worst. And then she's returned. We find out what went on. And then there's the other, puzzling, chilling stuff. You know, she was given toys, sweets, even a puppy to play with. She was left with the puppy, but we've had to give it away because it wouldn't get on with our other dog. She thought she was in some kind of fucking game. She thought she was on holiday, and that Mummy and Daddy had to go away for a while because of work. Wicked beyond belief!

'I can't tell you . . . it's so strange . . . so terrifying, to have your child taken and *kept*. Like a trophy or something. The police are really worried. They think he'll kill next time. I keep saying to myself, she came back, alive. She *will* get back to normal eventually. She's young and getting expert help. But . . . but I don't know about me. It's made me think *so* much. Look back. Remember. I can't stop thinking. I tried to get my mind back together again. On the straight and narrow of everyday life. I gave myself a few months. It's no good, though. That's why I waited so long after you wrote to me. I tried not to *need* to talk about anything to *anyone*.'

Danny was offering him an uncertain smile in reply. 'Aye, I wondered 'bout that. I mean, I'm happy to meet up wi' ye and everything under the circumstances, but I don't understand. Yer Katie's back. *Alive*.'

Christ! He refused to believe that Danny could be so

doltish. This was a bloody high-IQ'd guy sitting in front of him. Maybe he dealt with some things in life by blanking them out. Just like himself. He tried again.

'Look, Danny. Rachel, my wife, has left me and taken my two daughters with her. Oh, she said that she thought they could benefit from the time together, and that I was catching up on my backlog of work so she never saw me anyway. They're going to our house in France. She doesn't want me there. She's leaving me, I know it.'

'But? But, how's that, then? I would've thought you'd all want, need, tae be together right now.'

He felt it was time to ram the message home. 'It's all *my* fault, Danny! It's me. I can't go back to how I was before Katie was taken. You've got to be able to see that. Surely? It's changed me. Or rather it's reminded me of the person I *should* have been . . . it's ju—' He felt himself faltering, verging on tears, and took a swig of his whisky before he could go on. Danny was staring at him, apparently impassive. So bloody cool while he struggled on. 'It's just that I can't get that time in the Unit out of me now. I can't sleep, I can't work, I can't fucking live. I don't think the Unit's ever really been out of me. I've just blocked it off. You don't have to look a million miles away to see why I became a bloody psychologist! It was an act of recompense. But whatever, it's come back on me. I'm fucking drowning!'

Danny was letting the silence hang for a moment. What was he thinking, for God's sake? Couldn't he understand what he was saying? This was serious. Nothing more so.

'Si? Does Rachel know? 'Bout the Unit?'

''Course not!'

'Nothing? I mean, she doesn't even know you were ever in there?'

He shook his head again. What the fuck was Dan going

down this track for? 'No. Nothing. I never got round to telling her. Rachel's a very . . . very strong person. When we were getting together, I did think of telling her but somehow . . . it . . . felt weak. And that's just it. If I could've maybe told her something about it in all the years I've known her . . . well . . . well maybe, just maybe it might have helped. But she never would've understood what went on there. Even the sanitized, edited highlights. Rachel's from a different universe than us. Mentally clean and stable.

'Besides, Mother would never want her to know. Too shaming by far. Mother was always trying to deny that there was anything wrong, right up until I went into the Unit *and* even when I was in there! I'm still a coward sometimes when it comes to my mother. At least I've got that amount of insight into myself. She was always adamant that I should "tell no one, *ever*", as she put it. And, there's one other very simple reason why Mother never wanted anything like this to get out. She's a class A snob. The last thing she wanted when I was going through university, then my post-grad and ever since, was any "stain" on my character that would be seen to reflect badly on her. And she saw my marriage to Rachel as a "good marriage", meaning Rachel's family had money and . . . and "breeding". *Christ.* I used to hate it when she used that word. Sounding like some Victorian matriarch! Though she had a point of sorts in me not telling. I'm not sure how Rachel would've reacted to any news of my past vulnerability. Like I say, she's strong, mentally robust. So we started out as a lie and the Unit days slowly, effectively, got buried. But, to be honest, with Rachel, I didn't need to be encouraged not to tell her. Anything about the Unit would've seemed alien to her. She really is from a different universe.'

Danny was reaching over to him, placing a firm hand on

his forearm. 'I'm sorry, pal. Really. No one could ever have predicted what was going to happen to you, to your wee girl, your family. But Katie's back. You need tae put this behind you. Get Katie better. Find a way to get Rachel back. I understand that you can't tell Rachel 'bout the Unit. You know we're all in the same boat. We've all got our secrets to keep.'

He leaned back out of Danny's comforting grasp. 'But that's just it. I don't want to keep any fucking secrets any longer! Keeping stuff inside is killing me. I want . . . I *need* to see the others.'

'What d'you mean?'

'I want to speak to Alex and Isabella, maybe everyone. I don't have to worry about Carrie. It's nigh on twenty years since she hit that one too many heroin highs, isn't it? What a bloody waste! Anyway, you see, it's time. Time to deal with things out in the open. There's always a price to pay in life and my one's come up. *Now.*'

Danny's face had tightened. He was stretching over the table at him again, voice now rasping, losing its calm edge. 'Simon? You crazy, pal? You can't just do something like that. It affects us all. Not just you. Anyway, it's over a quarter of a bloody century since we last saw them. The others could be anywhere. How the hell you goin' tae find them? Apart from Alex, of course. Our November letters ensure we'll always know where she is. *Fuck!* You've not told her, have ye? I hope she's not been reading the papers.'

'Calm down. No, I've not been in touch with her. I wanted to talk things through with you first. And no, she won't have read about it. She'll have been in the Med at the time, getting a bloody expensive tan, no doubt. Remember, she's told us about that. Showing off. She always goes away for three months. She'll have missed all the coverage about my Katie.'

He noticed Danny's face relax and then tighten up again as he pressed his original question. 'But look, Simon, how *are* ye goin' tae find the others? It'll be impossible, after all this time. You're mental, man! Mental!'

Simon felt a strange smugness as he answered. Dan was out of order calling him mental. No, it was just the opposite. It was time to start behaving sanely. He leaned back again, away from Danny's intensity. 'I've always known where the others are. Where the whole *happy* family is. Call it a safety net.'

He watched with a tinge of satisfaction as Danny slumped back, shock at what was unfolding registering at last. 'I . . . I . . . fuckin' *hell*!' He stopped. Simon could see the thought passing over Danny's features before he asked his key question. 'And what about Isabella? You're not going to try and contact her? I mean, she's not important. She's got *nothing* to do with this. You know that.'

His answer was firm. 'She might have. We don't really know. We never really knew. Did we? I mean, given your relationship with her . . . I . . . I thought that you might have . . . have . . . kept track of her. Maybe even *spoken* with her.'

Danny almost lunged at him now, banging the table and splashing his pint all over the place. 'No, pal. *Absolutely not!* Abby's got nothing to do with this. *Nothing!*'

Simon held up an appeasing hand and moved the drinks back to the centre of their table. He believed him. Almost.

23

The meeting with Danny had exhausted him. He was grateful to be home. He was beginning to get used to the silence of the house. The silence from fellow humanity anyway. The wind and sea still kept him company. For that he was grateful. He glanced into the small, normally cosy living room. He'd brought down both the girls' night-lights. They didn't need them now since Mother had provided them with replicas for the bedrooms in her house *and* for the house in France. Typical empire-building and territory-stealing. He shoved the thought away and sat down. Watching the children's lights with their soft gentle glow and amusing cartoon characters emblazoned on the sides could become a nightly ritual for him. It was calming. And it made him feel somehow closer to both his daughters. The lights usually gave some semblance of warmth to a room, making it seem more welcoming.

But tonight everything felt cold, stale. He leaned his aching head back on the sofa, cradling one of the girls' soft toys that they'd grown out of, forgotten in that afternoon's excited rush to pack and leave. He was happy they'd left it. The tatty blue elephant had become his constant companion these few months. He'd got used to it. He roused himself and stood up, settling the toy back on the sofa, upright, as if it was watching the blacked-out television. The wind wasn't giving any quarter tonight, and he moved through to his beloved study and threw the window open. But the gusts were too strong and he pulled it to, but not all the way. He wanted to keep chilly. The journal lay open before him. Tempting and ready.

I'm not sure what I feel about tonight. Seeing Dan so strong and easy with himself was in part inspiring and in another depressing. How a man such as he could have rehabilitated, no, reinvented himself so successfully leaves me fighting for breath. I believe that he has never given a backward glance to that time in the Unit. Maybe living in isolation as he does makes that possible. He's at one with the land, with nature. Maybe he can console himself with that.

But for me? Well, every day of my life since then has been spent in attempts at denial, reparation, despair, a handful of moments of happiness and, above all, GUILT. Undeniably so. I ache to unburden myself. It's clear that Dan does not feel the same. How could he? He has no children. He is a different creature from me. A different species, psychologically! I can't help but envy him that in some way.

Abruptly, he stopped, screwing the top back on his fountain pen. There was something else he had to do. Fumbling through his uncharacteristically untidy desk, he retrieved it. He slid the photocopied letter towards him. Funny he'd felt the need to copy it.

Dear Alex

My first task must be to apologize in advance for contacting you. I know what we promised all those years ago, but events in my life have taken a turn that affects us all.

I don't know if you read the newspapers. However, even if you do, you may have missed the story about me and my family. Or, equally, it may not have registered, so much time having passed since we all last met together.

You will remember that time I am sure. It was 1979. It was another ragingly hot summer. We were having a picnic at St Monans in Fife, by the sea, where I now live. Looking back, I find it all a bit bizarre, surreal. A Unit reunion. A reunion of those who had been joined in illness and in . . .

He slammed a hand down on to the paper. No need to read any more. He knew the thing line by line. He'd written it, after all. With slow deliberation, he ripped it into a dozen pieces. Then, for a reason he didn't even bother analysing, he leaned through the open window and watched the pale, ragged squares sucked by the wind towards a gloomy, grey sea.

Slowly, almost painfully, he moved his cold limbs and headed back to the living room. As he switched off the children's lights, sobs tearing at his chest, he reached for the little blue elephant and prepared to weep the night away.

24

He was freezing and getting wet. Each time a particularly hefty breaker hit the shore, it sprayed up over his garden wall and caught him hunched in the corner of his wooden bench. He didn't care. It was only a bit of harmless sea-water. Besides, he enjoyed the taste of salt on his lips. It was sensation after all. Something to test his increasingly numb body.

He surveyed his garden and the beautiful stonework of his house, perched right at the water's edge, only yards from the church. He'd wanted to own this house, this garden, since the first day he'd set eyes on them in the sixties. That was when his parents brought him on the first of many and surprisingly – given the usual hell of family life – enjoyable summer holidays to this loveliest of fishing villages of the East Neuk of Fife. And he'd made no secret of his desire to live here. It had been back in . . . July maybe? Yes, July of 1979. That reunion picnic . . .

'I mean it. I've always loved that house. I'm going to buy it one day.'

'Sure you will, Si.'

'I will, Carrie. I will.'

Danny had slapped him affectionately on the back, making him cough into his can of beer. 'I know you will, Simon. I believe you. You'll soon be a better heid doctor than old Dr Laurie!'

The waves of their giggling banter had made him almost

happy. For a minute. But he'd had to have a moment alone. Take in what he felt. He'd gone down on to the pebble beach, just a few feet below the grassy headland where Anna and Sarah were sitting. And invisible to them both.

It was weird. Everyone *seemed* the same. Carrie was more jittery than he remembered. But she was on something. Not just spliff. Lydia was significantly thinner but irritatingly jollier than ever. Alex had grown her hair. And scowled most of the time. Situation normal. He'd seen a bit of her and Lydia at parties during the past eighteen months. They were on the same social circuit, but he kept them at arm's length. Best policy. Especially with Alex.

He found a dry rock and sat, sipping at his beer. None of them had talked, really *talked* since arriving. It was as if they were all on some superficial trip. Well, he'd have to wait and see. Above him, he pictured Anna and Sarah. Sarah, who was now apparently a fully qualified member of the Unit staff. No more 'baby nurse' for her. He saw that she and Anna had laid their blankets out in an area of no man's land, where churchyard ended and spongy grass began. In front of them stood a line of black, jagged rocks. Beyond that was the flat, pebbled beach where he was hiding. Far along to his right, he, and the nurses, could watch Ranj playing a game of improvised cricket with Lydia. He listened as Sarah raved about the 'Auld Kirk' – the very best example of darkly brooding Scottish ecclesiastical architecture – literally clinging to the headland, protected from the wildest seas by only a few yards of cemetery, holding the long-buried and the recently lost. He wanted this place. For himself. He gave a silent laugh and tuned into Sarah's chatter . . .

'This must be one of the most spectacularly placed churches in Scotland. It's fantastic!'

Anna was definitely in agreement. 'Yes, it's wonderful. There's been a chapel on this site since at least the thirteenth century. The story goes that this one was built about a century later by one of the early Scottish kings, David II, allegedly as a kind of thank you.'

'"Thank you"?' Sarah sounded surprised.

'Yeah. Apparently he was crossing the Firth of Forth in a ferocious storm that shipwrecked others. But, miraculously, he survived unscathed. So, bless him, he gave us all this marvellous church. The actual village is named after a medieval monk called Saint Monan. He worked as a missionary in these parts and was said to have been murdered by rampaging Danes.'

'You're bloody knowledgeable about local history!' Simon had to agree with Sarah there.

Anna was laughing. 'Comes from having a husband who drags you round any and all historic monuments at the drop of a hat!'

Sarah laughed back, and he moved a bit closer up the rocks, peering up at where they lay, as she changed the subject. 'D'you think this was a good idea? Getting them together like this?'

Anna was frowning, squinting through the glare of the sun's rays to where Danny, Alex and Carrie were chattering. 'I think so. We usually try it. But, more often than not, patients decide that once they're out they don't want to keep in touch. As a group that is. You often find that ex-patients will keep in touch in twos and threes, that sort of thing. But we did have one group that met en masse. It was early on, when the Unit first opened, about four years ago. I'm still in touch with a couple of them, actually. They're doing well. You know, there's nothing to stop you keeping in touch with former patients as long as the professional and ethical boundaries are maintained. Meaning, discussion of other ex-patients' problems or having a rampant affair with a former patient are out. Anything else probably does both of you good.'

Sarah was looking thoughtful. 'But . . . but how do you organize such a thing? A reunion like this, for example?'

Despite the bright sunlight, he could see that Anna's face had taken on a seriousness. 'It's a tricky one, really. Any interest in a reunion has obviously got to be voluntary. Usually Adrian or I get in touch with former patients and suggest it. But after that, the impetus has got to come from them. This is quite a good turn-out. Only two missing. Innes is away on holiday with her parents, and Isabella didn't respond to the invitation. Fair enough. That's her prerogative.'

Sarah was sloshing the wine back. 'Tell me, who of this lot's been keeping in touch?'

Anna was refilling her glass. 'As far as I know, Simon, Alex and Lydia have been in touch a bit, I think.'

'That's an odd combination, isn't it?' Simon felt a stab of irritation at Sarah's comment. Cheeky cow! What did she mean?

Anna was shaking her head. 'Actually, Sarah, it isn't that odd. There's a lot of evidence to show that patients like these tend to bond after release on social-class grounds. Not surprising at all. Just think about it. When they're in the Unit, they're in the same situation, the same physical place. They're also all ill and in need of treatment. But after release they have to return to their "real" lives. Well-off, educated kids, as a rule, don't mix with their opposites. I mean, what have rich-kid Lydia and council-estate Danny got in common now? Nothing. But, inside, I wasn't surprised at the Carrie/Simon relationship, for example. It was symbiotic in a perfect kind of way. Simon gets the attention and protection of a tough and sexy girl. Carrie gets the kudos of being admired by, and having power over, a top-drawer guy. She won't enjoy that privilege again in her life, I feel, by the looks of her.'

He had to stifle the laugh. Christ! Psycho-babble gone mad.

Sarah was in more serious mode now, bobbing her head in Carrie's direction and stating the obvious. 'Drugs?'

Anna's face was sad in reply. 'I fear so. The follow-ups we did last year went badly. Caroline's relationship with her family has utterly collapsed. She's moved out into some kind of squat in Leith. She's nineteen now and can do pretty much what she wants. As long as she isn't caught breaking the law. And for some reason she hasn't been busted yet. It's only a matter of time, though. She was showing me her engagement ring this morning. She's hooked up with some unsavoury-sounding jail-bird and swears blind she's going to marry him, settle down, have kids, the whole caboodle. And she's pregnant.'

'Jesus! Is there nothing we can do for her?' The answer to that was obvious to him and, it seemed, to Anna.

'Not if she doesn't want help. The worst thing is, she denies there is a problem. I fronted her up about the track marks on her arms. She just shrugged, put a shirt on to cover them and ignored me for two hours. Still, she seems to be having a good time.'

He saw them both turn to watch as, barefoot, Danny, Alex and Carrie, clad variously in cool shirts and shorts, wandered out of sight down to the faraway rocks at the opposite end of the beach. He wanted to know what they were up to. In the distance he could see that Ranj and Lydia had quit their game of cricket and were heading back for a drink. He moved along out of sight, watching Lydia's exuberant arrival at the nurses' blankets.

She plonked herself down, grabbing for a bottle of orangeade. 'Boy, it's bloody hot! Ranj is on his way. Where the others, by the way?'

Anna nodded to her left. 'Dunno 'bout Simon but Dan, Alex and Carrie have gone down to the rocks over there. Maybe they're having a look in the cave now the tide's out.'

Lydia was guzzling her drink. Then she bounced up. 'Think I'll go and join them.'

He edged away, determined to follow. He wasn't going to miss out on any action. But Dan and the others had moved much faster than he had, and suddenly he heard shouts coming from the cave beach. He heard Anna's bark above him.

'Sarah! Ranj! Hear that? Quick, get up!'

He heard their feet thump along the springy grass, but he'd misjudged the distance over rocks. He was last to reach the cave and had to wait until his eyes adjusted to its darkness.

Within lay a weeping Lydia, a thin stream of blood flowing from her mouth where the lower lip had been badly split. Lunging at her was a demented Carrie. Danny had her in both arms but needed the help of Ranj and Alex to pull her off the writhing Lydia. Anna was kneeling down comforting her, a brilliant white handkerchief soaking up the bright red blood.

'Stop it! Stop it! Stop it!' Sarah, to his astonishment, was on the edge of hysteria or rage. He wasn't sure which.

Anna was cooing at Lydia. 'Sssh, sssh. It's okay. Okay.'

But Carrie's screaming drowned out her soothing words and the cries of the gulls above. 'It's not fucking okay! That fat, ugly bitch is as bad as ever. Eavesdropping on our private conversation. Listening in. Little cunt!'

'Fuck it! Just leave it, will ye!' Danny pushed Carrie to the ground and ran away out of sight.

Simon caught his look of anger and fear as he brushed past. Then he noticed Sarah surveying the wreckage of their day. And he knew that she was thankful beyond words that these bastards were no longer in the Unit . . .

He was snapped back into reality by the freezing spray of an exceptionally strong wave. From his pocket, he withdrew the plain postcard. She hadn't taken long to respond to his letter. Just a couple of weeks. Not long at all for such a big decision. What did that mean?

Agreed. 8 p.m. Nov. 8th – how apt. Your place, St Monans.

Alex

But it was the terseness of the answer, rather than the speed of it, that had him most worried and fearful. Twenty-odd years since their last meeting there, up on the headland, and one or two parties since. He had absolutely no idea of the Alex Baxendale that he was about to confront. And, if he was honest, he'd never been able to fathom her. Nor, he guessed, had anyone else. Danny would be furious, but he'd come along. Present the reunion as a fait accompli and Danny would come. No doubt.

But never mind Danny. His thoughts slipped back to Alex. No matter what they'd all been through, experienced together, *she* was the one he hadn't a clue about. Had never had a clue about. Certainly, he could postulate several professional psychological theories about her, as he remembered Alex from the past, and from her annual 'missives', as she loved to call them. But what of her now? Whatever she was like, whatever she'd grown into, it wouldn't be long before he found out. In two days they would meet again. And he was fully aware that the thought more than unnerved him.

25

'It's a bloody awful night. You sure she'll get here okay? She *is* coming?'

Simon sipped at his drink and watched as Danny looked for the umpteenth time out of the small living-room windows. Rain was battering itself against the panes, and the wind shot in unpredictable gusts down the chimney, blowing billows of smoke from the log fire on to the hearth. He wished Danny would sit the fuck down! So the man was edgy. Big deal. So was he. So would they all be. And where did Dan stand in it all anyway? He'd been as sympathetic as he reckoned Danny could be. But what about Alex? What was she like now? What would she have to say about his nightmare situation? He glanced out into the night, imagining her at whatever stage in her journey she was.

He felt Danny's tension hit him full force again, and he offered more reassurance. 'She's coming. Believe me. Look, there's her card. You know where it is. On the mantelpiece.'

At that, Danny's restless checking out of the windows stopped. Simon watched him give a cursory glance at the postcard, which he'd brooded over for hours when he first arrived. At last, he sat opposite Simon and took a long mouthful of beer, impatiently tossing the end of his cigarette into the flames. 'So, how long did you keep in touch with Alex, after the Unit? Apart from our yearly letters, I mean?'

Simon gently leaned his head back against the lace antimacassar. 'Not long. And it wasn't really "keeping in touch".

We sort of kept together by accident really. Someone Lydia's dad knew also knew mine, and there was some connection with a friend of Alex's family. We ended up being invited to the same parties, weddings, dinners. But I stopped seeing her and Lydia towards the end of 1982. I was starting my postgraduate work. Kind of shut the whole world out then.'

'Did Alex and Lydia keep meeting?'

Simon shook his head. 'Doubt it. It was me Lydia liked. Not Alex.'

He felt Danny's scrutiny as the next question was fired at him. 'And did you ever see Alex on her own? That would've made more sense.'

Simon smirked, aware of what his visitor was up to. 'Not a chance, Danny, mate. Being alone with her was the last thing on earth I would've wanted. I think you know that. Let's be honest, neither of us liked or took to Alex in any way. She didn't invite that sort of response now, did she?'

Danny offered him an uncomfortable smile of acknowledgement. 'Eh, you've got that right. She was . . . was *creepy*. Every time she walked into a room she changed its atmosphere. Quite a power, when you think about it. Especially if you're an adolescent. I mean . . . she had that sort of animal aggression, but what made it worse was that you knew that wasn't all she had. Like us all I suppose, you knew she had a lot up top. She was bloody clever. Scary combination.'

Simon inwardly agreed but wanted to stop things there. Speculation about Alex was a waste of time. She'd be here in minutes. 'Cool it, Dan. You make her sound like a bloody Lady Macbeth. She was just a middle-class, pretend hard-nut girl of ambivalent sexuality. Off her trolley like us, all because of seriously bad parenting.'

Simon wanted a subject-change and went for it. 'Anyway,

what about you? Did you try to . . . eh . . . keep up any connections with anyone in *particular*, and not let us know?'

'I told you before. No. I wanted to.' Danny sat up a bit, animated now at what still seemed, to Simon, to be Danny's favourite, if obliquely expressed, topic of conversation. 'But wanting and doing are very different things. That picnic thing we had here in '79 was the first and last time I'd seen anyone, any patient from the Unit. Sure, I had follow-ups with Dr Laurie and Anna. I think I saw that student, Sarah Melville, at one of the sessions. Well, she wasn't a student any more. You know what I mean . . . a . . . a proper psycho nurse. But that was that.'

Simon went next door to the kitchen and came back with another cold beer. He stood over Danny, handing it down to him. 'Ah, that wretched picnic. Lydia went on for the best part of a year about Carrie splitting her lip. What a bore she was about it. On and on and on.'

Danny was twisting uncomfortably in his seat, staring at the fire as he spoke. 'Did . . . did Lydia *hear* anything that day, d'you know?'

Simon shrugged. 'Who knows? She was always a bit of a nasty little game-player, at her worst. I know Alex used to try and get it out of her when we met. What she was doing at that picnic, trying to listen in, snooping, all the usual attention-seeking Lydia stuff. But no joy, as far as I know. She remained tight-lipped, so your guess is as good as mine.'

'But that's a bit worrying, isn't it?' Danny was frowning now.

Simon knew he needed to keep Danny calm. 'Not really. I know where she lives if we ever have to ask her anything.'

'By the way, how the *fuck* d'you know where the others live?'

He let Danny sweat for a minute. 'It's really not that difficult. Most parents of our generation don't move house. They're always listed in phone books, and the older they get, the easier it is to chat them up and get them talking, about their children and their whereabouts. Failing that, over the years I've called in a favour or two from a solicitor friend of mine. He occasionally uses someone to track people down. It's never been a great challenge to find out where everyone is. Everyone that matters, anyway.'

Danny was letting the silence lie between them. For that Simon was grateful. He wanted a minute to ready himself for Alex's arrival. He was much more nervous than he must seem to Danny. He sat back, taking long, slow breaths. Silence, except for the occasional spitting of the log embers, accompanied by the hammering of the rain, was all fine by him, for now. He took another look at Danny. He was an odd-bod. Hard to read. For one thing, he had no idea how Danny felt about seeing Alex again. He was clearly uptight. But then, that was hardly surprising. Could he trust Dan? To support him? He didn't know but comforted himself with the knowledge that it was Danny who had got in touch with *him* when he heard about Katie. That was a kind act, wasn't it? He sneaked a glance at the man, still staring at the embers. Or did he have another reason? Wanted to check that he, good old Si, was still 'on-side'? Not going to be a loose cannon?

He shook the unwelcome questions and doubts away and thought about Alex. Alex was coming here! Over twenty years since he'd last seen her at that God-awful picnic and those dreadful snobby parties . . . Jesus! What was she like now? Not a skinhead any more, surely. She'd almost grown out of that in-your-face rebellious phase when he'd last seen her.

His eyes came back into focus on Danny's empty chair. What the hell? There was the sound of muffled voices in the hall and then she came in.

'Life's obviously treating Danny rather well, don't you think, Si? Yes, Mr Rintoul. Glad to see you've put on weight. And muscle. God knows you needed to.'

Danny was standing behind her looking astounded, awkwardly bent forward, hands hurriedly smoothing down crumpled jeans. Alexandra Baxendale was transformed. The hair was long, glossy and very dark. The make-up was thick. So was the dark red lipstick. The face was still strong-featured. Especially the jaw-line. The overall facial effect was certainly not soft, though there was a distinct sensuousness about the full lips that she held naturally or otherwise in a tempting pout. That was a feature of hers he'd never before been aware of. Perhaps it had been cosmetically enhanced along with some other body parts? The outfit of black turtleneck and slinky black trousers deliberately showed off her curves. Unfeasibly prominent breasts made Simon more sure than ever about the cosmetic surgery argument. But what *was* unarguably natural was her athletic, muscular but distinctly feminine body. She worked out. Looked after herself. Quite simply, she was very, very sexy.

She handed her raincoat dismissively to Simon, addressing him as if she saw him every weekend, her voice deepened and roughened as if from too much smoking and drinking. 'God, Si. Hope you've got a decent Scotch. I'm parched. Nice little cottage, by the way. So you bought it after all. Clever, Si.' Her gaze taking in all it needed to at this stage.

He poured the large single malt and handed it to her, trying to keep his hand steady. He motioned for her to take a chair between him and Danny. Danny was trying to spark up conversation. 'You look very well, Alex. Do y—'

But she cut across him as if he didn't exist. 'Hah, Simon! This little get-together almost had me asking when Carrie was going to arrive. Really! That would be our little quartet complete, eh?'

Simon shifted to face her. Christ, she was still a cold bitch! And she was playing with them. The spectre of Carrie and the significance of the 'quartet' screamed at him, though he ensured that he kept an outward cool. 'Funny, Alex, very funny.'

He waited for her reaction to his challenging sarcasm. And felt Danny stiffen in his chair, as he did the same.

But all she offered was an ugly moue of her lips. 'Oh, well. Far from surprising, I suppose. Carrie was born to die from an overdose. It was axiomatic.' She raised her glass as if in a macabre toast. 'Anyway, I think we should get on. Si, I want to know what you've been discussing since . . . since all this nasty business of yours.'

She waved her hand in a non-specific direction and sipped at her drink. Simon was reaching his limits already, finding it hard to seem unruffled. Trying not to let his anger show. For fuck's sake! She's just casually passed off the abduction, assault and imprisonment of his Katie as 'all this nasty business'.

He raised his glass to match her and answered enigmatically, 'In a moment. Another drink, Dan? Whisky this time?' He got up and went over to the drinks table, playing for time. She was *not* what he had expected. Though expectations of what someone would be like after so long were sheer folly. But he had to admit it. Alex was bloody impressive. Physically. But she was still Alex. Something about the sneer of the mouth and the stare of the eyes clearly remained eternal with her. An external manifestation of the immutable aspects of her character? Perhaps. And still a queen bitch but using sex now as part of her armoury. The skinhead Alex of old had largely hidden her sexuality. Felt uncomfortable with it. And so she'd buried it. Apart from . . . well, no, he didn't want to go down that road just yet.

Anyway, she'd obviously learned how to use it during all these long years. No doubt used it against both genders. But, on the whole, she was a push-over to analyse. Ten minutes in her company and he could see it. Control. The big issue with her. Not surprising, given what he knew of her upbringing. And violent? Possibly in bed. A penchant for S/M? Maybe. No, probably. But as a dominatrix only. She'd do the fucking. Perhaps difficulties with penetrating Alex went beyond fathoming her personality. Whatever, he reckoned she was definitely an 'on top' woman. And she was planning to make Danny's life a misery tonight. Prick-tease the poor bastard with those flirtatious looks and periodic touches of her hand to his knee. But one thing was obvious. She was hiding her anxiety at this meeting well. Very well. An effective act. That worried him. If he had to make a guess now, before they even talked, he reckoned that she was going to stand in his way.

Her voice, low and languid, boomed out. No hard-nut, tough-girl, put-on accent now. In fact she was sounding unnaturally and suspiciously sympathetic. 'I'm glad your little girl's back with you, Si. How is she?'

'Hard to know.'

She looked back at him, puzzled. He went on. 'She's not living with me. Neither is my wife or my elder daughter, Lily. They've been at my mother's for some months now or at our house in France. Just as well, or we couldn't be meeting here, could we?'

She sneered at that. 'And the police? They know damn-all then, in essence?' Her tone sounded strident in the cocooned, low-ceilinged room.

He stood up and attended to the fire. 'Yes, damn-all. I'd say that was a fair assessment. The abductor has simply disappeared into the ether, just as he did following the other abductions. It's like he never existed. However, my daughter's remaining injuries, albeit psychological, indicate otherwise.'

He waited for her response. Instead, she stood up and moved two paces towards the hearth, sipping away at her Scotch. Then she turned round and faced them, her body erect and towering above them as he and Danny sat back in their seats.

Simon gave her the floor. She seemed as cocky as ever. He glanced at Danny. The man seemed transfixed. A powerful woman was just too much for the guy. Danny was typical of so many rapists. Terrified and suspicious of women. Yet clearly in awe of this one. Well, *he* wasn't that easily impressed. He had a fuller picture of her now. A before and after picture. Despite her brazen and icy exterior, he had a good idea of at least some of what that mind ticked over on. You didn't have to be a clinical psychologist to work that out. Your most basic pop psychology could do it.

She was taking control. Her gaze was directed primarily at him, with the occasional condescending glance at Danny peppering her statement.

'Now look. What we're about to discuss tonight we all promised, twenty-six years ago, *never* to mention to *anyone*, including each other. Some of us broke that pact in 1979. I trust, since then, we have all kept it. Though, let's remember, we all kept in touch for a reason. A simple note to each other every November 8th to let each of us know where we were, how we were. A little act of mutual trust. And now here we are. On this night of all nights. This November 8th we've substituted our annual missives for this. That makes me worried. *Very* worried.' She stopped, looking down at them in turn, assuming the stance, Simon presumed, she used when dealing with lovers and underlings.

She continued, the tone of her voice, if not the accent, familiar to them all. 'Another November 8th we all made that pact, and I, for one, *despite* recent events forcing our hands, am deeply reluctant to break it. Even now.'

Simon recognized the steel of old in this transformed version of Alex. She wasn't going to be easy. He sat back dreading what was to come, and brooding over what appalling clash of events had brought them all to this. He'd always known there'd be a reckoning. And tonight was it. Or rather, the beginning of it. He hoped Danny would be on his side. He'd need that. He could feel his own tension levels rising by the second. It was going to be a bloody few hours.

26

The door shut with a firm shooting of the bolts. Just before, Danny had managed to catch the glance of a red-eyed Simon and mouth an 'It's okay, pal.' He drew his jacket collar round him and started through the rain towards Alex's car. He watched with amusement as she picked her way in high heels over the muddy water, her athletic figure skipping across the puddles towards her vintage Mercedes Sports. He followed in her splashing wake.

'"It's my fault . . . it . . . it's all my fault! My wee girls! My wife! They . . . they'll never ever come back! I did it! It's my punishment! G . . . od! I'm sorry. Please, it's best if you go now. I'll . . . I'll call you tomorrow, Dan. I didn't want to be like this. I'm sorry." God what a moaner!'

Danny smirked at Alex's uncannily accurate, if somewhat exaggerated, aping of Simon's last outburst. She'd always been a good mimic. Merciless to her Unit victims, both staff and patients. As he pulled the seat belt around him, he suddenly realized exactly where he was. And he felt distinctly uneasy. Alone with Alex for the first time after all these unknowable years. What . . . no . . . *how* had she turned herself into this stunning sex goddess? Whatever he'd expected, it would never have been this. That she was rich, professionally successful and had married money didn't surprise him. But this oozing of self- and sexual confidence was about as far from the adolescent Alex as it was possible to imagine. That adolescent Alex whose tough skinhead exterior had hidden a marked, though impenetrable, vulnerability. Dr Laurie had tried often enough to get through to her. And failed. She still seemed impenetrable, but now it was clothed in an alluring aloofness that he knew would get the sexual interest of many, male or female. She retained that dykey thing about her, but straight, red-blooded males would like that too. She had it all in the looks department. And she knew it.

Mind you, her hard face was not really to his taste, but many others would find it a sexy challenge and come-on. In a firm attempt to keep any trace of his thoughts from her, he kept a careful eye on the rain-soaked road, while trying to slump in a relaxed pose. The chain-smoking might give him away but she didn't seem to notice. He'd lit up immediately. It was a smoker's car. Though spotless, it had the smell of stale tobacco that you could never hide. He leaned forward to flick his fag into the ash tray and, not for the first time since they'd set out, felt her gaze. This time he returned it. She had a studied, raised-eyebrow expression: a cynical, facial pose that she'd used several times during the past three hours. And countless times during their Unit days. Her strident tones were tinged with sarcasm.

'Fucking cry baby. What an absolute arsehole Simon still is. I'm completely bloody gobsmacked that he's got himself a grown-up job, got a grown-up life. He just lost it in there. Like a bloody baby. He always was a bit of a spineless prick.'

Danny checked his annoyance, instead grinding his cigarette butt out more firmly than was necessary. 'Perhaps it was because you were pushing him, Alex. There was no need to keep bringing up what a bitch his mother was *or* slagging off his wife. You don't even know her, for fuck's sake! The man is hurting. Can't you see that? What's happened to him is a living hell. That's why he was throwing so much booze down himself. That and your needling.

He was relatively all right when I first went round. It's a real fucker seeing a guy in that state. Practically sobbing his heart out. I tell you, Simon'll need a sight more gentle handling than that in the future.'

He waited for some smart-arsed rejoinder from her, but instead she let the silence win. For two minutes.

'Well, Danny, you're obviously not going to be getting the last bus back from this godforsaken place at this time of night. Pointless dropping you at the village bus stop. I'll take you all the way back. What part of Edinburgh does this mate of yours live in?'

He zipped up his biker's jacket even further – as protection against her as much as against the cold he'd just escaped outside. 'Easter Road. Thanks for the lift. Simon had said if it got late I could stay but . . .' He paused for a few seconds until the reassuring tarmac of a proper road greeted them. She was turning the heater up as rain lashed its way against her windscreen, and she stole a quick glance at him again. He knew he was looking stony-faced. And bloody tired.

'You frightened of my driving, Dan? Don't be. I might be over the limit, but I can handle this car. It's called power *with* control. Hard to find.' He said nothing and she tried again. 'Well? What d'you think of tonight? Like I said in my note to you, I should've kept quiet last year about nothing exciting ever happening. Christ, what a turn-up. Unbelievable. Well? What did you think?'

He wasn't letting her get away with it. 'Why didn't you let me know Simon had been in touch? At least I had the decency to write to tell you what had happened to him and that I was going to meet him. Simon's a bloody liar. He said he hadn't been in touch with you.'

'Oh, get over it, Danny. Yes, I enjoyed your letter, but I

was worried about you being able to keep a lid on things. I don't know why Si didn't tell you. Fuck it, we're all liars in one way or another. But anyway, what did you think of tonight? Hah! Tell you one thing, though. Si turned out better looking than I thought he would. Studious but sexy. Yeah, turned out much better looking than I would've thought.' She paused, obviously for effect. 'And so did you, by the way.'

He refused to look at her. She let her wedding ring tap tantalizingly, suggestively, on the gear knob, waiting for his response. Then the crimson nails of her other hand started a slow tattooing on the walnut steering wheel. Jarring but flirtatious. He had the definite sense of being played with. Part of him regretted accepting her offer of a lift. He was going to be her captive audience. But he had his own reasons for wanting to be alone with her. He'd just better keep his wits about him, that was all.

He ran his fingers along his stubbled jaw line, determined to seem casual but thoughtful. 'I feel fuckin' sorry for Simon. Poor bastard. I can understand how he feels. I don't have kids, but I've thought the way he has over the years, from time to time. Haven't you?'

She'd stopped her gear-knob tapping and moved the hand to her slinky-trousered thigh. 'Not really. The past is the past. We were loonies in the past. We're not now. I hope. Well, I'm not and you don't *seem* to be. The thing is, all this business is not about what happened to his *daughter*. Of course that's hell. But this whole thing, though, it's really about two simple things. His obviously *shit* marriage. And his *cow* of a mother. The mother was always a problem. Remember those countless sessions with Laurie as he forced Si to admit that his mother hated him? Excruciating. As for the marriage? Well, as I recall, Si was always crap with women. Every damn one of us in the Unit terrified him. Shit scared of us he was. Scared of the effect we had on his dick. *Fool.* No, the thing with his daughter was just very bad luck. It's Marriage and Mother. That's what's up.'

He dared a glance this time. 'How d'you mean? What's that got to do with what he wants to do? Other than have an honest relationship with his wife and have his family back.'

Alex gave him a hoot of forced laughter, tossing her hair back against the leather headrest. 'Honest relationship? Oh, come on, Danny! What fucking planet are you on? Not one of us is capable of an honest relationship! And I bet you we've all had shit things happen to us in our lives since we left the Unit, but it hasn't made us do a Simon! He's fucking losing it.' She turned her head to him again, for emphasis. 'And you *know* that's a danger to us all.'

'But look what happened to him, Alex! *That.* Of all things! Christ, it's like it was tailor-made to punish him!' He reduced his voice to a near whisper, almost talking to himself. 'To punish us all.'

She practically spat at the windscreen. 'Pah! Christ, Dan, you even sound like him. You'll be thinking it's some divine retribution thing soon. Nemesis! Watch it, or you'll both end up in another Unit. Look, I know it's a really shitty thing to happen and a bit weird, but it still can't excuse him becoming a loose cannon. He was always the weakest link, you know. He was always going to abort some day. That's why I made it my business to see him for a while, after we all left the Unit. Just to keep an eye. Anyway, I think we held back the tide tonight. Time'll sort the rest out for us, I'm sure. I've a mind to go and speak with that bitch of a wife of his. Tell her to get her arse back home with his, *his* kids. That'd stop all this nonsense.'

He marvelled at her aggression. As potent as it had ever been. Just packaged differently. But there was something else that Simon had told them that was bothering him.

'What about this Sarah Melville thing? That's bloody unbelievable. God, if I was Si, I'd think the fates *were* after me, I tell you. It's spooky.'

She gave him a quick glance in reply, followed by a nonchalant shrug. A bit too forced, in his opinion, as was her over-light tone of voice. 'Oh, come on. It's not that weird. Sarah Melville mixes in a small world. It's only because Simon found himself in the position of needing a child therapist for his daughter that he came across her. It was *chance*. Pure chance. Yeah, yeah, so poor, deluded Simon sees it as some part of some quasi-supernatural conspiracy to force him to look at his past. That's bollocks. Jesus, Sarah Melville was probably more shocked and embarrassed by being confronted with an ex-patient *and* in her girlfriend's house to boot! Anyway, apart from Simon bumping into her, she's a total irrelevance. Funny, though, I always knew she was a dyke.'

That was rich coming from her, and he wasn't sure if she expected a response. But he wasn't going to give her one. He leaned back into the luxurious leather as they drove on in silence, the squeaking of the wipers and swish of the tyres through rain the only noise. Alex had put two cigarettes in her mouth, lit them, and was passing one on to him, its tip ringed with a kiss of scarlet lipstick. The little flirt!

He accepted the cigarette with a curt nod but otherwise ignored her, instead staring ahead into the middle distance. Un-bloody-believable. She was out-and-out teasing him. What did she expect him to do? Wrest the wheel from her? Drive to the nearest lay-by and fuck her senseless? Or maybe she wanted him to rape her? She, like the others, had always been fascinated by his 'rapist-at-fourteen-years-old' status.

She was the one to break the silence first. 'Penny for them?'

He said nothing.

'C'mon, Dan. What's in that clever head of yours? Worried about your sheep or whatever it is you do back home? *God*, how can a guy with your brains live where you live? Or are the Western Isles populated by Heiland lovelies? *Do* you have a lovely little crofter woman at home, keeping things warm?'

'Fuck off, Alex.'

She tossed her head back again, showing off the mane of black hair. 'No need to be so touchy. But then you always were touchy about *girls*. Well, no, only one girl. The lovely Isabella. I s'ppose no woman has ever held a candle to her, eh?'

This time he looked directly at her, secretly relieved that she'd brought up a subject that had been festering within him for most of the evening. 'Oh, *please*. But, since you raise the subject, that was a pretty stupid idea of yours to get in touch with Isabella. I'm glad Simon didn't hear it. I talked him out of that course of action a while back, when I first met him. Anyway, Isabella's got nothing to do with this.'

She changed gear roughly as she spoke, taking out her irritation with him on the car. 'Of course she has! If, *if* Simon's going to go all loose cannon on us, we need to be prepared. We have to speak to both Lydia and Isabella. Just in case. I mean, I think Si will calm down now. But he's still unpredictable. He's got addresses for them both, as you well know. He might just get in touch with them on impulse. We need to spin a line and explain to Lydia and Abby that poor Si's not too well and may start causing us all a bit of trouble and embarrassment in the future. I mean, let's face it, we've all got our lives to lead. Who wants our days in the Unit exposed? I certainly don't intend to let it all, let anything, hang out.'

She was making him angry now. 'This isn't about Isabella and you know it. You s—'

She cut across him, trying to change the subject. 'I was glad to hear that the obsessive nut has kept track of the others. And by the way, I know you took his address list. I saw you in his study. Hardly difficult to do, given Si's pissed-up state and the fact that he was boring the arse off me about his bloody wife. Too het up to notice what you were doing.'

'You know he's got our phone numbers and everything? I didn't know he'd gone that far. I think it's a bit mental, all of it, *and* him keeping track of the others. But I wanted a copy on disk. Just in case. I th—'

She cut back in, laughing, before he had time to make any justifications about why he took the list. 'C'mon, Danny. You took a copy because you wanted to know where Isabella is and what she's doing. You're so transparent. But since you've got it, I want a copy of that before we part company tonight. I've got the laptop in the back. Just for my own peace of mind. Like you say, just in case . . .'

She lit another cigarette, without offering him one, and blew a distorted smoke ring at the windscreen. Straight away she took another drag and breathed a gentle kiss of smoke at him as she smiled, her tone back to sarkiness. 'I'll tell you this, though. If Isabella's going to be talked to, it would be better if *you* did it. I think you and I should start making a plan. We've managed to hold Simon back from any . . . any precipitate move. He's agreed to more discussion and thinking, thank God. But I don't know how long he can be kept back. I think you should contact Abby. After all, you do still have her best interests at heart. Don't you?'

He'd had just about enough. 'Leave it, Alex. Anyway, what about Innes Haldane? We never talked at all about her tonight.'

'That's because, like Sarah bloody Melville, she's a complete irrelevance.'

He peered through the rainy gloom. Conditions were atrocious. Alex had stopped talking as she took a rain-soaked corner too fast, the rear of the car threatening to fishtail. But she quickly sorted it out with another rough gear change. She started in again. 'Innes Haldane was a naive fool. She didn't know what the Unit was really about, silly cow.'

'That's rubbish, Alex. Innes wasn't stupid and she was close to Isabella.'

'She was close to Isabella for only a while. Remember? That all fell by the wayside. Innes was clueless. Like I say, an irrelevance. I don't know why Simon even bothered keeping track of her. So, she's a divorced Civil Service lawyer, living in London. How typically and tediously conventional. She'd probably run a fucking mile from any reminder of the Unit. I think we leave her well alone. And she'll leave us alone. Anyway, stop changing the subject. If you'll be bloody honest with yourself for one minute, you'll admit that you'd use any excuse to get in touch with Isabella. I know you. Lie away to yourself, but you can't lie to me.'

She took another drag as she let the stinging – and he had to admit truthful – accusation sink in. Then she was off again.

'Anyway, don't worry. I think we can handle all this. Certainly in the short term. I need to do some thinking. Bloody Dr Simon Calder! A loony, treating loonies. Bloody marvellous. Well, I've got plans for him. I'm not going to let him or anyone else get in the way. Never have, never will.'

The bravado was loud and brash. But not totally convincing. He could see that under the showy veneer she was unsettled. Although he didn't doubt that she wouldn't let anyone get in her way. Never have, never will. Too true.

Psychodrama

The next few weeks

File note from Dr Adrian Laurie, Consultant and Medical Director, APU
21 December 1977
RE: Patient, Alexandra Baxendale (d.o.b. 12.9.62)

In consultation with Anna Cockburn, I am here recording some diagnostic notes concerning patient Alexandra Baxendale. I have today been considering whether to recommend the transfer of this patient to the main hospital, specifically to Ward 21, the secure facility.

I and my nursing staff have noticed a distinct deterioration in her condition of late, exhibited by prolonged periods of sullenness and uncommunicativeness. Further, there have been unpredictable verbal outbursts against staff and patients, and at least two observed incidents of threats of physical violence.

Alex continues to refuse to participate in group therapy and has been plagued by regular nightmares. These latter I have identified as coinciding with the playing of a 'practical joke' on the patient at the Christmas party, the reason for which we have been unable to uncover.

The patient remains acutely disturbed. Indeed, although her admission to the Unit was followed by a brief improvement, she has shown a distinct deterioration in recent months.

However, I have, on balance, decided against removing her from the Unit, judging that since all patients will be sent home soon for Christmas, we will reassess her on her return in the New Year. However, I have advised that Sister Cockburn should warn the patient's parents to remain vigilant throughout the holiday break against any self-harm she may do, and caution them that the possibility of the patient acting out violently against others remains a real possibility.

Copy to: Daily Nursing Log
Copy to: patient file, A. Baxendale

27

'How long's Guy away for?'

Alexandra Baxendale looked at her lover and smiled. 'It's one of those bloody Middle East jobs. Sucking up to the rag heads and all that. He'll be gone at least a couple of months, thank God.'

Her lover slid out of bed and stood naked, hands placed provocatively on thighs. 'D'you think he knows? About us?'

Alex threw her head back and roared. 'Ha! You must be kidding! He'd be very, very cross. And I never like upsetting him because I like his money.'

'But you've got your own money? You're rich.'

'Oh, my dear girl, you can never be too rich. This house is all mine, bought with the filthy proceeds of years in the City of London! But my prodigiously clever husband is *really* rich. And you don't want to upset someone like him. Thing is, Guy probably wouldn't mind if you were a bloke. We've had one or two threesomes with his mates in the past. But he'd be *very* pissed off knowing that I was fucking women.'

'Wo*men*?'

'Just a turn of phrase, darling. I'm only fucking you. No, fucking a woman would be too threatening to him. Guy's pretty adventurous for an anally retentive, ex-public-school boy in his fifties. He loves me tying him up and giving him a good beating. He likes that more and more. It means he has to perform less and less, which I think he prefers, *and* it suits me. A couple of years ago he was having real trouble getting it up in straight sex. So I suggested a few . . . *modifications*.'

She watched as the slim outline of the girl, nearly half her age, disappeared into the bathroom. The mobile kicked off – she reached down, finding it among the various items of underwear strewn on the floor. The sun picked out the faint scarring on her forearms that plastic surgery had almost obliterated. She paused a moment, as if seeing them for the first time.

She was on her own now, thank God. She hadn't particularly enjoyed the encounter. The girl was getting too nosy, too familiar. And very shortly, she'd get too clingy. She'd have to strategize a way out. Soon.

She ran her fingers over her forearm. The faint raised scarring had her attention today. Some days were like that. Most of the time she forgot about them, and when others, such as lovers, noticed, and were insensitive enough to ask, she passed them off as some childhood accident. On one or two memorable occasions, she knew she'd met a fellow traveller. The fellowship of self-harmers. When that happened, they wordlessly compared scars and moved on. But Laurie had never allowed her to move on when it came to those scars . . .

'And so, Alexandra, we can all see how new some of those wounds are on your arms. Would you tell us please when you did them? Where were you, what was going on?'

Silence.

She'd made sure to wear a vest, and crossed her arms more firmly than before, the purplish red zigzags on show for all to see. She was glad to see some of the jolly company wince. Simon for one. Fucking pansy! Danny had just raised an eyebrow. Bastard! Laurie was looking round the room, checking them all out and inviting others to ask the obvious. But no joy today for Laurie. He'd have to try again.

'Well, Alex? Apart from the fact that I think it would do you good to talk about it, I think you owe it to the others to explain why you've come back after the Christmas break in this state.'

Silence.

'Isn't anyone else interested to know?'

Nothing.

'Well, let me enlighten you all. Alex has been having a pretty bad time of it at home this past week or two. You ran away overnight. Twice. And then your parents locked you in your room. They found you some hours later, on Christmas Eve, with cuts on your arms so severe that you spent several hours in casualty during the early hours of Christmas morning. Would you tell us why, Alex?'

'Get tae fuck!'

'Would anyone else like to ask Alex how she is?'

'Al—'

'Shut it, Lydia!'

Danny had shut the fat bitch up. Good. Though his smile and wink were no friendly act. And Laurie wasn't going to let him get away with it anyway.

'Danny, why did you cut Lydia off? No matter, Lydia, speak up. What did you want to say to Alex?'

And the cow was squirming now. Wanting to be seen as Miss Goody-Goody in front of Laurie. But Danny had his 'don't fuck with me' face on. Tough choice!

'I . . . I just . . . just wanted to ask Alex if she'd hurt herself because she was upset at what happened before Christmas. At the raffle.'

She'd lost it then and launched herself at the fat cow. It

took half the room to drag her off, and one or two of her cuts opened up again, smearing blood all over Lydia's stupid dress and her fat, ugly face. Fantastic!

Laurie had forced her to apologize to Lydia, then made her sit back down and talk about Christmas. But she'd not talked about the raffle.

No, she'd got the message.

28

She pondered Simon's address list for a last time, staring at the most worrying entry of all, until it blurred out of focus, and finally threw the sheet of paper on to her desk. She sat back and looked down from the converted attic that was her office, to the garden below. The rain was unremitting, pebble-dashing Guy's greenhouse and turning her carp pond into a boiling cauldron.

She fingered the photos in front of her, stopping at one. The rows of sullen faces, with just a glimpse of the beauty of the Argyll countryside behind their heads. At least the staff were trying. Ranj, Anna and Sarah were all sporting tight smiles. As well they should. Ranj's fancy camera had taken a clear picture that day, the expressions finely delineated. As for the patients? Their surly features would mean nothing to others. The atmosphere that still emanated from that one curling photograph made Alex feel like it had been snapped yesterday. She shivered, and spread out the sheaf of other photos. Funny she hadn't kept up with her photography. She'd really been into it. The posh camera her parents had bought her – presumably to de-guilt-trip themselves over her admission to the Unit – had been well used. The camera club at school had been one of the better ones. She'd been good at taking her subjects unawares, even in secret, though not intentionally, well . . . maybe, sometimes. There was a little bit of the voyeur in her, she had to admit. She half smiled at the thought and shuffled through the pack, each image setting off a crystal-clear memory . . .

Sister Anna writing up reports in the Nurses' Office: hot as hell to look at. But cold and controlling in bed, she'd been sure. Pretty cold and controlling as a nurse, come to think of it.

Sister Anna and Dr Laurie in conference in the therapy room: he'd always had a hard-on for Anna, and dear Sister had known it. And enjoyed it. And played around with him. Same old, same old.

Ranj in the garden: clever, good nurse under the circumstances. And knowing. Sadly, not knowing enough.

Student nurse Sarah coming upstairs on night duty: her first night duty . . .

'You'll be fine, I'm sure. But any problems, ring extension five three five. It's a number that operates only at night. That'll get you through to the main hospital night-duty desk, just down the road. Okay?'

Alex opened the record-room door another half inch. She could see both Anna and Sarah perfectly clearly under the hall light outside the Nurses' Office. Anna had her coat on and was giving Sarah a final pat on the shoulder.

'Those who need it have all had their night medication. They'll sleep like babies. Some babies, eh? Right, see you tomorrow morning at the handover. Bye now.'

Alex checked her watch. Ten o'clock. Bloody hell, Anna had certainly overstayed to check Sarah would be okay. She'd be okay, all right. She listened as Sarah set the locks, and her footsteps started clicking along the hallway. She heard her stop at the TV room, and there was a muffled instruction to whoever was in there to switch it off and get to bed in ten minutes.

Alex busied herself with the pile of 45s on the floor. A creak of the door. She turned round, still at a crouch, and raised an eyebrow at Sarah.

'Ten minutes, Alex. Then it's time for bed.'

She didn't answer. Just smiled.

Fifteen minutes later, she finished swilling out the toothpaste, wiped her mouth and pulled the bathroom light-cord. The upstairs corridors were in near darkness now. As she walked towards the female dorm, she saw Sarah approach from the other end. She must have been checking on the others. At the night-duty bedroom door she watched Sarah stop with her hand on the handle and look up.

Alex met her gaze. But didn't smile this time. Neither did the nurse. By the time Alex had reached the night-duty bedroom, Sarah was inside, the door shut.

Everyone else was asleep. Carrie had definitely had Largactil tonight. She'd seen Sarah giving her a dose earlier. Maybe Lydia too. Whatever, the fat cow was off for the night, snoring away, drugs or no drugs. Alex stripped down to skimpy tight t-shirt and knickers, and lay down on top of the covers. It was cold but somehow she didn't feel it. She wasn't staying long.

It took only the gentlest of knocks. Sarah was standing in darkness as Alex moved uninvited into the nurse's bedroom. She closed the door with a click and stayed leaning against it. There was a momentary stand-off. For a flicker, Alex thought she'd blown it. Then, in silence, Sarah reached around her to turn the lock, and with her other hand lifted up Alex's t-shirt, her touch warm on her shivering belly . . .

'You can't stay here, Alex! Neither can I! Anna's got to stay behind because Innes has the flu. But you've *got* to go. Everyone has. We just can't stay. Neither of us. You must see that?'

Alex watched as Sarah crouched down by the stream and began rinsing through the last of the group's breakfast dishes, constantly looking around her like a timid animal. Just like when they were in the Unit these last few weeks, when Sarah couldn't help flashing nervy looks over her shoulder, as if she expected Anna, Lydia, Ranj, Danny, *anybody* to come running up pointing accusing fingers. Alex looked away from her. There were no witnesses. Only acres of desolate Argyll countryside. The bloody group were back at the huts, cursing the failure of the hot and cold water system, and packing their rucksacks for the day's orienteering and night-under-canvas expedition.

Sarah was still refusing to look at her. Alex tried to get her attention for the umpteenth time. 'But why do *you* have to go? Why can't *you* look after fucking Innes, then I can "get ill" too? Once bloody Innes is asleep, we'll have the whole night to ourselves.'

She wasn't winning. Sarah was shaking her head, still bent over the dishes. 'No, Alex. A senior member of staff has to stay behind if someone's ill. And that's going to be Anna. That's just the rules.'

'Fuck it! I thought this stupid holiday was going to give us some time away from the others. Fine. Okay. What about just a couple of hours tonight, then? I thought we could sneak away at the orienteering thing. If you make sure we're in the same team, it'll be easy.'

Sarah was looking at her, at last. She stood up. Was she going to kiss her? Relent? Agree to an adventure tonight?

'That's not going to happen, Alex. It's too dangerous. I can't just disappear with you and leave Ranj to look after everyone. What the hell's he going to think?' She was taking a step back now. 'Look, I've been meaning to say this . . . I mean, speak to you for a while. Things . . . things are . . . well . . . they're getting out of hand, don't you think? We've got to be careful. You still want to see me, don't you, after you're discharged, when we can . . . do things . . . I mean, see each other more safely? Maybe we should hold off until then. Just for while? Well . . . ? Say something, Alex.'

She didn't know if she was already shivering from the cold or if it had just started. She felt sick and stumbled back as Sarah tried to touch her arm. 'What? *What*? What're you trying to do to me? You said before we left the Unit that the camping holiday would be "perfect" for us. Your very words. *Perfect*. And what have you done since we arrived? Tried to avoid me every fucking day. And now it's our last day. You're a shit, Sarah! Happy to fuck and fumble on night duty, when you've drugged everyone else up to the eyeballs. Well, just you wait! I'll fucking show you. You can get struck off for what you've done! Struck off! If not put in bloody prison! I'll show you!'

She felt the heat of the tears on her cold face, and turned and ran, tripping over a dead tree root, Sarah's last words fading behind her.

'Stop it, Alex! Stop! Don't do anything stupid! Anyway, no one'll believe you! No one! Think about it. I'm telling you . . .'

29

She wandered through the empty house, sipping from the over-full glass of cognac, trying to ignore the battering of the rain, and the now howling wind ripping through the trees in the garden. Guy had woken her up calling from Dubai and telling her how much he missed her. Nauseating. She sat uneasily by the French windows. The light was off, and outside she could make out various swaying shapes, including the tendrils of the delicate young silver birches, standing sentry, halfway down the garden.

She'd brought some of the photos downstairs and placed them on the dining table, her hand resting over them, as if to shield them from others' prying eyes. She was glad Guy was away for the next few weeks. She needed both privacy and solitariness. She'd be happy to wish him away forever. It was a farce. A mockery. They both knew – though you'd have to torture it out of him to get Guy to ever admit it – that their marriage was a bloody sham, one of convenience. She'd regretted it almost as soon as she'd done it. But it had seemed a . . . a . . . *useful* . . . even prudent, thing to do at the time. She'd been trying to make a very difficult transition from years of hard working and living in London, and make it as a big metropolitan fish back in Edinburgh. *And* start a new career as an internet entrepreneur. She'd always been a pretty good networker, until she'd burned a few too many bridges. It was when the City got all PC and so-called 'workplace bullying' was the buzz phrase. *Bullying.* Bollocks. If people couldn't keep up, then they should be out on their ear – man or woman. She'd never had any truck with women who moaned about the City being hard for a woman. Sure, you had to be a ball-breaker. But women could and did – at least the successful ones did – use *all* their charms to great effect, herself included. Granted, if you were a guy, you had more strenuous ways of getting what you wanted. She'd known of senior traders kicking underlings in the balls in the Gents, of fist fights in the champagne-swilling watering holes of EC2, and a myriad of other episodes that would chill ordinary folk to the bone.

What *was* unfair was that when she felt entitled to do the same, she was penalized for it. Just because of her gender. God, it would have been funny, if it hadn't ended up with her head on the block . . .

'Alex, none of this is being officially recorded. Frankly, it's to save the company's good name and not your own, sadly now tarnished. There is no doubt that you punched, kicked, slapped, and scratched Louise Bailey, one of your team's most junior traders, in the women's toilets of Corney & Barrow. I concede that there were no independent witnesses. *But* those who were in your group in the bar noted your disappearance to the toilets at the same time as Louise, and another female team member found Louise in what can only be described as an hysterical state, on the floor of a cubicle, bruised and bleeding. You had apparently left the premises.

'I'm forced to say, Alexandra, that there have long been whispers about your . . . and I *will* use the term here . . . your workplace *bullying* methods. The company has seen fit to ignore these because of the money you've made for us. But this is a whole different ball game. We're going to let you go quietly. Louise isn't pressing charges. The case would be a hard one to pin on you. I've no doubt you'd make a fine and convincing showing at court, if it came to that. But it won't. The company couldn't have those type of headlines splashed all over the press. However, I will give you one final warning. A *promise.* I will do everything in my power to discredit you and have your licence to trade revoked if you ever, *ever* try to get another job in the City. And that stigma will follow you everywhere, believe me. So, you're in a Catch-22 position. You may still have your licence but you cannot trade. Consequently, I suggest that you embark on a career change. *And* get some psychiatric treatment . . .'

She winced at the humiliating memory. Then smiled. She'd still managed to play hard-ball and get a decent pay-off on the QT. When she'd made it plain that she was willing to trash her own City reputation just to get back at the company and force things into the open, they'd caved in. On the money side anyway. She'd wanted out of the City for a while. It had been boring her. And that stupid little bitch Louise had asked for it. She hadn't been the first either. But she'd been a squealer, unlike the others, who knew what initiation they were in for, and knew to grin and bear it.

She threw back the last of the cognac. It would definitely help her sleep. She stood up. She could safely leave the photos lying about. She wasn't expecting any visitors tonight.

The bed was cold when she got in. She stared at the ceiling, watching the rain's shadows run black rivulets down the walls. She was drifting off, the feeling of falling a welcome one to her. But it wasn't going to be that easy. She jumped and was hyper-alert and awake again. She sat up. An unbidden memory had been prising its way through her subconscious, not for the first or last time. It must have been looking at those damned photos that had done it.

Christ, the last day or two she'd spent more time living in the past than now. But this one? Maybe it was because Guy had said he was looking forward to coming home for Christmas . . . Christmas . . .

'Double o seven. Lucky for more than James Bond, it seems . . .' The layers of tissue paper had come off easily, her excitement building with every vigorous rip. It had taken what seemed like an age to actually acknowledge what she was seeing. In reality it had to have been a mere split second. And she knew immediately what was going on. She remembered punching her way through the crowd, all eyes and mouths like round, shocked O's. All heads craning to see what she was fleeing . . .

'It's all right, Anna, I've found her. Leave it to me. No, honestly. I'll be fine with her.' Sarah's voice had drifted through the back door and into the frosty night. She ignored it and hunched into her parka, enjoying the view. This garden bench was her favourite. Stuck bang-up against the house wall, it was in a raised position at the top of the grounds, and the view was always remarkable, stretching seemingly for miles across lawn, until the eye reached the arbour, where the swing was. All was glittering snow and ice. The sky was clear. A half-moon – more than enough to light up the sparkles of the snow-covered lawn – picked out Sarah's silhouette as she approached.

'Alex, you can't stay out here. It must be minus five. You'll freeze. Look, you're already shivering. C'mon, let's go inside.' She again ignored Sarah, who at least had the sense not to try to touch her.

She was aware that her face must still be blotched red with the tears, and she retreated into her parka hood as far as she could. Her breathing had returned to something like normal. She could at least smoke now and drew deeply on the roll-up. It was made out of old dried-up tobacco, but she was out of normal fags and what the hell, it was a fag, after all. She felt Sarah shift a few inches nearer to her on the bench. In truth, she was glad it was Sarah and not any of the other staff. Well, glad it wasn't Anna or Ranj. Laurie wouldn't grubby his hands to try to deal with her, with any of them, outside the formality of a bona fide therapy session. Controlling bastard. But he'd bring this episode up as soon as possible at their next session. There was no doubt of that, and the thought made her nervous. The others would know that too, and it would be doubly worse.

She waited for Sarah to try again. At least they'd made it up since the camping fiasco. Well, sort of. If Sarah only knew that what had happened had been largely because of her. Her fault really. But Sarah had been nice, though nervy around her, since then.

'Alex, what's going on? Please tell me? What happened in there? Here.'

She was offering a fag. A proper one, and some neat vodka. Fine, she'd accept both, happily and greedily.

'What happened with the raffle? What's with the rope, the knife? It's some kind of perverse joke, right?'

She found her voice for the first time. 'Joke! Yeah, Sarah, that'll be right! That's why I'm shaking, freezing my tits off out here and smoking and drinking myself to death! It's all one big j—'

The shaking suddenly got worse and she allowed Sarah to prise the vodka bottle and the cigarette from her hands. She slapped both palms to her face, the tears oozing out.

'Something happened. Something we'll all be paying for one day. Believe me . . .'

*

An exceptionally loud howl from the wind snapped her out of the memory. She slid back under the duvet. If she was honest, she knew this day would arrive. How could it not? Not with a fool like Simon around in the world. He might be academically bright, but she'd never had a particularly high opinion of his other qualities. And she had to keep an eye on Danny. He'd always been a selfish bastard, as far as she was concerned, so he should be okay. And the others? Well, that remained to be seen. Whatever, she needed to do some hard thinking and planning. She wasn't, after all these years, going to have her life fucked up again. Not by anyone.

Psychodrama II

The same few weeks, and 1977

File note from Nurse Sarah Melville to Sister Anna Cockburn
21 December 1977
RE: Patient, Alexandra Baxendale (d.o.b. 12.9.62)

Following last night's episode with the raffle, after which I spent some time talking Alex down, I have still been unable to find out what was going on.

It's perfectly clear that the genuine prize was switched. How, I can't think, except that I know the wrapped prizes were left unattended in the Nurses' Office at night before lights out, while whoever was on night duty was doing their rounds. What's also obvious is that this 'prize' was meant for Alex and so Danny, as the 'lucky dipper', had to be involved. They'd all told each other what numbers they had drawn for the raffle, so Alex's 007 was well known.

I confronted Alex with the fact that Danny had to be involved, but she wouldn't be drawn. She just kept saying 'Bastards!', so I assume she knows who did it and that it wasn't just Danny.

I am also no clearer about why the fake prize of rope and knife should be so upsetting, nor where they got these items or how they got them in. However, since the Unit is not a prison, the free movement of forbidden items (Carrie's past marijuana supplies, for example) will always be an issue.

In short, I have managed to get precisely nowhere with Alex.

Sorry.

Copy to: Daily Nursing Log
Copy to: patient file, A. Baxendale

30

Sarah Melville stepped out into the freezing air, fighting her way through the madness of the Glasgow Christmas shoppers to reach the relative serenity of the underground car park. The security locking of her dark green Range Rover beeped its greeting at her. She climbed up into the luxury of the leather seating and sat, eyes closed, as she allowed the past hour to wash out of her.

Her last client of the day had been wearing. She always was. That was why she'd recently manoeuvred her into changing her appointment time to a Thursday evening. The very last appointment of the week, barring client emergencies. Tomorrow was the usual Friday lecturing and an afternoon conference speech. A breeze.

She turned the ignition, allowing the CD player to fill the vehicle with the low-level, soothing balm of Celia Cruz salsaing her way through a throaty rendition of 'Te Busco' – the only music of choice on such days. Full concentration was required until she hit the A82 with the magnificence of Loch Lomond opening out on her right-hand side.

After a wearying and difficult drive in blinding sleet, the full-beam headlights picked out the white-posted driveway entrance. The Range Rover slithered round an icy bend, snaking its way to the entrance of the exquisite, loch-side converted baronial mansion, the stone-carved name plate KINNAIRD HALL a welcome sight. Her own analyst had given her the tip on this place. The owners, who were running it as an hotel, at a catastrophic loss, had gone bankrupt, and developers had bought the building and carved, albeit expertly, a handful of luxury apartments out of it, keeping a couple of the best features: the swimming pool and the huge roof terrace with a bookable function room attached. A very unusual home. Worth every penny.

She wandered into the vast hallway of her ground-floor apartment, ignoring the ringing telephone, always an essential accompaniment to her homecoming if, like today, she'd kept her mobile switched off.

Ten minutes later she headed for the swimming pool. She had it all to herself. Bliss. Twenty metres of blue oblivion. She executed a perfect dive into the deep end and lost herself in fifty glorious lengths. Fifty lengths. One kilometre. A neat number. A tough, cleansing swim. She was reluctant to leave the side of the pool, but, knowing the habits of the other residents, she could expect the guy from the top floor to be down in a few minutes, and sociable chit-chat was not what she wanted tonight. She made her way back to the flat, and, after showering, strolled into her study, bringing back a tray of whisky bottle, soda, tumbler and leather folder, bulging with paperwork. Outdoors, the wind slammed the sleet against the glass, but she sat back in a towelling robe, warm and invigorated.

She slurped greedily at the burning liquid, knowing that it was foolish to follow hard physical exercise with hard liquor. Tonight was an exception. Though inwardly calm, she'd noticed on her drive back that her gear-changing hand was far from steady. Easy to see why. She put her paperwork to one side, giving in to the most persistent thought of the evening.

Somehow, in the back of her mind, under the most protective of subconscious layers, and occasionally in her worst dreams, she'd expected something like this. Though Simon Calder's reappearance at Debbie's, of all places, hadn't been the one she'd expected, imagined or feared. However, there was no getting away from the fact that when he started making a name for himself on the Edinburgh clinical psychology scene, she had wondered what she'd do should they bump into each other. In reality, it wasn't that likely. But possible. Most probable was an accidental meeting at a professional social do. And she knew herself well enough to recognize that her decision to get out of Edinburgh, retrain and immerse herself in psychotherapy had, albeit very vaguely and peripherally, taken the odds on such an encounter into consideration. Basically, it had been there somewhere, although in the very far background. But it *had* been there. As for the chances of meeting any of the others, including the one she most dreaded? Not a chance. She had no idea where they were and was sure they'd forgotten all about her. Even Alex.

The unbidden image of the fifteen-year-old skinheaded tomboy flashed through her mind. She hadn't thought of Alex for an age. Occasionally, the dream world introduced distorted and disturbing versions of her. But she hadn't had any of them either, not for years. She refilled her glass, letting her memories flow back to a few weeks before. The conversation with Debbie after Simon Calder had gone kept replaying itself.

'God, Sarah, that's a turn-up, eh? You didn't tell me you'd worked in an adolescent unit.'

The lie came easily. Too easily. ''Course I did. Shit, Deb, we've been together so long we can't even remember those early courtship conversations.'

She hoped the joke would cover her anxiety and her lie. But Debbie's memory never failed her.

'No, I would've remembered. I mean I knew you'd

specialized in adolescents at some point, but I didn't know you'd done work in a unit, and the APU no less. When was that?'

'Oh . . . seventy-sevenish for a couple of years.'

'A couple of years! Bloody hell, you're a dark horse. Seventy-seven? That was in its early days, wasn't it? Who was in charge?'

She had no choice now but to keep up the conversation. If she could keep it to who worked there and general talk about the Unit, all well and good. 'Eh . . . it was a guy called Adrian Laurie.'

She watched Debbie frown and then smile in recognition. 'Ah, yeah. I read loads of his stuff when I was training at the Tav. I think he had some important things to say, but, as I recall, he suffered a bit of a backlash and headed abroad. The States, I think. And then of course, the APU shut, didn't it? Too expensive for one thing, and Laurie's theories were becoming unfashionable. Anyway, you would've quit the scene long before then and been in your psychotherapy training.' She paused and smiled admiringly at her. 'Well, well, well, Sarah. You are a one. What an interesting professional period that must've been for you, clever girl. But you're an even better asset to the world of psychotherapy.'

She tried not to stiffen as Debbie stepped forward to put her arms around her. Though maybe she could use the occasion to distract her from any further Unit talk. But Debbie wasn't going to give her the time. She felt a light kiss and then a squeeze to her waist as Debbie nodded towards the kitchen. 'C'mon, let's open a bottle of robust Rioja and play some of that salsa you so love, and you can tell me all about poor Simon Calder . . .'

*

The snow was really beginning to pile up outside now. She shivered, despite the fact that she had the central heating on full blast. At the end of the day, Debbie seemed more in awe that she'd worked in the Unit than offended or puzzled that she hadn't mentioned it during their five-year relationship.

Strictly speaking, neither of them should've gone on to talk about Simon Calder in such detail as they had. But lovers, husbands, wives, close friends in the same profession always did. Of course there were ethical boundaries. Every good professional knew that. But Debbie had sold her with a winner. Little Katie Calder needed help, and her father's current behaviour, which wasn't helping matters, was seeded in his past. So, what was his past? For her part, she could convincingly plead that twenty-six, nearly twenty-seven years was a long way back to remember, which Debbie accepted. If only she knew how clear her memory of him, of them all, of *that* time was.

But, strangely enough, it was what Debbie had said to her about Simon Calder, rather than the other way around, that had stuck. And brought back crystal-clear memories of 1977 . . .

31

The scattered detritus of the previous night's party was all around them. Sarah watched Anna come back in, grave-faced, and close the door. She moved to a vacant chair by the still-illuminated Christmas tree, accidentally kicking a plastic beaker out of the way. She observed the faces of her assembled colleagues: Adrian Laurie and Ranj outwardly impassive, Anna furious. And the American psychiatrist from down the road, Matt Benson, fresh and alert. Brightly confident, he was taking the initiative, rather cheekily, she thought. He'd obviously decided that his mere presence at the incident gave him the right to be part of the post-mortem.

'It's a set-up that *had* to involve Danny Rintoul. To give the "wrong" prize, you have to have someone on the inside. And since it had been known for some days who was going to do the picking out of the hat, Danny's your man. And what the hell's going on that kids can sneak a thing like a hunting knife in here? To get hold of something like that would take some time and planning. Yeah, it was a definite set-up.'

She smiled to herself. Ranj, clearly irritated at this indignant stating of the obvious as if it was an incisive deduction, cut in. 'That's clear, Dr Benson. I think we'd all have to agree with that. There was nothing fortuitous about this incident. We know it was planned. It's extremely worrisome to me too that a dangerous weapon such as this knife can make its way in here. Potentially, it puts us all in danger, staff and patients. However, I don't see how we can prevent it unless we wish to introduce the kind of personal searches and authoritarian regime found in a secure institution for the criminally insane. I've worked in those places, and that's not what I came to work *here* for. Thankfully, we're not gaolers.'

She sat up in her chair, enjoying Ranj's demolition of Dr Benson. But she had to watch herself. Best to pre-empt questions and keep them off the subject of her conversation last night with the distraught Alex. She directed her attention to Ranj. 'When you were handing the prize over to Alex, didn't you notice anything about it? The weight, for example? I mean, a year's free pass to the Odeon and a box of chocolates smaller than the runner-up box are a bit different to rope and a knife.'

Ranj met her eye and held it. 'I did think it was a bit heavy, Sarah. But I didn't wrap the prizes. You and Anna did. I knew that the first prize was multi-wrapped, but that was about it.'

It was unusual for Ranj to be defensive. She felt Anna, to her left, stir and lean forward in her chair, nodding at Ranj. 'Yes, that's right. You couldn't have known, Ranj. That apart, the one interesting thing is when and how the substitution was made. As you said in your handover note, Sarah, all the wrapped prizes were kept in the office these past few days, until practically the last moment. The only vulnerable time was at night, when the staff member on night duty was doing the final rounds. As a rule, the office isn't locked then, because all the kids are, or are meant to be, in bed. Obviously there was a switch, and someone now has the genuine first prize, although I'd be surprised if they'd dare to use the cinema pass, no matter how valuable it is. Too easy for us to catch them. Adrian? You want to say something?'

'Yes. The substitution, the wrappings, all that is ancillary to the other central questions. Namely, what is the significance of the rope and knife? And why was it aimed at Alexandra Baxendale? Why did it elicit such an extreme reaction from her? There can be no doubt that whoever planned this knew precisely what effect this would have on Alex. The items are obviously symbolic.'

He had stopped. She knew he wasn't finished. It was just one of his well-known tactics. He was looking round at his staff, making sure he had their absolute attention. Then continued. 'But symbolic of what? Anyway, I suggest we get this place cleaned up and exercise hyper-vigilance today. Sarah? If you get the chance for another tête-à-tête with Alex, see what you can find out. Okay?'

Sarah knew Alex had been avoiding her all day and had been planning her moment. Alex was good at that. She must have followed her through to the annexe. As she was replacing a file in the Records Office, Sarah heard the click of the door and its lock being set. There Alex was, leaning against the door, in skin-tight vest and baggy camouflage army-surplus trousers.

'Alex, you know you can't come in here. It's out of bounds. And you certainly can't smoke in here.'

She regretted the didactic tone immediately. She watched Alex take a longer draw of the roll-up than usual and blow perfect smoke rings in her direction. 'Yeah, that'd be a laugh, if all our records went up in smoke, eh?'

The girl looked tired. Already slim, she seemed to have lost pounds in a day. But gone was the vulnerability of last night. The tears, the sobs, the . . . outpouring.

'You okay, Alex? What is it? What's up?'

She thought Alex was going to make an advance and

steeled herself not to respond. Instead, the girl took another long, slow drag at her cigarette. All insolence and . . . yes . . . a hint of flirtation. 'Oh, nothin's up, baby nurse Sarah. Just swinging by.'

And then, without another word, she unlocked the door and was on her way out, only pausing to smile. 'I'm fine, thanks. Oh, and that stuff I told you last night. All bullshit of course. Complete crap. Yeah, we had a laugh, but it was all good clean fun, as they say. Just a big nasty joke. That's what too much vodka does for you.' She was heading out of the room, her last remark uttered *sotto voce*, as she entered the corridor.

'And you don't half look gorgeous today, baby nurse Sarah. See ya!'

Sarah followed Alex out of the room and watched her self-consciously swagger down the corridor that led to the Unit house proper. She stopped only once, to grind her roll-up butt into the carpet with an over-sized Doc Marten's boot. Very Alex.

Sarah left it five minutes before going back to the main Unit building. Ranj was in the Nurses' Office in a better mood than before. 'Hey, Sarah. How you doin'? You look . . . I dunno, worried. Come, tell me all about it. Coffee?'

She had to sound out her worry with someone. Ranj was probably better than anyone. Anna would question her questions and Adrian was a non-starter.

She nodded her assent to coffee and sat down opposite him, talking slowly, as if she wasn't sure what she wanted to say. 'Ranj? Why . . . why would a patient tell you an . . . an unbelievable though disturbing story, which clearly disturbed *them*, and then almost immediately afterwards retract it as a "joke"?'

'Alex?'

'Not specifically. A few of them have done the sort of thing I'm talking about. Just wanted to know your take on it, as an old hand at this game.' She didn't like lying to Ranj. But it was necessary.

He handed her the coffee, sipped at his own drink and sat back, feet on the chair next to him.

'Righto. There are obviously levels of story-making. There's no one in the Unit that is a complete deluded fantasist. I mean, not living in this world. Lydia's probably the nearest to that when she's really in the darkest part of her bipolar world. The others? Well, Carrie, Danny and Alex *will* make up stories. But they're usually acts of bravado. Indications that they feel they're not getting enough attention. They also like to wind we staff up, in case you hadn't noticed. A simple "pull the other one" usually suffices and stops them in their tracks.'

It wasn't enough for her and she racked her brains to think of a way to get more out of him. 'But what if they're, say . . . very down, or even very upset at the time, and they seem to be convincing?'

'Yeah, well, whatever the circumstances, I think it's key to listen, really *listen* to their story. Chances are it's saying something about what's going on with them. It may be a rewriting of some trauma in their past, it may be a kind of allegory of how they see their life. It'll be symbolic in some way. Unless it's just one big massive porky, purely to get your attention. And then you have to ask yourself why, *at that particular time*, they want your attention.' He paused to smile at her. 'That make sense?'

She returned the smile and nodded.

He drained his mug and sat up. 'Anyway, that's enough about fantasy. Did you get any further with Alex today? She say anything more about last night's fun and games at the raffle?'

'Nope. I tried again just now but nothing. I don't think we're going to get to the bottom of it.' Her final lie of the conversation came easily.

The simple truth was that she didn't want to know what last night was about. Right now, she'd happily see the back of Alex for ever. The girl was beginning to scare her. She'd be happy to see the back of them all. And as far as last night was concerned, she was going to consign it to history. After all, Alex had been barely coherent. It wasn't even a story she told. More a series of borderline hysterical claims. Just kept insisting that the raffle 'joke' was because of something she'd done, something they'd all done, 'Something so bad, no one will forgive us. Ever. And I mean *ever*.' Then, when she pressed Alex on the rope and knife issue, things started to get more worrying. 'What's the worst you can do with a rope and a hunting knife – go hunting? Hah! You could say that! And *where* do you think we last had rope and a knife before tonight? It wasn't in here, that's for sure. Think. It's not difficult . . .'

The implications seemed . . . *felt* . . . sinister last night but now . . . she wasn't so sure. Certainly, something had upset Alex – deeply – and the raffle episode was far from a light-hearted prank. But other than that, who could say? These kids, Alex in particular, were utterly unreadable when they wanted to be. Liars, deceivers, even cunning strategists at times. From now on, all she cared about was managing the Alex situation until she was eventually discharged. Patients couldn't stay here for ever. The average was eight or nine months. No, Alex would go at some stage. And that couldn't come soon enough. What a bloody mess things were in. She'd been nothing short of a fool. She needed her own head examined, risking everything like that. Reckless. Reckless and stupid.

32

Sarah had switched off all the electric lights and lit candles. That way she could see outside. The wind was still hammering the sleet against her windows and the surface of the loch was one huge black chasm. She wandered over to the third filing cabinet in the spare room that doubled as her home office, keys clinking in her hand.

With trembling fingers she pulled it out from the bottom drawer. Back at the window, she put on her reading glasses and peered at it, the candlelight flickering shadows across its still glossy surface. Breathing deeply, she allowed herself more whisky. The photo was in remarkably good nick. Probably because it had been kept in envelope after envelope over the years. She had moved it around with her all her life, though she couldn't remember the last time she'd been able to look at it. It had assumed the quality that photos of dead loved ones acquire. Almost living reminders of them. You know you have them, but it's usually too painful to look, since they remind you of what you've lost. And yet you keep them. Talismans. Kept out of love.

But the similarities stopped well before then. Yes, she'd kept it, yes, she couldn't bear to look at it. Why had she kept it? Easy to self-analyse on that. She'd kept it for the same reason that she couldn't bear to look at it. As a reminder of her shame. Her stupidity. Her vanity. Its presence in her life also reminded her of what she hadn't dealt with. In her own therapy and analysis over the years, she'd alluded to 'problems with a particular patient' in her early professional life. Her astonishingly astute psychotherapy trainer and personal therapist had almost managed to get more out of her, but she'd resisted. If her therapist had had an inkling of what her euphemistic phrase really meant, she wouldn't be where she was today. Without doubt, if her own decent and principled therapist had got wind of the truth about her and Alex, that would have been the end. She'd have seen Sarah thrown out of the profession, maybe worse. No, she'd successfully implied that it was a difficult professional problem, not the breaking of that most sacred of professional ethics: do not get sexually involved with a patient. Especially a severely disturbed fifteen-year-old girl.

God, she shuddered to think of where she might be. She let the candlelight flicker again over the faces. Apart from the then characteristically awkward-looking teenage Simon Calder, where were all the rest? What had become of their lives? She shook her head at the photo, her fingertips brushing over the faces, most of them . . . what? Gloomy? Uneasy? Frightened? That bloody camping holiday and that bloody orienteering fiasco. They'd found the kids all right. Safe, well, though reeking of booze and resolute in their denials that they'd been drinking. And then there was Alex's story . . . that weird unsettling story, if you could call it that. More an irrational outburst with some disturbing claims behind it but most probably attention-seeking lies and embellishments. She thrust that to the back of her mind, thinking again about her own lucky escape. Not only might she (and Anna and Ranj – hence Anna's fury that day) have been prosecuted for professional negligence if anything had happened to the kids, but if the Alex thing had come out she'd probably have been sent to prison.

She blew out the candles and meandered her way through the rooms of the flat, restlessly pacing, whisky glass in one hand, photograph in the other, eventually settling back into the living room. The snow had stopped falling, and she could see the ripples in the waters of the loch. Loch Fyne. That was the one good thing that had come from the camping débâcle all those years ago. It had introduced her to the beauty of Argyll and this marvellous loch in particular. And here she was, living in luxury by its edge. But how different it could have been . . .

'Well, just you wait! I'll fucking show you. You can get struck off for what you've done! Struck off! If not put in bloody prison! I'll show you!'

She'd been waiting for something like this and had her riposte ready. She watched Alex trip over a tree root and shouted her reply, 'Stop it, Alex! Stop! Don't do anything stupid! Anyway, no one'll believe you! No one! Think about it. I'm telling you . . .'

She bent down by the river, picked up the bucket of clean dishes and headed back to the camping huts. Christ. This was the last thing she needed. She didn't think Alex would do anything rash right now. She thought Alex would be too embarrassed, shy even, to draw sexual attention, especially *that* sort of sexual attention, to herself, which she would undoubtedly do if she caused some big allegations scene. And, though she hated herself for it, hated herself for all that she'd let happen, she knew that she'd be able to deflect Alex's accusations with the 'crush' defence. Patients often went through a phase in their treatment when they developed crushes on particular members of staff. And everyone knew Alex was a little troublemaker. No, if the worst happened, she knew what her answer would be. As she entered the clearing where the huts were, she relaxed. All seemed normal. There was no hysterical Alex, crying rape.

She knew Alex. She'd be sulking in her bunk. Chain-smoking and ignoring everybody and planning some sort of bad behaviour. Better keep a close eye.

She wasn't aware of losing sight of them. Darkness had fallen by 5 p.m., and they really should have bivouacked by then. They were running bloody late. She checked her own compass and map, and saw the flicker of two torches ahead. Simon and Carrie.

'Don't get too far ahead, you two!' But she doubted they could hear. The wind had really picked up during the past hour, and its whistling through the trees drowned out most other sounds, except for the loudest of Carrie's laughs.

But the moon was well-nigh full, so at least she could see their two silhouettes pretty clearly. She checked the map again, squinting at the cross where they would overnight. 'Damn!' She'd stumbled over a log. Map, compass and torch went flying. The black rubber torch was pretty much indestructible, and she saw it beaming through the damp bracken and leaves on the forest floor. 'Fuck it!' She wiped herself down, retrieved the map and compass, and was on her way again. God, she hated this. Still, she was happy that she'd taken on Carrie and Simon for her team. Poor Ranj. Stuck with an insufferably sulky Alex and a moody Danny. Though he did have Abby to brighten his group up. Instinctively, she did her regular check ahead. No torch lights. Cloud had covered the moon. Apart from the strong beam from her own torch, everything was blackness. Fantastic!

'Carrie? Simon? Hey, where are you! Hold on! Carrie! Simon, get back here! Come on!' Hell, they'd never hear her above the wind.

And then it happened. Her own hundred per cent reliable torch gave out. Not even a warning flicker. She shook it, pressed it to her ear. Shit! The bulb must've been damaged in her fall. The delicate glass was now rattling about inside the torch head. Shit, shit, shit! No spare bulb and no back-up torch. She had a candle and her cooking stove. Both bloody useless in these conditions. She stopped and leaned against the nearest tree. This was serious. She couldn't move safely onwards, but she had to find the kids. Why the fuck had she been so cocky about that damned torch? Ranj had told her she should have a back-up. Even offered her a little plastic Ever Ready thing with spare batteries. But she'd refused. What a fool! The moon was floating in and out of the clouds. She could move when it was out, but then she'd have to keep stopping and starting.

And the kids? They were already galloping ahead anyway. Just before her fall she thought they were trying to do a runner. And now she had no way of catching them up. Well, there was nowhere for them to go, except the rendezvous point. They weren't stupid kids. Far from it. No, they'd make camp where, she hoped, Ranj, Alex, Abby and Danny were waiting for them. As for her? She'd have to sit it out until there was a cloudless patch of sky and she could safely run on.

She let herself slide down to the damp ground, relieving the weight of her rucksack against the trunk of a tree. It was only then that she realized her own situation. In the middle of nowhere, alone, no light, and about fourteen hours until daylight. She had all the right wind and water-proof gear but still she shivered. She kept looking up through the branches, but the moon had completely disappeared. She did have her whistle, though. She reached into a side pocket of her rucksack and brought it out. That was one safety measure that Ranj had insisted on, for all of them. The noise from it would have carried well over this terrain but for the bloody wind. Anyway, Ranj said the whistles were for 'absolute emergencies' and this didn't really qualify. Except that the kids were on their own.

She pulled her hood tight and leaned her head back, eyes shut. What to do? An owl's hoot penetrated the whoops of the wind, as did a rustle behind her. She scrabbled to her feet and swivelled round, the weight of the rucksack nearly felling her again. 'Carrie? Simon? It's Sarah. Is that you? Hey!'

Her words were carried away on the wind, into nothingness. She could feel the increase in her heartbeat. She had to get out of here, moon or no moon. She could still see her compass and knew in which direction to go. Head bent, she took each step slowly, whistle in one hand, compass and plastic-covered map hanging round her neck. And then she saw it. The faint beam of light shining behind an incline a few hundred yards away. The kids! Thank God! She peered ahead. Only one beam. Carrie or Simon? Whoever, the other one couldn't be far behind. She reorientated herself towards its source, feeling the relief that comes after a build-up of tension. As she climbed the incline, she could still see only one torch beam, fanning left and right, as if looking for something. Or someone. And then she heard it. The shrill sound of a whistle, penetrating clearly through the wind. Oh, no, the kids! Her hand was tight round her own whistle, and immediately she replied with three long blasts.

'Here! I'm here!' Three more blasts. Three returning on the wind. And then the torch beam started bobbing up and down, its owner obviously running towards her.

'Carrie? That you? Simon?'

The figure was nearly upon her, slithering down a mossy hump.

'Sarah! Thank goodness!'

'Ranj, what the h—'

But he was shaking her by the shoulder. 'Listen. I've lost them. Abby, Alex and Danny. Where's Simon? And Carrie?'

Her initial relief had been replaced, yet again, by rising panic. 'Oh, God, no! I lost them. I fell . . . my torch broke . . . I've been calling them. Oh, God, Ranj, what the hell's happened to them? We've got to find th—'

He cut across her. 'Okay, wait a minute . . . Right, come with me up to the top road. The Land Rover's there. They can't be far. Come on, move it!'

A heaving flurry of snow slammed itself against the window, chasing the recollection away with a jolt. The photograph that she'd just brought alive lay before her, her eyes re-focusing on the rows of faces. Ghosts. She recalled that there had been staff post-mortems aplenty, analysing that night's events. All were agreed that the patients had deliberately gone missing. It had been a planned operation. Why? It had been impossible to find out. It was pretty obvious that they had been drinking and, it was assumed, smoking dope at some point, given their glazed, spaced-out demeanour. As far as the staff were concerned, Carrie had been in the frame for supplying both, but there had been no proof. No one had talked. Exactly where they had been and what they had been doing until they were found huddled and shivering at the side of the top road remained unknown. Alex had offered her some weird story that she kept to herself, but, at the end of the day, the staff agreed to leave it, apart from a couple of lectures about drink and drugs that everyone, staff and patients, knew were a waste of time. In all probability that night had been some attention-seeking ploy that had gone wrong, and they'd got themselves lost and frightened. City kids out of their depth. But somewhere deep down, she'd never really bought that. She couldn't of course discuss this with any of the staff, but she felt that this was an Alex-instigated act of revenge, in response to their row that morning. And just how far that act of revenge had gone she could never be sure. She'd never felt comfortable about the whole episode. Although she and Ranj had got a bollocking from Anna, who in turn with Laurie had the thing squared away as 'extreme acting out', she couldn't help wondering for months afterwards about the convenience of this explanation. That night Anna had been scared stiff too. They'd all have been finished if the kids had come to harm. Anna had vetoed calling the police 'until they were sure' they really were missing. Sarah had always considered that a dangerous, self-serving and wrong decision.

Yes, it had left a bad taste, even though it was soon forgotten as a topic of conversation in the Unit. Except. Except that the atmosphere was never the same with that group, and she was glad when they'd all gone. Every last one of them, including a much chastened and quietened Alex. But she didn't think she was a healed Alex. In truth, had the Unit done them any good at all? Didn't that débâcle of a reunion picnic not prove her case? That fight at the end. She and Alex had managed to avoid each other quite successfully all day until then. It seemed that they both wanted to forget about what had happened in the Unit. And that suited her fine. It had been tricky. She'd never forget when she and Anna were lying on the rug, near the rocks, by the Auld Kirk, and Anna started going on about, or rather referring to, professional and ethical boundaries. No affairs with patients! She'd just wanted the ground to open and swallow her up. In hindsight, it was bloody useful that there was a rumpus. She'd been feeling more and more uncomfortable in Anna's presence. Almost as if Anna could read her guilty thoughts. Rubbish of course. Anyway, the chaos of the fight showed that very few of the former patients had been released into the world any better than when they had come in.

Even Simon Calder, despite his achievements, was struggling. Something that Debbie said about him was nagging at her. She needed to find out more. She headed back to her office, photograph in hand, and returned it to its locked drawer. She threw the filing cabinet keys on to her desk and slumped down in her chair. She should have known. The spectre of the Unit was rearing its head after all these years. Given a lifetime of avoidance and denial, she had no choice but to follow where it led.

33

'You know the drill. Strictly observed feeding times.'

'Yeah, yeah. How many hundreds of times have I cat-sat for you, Deb? Now go. See you in a couple of days. I've got your return-flight details. I'll pick you up on Friday night. Enjoy the conference. It's in Barcelona, for God's sake. You've got to enjoy it. I bet it'll be a junket. Oh, and bring me back an excellent Rioja!'

Sarah stood in the cold at the front door, smiling and waving, watching the taxi's brake lights flicker and disappear round the corner into the night. She double-locked the outer and inner front doors and wandered back into Debbie's living room. The two Siamese were lounging imperiously on one of the sofas. She settled at the dining table, sipping at the wine they'd been sharing at dinner. She had decided on tonight's course of action as soon as she knew Debbie was going away.

It was outrageous, wrong, breaching every ethical boundary. After tidying away the dinner things, she made her way through to the back of the house, clutching a large brandy – Dutch courage for what she was about to do. Debbie's office was spacious and looked out on to her wild garden. Tonight it was in darkness. No outside lights on. Although the garden and, in their turn, the back rooms of the house couldn't be overlooked, she pulled the blinds down anyway. An irrational act, born out of guilt. The keys to the locked patient files were kept elsewhere. She knew where.

The filing was logical. All patients had an ID number only. But the key to cross referencing the numbers with names was also readily at hand in a different locked drawer. Patient number 1,571. Katie Calder. She scan-read through the session notes, looking out for any mention of Simon Calder, and then she came to the most-recent entries.

It is altogether common for there to be marital difficulties following the kind of pressures that Rachel and Simon Calder have experienced with the abduction and assault of their daughter. From previous discussions with Rachel Calder - again already recorded - it has been clear to me for some time that Simon Calder had no intention of taking part in the family-therapy sessions. My invitation for him to come to see me was readily accepted, somewhat to my surprise. I found him in an intense mood, though making a reasonable show of appearing relaxed.

However, when it came to it, he was extremely forthright and implacable about not attending Katie's sessions. I intentionally let it be known that I had been speaking to his wife about him. This surely cannot have surprised him. Also, I made him aware that Sheena Logan and I had also been talking and made reference to his past. In essence, Sheena knows very little about his psychiatric past, other than what she had to know when he accepted the post. It is a very long time ago, and records will no longer exist. However, the uncanny coincidence of Sarah being a member of staff in the APU during Simon Calder's time there is useful.

Though Sarah herself, understandably, could not remember enormous amounts of detail, she did scotch Sheena's and my speculation that he had suffered sexual abuse as a child. No, he had a complex mix of psychiatric disorders associated with his unloving and domineering mother, tied to having been a twin, the other sibling having died at birth and the mother somehow blaming him. I imagine that led to some fairly serious disturbance in adolescence.

It is through Rachel Calder that I have gained my best intelligence on Simon Calder. It seems that, unbeknown to him, his wife is aware that he keeps a daily journal. He apparently writes it every night once she is in bed and keeps it under lock and key. Recently she managed to sneak a look at it – no easy task, since she says that her husband is 'obsessively secretive' about everything to do with his study. Over the years she's assumed that this is because he may have confidential patient files there, and so the room is effectively out of bounds. However, she has said, with stark honesty, that her trust in her husband has completely broken down. She has taken advantage of his distraction of late and managed a glimpse at a couple of the journal entries and felt so concerned that she had to talk to me about it. She related the following: 'He talks about memories of something he calls "that time before". I don't know what he means. He says that time has always been "buried deep but constantly nagging". He talks about nightmares that have come back, ones he had years ago. About something I think when he was very young. And he talks about drinking too much. In secret. I didn't even know he was! Simon's never been a heavy drinker in all the years I've known him. He doesn't like being out of control. And he says a strange thing. "All is deceit. Lying. Guilt." He talks about how no one can know why what's happened to Katie has hit him harder than anyone else, including me. I think it's to do with this . . . this *thing* that happened when he was young. Anyway, he goes on to say something really odd. "There are others" meaning, others who know. Know what? And there was another entry. Something about a game that had gone wrong and that would stay with them all - whoever "all" are - for ever because what "they" did was "the absolute unforgivable . . . irreversible".'

The hit as she threw the entire triple brandy-shot down her throat almost induced immediate vomiting. She stood up, consciously trying to slow her breathing and counteract the nausea, and then, when it had subsided, she eased herself back into the chair. She read and reread the entry three times. She'd understood the significance of every word. There was no mistake. With a shaking hand, she closed the file. Hurriedly, she put the file and the keys back in their rightful places and switched off the office light. Suddenly aware of a scratching at the door, she moved into the hallway and padded her way down the stairs to the kitchen, the cats hungry and noisily insistent behind her. She ignored them, instead looking for the bottle to refill her glass. A foolish act, she knew, but the only answer at that moment. As she sloshed the liquid in, the smell of it turned her stomach, decisively this time. She leaned over the sink and vomited. The shock had been too much. But from that moment onwards, she knew exactly what she had to do. To be sure.

* * *

She walked into the freezing winter sunshine of Lochgilphead, gasping in lungfuls of air. The local newspaper office behind her had been small, stuffy and cramped. But her sense of claustrophobia had nothing to do with that. She carefully folded the photocopied articles and headed for her car. She looked at her watch. She'd get there, as planned, by twilight.

She'd never returned to this exact spot since the camping holiday. She'd driven down to look at the outward-bound centre. Still there and, unbelievably, looking exactly the same. Nobody in residence. Four twenty. The sun had almost had enough for the day. She parked on the high road, pulled her backpack out of the boot and set off. Within half an hour she thought she was there. A compass and plastic-covered, weather-proof map had been easy to find in town. She squinted at where she thought she was. She was going to need the torch soon. It was foolhardy coming out on her own at night, no one knowing where she was. But it had to match the timings of before. For greater verisimilitude. Besides, she wanted to *feel* again what it was like for her. More importantly, what it must have been like for the others. Two in particular.

She couldn't be sure that she was on exactly the same path. Chances were she wasn't. A forest path was a forest path. She was no expert hiker. But she knew where she was heading. She'd mentally marked on the map where they'd peeled off. Carrie and Simon. And where had they rendezvoused with the others? Where had Alex, Abby and Danny given Ranj the slip? They would have to have gone down to the loch-side and doubled back. It was the only answer. She would do the same. The torch was needed now and she smiled to herself as she patted the reassuring shape of the Maglite back-up in her breast pocket. This wasn't going to be like last time. The cut down to the loch was slippery, and she must have slithered more than walked. But she made it. She took her bearings again and then pulled out the photocopied cuttings. She wanted to be sure she was heading to the right place.

She couldn't be certain this was it, but shortly after the village of Minard she saw a path to her left. It ended in a clearing right by the loch-side. She looked around. Yes, on a moonlit night all would be visible, and even if you had a few torches about the place, the thickly forested pathway would hide them from the main road. She walked towards the water's edge, toeing a few loose rocks with her boot. She bent down to touch the surface of the water. Freezing. To her right was a raised bit of rock and moss, almost like a natural diving board. There was even a ready-made little flight of rocks like steps leading up. She jogged up them. The height was surprising. She shone her torch downwards. It was quite a drop. To her right, someone had hung a monkey rope from an overhanging tree bough. For swinging and jumping into the loch in the summer. Kids laughing. Kids playing. Kids . . .

She shivered and carefully picked her way back down. She'd seen enough. The walk would be tiring, but she'd stay on the main road and maybe hitch a lift to her car a few miles on. It was remarkably still on the loch. No wind. No moon. The opposite of last time. There were owl hoots and rustlings like before. But this time she wasn't scared of the journey. Only scared of what she now knew. And what she should, what she could, do about it.

With a final backward glance at the blackness of the loch, she headed up the path to the main road, tears beginning to burn at her eyes. Burning with her own shame and guilt.

Reunions II

The same few weeks

Handover note from Sister Anna Cockburn to Charge Nurse Ranjit Singh
22 December 1977
RE: Patients, Danny Rintoul (d.o.b. 5.3.62) and Isabella Velasco (17.6.61)

Probably due to the other disruptions currently infecting the Unit, I think we have all missed yet another shift in patterns here. I have become aware that the previously close relationship between Danny and Abby has cooled, distinctly.

As we have discussed many times in our staff meetings, we all had a suspicion that this relationship was on the point of becoming sexual. For obvious reasons that could not be permitted. If it has already happened, then we have not been monitoring both patients thoroughly enough. However, on balance, I feel that matters have not reached that state.

I have discussed this further with Adrian and we agree that any emotionally bonding relationship that Danny can have with a female without an active sexual factor is to be encouraged. Danny is clearly very fond of Abby, who is of course extremely attractive, and on the whole we think that this relationship, if kept at friendship level, could be good for both patients.

However, there has been an inexplicable change in atmosphere between the two. It seems that Danny has given Abby the cold shoulder. Rather surprising. Further, I don't think it is because he no longer cares for her or admires her – I have seen those puppy-dog looks he still gives her when he thinks she (and everyone else) can't see him. No, he seems to be under great strain and will not let Abby in (or any of us for that matter), hence his outbursts of pent-up frustration and anger.

Heavy monitoring of both for the next day and night. Roll on the Christmas break!

Copy to: Daily Nursing Log
Copies to: patient files, D. Rintoul; I. Velasco

34

The journey back had been hellish. Trying to cross the Minch at this time of year always was. Although he could count on one hand the number of times he'd gone back to the mainland since he'd settled in the Western Isles. He lived here for a reason. He liked the solitude, the idea of being cut off from the rest of the world. A feeling he enjoyed, especially during the winter months, when ferries and planes had their problems getting here. No, he didn't enjoy the outside world. Even Stornoway was too loud and too busy for him sometimes.

He'd just been over to his neighbour's croft to thank him for seeing to his dogs and sheep while he'd been away. An ailing ewe had been found dead in the snow, but that had been expected, and he shooed away the neighbour's apologies. The neighbour had insisted on immediately opening Danny's gift of a single malt, and they'd got through half of it before Danny could take his leave and make the very slow and careful two-mile drive through the snow, back to his croft.

At home, he sat by the peat fire, sipping at his own supply of single malt. The journey, the whole couple of days, had unsettled him to the core. Could he really have fooled himself that they would never meet again, when they had all kept their bargain to keep in touch every year? Albeit in the most terse and tenuous way, as far as he was concerned. And hadn't it been he who had initiated further contact with Simon? He'd thought long and hard about that. When he'd read the newspaper reports, he'd just about passed out. He'd been surprised that Simon hadn't contacted them all. And Simon had taken such a long time to reply to his own letter of condolence about the wee girl. That had forced him to write to Alex. She'd responded in a devil-may-care way but, crucially, had supported his decision to get in touch with Simon.

He worried about that. Simon mustn't know about his telling Alex behind his back. Anyway, she'd been okay about it. She'd known nothing about the kidnapping of Katie Calder. Simon had been right. She'd apparently been sunning herself somewhere abroad at the time. But, having met her now, seen her, he was sure she was as freaked out by it all as he was. She just hid it a bit better.

He poured himself another drink and stared down at the photograph and the address list cradled in his lap. That random act of child kidnapping had set Simon, set him, set them all, on a journey he would like to get out of. Opt out, just like he had fifteen years ago, when, in his mid twenties, he'd decided to bury himself here. He'd done ten years hard working and hard playing on the rigs and he'd thought the life suited him. But it hadn't. Once here, he thought he'd found his paradise. But it wasn't going to be that easy. That his fate depended, had always depended, on a few others had been easy to hide from this place at the end of the world. Except for those November 8th letters. He hated that date. So much so, that he usually spent the evening on that day in a Stornoway hotel room getting mindlessly drunk. A completely understandable ritual to him. At least it prevented his home, his croft, the few neighbours and others he saw regularly from being contaminated by that day.

He marvelled at his ability to shut off, compartmentalize what was bad. He was very good at that. It had served him well. It allowed him to live. But he was involved now. It was only a matter of time before the wretched Simon would be calling him up, asking for advice, for a sympathetic listening ear. And Alex? That uncomfortable but ultimately useful drive back from Simon's had been instructive. He didn't trust her a bit, but he recognized some form of alliance with her. She'd been dragged into a situation she too desperately wanted to deny. He fingered the Unit camping photo, gently smoothing back its curling corners. The tip of his forefinger stopped on the face of Isabella. What would she look like now? What would she be like now? Her personality, her nature. People didn't change that much, did they? Not people like them.

35

He knew he would still have recognized her had she been ninety. Although there were several women of the right age disembarking, his eyes could settle on only one. She'd always been, and would always be, beautiful. He felt his stare on her to be as piercing and unwavering as if it had been a laser.

He'd had three weeks of sleepless nights since getting in touch with her, and now here she was. She walked slowly, tentatively, across the tarmac to what passed as an arrivals lounge in the tiny, oblong-shaped building that was Stornoway Airport. Apart from her looks, the second most obvious thing about her was that she had the air of affluence. Presumably quite a few rich women passed through this airport. Local politicians' wives, landowners' wives, the occasional minor celebrity. But she was London rich. The confidence, the bearing, said as much. The impeccably tailored trousers and soft buckskin three-quarters-length coat reeked of class. He suddenly felt woefully inadequate in his faded jeans and ancient leather biker's jacket. In the remaining two minutes that he judged it would take for her to reach the lounge, he pondered the letter he'd sent her. Word for word, he knew it by rote. It had taken ten hours, a billion drafts and bottle of the hard stuff to compose . . .

Dear Isabella,

I imagine I am the last person on earth that you would expect to hear from. The days of the Unit are so long ago and I am *sorry if this upsets you or makes you feel down. I got your name and address from a list I have seen. A list of everyone in the Unit in 1977. Simon Calder has it. You remember Simon? I had to write to you, as this affects us all . . .*

His head jerked up, and involuntarily he stood to attention as he became aware of a movement a few yards to his right. She'd come through into the terminal building more quickly than he thought she would. Without hesitation he was moving towards her. *What a moment!* And there she was, flesh and blood, standing five feet from him. A clearer vision of loveliness than the one just glimpsed through plate glass. There were a few crow's feet around the chestnut-coloured eyes. A very attractive feature. Skin – smooth, tanned. Hair – still blackest black. He tried to check this unbidden sexual assessment, but it was difficult. She was, quite simply, lovely. He watched her scan the handful of meeters and greeters, her gaze stopping on him. There was no smile. Just the faintest nod as she searched his face, making sure.

He stopped in his tracks but, after a moment, took a shaky step forward. 'Hello, Abby. Let me take that.' He knew his voice sounded hoarse, rough.

And he could kick himself! The old-fashioned, chivalrous act of offering to take her bag made him feel even more inadequate than ever. He must seem like a bloody caveman! Her unspoken refusal with a casual flick of the hand was tantamount to a physical blow. He'd better shape up. Behave like a grown-up, modern man. Not the love-struck fifteen-year-old he had once been. But her first utterance to him in twenty-odd years turned him over, his heart hammering.

Her voice was deep, still distinctly middle-class Edinburgh, with very clear diction. A sexy voice. Of course. 'Is there anywhere else we can go or is this it? The place is even smaller than I expected.'

The implied disapproval of her surroundings momentarily threw him. *She hates the place. She hates me. She's regretting coming here.*

He made a clumsy attempt at taking control. 'Well, it's just that I thought you'd want a rest after all that travelling. There's actually a very quiet area round the corner here. See that table there? What can I get you? Eh . . . they do alcohol too, if you want it?'

'Coffee. Black.'

He parked her and her bag in the quiet corner and walked briskly away to the drinks counter. Her back was facing three quarters towards him, and she was partly obliterated by a pillar. But, just as he joined the queue and turned to look at her, he saw her whip her head back round and look down at her hands resting on the table. She'd been watching him. Assessing him.

He watched her back rise and fall in one wave. She seemed to be giving a sigh of relief. At the long café queue? Maybe she was thankful for the few minutes she now had to compose herself. Despite her apparent coolness, surely there was no way that this couldn't be a huge moment for her too? She'd come all this way, hadn't she? Yes, she must be apprehensive, at the very least.

He looked more closely at her. He saw her fiddling with the salt and pepper pots, as if unable to keep still. Sure enough, her hands were shaking. She'd had what? A couple of weeks to think about this meeting – if not twenty-six years, if she'd fantasized about it as much as he had – and maybe she realized that still she'd fucked it up. Was this her in her usual defensive mode – remote and snooty? She'd had a bit of that attitude in the Unit, usually when she was depressed or tense. Or was she genuinely regretting her arrival here? What did she think of *him*? He'd obviously changed radically in a physical way. He looked what he now was: a toiler on the land. Gone was the puny, awkward adolescent of old. Instead, she'd been confronted by a physically strong man of the soil. He didn't think too much about his looks, as a rule, whether he was handsome, rugged, and all that. But he'd never had any trouble in attracting women. Even on a remote island. So, he reckoned he must look okay. Did the way he'd changed surprise her, disturb her? No man looked quite like him in any city, let alone the chichi parts of London that were hers. He watched as she straightened her back and flicked her hair behind her ears. Suddenly he felt disappointed. It was going to be hard to read her. Know what she was feeling, guess what she was thinking.

He caught her taking a final, deep, calming breath before he returned to the table, coffee cups clinking in his trembling hands. The space was more cramped than he'd like, the proximity of bodies unavoidable. He slid his roll-up tin out of his breast pocket, noticed the NO SMOKING sign on the wall beside them and shrugged.

She was trying out her first smile. 'Go on, they'll never notice round here.'

He was enjoying her smile, and her encouragement to break the rules. It was a promising sign. He shook his head and nudged the tin box to one side. 'Nah. Don't want to attract attention. This place, the whole island's a very small place. I really don't want to bump into anyone who knows me today. I don't feel sociable.'

The hiatus was momentary but enough. The laser look again – blue eyes to brown, brown to blue – took only a split-second, but it had blasted him – and her? – back to those long-ago shared times. To his disappointment she was first to look away. In consolation, she was the first to speak again.

'Danny? Tell me more about Simon. What's going on with him?'

Her directness took him by surprise. He thought there'd be a preamble, with him thanking her for making the trip and . . . and . . . and what, for God's sake? Abby had never been one to beat about the bush. He seemed unable to stop himself twisting in the too-small seat. The fidgeting reflected his unease about the . . . half-truths . . . no . . . the outright lies he'd concocted in his letter to get her here. If Simon knew what excuse he was using. Still, he couldn't tell her the truth.

As he thought through how he was going to get things going, he began a mesmeric ritual of slowly rolling tobacco between fingers and thumbs. It was a kind of therapeutic necessity for him in non-smoking places. The act was almost as good as lighting up. He knew she was trying not to stare as he licked the sliver of rice paper with a delicacy that obviously fascinated her. And, instead of lighting up, he placed the perfect tube in front of him and swivelled it round and round on the table as he talked on in a low voice.

'Look at these.' He reached into the inside pocket of his jacket. 'This is what I told you about in the letter.' He scrutinized her changing expressions as she began reading the two newspaper articles.

She had bent her head to look at the photocopied stories. He wanted to stroke that glossy hair, with its perfect middle parting, touch those hands with their three silver rings, none on her wedding finger. Suddenly, her head shot up. 'Good God! Simon's daughter abducted? And . . . oh, God, *assaulted.*

But the whole thing's dreadful. *Appalling.* And . . . oh, right, she was returned, alive. Thank goodness. *But this is just any parent's worst nightmare.*'

Paradoxically his voice was rising as he leaned closer to her, issuing his carefully prepared combination of lies and half-truths. 'I know. It *is* the worst. But listen, I told you in my letter that we might be in danger because of this. Simon's crazy. I told you, he's kept this list of us all, where we live, if we're married, kids, our jobs. Everything! Here, have a look. I added Simon's details to it myself, so I'd have a complete list of everyone together.' He flashed her the list quickly and then retrieved it, slipping it inside his jacket, before going on, leaving her staring in obvious concern and shock at the newspaper cuttings.

'See, Abby, he's got a notion into his mind that we are somehow responsible for what happened to his daughter. Not like, directly, but in some kind of . . . crazy . . . mad supernatural way, he says his time in the Unit brought this on his head. And that we're all to blame for being so horrible to him then. I don't think we were any more horrible to him than anyone else actually. We all took our knocks from the others, depending on how the group was feeling. Anyway, I didn't expect this. I thought he was quite sane. Thing is, I do think he's sick in the head now, really sick. A—'

But she was interrupting him. 'Then go to the police about him, Danny! They need to know.'

He shook his head, hands upturned in dismay. 'Look, Simon's a fuckin' clinical psychologist! D'you think if he's a danger and losing it he won't be able to hide it from most people? Of course he will. Christ! Alex and I had one hell of a night with him when we got together. She says that this thing with his daughter and that bitch of a wife going to live with his bitch of a mother has really done for him. You must remember about his mother, surely? A dangerous woman then, still is now by all accounts.'

He held his breath as he dared to touch her for the first time in twenty-six years. Three fingertips to the back of her cool, soft hand. 'Abby, I'm only telling you all this to protect you. Just in case Simon really goes off the rails. Just to warn you.'

She was letting his fingers stay! Thank God. 'I know that, Danny. And I'm grateful. I just don't see why he should take against us all. Maybe I should go and see him myself.'

This wasn't what he needed to hear. He sat back now, fingers and body withdrawn from her. He was beginning to feel frightened. Her request was a reasonable one. He hadn't thought this through properly. He had to get her out of this line of thinking. 'No, don't do that. It might set him off more. He met with me and Alex, which I'm glad about. It let us see just what a state he's in. But I think we should keep it at that. I mean *if* he does get in touch with you now, don't talk to him. Don't get involved. Tell me and I'll deal with it.'

He had to keep her away from Simon. And yet, what he was doing was, in effect, a pre-emptive strike, in case Simon did exactly that and approached *her*. And, of course, there was the other reason for wanting to keep her close. He just couldn't help himself.

He watched her with a mixture of joy, relief and some guilt. She'd believed his story. Of course. Why shouldn't she? It looked like she thought he'd finished his tale and she was about to say something. Instead, he pressed both hands to his temples. It was a dramatic gesture but genuine, as he pulled the worried features of his face taut. 'Just always remember, I'm trying to help you, Abby. That's all that matters to me.'

And despite what other lies he'd told her, that was largely true.

36

'How much longer can you stay up here?'

He knew his tone was beseeching, pleading. He was transfixed on her as she touched and caressed the pale slivers of stone pointing to the sky.

'These are amazing, Dan. I'd never even heard of the Callanish Stones. It's just like a mini-Stonehenge! This place. It's beautiful. The whole island's beautiful. I can see why you've been very happy here.'

It was incredible. The speed with which they had been swept up into each other's lives had surprised him. Surprised them both. All in just a handful of weeks, what, two short months only? She'd initially been toing and froing from London as much as work would allow. But these last few weeks, she'd practically been living with him, spending more and more time away from work, away from her other life. The intensity of what had been happening between them had shocked him initially. And yet now, it didn't. Their circumstances were, after all, unique. The intensity had come from that. Not subject to so many other lovers' rules of involvement. There had been little or no caution after the first sexual encounter. Both had plunged in. What had continued to surprise him was that *she* seemed to feel the same. It was *she* who was making more of the sacrifices, staying up here longer and longer, putting her life back in London on semi-permanent hold. Adjusting to his way of life, which was undoubtedly far less comfortable and far more primitive than her own. But that didn't matter. They both knew what they were doing. Making up for lost time. Twenty-six years of it.

He thought back to that awkward and frosty first meeting at the airport. His giving her his 'story'. Lies which he'd never yet righted . . . he shoved that part of their shared time away. Yes, he remembered that first visit so well. She'd been booked into the best hotel in Stornoway, reluctant to give up any comforts or city routine. But she'd accepted his invitation to show her around Lewis. And he'd saved here for last . . .

She'd looked doubtful as they'd trudged along a hilly gravelled path, the odd stray sheep skittering away from their heels and back to its flock. The chilly wind had picked at the collar of her fleece, and turned his own face white with cold. Suddenly, to his surprise and joy, she was pointing back from where they'd come and was laughing a few words to him. Words that had been carried away on the wind and he'd missed them. But he'd watched as she made a playful sprint to catch up with him and what he'd wanted her to see. Then she'd stopped dead.

The ground had levelled out. Atop a grassy plateau stood the stones. A mini-Stonehenge indeed. But, according to the engraved information plate, the Callanish Stones predated Stonehenge and the Pyramids. She wondered at the circle – surprisingly small, she'd said – with a few peripheral stones forming a kind of corridor or avenue leading to the centre of the collection. She went to each stone, a long grey finger pointing skywards. It seemed that she couldn't help herself as she weaved in and out of them, touching, feeling each one . . .

*

And here she was doing it again. She turned around, stood facing him, her back to the centre stone now. 'This place feels so special. Spiritual. Peaceful. So peaceful, Dan. Perfect.'

He watched her pulling herself away from the stones and taking in her surroundings. To her right, down the hill, lay Loch Roag, with what must have been the ruins of an old croft. And, in the distance, she could see his own croft. 'What a place to live. You're lucky, Danny. So bloody lucky!'

He was standing immobile, staring, as the wind attacked her hair, turning it wild and swirling it into a nest of Medusa tangles. After a minute he managed to move towards her. 'How long? Tell me.'

She reached both hands out to him in a languid, consciously flirtatious movement, and immediately he had her pressed against a stone. He lost count of the time it took for her to eventually push him gently away, to look into his eyes. 'I'll take a few more days off. And spend every minute of them with you. *Every minute*.'

He smiled at her, huddled into the duvet in the living room, staring at the log fire. He knew she was naked underneath. Still warm from their love-making. As he closed the door, he thought back to the first evening they'd been here together. He'd made her laugh when he'd brought her back from the stones, standing awkwardly in the hallway, until she managed to get it out of him. *The bedroom was too cold for love-making!* The chimney in there was blocked, and he couldn't light a fire until he'd cleared it. She'd laughed at that and assured him she was neither too old nor too shy to do it on a mattress in front of the living-room fire.

He knew that she *had* to leave tomorrow. No more excuses left for bunking off work. And for old times' sake, they'd settled down in the living room again. They always did this on the last night of her visits.

He pulled his jacket tight to his throat and headed out to check the dogs and the outbuildings. All seemed well. He turned back and was walking to the side door of the croft and then stopped. The living-room curtains were only half shut. She was sitting up now, staring at something thoughtfully. What was she doing? He saw her reaching up above the mantelpiece and pulling a photograph from its Blu-Tacked place on the wall. *It was that photograph.* The Unit holiday snap. It had been stuck up there for ages, but was usually obscured by red bills, bank statements and the like.

He'd shown it to her on the first day as he dropped her at her hotel. He'd slipped it out of his pocket, and they'd talked about it while sitting in his truck. She must have thought it was a funny thing for him to do. She'd forgotten that each of them had been given a copy of it. He'd asked her a lot of questions about that day. That time. It had seemed to break the ice for her, and she'd found a way to talk to him about the Unit. They'd talked about it for quite a long time, about the bad times, and then he knew it was all going to be okay. He could relax. Really loosen up. He'd even managed to crack a joke about Lydia and her bandaged knee.

He peered through the curtains, a voyeur spying on his own home, his own lover. She was lying back on the cushions, looking at her image from the past. So young. Tracing a finger along them all, no doubt wondering at their fates. She had her eyes closed now, and he could hear the crackling of the fire, smell the pungent but comforting scent of peat smoke permeating the room and filtering from the chimney.

A moment later, he deliberately banged the croft door too loudly. Pulling off jacket and shirt, he appeared in the living-room doorway. 'Hi. Can't say I'm sorry if I woke you. It's our last night and I want it to go on for ever.'

Without a reply, she knelt up to meet him, letting the duvet fall from her body, her hands moving to his crotch, as she began undoing buttons.

37

'He's evidently not fit to be back at work if he can't deal with something like this! Let's look at that e-mail again. Right. *Dr Calder, herewith new patient list for consideration. Four patients. Fifteen-year-old female with eating disorder; 52-year-old male with OCD.* That's obsessive-compulsive disorder to you and me, Dan. What else? *A 44-year-old male with psycho-sexual disorder.* Interesting. And here we go. *We've also had repeated inquiries from a male with post-traumatic syndrome stemming from the gang rape and kidnapping of his young daughter. He has specifically asked for a consultation with you. Further details in inquiries file.*'

Alex flung the e-mail printout on to the table and turned to face him, eyes narrowed. 'Frankly, Danny, I wouldn't give Simon's employers any gold stars for sensitivity, though they may have thought he should get back in the saddle pronto, for his own sake. But really, he's going to confront stuff like this as long as he remains in the career he's in. He sends this to us, expecting our sympathy! What the fuck can we do about it?'

Danny sat at her expensive mahogany dining-room table, shaking his head, as much to himself as at her. 'For fuck's sake! Have a heart for poor Simon. When he'd calmed down, I got him to call the Clinic Director then and there. He knows her quite well. Someone called Sheena something or other. Anyway, apparently they've got a new secretary in the department. Doesn't know about Simon and she said that the patient asked for Simon by name. Said he'd been treated by him in the past. Simon says he's never treated anyone with that profile. Weird, eh? Of course it made Simon worse. I had a hell of a job calming him down.'

He watched her. Typical Alex, putting the whisky away. Situation normal. She flung her head back in disagreement. 'It's probably some undercover tabloid journalist trying to get a story. Or, maybe it's a genuine patient who had read about Simon in the paper and thought, oh, I'll see if I can fast-track and get that bloke to treat me. He'll understand, etc. Anyway, I think Si should take the patient on. It might be just what he needs. To think about someone, something else now. Instead of his crumbling marriage. You know, he phoned me up the other day and told me that his mother had openly taken against him, siding with the wife! That doesn't surprise me. His mother was always a bitch to him. Pure poison. That's why he was in the fucking Unit in the first place, as you well know. God, remember those endless hours in group therapy talking about her latest shit with Simon! Thing is, I think the wife should either leave him or stay with him. Or Si should get rid of her for good. Divorce the bitch.'

Danny raised a hand at her and let out a mock-laugh. 'No chance. He's the sort of guy who needs a family around him. Unloved as a child, he needs at least the trappings of stable family life. He had that once but not now. The child's kidnapping has ruined his marriage. But look, I think you should've got Simon to come here. I'm not happy being here without his knowledge, Alex. I mean it. We need to sort this out once and for all. Take a decision. Anyway, I can't just come down from the fuckin' Western Isles at a minute's notice. I've got a croft to run. And it costs a fuckin' fortune to get here.'

He stood up and began pacing Alex's long dining room. He'd just about had it now. He wanted to get a word in edgeways. He had things he wanted to raise. But he knew that Alex, as ever, was determined to take the lead. He recognized her uncanny ability to take control, even in those very situations where she had the least right to. Her urge for control always suggested it was on the dangerous and, to some, sexually enticing side of violence. That's how she'd been in the Unit, minus the overt sexualization. That would have been too troubling for her at the time to face publicly. To any normal adolescent. And she'd been far from that. They'd all been far from that . . .

He drifted back into her surprisingly emollient tones. 'Danny. Please sit down and please calm down. I told you what's going on with Si, his family. He's severely fucked up, that I do know. I think we can both agree on that. But I also want us to agree to hold him back. We need time to think, given what's at stake. Anyway, I think I might stay in closer touch with Si from now on.'

He stopped the pacing and answered her with a sarcastic laugh. 'Hah! How close?'

It was a cheap shot but he knew he was right about one thing. Alex wouldn't hesitate to use her sexual power on *anyone* if she thought it would help her. She'd already tried it on with him during that wretched car journey after the reunion at Simon's. But from the look of her, he thought he might have gone too far this time.

'Fuck off! You should be thanking me, not insulting me. If I can control Simon, then we might avoid being in the shit! You've been in close touch with him up to now and he's still going off the rails. Let me try.'

But he was going to stand his ground. 'Yeah, well, you have got the equipment, after all. Mind you, I think his head isn't on sex right now, hard though that might be for you to understand.'

The slap of her hand as it made contact with his cheek was loud as a whip-crack. He sensed that it had been planned as a dramatic, even flirtatious gesture, but Alex didn't know her own strength, and he was amazed to see in the wall mirror a trickle of blood beading along his cheek from the cut that her hefty ring had opened up. It hurt. Strangely, Alex seemed more shaken than he did, and he simply wiped a knuckle across his face. She, meanwhile, was helping herself to as much Scotch as she could fit in her glass. She was losing her usually water-tight self-possession.

He turned his back to the room, staring unseeingly out of the window into the black depths of the garden. Alex was speaking to him again. This time her tone was apologetic, though barely under control. 'Danny? You said something about "taking decisions". What d'you mean?'

He turned back to face her, pulling out a ready-rolled cigarette, and joined her at the table. The bleeding cut apart, he knew his face looked tense and tired. Alex had pushed a clean ash tray towards him. A peace offering of sorts?

'What's been going on, Danny?'

The cigarette had stopped midway to his lips, his face a darkening scowl. He did and didn't welcome the prying question. He put a finger to the cut on his face to check the bleeding and kept silent, refusing to answer her. It looked like Alex was going to prompt him again, but she'd obviously decided to hold back and wait.

He kept his head bent and eventually, when he began, he seemed to be talking to his cigarette, as he rolled the orange, glowing ember into a point against the side of the ash tray. 'Right, it's time you knew about this. There's no other way to put it. I've been seeing Isabella. I did as you suggested. Spun her a line about Simon. The last thing we wanted was for him to be getting in touch with her, but, if he did, I wanted her ready to dismiss his claims. I mean, what happened to his daughter, that obviously got her attention. Naturally, she felt really sorry for him. But I just needed to give her a bit, no, *much* more to make her wary. I made out he had really lost it. Had become irrational and paranoid, believed that somehow we were all to blame for what happened to his daughter. Basically, I said that he was *dangerously* mentally unstable. I know it was all a bit out of order, but I had to sound her out once and for all, and, as I thought, she was solid. Clueless. But . . . something . . . I dunno, I can't explain it . . . as I say, we just began seeing each other. She's been up to my place. And we intend to see more of each other. A lot more. You can make what dirty, smutty remarks you like to yourself, but I'll tell you this. Yes, we are both having "a thing" and it's a lot more than just shagging. I was certain when I first met her in the Unit that I'd never meet anyone like Abby. I never did. I don't try to understand it. I just know it. We fit together in a special way. And if only I'd listened to her that day I . . . fuck it. Forget it.'

He'd finished abruptly. There was only silence in return, as Alex swallowed her shock, along with the whisky. Tough. She'd been the one who'd encouraged him to get in touch with Isabella. Had she really wanted him to or was she just doing a bit of general stirring? From the look on her face, she never believed he would do it, let alone that things would turn out like this. And he'd just given her a distinctly watered-down version of what was going on with him and Abby. God knows how she'd react if he told her the full intense truth of their relationship. And exactly why did the news so clearly disturb her? Jealousy? Of whom? Himself or Isabella? Or maybe it was that he, Danny Rintoul of all people, a man she thought she could control and second-guess, had acted on his own. Acted on an eternally held desire. Whatever, the news had come as a bombshell, though she was keeping her voice low and calm, the tone falsely flippant.

'Hey, Dan. You kept that quiet for long enough . . . okay . . . I see.' She was leaning towards him, waiting until he met her eye. 'So, what you saying? That you're *in love* with her? Christ, Dan! I said you should sound her out, but isn't this . . . *this* taking things a bit too far!'

The sarcasm was thick on her voice. He ignored it. 'I've always loved her. And that's why I need to tell her the truth. I may lose her. Lose everything. But I've got to do it. I think we should stop pissing about.'

She exploded exactly as he expected her to. '*What!* Oh, *come* on! In God's name, Danny! Tell her the truth? She's a fucking Girl Guide! She'll blab her mouth off. That'll be fucking it! The end for us all! Now stop this adolescent puppy-love crap. Shag the arse off her, get her out of your system, and grow up!'

Part of him wanted to strike her. Instead, he gathered up his jacket, snatched his cigarette tin off her table, scratching it on the way, and headed for the door. 'I'm going now. You'd better have a long, hard think, Alex. This business needs sorting out. I'm willing to give you some time. God knows I need it too. I'm not due to see Abby again for a bit. But, equally, I can't force Simon to go against his deepest wishes. This needs facing up to. And we should've done it twenty-six years ago.'

He heard the echo of his door-slamming fade into the building, followed moments later by his footsteps crunching their way down the gravel path. Then he paused and took a few steps back, looking through the living-room windows.

Alex was on her feet now, Scotch in hand, shouting at the top of her voice to herself. '*If he tells her, I'll fucking kill him. Kill them both. Him and his Girl Guide!*'

He winced as he watched her hurl the crystal glass into the fireplace, where it shattered into a dozen pieces. With a pitying shake of his head, he went on his way.

38

He was missing her. There was no doubt. He'd never experienced that with anyone. Not even Sian. Sian . . . she was staying away from him now. She'd sensed something and the fact that he'd avoided seeing her, apart from a couple of monosyllabic phone calls in the past few months, had led her to give up. Or rather, she'd decided to leave him be for an unspecified period of time. Well, that period of time would have to be for ever, now he had Abby. But Sian was a toughie. She'd survive. Theirs hadn't been a love job. Just good sex, companionship, no commitment. But her brother Ian was a different prospect. He could feel Ian's puzzlement and hurt. They'd been mates. An odd couple, though. Funny that a gay man and a straight man could be close. But Ian was an interesting, generous and entertaining guy. And as for himself? He didn't care a toss who anyone slept with. Each to their own. And Ian had trusted him – quite justifiably – with his 'secret'. To be outed, even in this day and age, on this island would be the end for Ian and his partner. No, he and Ian had enjoyed a great friendship. Until now.

He wandered out the back door and stood enjoying the end of the day. His croft offered a breathtaking view up the length of Loch Roag. This freezing January evening it was a deep mauve. And still. So still. He leant against his back wall and lit another roll-up, the plumes of his exhalation hanging near-stationary in the cold air. The entrance of Abby into his life had added so many complications: the

Sian thing, his friendship with Ian, the physical distance between them when Abby was in London. She so belonged here now and he felt her absences. He didn't quite know how she could take so much time away from her London life and work, but she seemed remarkably flippant about it. Said that after twenty-six years, it was time for her to get her priorities right. Too true.

Finally in all this, there was the issue of his keeping her a secret, hidden away. This wasn't too difficult in these coldest, darkest and most inward-looking of months, when people kept themselves to themselves, hardly seeing another soul for weeks on end. But why was this so important to him? Abby had raised, more than once, the issue of why he didn't introduce her to anyone. She'd thought it was because he'd have to lie about how they first met. The Unit days were not for others' consumption. And so she'd encouraged him to bend the truth and spin a line saying that they knew each other from Edinburgh, years ago, and had met again through a mutual friend. Truthful, as far as it went. But he didn't want to examine too deeply his own motives for keeping her a secret. He just wanted some absolutely exclusive and 'perfect' time with her. And the future? Well, he shied away from that one . . .

He took a last loving look at the view, ground his cigarette end out in the yard and went back into the warm. The fire was still roaring and he sat down in his comfy chair by the hearth, whisky bottle and glass to hand. Twilight was fading fast, and he saw the first chunky flakes of snow fall outside the window. Without any wind the fall might be heavy but there wouldn't be drifting or blizzards. His flock should be okay. Strange, over the years he'd loved, cherished, solitary evenings like this, just thinking about his animals and enjoying the fire and the single malt. Now, somehow, it was different. It no longer offered the security of solitary self-sufficiency. It just felt lonely.

He reached up to the mantelpiece for the photo. How his adolescent life had caught up with him in such an unexpected way. Although by the time that wretched photo had been taken, he knew that he'd be tied to at least some of them for life. But Abby? No, he thought that one was gone . . .

'What the hell happened last night, Danny? Where did you all go after I left you?'

'I told you, Abby. We got lost. Just like you did. You said you'd see us up at the fork in the high road. But you fucked up too. It was blind luck that we all eventually bumped into you. And yes, I know we had the orienteering compasses and maps, but we're all crap at that. And anyway, you know we'd all been smoking dope and drinking. We . . . we just fucked up with the directions, y'know? At least we found you eventually, so we could wait out the night together. And yes, I know we were grumpy and weird, but we were fucking freezing and knackered and we'd done too much bevvy and dope! End of story.'

Her face said it all. She didn't believe him. He wasn't sure the staff did either, although their relief at finding them all safe and well seemed to have foreclosed any possibility of interrogations or post-mortems on the night's events. Sarah Melville in particular seemed purely relieved, not a trace of anger. Simon had told him about eavesdropping on a completely livid Anna, who really tore a strip off both Sarah and Ranj, outlining in no uncertain terms what would have happened if any harm had come to the patients. Professional disgrace, careers finished and quite possibly a court case. That was a laugh, said Si! But that was also good. It concentrated the staff's minds and kept them preoccupied with their own stuff. He hoped to God Si was right about that.

Her voice broke back in on his thoughts. '. . . did you?'

'What . . . sorry, Abby. Did I what?'

'What is *wrong* with you, Danny? Did you hang around by the loch after I left? I hope you didn't. You promised.'

She was waiting for an answer. Even within his confused, panicky and exhausted state, he knew this was it. A chance to change everything. His whole life at stake with just a few words. But he wouldn't. Couldn't. Not even for Abby . . .

The howl of the wind snapped him out of it. He smoothed a hand over the photo and looked out of the window. He'd read the weather wrong. Not like him. Maybe his desperate attempts to be optimistic were stretching to everything. It was going to be a bad night, in more ways than one. She was due up for a visit tomorrow. It should be a time of happiness for him. But it was time for something else. Time to tell her the truth. A truth he should have told her twenty-six years ago.

Four months later

File note from Dr Adrian Laurie, Consultant and Medical Director, APU, to Sister Anna Cockburn
7 January 1978
RE: Patient, Innes Haldane (d.o.b. 3.4.62)

As you know I have spent the initial post-holiday group-therapy sessions monitoring how the group are, after spending time at home with their parents. Some have had their fair share of excitement, such as Danny's physical fight with his father, Alex's absconding from home, and Lydia's burning down of her father's garden shed.

They are all setbacks, and we will discuss them individually at the next case conference. However, it is Innes that is causing me some concern this week. She has returned from home clearly depressed and, unusually for her, monosyllabic. She refuses to engage in group therapy. As we know, with some others this is attention-seeking behaviour and normally the precursor for some dramatic acting out. But Innes does not display in that way. I advise careful monitoring.

Copy to: General Nursing File
Copy to: patient file, I. Haldane

File note from Sister Anna Cockburn to Dr Adrian Laurie, Consultant and Medical Director, APU
8 January 1978
RE: Patient, Innes Haldane (d.o.b. 3.4.62)

Last night I managed to engage Innes in conversation. She admitted that her festive break had been 'a disaster'. Her mother, clearly ashamed and embarrassed by, as she put it, Innes's 'incarceration', insisted that she, Innes and Innes's father would, throughout the holidays, tell all family and friends who visited that Innes had been away at boarding school. Denial was the order for the two-week break. I have to say that I am worried about this. I feel that the shame, embarrassment and denial fed to Innes by her mother may stay with her for a very long time, whatever the outcome here is.

Copy to: General Nursing File
Copy to: patient file, I. Haldane

39

'Frankly, Innes, this couldn't come at a worse time. We're critically below acceptable staffing levels. I mean . . . can you give me some idea what this is about?'

'No.'

The sigh of exasperation had sounded deafening in the high-ceilinged office. 'All right. Take a fortnight. But this may reflect badly on you at your next evaluation. And as for any promotion board . . .'

Reluctantly, she allowed the morning's conversation to play back and forth in her head as she rode the Docklands Light Railway towards Greenwich. She'd been taken aback by her line manager's lack of sympathy, perhaps expecting a more understanding 'woman-to-woman' encounter. Well, she'd misjudged that. Badly. Maybe she should have kept up the 'viral illness' fiction. Now it was surely exposed for what it had been. But, after all these years of loyal service, she'd honestly expected to be allowed some compassionate leave to deal with 'deeply personal matters'.

She let her eyes drift down to the waterside walkways outside Canary Wharf station, already bustling with lunch-break office workers in sharp suits and smart dresses. Well, if her decision was going to terminate her Civil Service career, then so be it. Perhaps she'd have to try the big wide world of commercial law again. If she could get back in at her age. Whatever, if she looked hard enough at herself she knew this was a time for personal upheaval. Long overdue.

She'd buried herself in work since her divorce five years ago. A divorce that *she* had wanted. A divorce that had left her very comfortably off. She'd even inherited a few of her ex's friends and welcomed them into her own circle. One or two into her own bed, on occasion.

She saw the sign for the Cutty Sark station appear and stood up. Outside, the day was warming up. She was tempted to sprint-walk the few hundred yards to the row of pretty former naval captains' cottages she knew so well but held off. She veered left and took a seat on one of the benches beside the great, three-masted tea clipper. As always, it was crawling with inquisitive tourists, weaving in and out of the rigging.

She sat back and tried to relax. There was time to spare after all, and it never really did to be too early. She hadn't been to see Liv for nearly eighteen months. But she'd had lapses before and had managed, as Liv put it, to 'plug back in' perfectly successfully. Usually when she was in trouble. Like before, during and immediately after her divorce. Like when her last bouts of panic attacks became so incapacitating that she thought she was losing her mind. But in all the years she'd been seeing Liv she had never, *ever* admitted to her time in the Unit. Never admitted it to anyone, friend or lover or husband.

And maybe there was a lesson in that. 'That Time' (as she always dubbed it to herself – maybe the others did too?) was consuming her. If she was to be honest with herself and look deep inside, it had been consuming her all her life, but had breached her sophisticated unconscious barriers only recently, when she'd arrived home on an ordinary weekday evening to hear the desperate tones of Isabella echoing out from the answering machine. Quite unquestioningly in many ways, she'd followed where Abby had led, without exchanging one word with the living woman. Now she was dead and it was too late. Now she felt as if she was shadowing a ghost. Many ghosts. And would keep shadowing and following. For how far and how long she had no idea.

The front door looked the same. Appropriately navy blue, the brass plaque announced that LIV KLEIBEL & KIM HARVEY were REGISTERED PSYCHOANALYTIC PSYCHOTHERAPISTS and had been in practice for over twenty years. A reassuring husband and wife team. The receptionist was new, as were the two bright airy extensions that had been built on to the back of the first floor. The decor of the treatment room remained the same, though. Liv's favourite choice. Light, soft colours and furnishings. Cocooning, embracing chairs. Fresh lilies, and, of course, Liv's obligatory burning candle. A comfort and a focus for the eyes, when the mind wanted to take over the senses.

'Well, then, Innes. Welcome back. *How* are you?'

The unusual but familiar inflection reminded Innes that this was no cursory, conventional inquiry into her well-being. It meant that Liv wanted, and expected, a straight answer.

Innes watched as the inordinately long, elegant limbs of her therapist stretched themselves out and away from the confines of her chair. It had been a hard session. For both of them.

'In answer to your worry about how *our* working relationship may be affected by the news you have given me about your adolescence, please, *please* put that from your mind. In here, in these sessions, you bring up only what *you* feel like. There are no "betrayal" or "lack of trust" issues where I'm concerned. However, I *am* pleased, as your therapist, to know an important bit more about your past than I did previously. When I consider what brought you here – your relationship with your mother, still troubling, though she has been dead for many years, your panic attacks and control issues, all of that and more – I have always been left feeling that there was something else. And that something else remained a puzzle to me. It is no longer.

'As you know, any decisions about your future must be yours. *But* given that you have travelled down this road remarkably quickly, I would strongly urge you to consider confronting your demons.'

Innes frowned. 'What d'you mean?'

'I *mean*, do what I think is already at the forefront of your mind. That is, to contact this . . . this Alex and Simon. They are, after all, the only remaining living, or at least healthy, former patients left. They are your only link to this intriguing past of yours. You know where they live. Your concerns about these deaths being somehow linked to your collective time in the Unit are clearly troubling you deeply. Maybe you feel the need to perhaps *warn* them, or at least explore further your theory that the Unit is somehow causing all these deaths and misery with some of those who were *actually there*. They may know about what's been happening in the way that you do. On the other hand, it's quite possible that they might be upset by your interest. They may know nothing about each other and be living in absolute ignorant bliss, having also buried their Unit days. From what you've told me, both Simon and particularly Alex were extremely disturbed adolescents who have now made something of their lives. And, if that is the case, this may leave a high motivation in them to excise the unpalatable past. I'm not saying that this *is* the case. It's just possible. But that is a calculated risk that you have to take. *If* you choose to contact them.

'This monumental period of your early life has returned to have significance in your life *now*, *today*. Whatever the truth behind these deaths, they have come into your life and collided quite spectacularly with your controlled and, most of the time, apparently contented, ordered existence. But I wonder? Given your history of anxiety, panic attacks, *difficulties* in forming successful and abiding intimate relationships, I'm left wondering if some of the answers lie in this past which you have suppressed for your entire adult life. You're a highly intelligent and very self-aware woman. You must have reached this realization yourself?'

Innes could feel the tears ready to roll, each of Liv's incisive observations cutting further and further into her own dwindling self-control. 'You're right. So right. I . . . I . . . I don't know why I never brought up the Unit thing in our sessions. I . . . I think somewhere deep down, I felt . . . I felt . . . *ashamed*. I can't really explain it in any other way. There's always shame in mental illness. For me. For many who have suffered likewise. But . . . but . . . at this moment, I feel as if I've been waiting for something like this to make me look at, face up to that time. But I've always held back. Until now.'

'That's fine, Innes. But what else is there? Other than shame?'

'I think you know what else, Liv. I'm scared. Terrified. And it seems with good cause.'

40

'Innes? Innes, it's Isabella. Isabella Velasco. I . . . I . . . Don't ask me how I got hold of you . . . I . . . we live quite close, you know, would you believe? God, you sound just the same. Just the same! Look . . . please don't be angry . . . I need to talk to you . . . see you. Can you call me as soon as you can? My number i—'

She clicked off the mini-tape player and sat motionless at the desk of her hotel room. Anyone watching her would have thought her mad. Obsessive. They'd be right. She'd known it was an odd thing to do at the time. Keep the tape, when she had no intention of answering the call. But something had *made* her do it. She'd tried to analyse why and given up. Part of her was glad she had. Another cursed herself for the act of foolishness. Playing it again, Abby's voice appeared even more infused with desperation. And something else. Fear? The guilt kicked in stronger than ever. She should have called her back. It was a plea for help. She should have called. It was as simple as that.

She'd gone over that particular ground again and again in her session with Liv in London two days ago. And hadn't felt much better about that issue afterwards. What she did feel better about was Liv's urging her to 'confront her demons'. And here she was again. In Edinburgh. About to do just that.

She turned to her laptop and stared again at the story she'd downloaded. The north London local paper, anxious to fill its pages in a slow news week, *had* done what she thought it would – a follow-up piece on a well-to-do resident.

Leading dental surgeon leaves generous legacies

Leading dental surgeon 42-year-old Professor Isabella Velasco, of 12 Belsize Park Square, who was found dead floating in the swimming pool of the Belsize Sports Centre last month, has left a number of generous legacies in her will, made public today.

The troubled Prof Velasco, who was found to have committed suicide, left the majority of her considerable fortune to charitable trusts and hospitals. She left £50,000 to the Eastman Dental Hospital, to be used in the specialist training of paediatric dentists. The sum of £40,000 is to be donated to Urban Medical, a charity that provides dental and medical care to the homeless on London's streets; Prof Velasco used to do occasional voluntary work for them. But, surprisingly, the bulk of Prof Velasco's fortune goes to two charities unrelated to her work.

The mental health charity MIND receives £100,000 with the proviso that the money be used for work directly related to young people with mental illness. But most intriguing of all is that a small Scottish charity, called 'Renewal', based in Edinburgh, which supports bereaved parents and relatives of children who have been murdered, has been left a colossal £220,000. Its director, Mrs Lavinia Henderson, said, 'It is quite an astonishing act of charity. It will affect so many lives for the better. We are very moved by the kindness of Professor Velasco.'

Prof Velasco leaves no children. The remainder of her estate was bequeathed to her former husband, an anaesthetist now living in New Zealand.

A couple of minutes later the information she wanted was on the screen.

'Renewal' – Aims and Objectives:

- To provide support to families and relatives who have lost children or young relatives through murder, manslaughter or any form of unlawful killing.
- To foster research into the effects on families of murder, manslaughter or unlawful killing.
- To distribute this research to the general public and professional bodies, with a view to increasing their awareness about the needs of those affected by such loss.

She re-read the information and sat back, puzzled. A small, obscure charity, no doubt doing important work, and one Isabella thought enough of to leave most of her fortune to. The why of it chased through Innes's mind as she wrote down an address in her notebook.

She found the offices surprisingly plush for a small charity.

'I'm sorry, Ms Haldane, we can't give out details about benefactors other than those already in the public domain. What I *can* say, though, is that we are eternally grateful for your friend's generous donation.'

Innes studied the firm face of the charity's Director. A woman in her sixties who, she knew from the charity's website, had lost all three sons in an arsonist's fire at a nightclub in 1976. Intimidating demeanour. Not surprising perhaps.

Innes tried again. 'But did you ever meet Isabella or have any contact with her? The thing is, as far as I know, she *hadn't* lost any young relative through death of any sort. It's very puzzling.'

The Director stood up, motioning towards the door. The battle had been lost. 'I'm sorry. All I can say is that I have no recollection of ever having met Professor Velasco. She clearly considered us a good cause, but her reasons for doing so must remain her own, and die with her. We'll never know.'

41

She'd spent the rest of the day sitting at one of the hotel's outside tables, drinking too much coffee and watching the tourists wander around the rejuvenated and gentrified Leith Docks. It had seemed a long wait until evening, but she knew it was the right time to try to make the visit. There was more chance of his being in then. But why not call him? His number was in the book. She'd vetoed that idea almost immediately. Too risky. Too easy to be turned down, hung up on. No, if she was going to do this, far better to try the personal approach. *And* she could always duck out of it right up to the last minute, couldn't she? And why Simon? As she made her way through the hotel lobby to her car, she thought that one through all over again. Of the two, Simon and Alex, as she remembered them, Simon was surely the more approachable. And he was a trained psychologist now. He, of all people, must know how to conduct himself in tricky situations.

But Alex? In Innes's memory, Alex still stood out as the hard skinhead with the hint of real physical danger about her. Of course she couldn't be like that now. As a former City trader and now internet executive, it seemed unlikely that she hadn't learned to control her temper and wayward behaviour. Though, you could never accurately guess just how much people *didn't* change over time. Part of her felt that there was a central, emotionally brutal core to Alex, which had its roots so deeply seated in her self from some horrendously dysfunctional upbringing that it was probably still there. The thought not only disturbed Innes, but she had to admit that it also left her almost afraid. Of course she had no evidence whatsoever for this speculation. But, on balance, knocking on Simon Calder's door seemed infinitely preferable to wandering into Alex's den.

The sight of the evening's golden sky as she crossed the Forth Road Bridge eased her nerves a little. The roads remained unclogged and she made it in good time, with the sun beginning to set as she took the winding road down to St Monans Harbour. As she zigzagged her way through the village, it seemed surprisingly busy. The usual gangs of bored teenagers hung around outside the quayside chip shop. Further up towards the top of the town, elderly holidaymakers took their last stroll of the evening before repairing to the pub or to an early bed.

She smiled to herself as she remembered her own happy childhood visits here. And then she remembered that the Unit had organized a 'reunion picnic' here in . . . '79 was it? Yes, she'd missed it, somewhat to her relief, because she'd been away on holiday with her parents. On her return she'd actually summoned up the courage to call the Unit to ask how it went. Student Sarah Melville, who wasn't a student any more, had been honest. The picnic had ended in chaos. Carrie had punched Lydia. Sarah said that she didn't know why and sounded as if she didn't care anyway.

Innes shook her head at the memory. Typical Unit fiasco. She shoved the thought away, and felt relieved that at least what she *wouldn't* be confronted with at Simon Calder's home was indiscriminate violence. As she crested the hill on her final journey down to the Auld Kirk and Simon's shore-side house, the expected peaceful landscape had changed. In the car park of the church and in the lane that led to the Old Manse, a police car and a van were parked. Uniformed men and women were coming out of the house and a handful of worshippers were leaving the church after an evening service. One group had collected and stood in a ragged semicircle, while the local minister, complete in cassock and dog-collar, was standing holding the hand of a clearly distressed old lady.

Innes parked, and tentatively approached a friendly-looking middle-aged woman on the edge of the group.

'Eh . . . I . . . I'm sorry, excuse me? I . . . I . . . I'm a friend of Simon, Simon Calder. Is anything wrong?'

She knew the question was stupid, but the woman turned with a concerned look. 'Oh, my dear, you know Dr Calder?' At this she laid a steadying hand on Innes's forearm. 'I'm afraid I've got an awful shock for you. Dr Calder's missing, presumed dead. They think he fell over the side of his garden wall. You see, over there? The wall goes down to the rocks and the sea. They think it happened the night before last. They found some of his torn clothing. It had become lodged in the rocks and . . . and . . . well . . . here we are. I'm very, very sorry, dear.'

Innes felt like she was going to faint. She leaned against a nearby parked car, hoping that the dizziness was going to fade as fast as it had overcome her. She patted her jacket pocket, listening out for the tell-tale rustle of the paper bag. Good. It was there. But, miraculously, her breathing was staying under control.

She was aware that the friendly woman had led her just a few yards into what was obviously her own garden and settled her in a wrought-iron chair. 'You sit there and get some air. It's a lovely evening.'

The woman then disappeared inside her house and returned within seconds, handing Innes a glass of chilled, over-sweet, home-made lemonade. But it tasted wonderful. She turned back into the woman's cooing tone, picking up the last phrase.

'. . . unbelievable, especially after what happened to his daughter and everything.'

'I'm sorry. What did you say?'

The woman frowned at her. 'Katie. Dr Calder's daughter? She was abducted last year. It was in the papers. You don't know about that?'

Innes thought quickly. She'd seen nothing of this. Would she have noticed it in the newspapers? It wasn't the sort of thing she'd read about. Too gloomy. She always avoided articles about things like that. And would the little girl's name have registered? Probably not. She had no idea Simon lived in St Monans until very recently. Whatever, the news was a sickening blow. She became aware that the woman was waiting for an answer and, despite her continuing nausea, the lie came smoothly. 'Eh . . . no . . . that's just it . . . I, eh . . . I've been away overseas for a long while. I was looking up Simon after . . . after not seeing him for a few years.'

The neighbour seemed satisfied. 'Oh, dear, then you're in for an even bigger shock. Not only was wee Katie abducted, she was missing for weeks. We all thought she was dead. Anyway, out of the blue, she was released. *But* the effect on the family. Dr Calder's wife hasn't been living with him here for a long time. Nor the wee girls either. I'm wondering if the strain, you know? If the strain made him just end it all over the wall? I know it's what the authorities are thinking.'

Innes tried to stand up, the woman's helping hand at her elbow. 'Thing is, dear, the police will probably want to speak to you. About when you last spoke to him. All that.'

Jesus! That was the last thing she wanted or needed! 'Yes . . . okay. I'll just need to go back to my car for something. Thank you for being so kind. Bye for now.'

She knew that it was the sheer fear of what had happened and the terror of being asked by the police to give answers as to exactly what she was doing here that spurred her on. Despite the ongoing nausea, she slipped down the narrow alley to where she'd left her car. As far as she knew, no one except the kind neighbour had even noticed her. With shaking hands, she turned the ignition key and manoeuvred her way through the winding village roads as quickly as possible, tyres screeching as she made her panicky way back to Edinburgh, one thought racing again and again around her head. *Danny, Abby, now Simon.*

Why?

42

Monday, 23rd, 2.15 a.m.

I have felt unable to go near this – my precious journal – for some while. But tonight, for the first time in so long, I have felt drawn to putting pen to paper once again. The reason is straightforward. Danny left this morning after staying here with me for a few days. To both our surprise, Danny and I have become quite close over the past months. He offers me an odd kind of comfort but comfort all the same. And without Rachel, and Lily and Katie, I need whatever comfort another human being can offer.

But, that apart, of late, a strange situation has occurred. One laced with heavy irony! Danny has been seeing Isabella Velasco! He didn't tell me at first. Possibly because when I had initially made such a suggestion to him he had rejected it out of hand. He also admitted taking a copy of my address list. I laughed. I didn't mind. Maybe seeing in black and white where he could actually get hold of Isabella proved too hard for him to resist. Danny tells me that he and Alex had discussed his contacting Abby during their drive back to Edinburgh that dreadful night we all met up here. I suspect she was just teasing him, but he seems to have taken the suggestion seriously. I was alarmed to begin with. And then curious. What was she like now? How did she react to being 'found'? Most importantly, what were her memories of That Time?

Danny had laughed at my initial interrogation of him. But he said I wasn't to worry, as everything was okay. Isabella was absolutely fine. 'Solid' is the word he used. Odd. But I knew what he meant. Anyway, he told me how he'd met her at Stornoway Airport, and, as she'd walked into the little terminal building, he'd almost passed out. She was more beautiful than ever! Had the same voice, though a bit deeper. 'Devastating', he had called her!

It wasn't until last night that Danny dropped the bombshell. He said that he'd met Isabella more than just the once. More than twice. In fact he'd been seeing a lot of her and something had happened. Something wonderful. They were in love! In love! Incredible!

But Danny is troubled now. He's found the greatest happiness with a woman he says he always loved. It could've been a fairy-tale, he said. A dream come true. Parted after all these years, then they find each other, and amazing! It's love!

However, Danny is a tormented man now. A difficult time is ahead for him, poor soul. I have listened to what both he and Alex have said about me holding back. But I predict that Danny will want to do the Right Thing by Abby. He's said as much.

For now, I'll let him take the lead. And then follow.

Alex allowed herself a generous sip from her single malt and flicked forward to a more recent page.

Tuesday, 14th, 3.20 a.m.
Danny's dead! I have never felt so overwhelmingly sad and afraid since Katie was taken. He's chosen to take his own life, deprive himself of the love of Isabella! I cannot believe it. The price for loving her was too high to pay. He'd said it was a punishment – loving Isabella. Like my Katie being taken. I understand what he meant – the skewed logic in that.

But I am puzzled. He seemed so sure, so determined to talk to Abby. To share the deepest part of himself. Said he'd decided and thought he could do it. What changed his mind, I wonder? What happened? And to choose the sea? Danny was terrified of water! It was a phobia he'd talked about in the Unit, and he'd mentioned it again recently when he joked about it being crazy to live on an island if you hated water! It looks like he punished himself in the cruellest way imaginable.

What am I to do? Should I contact Isabella? No! That would be wrong, since how could I explain Danny's death to her? I could give her the reasons why. But it would ruin her life, surely. No, I need to think. And speak with Alex again. I can't help but feel she enjoyed breaking the news to me. Alex hates me, I'm sure of it. Thinks me weak, spineless. Well, let her think that.

Alex allowed herself a twisted smile at that. Shit, these were a goldmine! She wished she'd been able to make off with more from Simon's place, but she'd got the main stuff. All the recent dangerous stuff. And those nursing notes. Very interesting. Where the hell had he got these? That worried her. If there was some source of old Unit notes, they could come back to haunt her. She shrugged the worry off for the time being. And then there was the photo. He'd kept a copy too. Not entirely a surprise. What was a surprise was that he didn't bring it out at their reunion with Danny. It's the sort of thing she thought Si would have done. *Oh, look, here we are all jolly together!*

She heard the trees stirring in the wind. Outside all was blackness. She moved away from the window towards the fire. It might be spring but it was cold. She shivered. She glanced back over to the windows. Funny, it was like someone had been staring over her shoulder from outside. Ridiculous.

Friday, 28th, 2.25 a.m.

This day joins three others during my time on this earth in being the very worst in my wretched existence. Isabella has killed herself! Alex told me. Again, ever the happy messenger of hellish news! I've read the newspaper reports online tonight. Abby too has drowned! She too has taken her own life away. To Heaven rather than Hell, I dearly hope.

I could have stopped her. I'm sure of it. If only I'd been given the chance. But this is it now. There is no more time to dilly-dally. Alex is against going to the authorities and telling them everything, but I think procrastination has caused a heavy price to be paid. It is time.

At last we are all being visited by the ever-present Nemesis, except Alex, who continues to try and resist the inevitable. But not for long, I fear. I will have to try a—

Alex put the book down. She knew why she'd found his journal open at this entry. Why he'd left the rest unread and got up so abruptly. She stood and wandered over to the window again. The wind was really up now. She opened the French window and allowed the wind to hurl its gusts into the room, immediately causing the flames of the fire to flicker manically.

I will have to try a—. At this point she knew Simon had left his study and opened his front door, grabbing a waterproof as he let the door slam behind him. The gale had whipped at his face as he'd walked down to the bottom of his garden. And he couldn't help but feel the sting and taste the salt-spray from the waves swirling against the rocks below.

The tears had surely hurt his eyes as they pricked their way through his lids and down his cheeks. Slowly he'd begun to beat a soft tattoo against the wall with his bare fist. He'd been aware that he was drawing blood but had felt no pain as he leaned forward against the wall, watching each wave dashing itself to oblivion.

The powerful tug on both his ankles had been swift but painless. And as Simon had toppled forwards, the wind had twisted his body so that his last glimpse was of the pale yellow light burning like a beacon from his beloved study into the stormy night.

Illuminating the face of his killer.

43

Innes had managed to get some sleep – with the help of medication. Bringing the tablets with her to Scotland had been a reluctant but, in retrospect, sensible precaution. As soon as she'd got back to the hotel, she'd had an emergency session with Liv on the phone. Just what she'd needed. No 'get a grip, Innes' type of advice. Rather, a lengthy exploration of what Simon's death meant for her and what, in relation to the other deaths, it might mean in the wider world. The talk hadn't brought any great enlightenment about the latter. Neither she nor guru Liv knew why Simon was dead, so all remained merely dispiriting speculation. But the morning had brought an even greater resolve for Innes, replacing the initial and lasting shock of her visit to St Monans. She was going to get hold of Alex Baxendale. The only living Unit person left she'd yet to make contact with.

As she drove the few miles to Alex's house she thought about the phone call. Alex had answered quickly.

'Alex?'

'Yes.' The reply clipped. Brisk. Unfriendly even.

'It's Innes Haldane. I hope you remember wh—'

'Yes, of course I do.' And then she'd remained silent. No inquiry as to how she'd got the number. Nothing.

'Eh . . . I . . . oh, it's too long to tell you everything. I'm not sure if you know but everyone's dead . . . I mean Unit people . . . I mean Simon's dead. He died yesterday. And

Danny's dead. And Isabella. I . . . I think we should meet. I hope you don't think I'm stupid calling b—'

'I know about them. You'd better come here. Tonight. Eight o'clock.'

As she approached Alex's quiet, leafy neighbourhood of vast detached houses in their own grounds – uncomfortably reminiscent of the Unit building – Innes felt relief in some way that she'd contacted Alex. She had a feeling that Alex knew something that could help her understand what had been going on, maybe cut a way through all this mess for her. On the other hand, of all the Unit patients it was Alex who had left her most puzzled. She had seemed utterly unknowable in the Unit, and Innes had to admit that she'd noticed very little, if any, change for the better in Alex during their time together in that place. It was as if Alex used to relish playing a kind of psychological cat-and-mouse game with Dr Laurie. They both knew what was going on, and the rest of the group were left as mere spectators rather than as participants in what was meant to be a group learning and healing experience.

The memory increased the apprehension churning in her stomach as she rang the bell. The door was opened with a wrench and there she was, sharply outlined by the porch light. Dressed in a dark blue silk shirt and matching trousers, Alex Baxendale looked well, prosperous, formidably attractive in a rather hard and brittle way. Innes would never have recognized her in a thousand years. The contrast from the butch skinhead of old as far as it was possible to get.

'Come in, Innes.'

Alex Baxendale's eyes were on her: a quick but thorough assessment. Innes allowed herself to be guided down a long hallway and into what was the living room, minimally but comfortably furnished with two soft leather sofas and chairs. A blue and gold rug lay underfoot, covering well-maintained wooden flooring. Unlike others who seemed to be blind to their surroundings when in a state of near panic, she always noticed every detail. A kind of displacement activity, she presumed, to keep the nerves at bay. With limited success.

She caught Alex's smile. More of a secretive smirk. 'Please, Innes. Sit down. Drink?'

Innes nodded slowly, desperate to appear composed. If Alex was going to be the vision of cool, calm and collected, she would have to try to match her. Not rush into things. 'Whisky would be good, please. I feel I need it, under the circumstances. It's an understatement to say "it's been a while", don't you think?' She knew she sounded stilted. Robot-like. And she waited nervously for a response.

But Alex remained silent as she busied herself at the drinks cabinet. Perhaps she hadn't heard her? Innes kept quiet and waited. In a moment Alex moved back to her, handed over the drink and headed slowly to the sofa opposite. She made herself utterly relaxed, as if home alone, shoes kicked off, bare feet tucked underneath her.

Alex was playing games, Innes thought, and bloody-mindedly resolved to keep quiet. She watched Alex take another sip of her drink, unrushed, and then she answered. 'Yes, twenty . . . six, twenty-seven years, isn't it? Amazing.' She neither looked nor sounded very amazed, and Innes awaited her next move. A stiff slug of her drink, and Alex continued. 'Look, Innes. I won't piss about. I must say that I'm more than a bit surprised to hear from you. Please tell me how, and why, you've tracked me down.'

Innes had resisted all offers of second and third drinks. Alex could put it away, all right. And hold it. What surprised her most, though, was Alex's seemingly calm, unruffled manner. After all that Innes had told her, there wasn't a chink in Alex's self-possession. It was utterly unnerving. But maybe that was because Alex knew so much already, a fact she had made clear to Innes in an increasingly haughty tone during the past hour.

But the main shock was when Alex had, quite unself-consciously, pulled up the sleeves of her shirt to reveal the traces of those scars. Though Alex seemed oblivious to the scars, the sight of them had taken Innes by surprise, reminding her of the other, younger, so different Alex of old. Innes had forgotten all about the scars, but they'd been much talked about in the Unit, both covertly, among gossiping patients, and openly, in group sessions. In the Unit days she had always found those marks, so livid and ugly, symbolic surely of profound psychic pain. Stomach-churningly awful. What in God's name could lead someone to inflict such agony and permanent disfigurement on themselves? For Innes, this issue had never been satisfactorily dealt with when they were all patients. Of course now, modern pop psychology had lots of fancy PC names and descriptions for it, as she'd seen outlined in the quasi-learned articles she'd read in the quality papers. All well and good in theory, but actually seeing the living proof of this, still evident on a grown, immaculately groomed woman, made Innes catch her breath. Alex might present a cool, balanced front, but it was those wretched scars that somehow gave the lie to it all.

'So you see, Innes, I, Danny and Simon had kept in touch on and off over the years. Isabella only got back in touch recently, primarily with Danny. I only met her once, in fact. I don't know why she got back in touch. No idea. Anyway, I was obviously shocked and saddened to hear of Abby's recent suicide. All these deaths are sad, but, I can assure you, the deaths are not linked. How on earth could they be, for goodness sake? Quite frankly, your theories about the Unit being involved are quite wrong. Simon had had a terrible time of it this last year, what with the abduction of his daughter and the breakdown of his marriage. From what I've heard, it sounds like he took his own life. Abby had been depressed, in a mid-life-crisis type of way, for a while. Maybe that's why she called you, who knows? I mean, she always was rather buttoned-up with her emotions. That was part of why she was in the Unit in the first place. It's perfectly possible that this emotional suppression re-emerged later in her life, isn't it? And Danny? Well, I believe that was a pure accident and it was found to be so at the inquiry. Pure accident. Unfortunate. But nothing more sinister.

'Look Innes. The Unit is a long time ago. I've put it behind me. Apart from occasionally meeting up with some of the others, the Unit has not played a large part in my life. If you don't mind me saying so, perhaps it is *you* who needs to think about how you've viewed that time in your past. Perhaps you've invested it with more significance, symbolism even, than it actually deserves. We were just a bunch of unbalanced teenagers. That's all. And some of us happened to keep in touch, in a loose, casual way. And some of us perhaps kept the experience buried within ourselves. And finally, some of us died. It happens.'

She couldn't help herself from being slightly unnerved by Alex's uncannily incisive ability to so accurately assess her own shameful attitude to her Unit days. But her utterances smacked of a prepared speech. Still, Innes remained silent and let Alex get on with what was fast becoming a lecture. 'You see, I feel that I must counter at least part of your extreme anxiety with a bit of down-to-earth common sense of my own. I have no problem with the fact that some of the group have died. People *do* commit suicide. Bad things *do* happen to people, like Simon's little girl being abducted. And as for Lydia? Well, who knows the truth there except that she'd been depressed, apparently. I'm sure it's true that some of us may never have got over, *really* got over our problems. I have severe doubts about the efficacy of the Unit. I'm surprised it stayed open so long. The thing is, none of us has any answers. Because there are none. Or at least there is no one "big answer". That's life, I'm afraid. Really.'

Innes wanted to leave immediately. The room was closing in. She was finding it impossible to keep her eyes from straying to those faint scars on Alex's forearms. And the realization that Alex had been in touch with others from the Unit, seemed to really *know* some of them as adults, was shattering. She couldn't quite pin down why, although part of her felt more than a passing hint of jealousy. It went deeper than that. Maybe if she'd answered Abby's call, not only might she have helped Abby but perhaps they would have become friends. Jointly made some sense of their past?

She snapped out of the thought as Alex lectured on. 'And, Innes, I just want to emphasize how misguided I think you're being. And I have to be brutally honest with you. I think your . . . how can I put it? Your *mission* to find out more about those of us who were in the Unit *and* our various fates in life is somewhat ill considered. And a . . . touch . . . *unhealthy*. Still, after our little talk, you might think differently on all this tomorrow. But I feel that you've had a wasted journey, both here to me and to Scotland in general. I'm sorry.'

Alex's tone now had the force of a dismissal. Innes was more than happy to leave the claustrophobia of the situation. And there was another nagging worry. As she stood up, she couldn't help but feel she'd been handled. Expertly managed. But she had no idea what to say next, except a mumbled thank you for the drink and a weak smile as she handed Alex her business card on the way out. 'In case there's anything else you remember, especially about Abby.' As she walked to her car, with Alex offering a polite wave of farewell, she felt the visit had been worse than useless. Alex had been in overriding control, and her devil-may-care attitude to each and every concern raised had left Innes embarrassed and confused. Maybe it was time to get home to London. Stop this nonsense. And just book herself a year's worth of self-indulgent sessions with Liv.

As she pulled out of the driveway, she could see Alex still at the front door, unwaving now, merely checking her off the premises. And despite more than half a lifetime apart, bringing with it perhaps the wisdom of middle age, Alex remained to her as impenetrable as she had always been.

44

Alex watched as the tail-lights disappeared round the corner. She headed back inside, threw herself on to a sofa and shut her eyes, reviewing what she'd just heard and seen.

She knew she'd been very smooth in her performance. Granted, she was in her own home, her own surroundings, but she had kept it together very well indeed. Outwardly at least. Innes Haldane's phone call that morning had just about finished her. She'd jumped to all the wrong conclusions. Frozen with shock, she'd consented to seeing Innes, not having the least idea about how she'd been tracked down. From the brief phone call she knew Innes's knowledge was limited. The knowledge she did have seemed to revolve around the recent deaths. That was fine. There was no hint of menace or *dangerous* knowledge evident in the call. Still, the intervening hours waiting for her arrival had been nerve-racking, working out how to handle Innes, what story to spin, if, as she thought and hoped, Innes was clueless.

And as for her lies tonight, delivered with such aplomb to Innes? Well, she was pretty much certain that she'd put her off. Granted, she had the address list and had been snooping around in the Hebrides, and round at Simon's place. But she had only got so far. Innes Haldane might be as intelligent as herself, but she had always been trusting and naive and, to that extent, a rather stupid woman. Although her visit and her nosing about in things left a nagging worry, there was something far more pressing. She wandered over to the dining table. Christ, the photos had been sitting here, in plain view, while Innes had been here! But she hadn't gone anywhere near and she wouldn't have recognized Sarah. Well, probably not.

She'd tracked Sarah down at her partner's place. Debbie Fry's house was registered as her business premises. It had involved a couple of cloak and dagger evenings, hanging about in her car. But she'd got lucky the second night. Both of them arrived together. They looked similar. Like sisters almost. Fit, tanned, short hair. Typical middle-aged dyke thing. But she knew who was who, all right. Alex shuffled through the photos she'd taken that evening and the next morning. And the ones of her place by Loch Fyne. *Loch Fyne*. The bloody cheek of it. Following her out there had been a bit trickier. She'd been able to get Sarah's practice address in Glasgow the same way that she'd found Debbie Fry's. She'd only opted to sit it out in Morningside at the Fry woman's place because she didn't immediately fancy a trek to Glasgow. But, having seen Sarah a couple of times, the initial shock, yes shock, had worn off. The other afternoon she followed her from her central Glasgow offices all the way to Argyll. It had been a tricky drive, but she surprised herself. *Loch Fyne!* What did that mean? Everything or nothing. And now, she had to decide what to do.

She wandered out of the living room. Her head was beginning to hurt. That episode with Innes Haldane was the last thing she'd needed. Time for another drink. She wrenched at the fridge door, the sucking noise as it opened and closed sounding unnaturally loud in the high-ceilinged kitchen. She filled the ice bucket and grabbed a half-full bottle of Scotch from the worktop. Maybe she'd make a night of it.

Back in the living room, she threw herself into one of the armchairs and sloshed a generous slug of whisky into her tumbler. She downed it in a oner. *Simon had been a fucking fool. It was all his own fault.* She downed another treble in two cold yet burning gulps. *He was a fool. He'd fucked it up for them all.* Danny was gone. *Shit.* And Abby? Well, inevitable really. And convenient. *Oh, Christ.* She raked a hand through her hair. Her head was killing her. *Too many thoughts. Too many memories. Stop it!*

She reached clumsily for the TV remote and started channel-hopping, rattling through the sixty-odd cable channels, first settling on one, and then flicking back and forth. After a few minutes and another huge drink, she angrily hit the standby button and the screen went black.

'*Fuck it! Fuck it, fuck it!*'

She raised an unsteady hand upwards and backwards and hurled the TV remote against the opposite wall, feeling satisfied as it shattered. She slumped back down in her chair, eyes closed. She might as well pass out here. It felt cold, though. Like a draught somewhere. Couldn't be. She tried to warm herself up with one more whisky, draining her glass before it slipped on to the carpet. *Shit.* The lighting was low, and she was almost out of it. She snuggled into the armchair, ready to drift off, confused images of Innes, Sarah and Simon flitting across the back of her eyes.

The cold had roused her. But she was too late. As she turned her head, she caught the sight of her muslin curtains flapping through the open French windows, but then her eyes focused on the immediate foreground. Hands were reaching over her head and covering her throat and mouth before she knew what had happened. And, in a moment, she felt the taut muscles in her face twist from surprise, to recognition, to horror.

The Unit

One hour later

Confidential note from Charge Nurse Ranjit Singh, to Head of Psychiatric Nursing Services
20 March 1978
RE: Adolescent Psychiatric Unit (APU)

My RCN representative has advised me to write to you, in confidence. However, please feel free to use the contents of this note should the need ever arise.

It has been with increasing anxiety that I have seen the last of the 1977 intake leave the Unit and take their respective places in the wider world. I think you are aware of how much I was looking forward to taking up my post here when the Unit opened in 1975. That hope and pleasure have stayed with me up until this past year.

I know I do not have to tell you how important group dynamics are to the success (or failure) of therapeutic communities. Patients are selected as individuals but also on the basis of how they will work as a group. Over these past nine months or so I have become increasingly worried, and I am now convinced, that fundamental errors have been made in the selection of the 1977 intake. This group have, by far, been the most difficult, most disruptive and, sadly for them, had the least successful outcomes in terms of their treatment.

We clearly cannot keep patients indefinitely, but we can refer them on, either to main hospital psychiatric services or to outside therapeutic agencies. This has not been done in any patient's case from this particular group.

I am very concerned that, in some cases, we have released highly disturbed, possibly even highly dangerous individuals into society. Enough chaos was wrought here these past few months. I fear that what may be unleashed in coming years to an unsuspecting world may be well beyond that.

45

There was more than enough light for them to see each other and their surroundings. He'd made sure of that. Beside each single bed was a low-wattage lamp. And he'd lit every second one.

Simon looked directly at Alex. Although the tape across her mouth prevented her from speaking, her eyes held plenty of expression. As she'd awoken from the drug he'd given her at her house an hour before, her attitude had gone from puzzled disorientation to fear, and now she was trying a look of defiance. He'd ignored that one and continued to do so. He was relieved that she'd survived the journey here and woken up at all. He'd had no way of knowing how a bucket of Scotch would react with the drug he'd injected her with to make her easier to handle. But she was alive. That was something. As for her surprise at seeing him? The man she thought a water-logged, bloating corpse awaiting discovery in the Firth of Forth was very much alive. Yes, despite the attempt on his life, he'd survived. Had lain low to make sure that his 'death' made it into the local press, and then he'd formed his own plans for Alex.

He checked her bonds. Legs spreadeagled and secured to the bed-ends. Hands, enclosed in handcuffs, were freer. He'd put in wall bolts with generous lengths of chain attached. All ready for her. Now, without a word, he left the room, closing the door of the female dorm softly behind him, refusing to acknowledge her struggling body or expression of pleading terror.

He took his time down the wide staircase, checking that everything was secure and as he wanted it. He paused on the lower landing to take a look at what he knew had been a male patients' bedroom, now an empty shell of peeling wallpaper with a single rusting bed-frame in the corner. The staff overnight rooms were in much the same state. The second male patients' bedroom was similarly kitted out to the female one and had obviously been used for something residential in recent years. He shrugged to himself. None of that really mattered now. Everything was his. He'd bought it all. The hospital authorities had been desperate to offload the place for years. A property developer had initially bought it, couldn't get the planning permission he'd needed, and was happy for Simon to take it off his hands. It was the opportunity he'd been looking for. The building. Its contents. Its land. Its memories. Its secrets. Its history. Its pain. They were all his.

On the ground floor, he wandered slowly towards the main room. The vastness of it, with its quadruple bay windows, still made him pause each time he entered it. Slivers of street-light were filtering through the huge wooden shutters. Like orange laser beams, targeting enemy points on the scuffed carpet beneath his feet. If only they had been real lasers back in 1977. Picking off each and every one of them as they lay in their psychodramatic comas. None of this would have happened. Relaxation exercises! He wished now that there had been other, rather more strenuous activities imposed on them.

Back in the hallway, he toed open the door of the study room. An old desk. Two chairs. Nothing else. It had always been a soulless room. He'd preferred to do his studying out in the garden when the weather was good, or in the kitchen between meal times. He moved through to the kitchen. It was still the same. Still had its now-ancient industrial ovens and cooker. Half a dozen round tables and stacks of grey plastic chairs stood against the wall. The place was deserted. Lifeless. Finished.

The room he wanted was back at the end of the long hallway. Glass on three sides. Two blinds tucked neatly up. The third, keeping prying eyes away from the outside of the building. He settled himself at the desk. How many nurses had sat here? Writing up notes? Missing things? Suspecting others? He could almost hear the murmurs of Anna on the phone to Dr Laurie. The hearty laugh of Sarah Melville as she joshed with Ranj.

He bent again to his task. Time to double-check it all. The papers. The tape. He pressed the play button on the cassette player, listening to the sombre tones of his own voice.

'We saw them from some distance away. The moon had come out and it was quite easy to see, what with the light reflecting off the waters of Loch Fyne, and we all had torches. There were two of them. When they saw us they began waving. Tentatively at first. Unsure. And then they realized that we were just kids. Nothing to worry about. I heard one of them say, "They're smiling. They're friendly. Allies. Not the enemy. We're saved!"'

He pressed stop. Enough for now. He was satisfied that the tape was working. He gathered up the entire package, ready to make his way back up to the top of the house. It was as he was clearing everything from the desk that he noticed it. It was a shock. He could have sworn he'd left that at home, in his study, where he'd read and re-read it with the night wind and sea spray pouring in from the open window. The discovery of it here among the others papers had shaken him and he needed to sit back down. Recompose himself before going upstairs and continuing with what he had to do. The pale blue envelope was becoming tatty from regular handling. He slid the matching coloured sheets from it, running a finger over the indigo ink. A fine, loopy script. He felt like he'd read it a million times. In that case, what harm would there be in reading it again?

The fact of it, her killing herself, he had to admit, had been a surprise. A shock. When he'd paid her a visit at her home in London some weeks before, her reaction to him had been, initially, remarkably calm. As if she'd been expecting something of the sort. She couldn't have been of course. She'd made him lemon tea, served in the finest bone-china cups and saucers, listened silently to his tale, and eventually wept. He'd liked her. In truth he'd liked her when they were in the Unit. She seemed so normal to him that he sometimes wondered why she was in there. But he also remembered how Laurie's sessions ripped the heart out of everyone, and Abby's dysfunctional family life had been laid bare, as had everyone else's. No, no wonder Abby had obsessive, control issues, which she kept fairly well hidden in the Unit but which surfaced in highly tense, withdrawn moods from time to time. A visceral, permanent, dug-in tension he could still sense in her, twenty-six years later. He guessed she'd just learned to live with it.

He stroked the first page of the letter. He knew now what had happened to her that day by the shores of Loch Fyne, more than half a lifetime ago. He understood. She was essentially a good person. Maybe she should have done more? Instead of walking away in disgust. But no, she couldn't have *known*, couldn't have predicted the rest.

He'd found it hard to be in her close company. She was indeed striking. In every way. A lasting and sensual beauty that would – would have – carried into her old age. How lucky Danny had been to have known this woman. To have been loved by her. In another time, another world maybe . . . maybe *he'd* have tried with her. Her sexual and other, deeper forms of magnetism were almost irresistible. But he'd put those thoughts away almost as quickly as they had emerged.

They'd talked about his life, her life. She was worried. Desperate. He had reassured her. It was only as he was leaving that she told him what had happened on the ferry. He'd almost collapsed at that.

He opened up the letter, head shaking as he re-read her words.

Dear Simon

I can't begin to explain what meeting you again has done to me. I wasn't afraid like you thought I might be. Just sad. So sad. It's clear that Danny had very much led me to believe the wrong things about you. About you being a bit mad and thinking it was somehow our fault, everything that had happened to you and your family. And he also led me to think, if not actually believe, that you were involved in Lydia's fire. It was wrong of him to do this, but, as you yourself said, he obviously wanted, maybe needed, to see me, and he was terrified that you might look me up first. For all that, all Danny's misrepresenting of you, I am sorry, although I cannot say that I regret having met Danny again, even if we started out from a position of deceit.

When I look at everything that happened all those years ago, my overriding feeling is one of guilt. I can never make amends for any of it. The odd thing is that if I really try hard to remember how I felt then, what I saw then, how it all was afterwards, despite what you said when we met, I should have known better. Things were different in the Unit afterwards. Things were tense beforehand. Strange. Perhaps that was part of the cause of what happened later. I don't know. I think you may have a better idea of why things happened. You are, after all, the psychologist.

What I can't understand – and I have thought this through again and again until my mind, my memory, reels – is why I didn't notice anything that night when we all met up again. True, we were all a bit worse for wear, with the whisky and dope Carrie had brought along. I mean, that was part of the whole thing, wasn't it? Running off to get boozed and doped up. Thing is, I wasn't enjoying any of it very much and the thing down by the loch did it. I stormed off, telling Danny that I wanted some space. He promised he'd be up at the fork in the high road, 'soon', as he put it.

I blundered about in the forest, probably thanks to having drunk too much, and got genuinely lost for some time, with no map, no compass. And then I saw you all. A silent, bedraggled, downcast group. But I just thought you were a bit drunk and fed up that the absconding prank had got us all lost, cold and tired. I've done everything I can to try and conjure up that moment when I met you all and we were waiting it out for the inevitable – for the staff to drive past and find us. I just don't remember anything specific. Maybe it was because I was being self-centred. I was sulking because Danny and I had had that row. As I saw it, he'd wanted to stay drinking with you all and larking around by the loch, rather than come with me. I just don't know why I never picked up on anything specific. And that is another appalling lapse on my part that I can never forgive myself for.

Anyway, afterwards I was unsure as to why things were different in the Unit. The evening did niggle at me and I did ask Danny about it, but I didn't really piece the two things together – that night and the atmosphere in the Unit afterwards. And within weeks I just wanted to do my time and leave. You know what it was like. Waiting for a leaving date. Waiting for the staff to finally decide when they thought you were fit to go back into the world. I became fixated on leaving. I wanted to get on with living. Living as normally as I could again. So after a while I blotted it all out. It was wilful ignorance on my part. And it is that knowledge that I can never reconcile within myself. Never.

As for your attempts to make amends. I am impressed at what you've achieved professionally and I believe you when you say that you want to heal others. I also believe that you now want all the truth to come out, whatever the consequences. These are all laudable actions and aims. However, you also mentioned wanting, needing, forgiveness. How you will achieve that I do not know. I believe that you are a changed person from the one I knew in the Unit. But I cannot dismiss the fact that you were involved. You were an active participant. I'm not sure and I don't think you have any clear idea about how you are going to make things right.

Whatever you hear about my fate, and I know since we met that you will take an interest in what happens to me, please know that the choices I have made have been mine alone. I have made plans, which, when carried out, you will see as absolutely fitting. And now I have only one concern in life. To do something to make amends. In relation to that, I have enclosed a copy of my will, outlining the substantial bequest that I am leaving to 'Renewal'. I think that action speaks for itself.

Finally, there is a separate letter enclosed for you to show to any authority you may think fit, if and when you want to. It outlines all I now know.

You will receive this package after my death. I don't deserve to live. I hope that I can find peace.

Let the pain of the past die with me,
Isabella

The lump in his throat wouldn't budge. She had been a beautiful and decent woman. But her hopes of peace, for the pain of the past to die with her, were impossible dreams for him at this moment. But not for much longer. Gently, he placed the pages back into their envelope and put it inside his breast pocket. Closest to his heart. Since receiving it, it had been his spur.

His mind swayed back, as it so often did after reading the letter, to wild imaginings of her last hour on earth. Imaginings they might be, but her actions were, as she'd promised, 'fitting', although only he, and Alex, could understand them. God, what it must have been for her, that last evening! He'd made it his business to find out as much as possible about that final hour. Inquest reports, press reports, interviews with locals, witnesses who saw her last – he'd built up a reasonable picture of what had happened, just as he'd done after the return of his little Katie. Like then, the need to know, or at least to add some sense of 'reality' to the awful event, was a necessary dealing mechanism for him. Each and every obsessive detail and the rest . . . well, the rest of it may have happened that way . . .

Her bag would have been packed. Towel. Goggles. All there. Perhaps she dumped the bag in the hall as she headed back into her study. The pale blue envelope was sealed with a gentle lick of her tongue. The other enclosures placed in the bigger, bulky brown envelope. Finally, she would write out the address in that fine, loopy script, picked out with delicacy by a cherished Mont Blanc he'd remarked on when visiting her home.

She'd then have locked up the house and headed for the sports centre. The chemist's at the end of the road would still be open.

'Ah. Evening, Professor Velasco. Swimming lessons tonight?'

She'd maybe tried an automaton's smile and looked around at the old-fashioned shop with its old-fashioned wares, picking out what she wanted. 'Good evening, Mr Maitland. Yes, swimming tonight. I'll just have those, please.'

Outside the shop, did she hesitate at the post-box? Then recover, watching numbly as the First Class slit swallowed up her packages? The walk to the sports centre, through reception, and down to the female changing area, would have seemed like a dream. Was her mind clear then perhaps? Empty? No thoughts left. Maybe she answered greetings by reflex, with an unfeeling rictus grin.

Forty-five minutes later she would have recalled nothing of the lesson. The gaps in her memory were getting worse. It was the drugs. The ones her GP had prescribed were useless. She had procured much more effective ones from work. She knew only too well how much to take to get through the day and how much was too much. Tonight she'd taken too much. But that was fine.

By this time she'd be sitting in her changing cubicle, swimming costume dripping wet, towel hanging limply in her hands. All around her, women would be chattering, showers hissing, hairdryers humming, the pungent tang of chlorine saturating the damp air. For how long she'd never have known, as she sat unmoving in the tiny space, curtain drawn against the world. The oblong, wooden shape of the cubicle like an upended coffin. Apt.

Then, after a while, she'd notice it. Silence. She'd draw the curtain aside. The place was deserted. Maybe she'd slump back on to the bench seat, fumbling for her small handbag inside the bigger sports holdall. Yes. It was there. She would take out the syringe and vial of clear liquid now. She'd stolen it, perhaps that very day, from work. To do such a thing seemed the final confirmation of the action she was going to take tonight. That and the purchase at the chemist's.

She'd watch herself in some out-of-body-experience way – a bit like he did sometimes – as she measured the local anaesthetic into the syringe and plunged it into first the left wrist, and then the right. The effect would have been instantaneous. Next, the chemist's paper bag. She'd slide out the razor blades, carefully unwrapping them from their folds of delicately thin paper.

As she wandered towards the door leading to the pool, she wouldn't remember making the cuts. But on either side of her lay the red trails. Through the door, and in five steps, she was in the blissfully warm water. Her last sight, the bobbing head of a child looking like a doll, high up on the balcony above . . .

46

Simon sat back in the old Nurses' Office, forcing his memory and his imaginings to take a momentary rest. He was now regularly feeling the need for strong drink to calm him. From the desk drawer he lifted out the half-bottle of brandy. He'd brought it here for this very purpose. He put the bottle to his lips and drank greedily, the burning sensation a comforting distraction. He put the bottle back in the drawer and sat back, one foot upon the desk. Now that he'd reread Abby's letter, she remained in his mind. And other haunting thoughts came back to him. She'd let it all pour out that evening he'd visited her. The image of her sad monologue, uttered in strangely calm, clinical tones, now grafted on to his memory . . .

'The day Danny died, the *Queen of the Minch* . . . yes . . . I remember the name of that ferry . . . I sailed on her so often, I felt I knew her. Anyway the *Queen of the Minch* docked ten minutes early. It had been a busy crossing. I was glad. There must've been about fifty foot passengers, all eager to make their way off the ferry and disperse into Ullapool or get on to the next stage of their journey. I know I looked a state but . . . but incredibly, no one seemed to notice me. Everyone was just interested in their own thing. I remember stumbling my way across the wet ramp, heading for the women's toilets attached to the booking office. Absolutely no one else had noticed me, even though I must've been ashen-faced, my body shaking, and I was ripping off my jacket and wrenching the hat from my hair. I was going to throw up.

'It was odd. It seemed as if the waves of nausea were paradoxically stronger now I was on terra firma, and I dry-retched into the bowl, again and again. When they subsided, I recall pulling at the roll of toilet paper and wiping my eyes. Just to staunch the non-stop stream of tears. At the wash-hand basins I soaked ice-cold water on my face again and again, and checked in the mirror for tell-tale blotches. I was convinced someone would stop me as soon as I set foot outside.

'And outside, the afternoon was mocking me. The sun, unbelievably, even had a hint of warmth in it. The single-decker bus was waiting for the alighted ferry passengers, and I dragged my rucksack and my weary body up into the empty back seat. The one nearest the toilet. At no time, then, before or afterwards, did I make any attempt to look at anyone, to talk to anyone – fellow passengers, boat crew and certainly not harbour police. I knew there was no point. The bus jolted and pulled out of the station, and I risked a look back towards the docked ferry. Like an X-ray, I imagined my gaze passing through the ship, into the grey waters of the Minch. Out where Danny lay. Tossing about on the waves. Cold. Dead.

'The drive from the ferry port seemed to take for ever. I left the bus at Inverness and transferred to another that was going straight to Edinburgh. Again I found a kind of haven in the relative security of the back seat. Cocooned into myself, with the occasional glance out the rear window, expecting . . . expecting what? Oh, someone or other to be in hot pursuit.

'By the time I was at Edinburgh Bus Station I knew where I was headed. Well, I had the List, hadn't I? The one Danny had taken from your house that reunion night. Danny had eventually let me have a copy of my own, complete with your own details, which Danny had added ages ago. Why? For his own sense of neatness and orderliness? Everyone on one page – at a glance. Very Danny. Anyway, yes, I had all their addresses. No problem there. But . . . and I don't know why I did this . . . I don't really know what I was thinking about all those hours travelling. Or if I was thinking or *feeling* anything. When I look back now, it all seems . . . I feel numb. Anyway, instead of boarding a bus for Fife to see you, I hailed a taxi and made for Cramond.

'The frantic hammering on the front door would've been enough to tell Alex that something was wrong. I could make her out, marching down the hall, peering at my distorted figure outlined through the frosted glass in the door. She'd unlatched it and I literally fell through. I stood, propping myself up with my back against the wall of her hallway. What a sight I must've made! Hair wild, a heavy rucksack hanging limply from my shoulder. I was dressed respectably in an expensive waterproof and smart, corduroy trousers, but I must have looked mad. For one fleeting moment I wondered if Alex thought I was the wronged partner of someone who, mistakenly, had thought she was her husband's mistress. Whatever, it was clear Alex hadn't a clue who I was. And as for Alex? I didn't question it was her at that moment. Didn't wonder at the transformation in her.

'I was shouting by then. "Alex! Alex! It's Isabella. Isabella Velasco. Danny's dead! Dead!" I do recall Alex looking as if she'd been struck across the face. But she'd rallied quickly and, in a moment, was steering me into her living room, pushing me down into a chair. I was crying again. Uncontrollably. A huge drink, brandy I think, was poured and force-fed to me within seconds.

'And then I remember sitting bolt upright. Staring at a blank TV screen. Catatonic. Alex was keeping out of my eye-line . . . maybe preferring to watch from afar. Maybe working it out. *Yes, this definitely was Isabella! Didn't she look the same? When she wasn't looking . . . demented? Haunted? What the hell had happened? Was Danny really dead?* It must've all gone through her mind. Maybe she was scared of me at that moment. But she risked a step forward to replenish my glass. I drank quickly but stayed silent, and closed my eyes. Then, without any warning, I jumped up. I needed the bathroom. The sickness was back.

'Alex had grasped my arm and frog-marched me to a downstairs bathroom. Alex . . . her face and jaw were taut . . . angry-looking . . . she was watching me kneeling over the toilet bowl, heaving and wiping streaming eyes on toilet paper. Just as I had at the ferry port.

'And then she spoke to me. Were these her first words? Couldn't have been. Yet I felt I was hearing her speak for the first time in over quarter of a century. She said, "Isabella? Abby? Here, let me help you." The next thing I remember was, like a biddable child, allowing myself to be led by the hand, back to the living room. And then she was being nice to me. It made me cry again. "I've a wet face-cloth here for you, Abby. With very cold water. Here." And then she was kneeling down in front of me, wiping my face like a baby's. "Abby? Come on. You're okay." And the combination of cold water and the soothing voice must've done it. I came to. I looked, really looked at Alex for the first time, and was at last taking in my surroundings . . . and then it hit me with full force. The delayed shock. The awful reality. "Alex? Oh, Christ! Oh . . . oh, help me! I must go to the police! He's dead. It's my fault!" I cried it a few times. And Alex held me down as I fought again and again to get up, out of the chair. But she held me down until the impulse to flee subsided. Then she lowered her face to meet mine, a hand stroking my cheek. "Listen to me, Isabella. Tell me what happened? Where have you been?"

'And I knew it was time to tell it. Tell my story. "We were on the ferry. From Stornoway," I told her. "We'd been seeing a lot of each other. He said that he wanted to see me safely across to the mainland after another idyllic visit with him. Maybe, I hoped, it would be the last time I would have to leave him. I had wild thoughts of living permanently with him, maybe marriage, who knows? I . . . I just wanted a . . . a last couple of hours with me . . . and . . . him. I was going to tell him that I loved him . . . then he went funny. Said we should go up on deck where it was quiet. Private. Then he told me . . . told me about . . . oh, God, how could I have missed it! He told me three times! I wouldn't believe him." And Alex was raising her voice. "*What*, Abby? What exactly did he tell you? *What*?"

'But I wasn't listening and wanted, *had* to go on with my story. "And . . . and . . . and then I just started hitting him. With fists! Really punching him . . . but the deck was wet. Greasy with oil. He slipped . . . fell backwards over the safety rail . . . I couldn't hold him . . . he just went over . . . he's dead! Deeead . . . !"'

The imagined screams of her anguish had stayed with him night after night. And again they'd returned on this most significant of nights. Pushing the chair back, Simon gathered up what he needed. He checked his watch. Any time now. Two minutes later, the side door-bell rang.

The motorcycle courier stood head-to-toe in black. Simon handed him the package.

'Well done for being on time. I wasn't sure. It's a bit out

of the way here. Okay, now remember, if Dr Logan's not there, call me immediately on my mobile. There's the number and here's something extra for yourself. It'll take you about an hour and a half to get to her hotel in Glasgow. She's on business there. She'll be registered. The night porter will *have* to rouse her. This is urgent. Top priority. Don't leave it with anyone else, and don't deliver it before 2 a.m. Got that? Timing is very important.'

He closed the door behind him, hoping to God that the courier could follow those simple instructions. The chances were that Sheena would hit the phone as soon as she'd digested the contents of the package. And then, timing would be of the essence. Now, there was only one other to arrive here before his tasks were completed. Before he'd played out his last, personal act of psychodrama.

With an inner weariness taking hold of him, he fetched another package from the old Nurses' Office and made his way back up to where Alex was waiting for him.

47

In the hotel car park Innes sat for a moment. Rational thought was beyond her. The experience of meeting Alex had been worse than she'd thought it would be – but in a different way than she had expected. She'd sat there, strangely impotent, as she let Alex take control. Most irritatingly of all, she'd allowed herself to be lectured. Yes, *lectured*! But mulling it all over on her way back here, she'd replayed the lecture in her mind. Something hadn't rung true about the whole encounter. Alex had been too relaxed, too incurious about everything. And, most of all, she was lying. About exactly what she didn't know, but Alex was lying. Innes cursed herself. *Jesus!* She, of all people, should have seen it earlier! It was part of her bloody job to work out if and when someone was lying! And Alex was a good liar but not good enough.

The journey back to Alex's was spent with Innes rehearsing her second attempt at tackling her. She didn't care if Alex had gone to bed. No, Alex was going to talk, really *talk* to her. And she wasn't going to leave the place without answers. The house was lit up just as it had been when she left. But there was no answer. She tried the front door. Locked. Round the back, her eye caught the fluttering of the muslin curtains as they billowed through the open French windows.

Inside, the living room was much as she remembered it. And yet not. Alex's empty glass was lying on the floor beside a chair, not the sofa she'd been sitting on earlier. And the television remote control was lying shattered in pieces in the far corner.

'Alex? Alex! It's Innes again! Alex! *Alex!*' She heard the heightened pitch of apprehension in her own voice and stopped in the centre of the room. Uneasiness was sending out a warning. *Wait a minute! Don't go upstairs yet.* She combed the ground floor. Nothing.

Okay. Next. Nerves ate away at her stomach again as she moved upstairs into unfamiliar territory. All five bedrooms were deserted. As were the bathrooms. She stood on the landing, scowling, and then started back down, the creaking of the old floorboards disconcertingly loud in the silence of the empty house. She was heading back for the French windows to secure them, when the mobile sounded. *Shit!* Her heart hammered as she fumbled to pull the phone from her jacket pocket.

'Yeah, hello?'

'Innes. It's Alex. Look I'm sorry about earlier . . . if I seemed unfriendly. B—'

Innes cut in. 'Listen, I'm at your house. I came back to talk to you. You've left the whole place unlocked. Where the hell are you?'

Alex's voice crackled through a patch of bad reception. 'You're *what? In my house?* Oh . . . I . . . hold on a minute . . . eh . . . I forgot about the French windows. Please just shut them behind you. Just forget them. Look, I'm calling you to apologize for tonight. I wasn't very . . . very forthcoming. I'm a bit . . . a bit uptight. Listen, there's a lot I need to tell you.'

'Okay. *But where are you?* It's bloody late now, Alex!'

'I know, I know. I'm a bit fucked in the head right now. And a bit pissed. I've no sense of time. Even less of a sense of place but I've . . . I'm here. At the Unit. I . . . I just wanted to have a look round. Knew I couldn't sleep tonight and thought, fuck it! I wanted to be here. Think about things. Come over. Meet me here. I need to see you. I need your help, Innes.'

Innes stopped walking through Alex's living room and stood at the open windows. She recognized something of herself in Alex's almost shameful confession that she was paying some kind of secretive, nocturnal visit to the Unit. She'd done it too, after all, even very recently. Yes, she could understand that. But could she face that tonight? Tired, confused. Was she up to it?

She sighed. 'For Christ's sake, Alex! What *is* going on? There's nothing to see at the Unit. Damn all. It's shut up. I've been out there.'

But Alex's voice filtered back through, unusually emollient. 'I know, but I'm . . . I need to be here. Just come over. *Please, Innes?*'

Innes closed weary eyes. She was too tired to think any more. The prospect of meeting up with Alex no longer appealed. On her own admission, Alex had said that she was drunk and that might mean aggressive too. Though . . . on replaying the brief telephone conversation again in her mind, Innes thought Alex had sounded more maudlin than combative. If that were the case and Alex was in a vulnerable state, maybe she could, this time, get a semblance of truth from her. Whatever was going on with Alex, she might as well confront it now. 'Fine. Okay. But I'm so bloody tired of all this. I'll be there shortly.'

Simon replaced the tape over Alex's mouth and removed the mobile from her tightening grip. 'She's coming, I take it?' He didn't wait for the nod of agreement. Instead, he turned his back to the room, checked his watch and strolled over to the window. Hands in pockets, he waited for the headlights of Innes's car.

48

She pulled up in the parking area opposite the old Unit building. As she locked the car, mild pricklings of anxiety started again in her gut. She had doubts as to whether this bizarre rendezvous was such a good idea. If Alex was in a weird mood and maybe drunk, what was she letting herself in for? Her abiding memory of Alex from the Unit, and not entirely exorcized by their meeting that evening, was of someone capable of violence. She'd always carried a nasty air of physical threat about her. On the other hand, she was here now, so might as well face Alex, whether drunk and gloomy or belligerent.

The great hulk of the old Unit building stood in darkness. Silent. Closed against the world. Everything about it said 'go away'. She clambered over the low garden wall and checked the front of the house. The ground floor was shuttered as before. Nothing. But . . . hang on? As she glanced up to the top-floor window of what was once the main female dormitory she saw it. A faint yellow glow. What on earth? Someone was up there. She started jogging round to the main entrance again, situated, perversely, at the side of the house.

'Alex! You there? It's Innes! *Alex, you there?*'

She stopped, spun through three hundred and sixty degrees, convinced she'd heard something, flinging rapid glances up and down the road, and checking back at the car before stopping where she'd begun. The main entrance door was before her. Open. She hadn't noticed that before. She took two steps inside the hallway.

'Alex? You in there? *Alex!* Look, don't muck around. Please, Alex!' The tentative steps turned into a brisk walk as she headed deeper into the building, heart-rate up, breathing shallow. She patted her pocket. The paper bag was there. But shit! Anyone could be in there. Druggies, vagrants. Where the hell was she? 'Al—'

The left hand was clamped around her mouth, the right hand and arm lifting her with ease, the whisper clear. 'Please don't struggle. You'll hurt yourself. Alex is fine. You'll be fine. Just come with me.'

She lost count of the flights of stairs as he bundled her up them with strength and agility. As her eyes adjusted to the gloom, she became aware of the familiarity of the place. The various doors and landings sucked her back over a quarter of a century to her last time here. She noticed a complicated matrix of scaffolding poles on each landing. The building looked like it was being propped up by them. As her captor kicked the door open, she knew immediately where she was. The ornate ceiling rose and cracked picture-rail had once been the object of hours of her attention, when at her lowest ebb and brooding in her bed, during those many sleepless nights. The knowledge of where she was dampened the shock of her abduction.

As he released her, the sight that met her stopped any thoughts of fleeing. She could have sworn that the spartan, metal-framed single beds were the same as those they'd used to sleep in. Alex Baxendale was sitting up as much as her chains would permit, a dark band of tape slashed across her mouth, her eyes swivelling from side to side in an oscillation of rage and confusion.

Innes felt the man release her and move round in front of her, his face eerily distorted, half in shadow and half illuminated by the lamp-light. 'I apologize for the use of force, Innes, but it was necessary. Will you please sit there? On the edge of that bed.' He paused to make sure she was looking directly at him. 'Do you know who I am?'

He took the opportunity to observe Innes while she was still in the relative oblivion that was shock. Yes, he could see that vestiges of the adolescent version of her that he had known were still evident. She looked puzzled and frightened. Understandable. But she had done what she was told. She was sitting on the bed indicated, chosen by him so that she would be facing Alex. Though dishevelled from the struggle, she was a good-looking woman. Strong-featured, intelligent face. It was Innes's misfortune that she found herself here. She hadn't been in his plans. There had been no need. No reason. But, along with Alex, she was the last survivor of the group to be left unscathed, until now. Maybe it was fitting that she was here. It was both their fates, his and hers, perhaps.

She didn't know how long it had taken for her to become aware, really aware. Seconds rather than minutes, no doubt. She felt sick. It was the shock. The room, the whole scene, had a dream-like quality. But it was more than that. How many times had she thought of this very room in the years since she'd left the Unit? Countless. She'd dreamed about it. About the whole place countless times too. And the patients? Seldom, until recently. And now here were the two of them. She and Alex. Alex in chains.

She looked at the man again. Properly. He was dressed, incongruously smartly, in an expensive business suit. The face was tanned, lean, behind the sleek designer spectacles. The dark hair close-shaved, almost a military crew-cut. He talked in a normal volume now, the voice educated Scottish.

Disarmingly gentle. She was in a world of shock, that much was true. Scared, yes. But this man had less of an air of menace about him than . . . than what? Melancholy? Any fear in her was fuelled not so much by him but by the sight of Alex in chains and the look of anger and fear on her face. Although she was trying to hide it under a pose of defiance, worryingly reminiscent of her Unit days. And failing.

And then she got it. Recognition registering. It must've been the shock, blanking out her memory. 'My God. *Simon*.' It wasn't so much how he looked, although there was something about the eyes and mouth. It was more the way he was standing. Still that diffident, almost awkward air. And he still had that earnest, near-pleading look on his face. The voice was lower, but precise and measured, with a hint of unintentional condescension. Just as she'd always remembered it. 'But I went to your house. You'd fallen. I don't un—'

He shook his head. 'As you can see I'm very much alive and well. I'll tell you about my "death" later.' He raised a hand. 'Now, I should say right at the outset that this . . . these events tonight are *not* about you. They concern *her* and others of us who were here in '77. However, you have, through your own inquisitiveness, become directly involved. Alex has told me about your meeting with her tonight and how you come to be here in Edinburgh. It's commendable and touching that you wanted to find out more about Abby's death. But I'm afraid you've bitten off far more than you can chew. What I am about to tell you will, I'm sure, upset you deeply. But in a way, your presence here may be of some use. You can be my . . . well, my *almost* independent witness.'

She felt she was coming to her senses a bit now. Felt less afraid, although the sight of Alex bound and gagged was more than unsettling. 'Why? What the h—'

'One moment.' She watched as he disappeared into the shadows and then, seconds later, came back into the lamps' spotlights, a bundle of papers and what looked like a small tape player in his hands. The furrows of concentration on his face grew deeper as he flicked through the paperwork.

He dragged a chair from the end of one of the beds and sat facing her, interposing himself, she noticed, between her and the door, just in case she tried to make a run for it. With legs crossed and the bundle in his lap, he looked to her as if he was just about to give a seminar in some relaxed academic environment. It hurtled her back to group-therapy sessions. He'd often sit like that aping Dr Laurie. And now, before he began, she couldn't help but notice the withering glance he threw at Alex.

'As you may recall, twenty-six . . . nearly twenty-seven years ago, at that benighted camping holiday, I, Alex, Carrie, Danny and Isabella went missing on an orienteering exercise. We got lost. Or rather, we didn't. We deliberately absconded. Isabella didn't want to do it but went along with it because of Danny. Anyway, it was actually Alex's idea. For some reason she was in a particularly filthy mood that day. That whole holiday. Looking back on it with my psychologist's eye, I recognize that Alex had been waiting to erupt. Violence I would have expected but what else ensued leaves me, even now, dumbfounded. You are not the only person tonight who is going to hear our story. Here in my lap is a copy of a package that my senior colleague, Dr Sheena Logan of the Royal Western Hospital . . . our old hospital, if you remember . . . yes, a copy of a package that she will receive in the next hour. I made a back-up to leave behind here.

'Anyway, as you are here, I'm going to share its contents

with you and I think it will speak for itself. This first excerpt is a description by me of what happened as we peeled off from the staff that night. The idea was to go missing for the night, have the staff frantic and then allow ourselves to be found, when we felt like it. Very typical Unit behaviour, as you may recall. Tormenting the staff. Our favourite pastime. When we were not tormenting each other. Or ourselves.

'That night, darkness had just about fallen and we had made our way down to the shores of Loch Fyne. We were in boisterous mood, having smoked a bit of dope and cracked open one of two bottles of whisky we had with us. Alex and Danny had an idea to steal a boat if there was one lying about, as it were. But there were no boats. We continued our increasingly aimless wandering, getting a bit bored, a bit cold. And then, down a track to the water's edge, we came across a clearing. There were two children there. They were obviously lost and had been out all day. They had duffel bags and toy machine-guns. They were playing some sort of goodies and baddies game. They were brave French Resistance fighters, trying to get back past Nazi enemy lines. Anyway, please listen.' A hiss and crackle. Then he found the place.

'We saw them from some distance away. The moon had come out and it was quite easy to see, what with the light reflecting off the waters of Loch Fyne and we all had torches. There were two of them. When they saw us they began waving. Tentatively at first. Unsure. And then they realized that we were just kids. Nothing to worry about. I heard one of them say, "They're smiling. They're friendly. Allies. Not the enemy. We're saved!"

'We asked them their names, where they were from, what they were doing, that sort of thing. They were shy and acted in a very naive, childish way. The girl especially. She let her little brother do most of the talking. He was obviously very protective towards her. But, looking back, I suppose they were just quiet, sheltered, country kids, really. And trusting. They were obviously relieved to see us, though, and told us that they were lost and that their mum and dad would be frantic. They lived further down the loch at Lochgilphead. At first I think it was our intention . . . it was certainly mine and Abby's, at least, to help them. Somehow get them safely home. But, almost immediately, Danny had started taunting the little boy. Grabbed his toy gun. And then Alex did the same with the girl's. Danny started saying things like, "We're in charge now, what you gonna do about it soldier?" Joking, really, but . . . on the edge of meaning, *really* meaning it. And Alex . . . well, she started it. She started laughing at them both, rifling through their bags that just had a bottle of lemonade and some biscuits in each. She emptied everything on to the ground, smashing one of the bottles in the process. And then she started telling the kids to stop whining about going home. Alex slapped the girl and she started crying. At that, Abby tried to intervene. She told Alex to lay off and walked away up the track. Danny ran after her and I could hear raised voices. A couple of minutes later, he came back. He looked angry and muttered something about us meeting her later up at the high road.

'And then Carrie started in. She started having a go at the girl, saying that she whined just like "fat pig Lydia". Carrie always had it in for Lydia. They couldn't stand each other. Of course Lydia wasn't there, so Carrie needed someone else to bounce her aggression off. And then she had the bright idea to "play psychodrama". "Let's make this little bitch be Lydia and put her and the other little fucker in the circle." That's how she put it. And so that's what we did.

We crowded round the children and trapped them in a tight circle. And that's where the similarity between that and psychodrama ended. Basically we were just terrorizing these poor kids, shoving and jostling them around, forcing them to have swigs of whisky. So much that the boy vomited. And then we made them drink more. Pure unadulterated bullying. We needed to let off steam and we were doing it at their expense.

'And then Carrie went to her rucksack and came back with a length of climbing rope and a hunting knife, and said, "Right, now let's really play the trust game." That's when the atmosphere changed. Carrie and Danny dragged the boy off and tied him to a tree. Danny kept saying it was just a bit of fun. But he slapped the boy into silence and the lad stood tied to the tree, quivering and wetting himself. Just watching, eyes wide with fear . . .'

Without warning, he leaned forward and clicked the tape to a halt, pulling it roughly from the machine. He'd been watching every flicker of Innes's face. Now it was time. 'The names of those children were Crawford and Fiona Hamilton. I would appreciate it if you would read this. Here.'

49

What was he giving her? She took the piece of paper and peered at it under the dim glow of the nearest lamp. It was a printout from the *Glasgow Herald*'s website.

archive/Glasgow Herald/27 September/1981.news.text
Bodies of missing children found in Highland loch

The remains of a brother and sister, missing for almost four years, have been found in the waters of Loch Fyne, about twenty miles north-east of their home, near Lochgilphead.

Strathclyde police have confirmed that the remains have been identified as that of Fiona Hamilton (12) and Crawford Hamilton (8), of Gair Lodge, Kylemore, by Lochgilphead. Fiona and her brother went missing on 8 November 1977, after going for a walk in the Kilmichael Forest.

Although police have never ruled out foul play, it is thought that the two children had a fall while climbing rocks close to the loch's shore. A spokesman said, 'Unfortunately, due to the length of time that the bodies have been in the water, it will prove extremely difficult to establish cause of death. Identification has had to be confirmed by reference to dental records.'

Last night, the children's parents, Eileen (40) and Alistair Hamilton (49), were said to be 'devastated' by the news. Friends and relatives said that the couple had been 'living in hope' that one day their son and daughter would be found alive, even though an extensive search at the time failed to find any trace of the children.

In the low light she reread the news report. And again. He saw her blink repeatedly and then she looked up. 'Oh, God. How . . . what . . . was it an accident? How did they fall into the loch? *Tell me! Simon, what happened? What . . .*'

She felt her voice trail away. She felt cold all over now. But that wasn't what was worrying her. Something was wrong with her mind. She wasn't processing the information. It wasn't going in fast enough. She felt sick, confused, scared. The surreal atmosphere was cutting across any attempts at rational thinking. Before she had time to steady herself, he was talking again. Ordering her to listen to him.

He handed her a sheaf of photocopied news cuttings. 'These are going to be in my packages. You'll see why in a moment. Go on. Read them out for *her*. Just the headlines please.'

Most of them Innes recognized. One by one she leafed through the cuttings, each banner headline screaming out at her as she parroted their chilling messages into the silence of the vast room. *'Girl Abducted – Police Fears Grow', 'Girl Found – Police Search for Serial Abductor', 'Father and Three Children Die in Christmas-fire Tragedy – Mother "Critical"', 'Inquiry Finds Family-death Fire "May Have been Started Deliberately"', 'Man Falls to Death from Island Ferry', 'Swimming-pool Death – Inquest Date Set'*.

She finished the eerie recitation, her head spinning. A few feet away, Alex had stopped making any kind of movement and sat slumped on two crushed pillows, her arms awkwardly pinioned above her head. Innes knew she had to put a stop to this. Or . . . or things would become uncontrollable. 'Listen. Please tell me wh—'

Again he cut across her. 'And this please. Read. Aloud.'

She peered at the yellowing magazine. 'It's . . . it's from the *Journal of Adolescent Psychology*, vol. 76, March 1975. You want me to read the passage marked in highlighter pen?'

She detected the slightest of nods. 'Okay . . . "The Royal Western Hospital in Edinburgh this week opens a new and innovative clinic. The Adolescent Psychiatric Unit (APU) is a specialist, residential centre for patients aged 14–19 years. It is planned that the Unit will house some of the most difficult adolescent patients but only those whom the Medical Director, Dr Adrian Laurie, believes will benefit most. Dr Laurie outlined his plans for the new clinic. 'It is aimed at the most intelligent young people who may have high levels of disturbance but whom we believe, through intensive, innovative therapies, can reach full psychological health once more and continue their lives without further harm to themselves or others.'"'

'This next, I want you to listen to very carefully.' He paused for a moment. He was worried about her. She looked as if she was going to pass out. Very pale, shivering, bewildered. Too bad, though. She was here now. And Alex? Well, she knew what was coming, one way or another.

He inserted the next tape, hearing his own voice sounding strangely unfamiliar, its utter calmness belying the truth of what was being said . . .

'Sheena. I considered it best to deliver my message, my plea of mitigation and understanding, if you like, to you. I feel that I have let you down very badly. I've let everyone down. My family especially. But, professionally, I want to use you as my conduit to try and make you understand why you found me perhaps less than forthcoming about my adolescent psychiatric history. I know that you and Debbie Fry have been trying to work it out. Well, here is the answer. You are an extremely able psychologist, and I imagine, given all the material you now have, it will not be too difficult a task to understand what I am about to say.

'The list of names you see in front of you are those of former patients who were resident at the so-called Unit described in the *Journal of Adolescent Psychology*. You will see my name among them. We were not the first intake, but resident some time after the Unit opened. Between 1977 and 1978 to be exact. A diabolical synchronicity of time, persons and place.

'During that time, early November 1977, the group was taken on a holiday to Argyll. We stayed at an outward-bound centre near Loch Fyne. One of our days, November 8th, involved an orienteering exercise. An exercise that ended in shambles, a fiasco. Late afternoon that day, some of us got lost. Or rather, we deliberately went AWOL. We wanted to give the staff some trouble. On our wanderings we encountered two children. A brother and sister, Crawford and Fiona Hamilton. In short, Fiona was tied up. Blindfolded, cut, raped, buggered, tossed into a loch to drown. The boy was tied to a tree, forced to watch, and then eventually hanged from that tree before his weighted corpse was sent to join his sister's at the bottom of Loch Fyne. The offences were committed by the patients from the Unit whose names are underlined, my own included. We were all monsters.

'Danny Rintoul and Alexandra Baxendale committed the most sexual abominations on the girl. Danny repeatedly raped and buggered, while Alex did the same, using the handle of a hunting knife. I attempted to rape her but, thankfully, became impotent. Caroline Franks beat and cut Fiona, but it was Alex who was instrumental in urging us to throw Fiona into the loch, having been told by the screaming girl she could not swim a stroke. Alex then instigated the hanging of the little boy. I wonder, Sheena, how you would explain that behaviour? Because I am largely at a loss even now, even with my training and clinical experience.

'I'd like to say that it was because we were all so mentally ill, to the point where we were unable to comprehend what we were doing. I cannot. I'd like to lay the blame at the door of the dope we were smoking and the whisky we were drinking too much of. I cannot. They may have been the fuel for what we did. But, in essence, they were just the incidentals to that horrific event. Not, most definitely *not*, the cause. The cause lay within us, as individuals, as a group. But I am powerless to analyse it any further. It remains a dark, the darkest of events, immune from neat psychological explanation.

'In addition to those mentioned, there was one other present that day, Isabella Velasco. Sadly, now dead. I had a long talk with her recently, before her death. I agonized about going to see her. But I'm glad that I did. She walked away from the group when she saw them begin to bully the two children. She and Danny Rintoul had a row some yards from where we were, and then she walked off, Danny saying that she wanted to be alone and would meet us all later up at a place known as the high road. But she worried about that bullying episode for weeks after, though she was strenuously assured by Danny Rintoul that all that had occurred was a bit of fun. Eventually she put it from her mind. But that was her mistake. You see, Isabella Velasco's absolute horror at realizing the truth of what happened that day has led her to take her own life, as you can see from the news cuttings I have enclosed.

'When I met her recently she seemed calm but in truth was in a very bad way. She had, through Danny, been informed of the awful truth of what happened that day by Loch Fyne. However, for some reason, she wasn't told the entire truth. Perhaps because Danny hadn't been given the time to explain all before he fell to his death from the ferry.

Whatever, Isabella was under the impression that he alone had done the awful deed, and gave no thought to the others' complicity. Perhaps because of Danny's history of sexual crime, she assumed he had revisited that part of himself on his own. In any event, the knowledge had been a double blow, since her renewed friendship with him after twenty-six years had also renewed her interest in her past at the Unit. She said that she had discovered a new-found need to look at her life then. Remarkably, she'd even gone as far as trying to track down her old medical records. Miraculously she had found some. How, I don't know. She made an oblique reference to "medical friends up north". She said that she was looking forward to revisiting her time in the Unit. She had blocked it out for so long. But now she had an overriding reason to face up to it, thanks to her burgeoning relationship with Danny.

'But she was to be in for . . . well, to say "shock" is a gross understatement, is it not? She could barely remain composed as I explained the truth of what went on and who was involved. She broke down at the recent memory of her running to Alex after Danny's death, thinking she would find help and support from that most dangerous of women. But after that initial panic-stricken visit to Alex, it was Alex who took it upon herself to keep in close touch with Abby. Not, as she tried to make out to Abby, through concern, but to keep a watching brief on her.

'Isabella struggled to take in all that I told her, and described her feelings at finding out what the others did, once she had left them at the loch-side. The news made her physically sick in my presence, such was the shock. You see, that day she merely thought she was leaving the group to carry on with some gratuitous bullying. How little she knew.

'However, she *did* tell me a few interesting things about her time in the Unit after the killings. She noticed a change in the atmosphere of the place. Atmosphere, you see, was always an all-important factor in gauging life there. She recalled, as did I, that the staff appeared to be aware of it but ignorant of the cause. Isabella herself withdrew from her one friendship with another patient, Innes Haldane. Innes had no part in the murderous events.

'There was, though, a deep effect on us from what we did. Alex had constant nightmares during the rest of her stay at the Unit. She was also perceived by the rest of us to be, paradoxically, the most brutal yet the weakest or least trustworthy of the guilty ones, though that position has been ruthlessly reversed by her in adulthood. But, knowing what I do about her, I don't think she was anything like the threat that at the time we thought she was. Yes, her subconscious in sleep may have given her away at times, but the conscious Alex was and is always on alert. Nevertheless we had to be sure, and thus we subjected her to pressures to ensure that she stayed quiet. In one case we played a practical joke on her, so threatening that we knew it would ram our message home. We knew Alex, how her mind worked. We all knew each other's vulnerable spots. Alex, once warned, would not break, not give us away. She would never, *never* have done anything to imperil herself. Not with her obsessive need for power – a need that has clearly grown over the years. She views the world as revolving for only her and she is omnipotent over it all. A true psychopathic take on the world, Sheena?

'And as for my own part. Yes, I am equally culpable and my punishment is already well under way. Can you imagine what it has been like reading the articles about my abducted daughter side by side with those about the

Hamilton children, all those years ago? The clash of destinies, fates. I couldn't believe it. And yet I could. It was a punishment. No doubt. But not punishment enough. I think Katie being taken and, mercifully returned, though harmed, crystallized all that I had ever thought about what we did. In the first place, I still do not know why we did what we did. It was a combination of time, place and the most terrible of group dynamics. And . . . and almost as soon as we had done it, we . . . how can I put it . . . we came back to reality. Realized the horror of what we had done. We immediately made a pact never to divulge it, never to discuss it, and we pledged to keep in touch for ever, contacting each other every anniversary. Every 8th November. We had to trust one another. One fell, we all fell. I know we lived on terror the next few weeks and months, fearing the bodies' discovery. But, incredibly, it never happened. And when they did appear four years later, it was like some blasphemous miracle. No evidence of the killings, no ropes, meagre human remains, incompetent police work. Yes, that's all the parents got, to live and die with. A sloppy and bungled police investigation. A rapid conclusion to "accidental death", which no one questioned.

'And what, all this time, did I think I was going to do? Go to the police? Possibly, probably. Tell the parents? I think that's what drove me. I thought of how I felt about Katie that short while she was missing and what it would've been like if she'd never come back. I had to do something. Would telling the parents be crueller than not? Anyway, I met with both Danny and Alex in recent months and discussed it all with them. In truth, I don't know what could be done legally now. What evidence is there? None. Nothing physical. The bodies were undiscovered for nearly four years. There was little left to examine. And the original police investigation had been grossly incompetent. No one had seemed to consider foul play. Nor had they looked, really looked, to see who else was staying in the area at the time. A posse of adolescent mental patients within spitting distance had seemed to elude them. Fools! No, there is no evidence. Just my word, and the, presumably, still provable fact that we were in the area on the night in question. But the biggest blow has just come to me. I have, after some inquiries, discovered that the Hamilton parents are both dead. Gone to their graves not knowing the truth. It is too much. Too much.

'However, none of that matters now. It's all too late. I have my own plans for justice, for self-punishment. As for the others? First, Lydia Shaw. She was not present at the killing of the Hamilton children, but she found out about it and said nothing; possibly, and I give her the benefit of the doubt, she didn't believe we could've done such a thing. She had apparently overheard some talk on the day we had a reunion picnic in St Monans, though wasn't quite sure what to make of it. I visited Lydia Shaw some time ago and found out then exactly what she knew. She was contrite and frightened. I said that something was probably going to come out but that I wouldn't involve her. I now know that Alex too visited her. That encounter was rather more threatening than mine, the consequences of which are there to see. I have been to see Lydia at her convalescent home, slipping into the grounds unnoticed, not wishing to invite innocent but intrusive questions as to who I was, why I was there. I wanted to see what state she was in. Sadly, Lydia became rather agitated at my visit. Alex had been there before me and put the fear of God into an already broken and largely irreparable Lydia. She knew about the deaths. And only Alex could have told her. Alex has done her work there, in more ways than one. I shudder at the memory of that visit. There's no doubt that Lydia will be convalescing for the rest of her life. A cruel turn of events for a woman whose main crime was to be overly inquisitive.

'One vital piece of information you should have. Danny's death was an accident. Not suicide. I know what happened. That is all you need to know. Again justice found its own way through with him as with so many of us. Those whom justice has left untouched, that is, Alex, I plan to confront. I have no life left after tonight. Sheena, please be sure to pass all I have sent you on to those who will require it.

'I regret only one thing. The death of Isabella. Perhaps I should have shown some restraint. Not told her everything and maybe, maybe, she'd still be alive. Perhaps my own selfish unburdening – oh, yes, it was a relief – in telling her every second of the hell we perpetrated was too much for her. I have no doubt that the rather . . . rather *extravagant*, yet highly symbolic way in which she chose to end her life was meant as recompense to those poor pitiful children and their parents. Although I doubt her penance will ever be appreciated. Not in this world.

'As for the rest of us? All the misfortune that has befallen us must be laid at our own doors. We thought we could escape responsibility for an act of such inexplicable evil that I can never begin to understand it, despite my own lengthy forays into the world of the mind. We have or will pay for that.'

50

Innes was conscious of Simon turning off the now hissing tape. But still her mind seemed empty. Unable to function. She was no longer cold. Only numb. She had a notion to stand up, perhaps flee the room, but her limbs refused to work. She tried to hurtle herself back to the fifteen-year-old she had been then. To recapture the atmosphere. How could she not have known? Not have heard something later? Her whole memory of them all had been transformed in an instant. Her memories were not of fellow mental-illness sufferers. Rather, they were all . . . Simon, Carrie, Danny – yes, Danny! And Alex . . . all *killers. Rapists. Monsters!*

She sensed another movement from him and looked up. With deliberation, he placed the tape recorder on the floor, wiping his tears away with trembling fingers. He stood up and walked over to Alex, ripping the gag from her lips with a ferocity that made her wince with the pain.

'It's all rubbish, Innes! Pure crap! He's mad! Don't believe a word he s—'

The instant change in his demeanour to one of threatening violence kept Innes silent. He spat the words at Alex. 'Admit it! Tell her what I said is true. Tell her, damn you! I want to hear the truth from *your* lips!'

Simon was standing over her, waiting. Innes watched as Alex stared straight ahead, refusing to meet his eye. Anyone's eye. Twenty-six years on, her behaviour was identical to her most insolent episodes in group therapy. But Simon was no Dr Laurie, and the whiplash of his hand on Alex's cheek echoed through the room. Innes watched as a chillingly unresponsive Alex lifted her head up from the pillow, gradually and deliberately unrushed, as a slow gash of blood meandered its way towards her chin.

But the blow had been too much for Innes. She saw where things were going and managed to get to her feet. 'Stop it! Stop! Simon, please. We must go to the police or something. Please don't do . . . don't do anything . . . anything . . .' She didn't finish the sentence. His look of fury kept her nailed in place, and, meekly, she lowered herself back down on to the bed's edge. But she noticed that he too was shaking, staring hard at the hand he'd struck Alex with, as if it didn't belong to him.

Despite her attempts at an impassive front, Alex was struggling to sit up now, eyes fixed in the middle distance. Still meeting no one's eye. Her breathing was laboured, the lamplight picking out the clamminess of her forehead. Unbidden, the memory came back to Innes – the memory of one particularly bad nightmare Alex had had after the Christmas raffle. She remembered Anna and Ranj had come upstairs and roused Alex. She'd sat bolt upright, sweat all over her face and body. Just like now. And that raffle! Only now did she realize the significance of the 'prize' of rope and knife. A diabolical practical joke.

She heard him shouting at Alex, his voice catching, almost like a sob. 'Tell her. Everything!'

Innes held up a shaking hand. 'She doesn't have to. I believe you, Simon. I do believe you. *Oh, Christ, Alex.*' She was aware of the tears falling down her own cheeks and welcomed them. At last something. Something to feel. She also felt her breathing quickening, the tell-tale choking sensation causing a fluttering in her chest and tightening of her throat. She wrestled in her jacket pocket and pulled out the paper bag. Aware of the looks of puzzlement from the others, she blew the bag into a balloon and started breathing into it and inhaling. After two five-breath cycles, she was calming down, though her heart-rate felt unnaturally high.

Silence, save for the sound of her folding up the bag. The hiatus was broken by the hacking cough of Alex. Innes looked at her and shook her head. She wanted out of this room, out of this place and, most of all, away from Alex. Away from them both. But she needed to go along with Simon for now, and *if* she could, try to talk him out of whatever he had planned.

She heard Alex cough again. A preparatory clearing of the throat. A noise Innes recognized from the past, when Alex would occasionally tease them all through group-therapy sessions and then, without warning, decide that it was time to do a bit of grandstanding. She was going to talk. At last.

'He's right. It was the day we went orienteering. You weren't involved in our group, remember? You had a cold or flu or something, and we'd fixed Lydia with that broken monkey-rope. Anyway, we were fucked off. We got lost. Were bored. Annoyed. We bumped into the kids. Just by chance.'

She stopped, wiping blood from her mouth, her body racked with a palsy of fear. It was obvious now that her defences had failed her. Perhaps because the worst was about to be heard. Innes nodded for her to go on, uncomfortable images already settling in her mind.

'Isabella didn't want to get involved. She wanted us to give them their toy guns back and leave them alone. The boy was getting annoyed and the girl? She was afraid. Shit scared. Anyway, Carrie and I told Isabella to fuck off. She walked away. Then Danny ran after her. I heard them arguing. Danny suddenly reappeared. Then we started the psychodrama thing. Soon Carrie had blindfolded the girl, like we used to do in the trust-game part of psychodrama. I think we used the bandanna that Simon was wearing that day. Anyway, Carrie wanted to role-play like a real psychodrama and make the girl be Lydia, I s'ppose 'cause she really hated Lydia. She was so fucking fed up with her. Anyway, the psychodrama game didn't really work. And then . . . and then it changed.'

She paused again, flexing her shoulders to keep upright. 'Carrie hit the girl to the ground. Her dress got torn. It was . . . it was obvious that she was older than we thought. Everything changed then. I looked at Danny. I knew what we were both thinking. So did Carrie. For fuck's sake. That Unit kept our sexual impulses and orientations so under wraps, no wonder we snapped. Sex is power, for fuck's sake. All about power. And anger. And we were angry. All of us. Hacked off to fucking death with the fucking Unit.

'Anyway, we had stuff like rope and a knife with us in our backpacks. The knife was Carrie's. Dunno where she got it. We tied them both up. Started stuffing the whisky bottles in their mouths. Forced the stuff down them. And down ourselves. More and more. The boy threw up and then we made him drink again. And then we were ready. We made the little . . . the little boy watch. We stripped the girl. Danny had her first and we all egged him on. God! Danny told me that he could still hear it in his dreams sometimes. The whooping sound we made . . . just like we were all at a football match or something. He . . . Danny . . . he raped her. Buggered her. He was an animal. Changed. But he made us all change. I . . . I used the knife handle on her. Inside. Everyone was laughing but . . . the . . . the boy was yelling for us to stop. Danny punched him in the face. And . . . and then Carrie . . . Carrie made Simon have a go. Shouted at him to do it. He tried but . . . but he couldn't get it up. She laughed at him. *Laughed and laughed and laughed. Hah! Hah! Hah!*'

Innes looked pleadingly at Simon not to do anything as Alex's hysteria rang throughout the room. She was mentally disintegrating in front of their eyes. The jangling of her chains joined in the mad cackling as she continued her sickening commentary.

'And then it was Carrie's turn to do something. Carrie, being as straight as they come, wouldn't do sex. So she took her knife and began making lots of little cuts on the girl's body. There was a lot of blood. The girl had given up screaming and crying now. We didn't even bother gagging her. No one could hear. We were in the middle of nowhere. By now, she just lay there. Her eyes . . . they just stared straight up. Unseeing. It was like she was dead. But she wasn't.

'And things changed again. It was like waking up. Suddenly we looked at what we'd done. I can't remember who wanted to throw her in the loch. Carrie, I think. The boy was hysterical again when he saw what we were going to do. Carrie made Simon lift the girl to the water's edge. She was . . . she didn't move, didn't struggle, but she was awake. She'd told us she couldn't swim. The boy told us she couldn't. But she must've known what was coming. Carrie made us all move to the loch-side and we all had to hold the girl and we tossed her in like it was a game. 'One, two, three!' Carrie shouted and she laughed. *We all laughed.* We watched as the body hit the water. The rope had come undone somehow but it didn't matter. The girl landed face down in the water, stayed there for a while and then sank. And then I . . . I saw Carrie turn away, smiling. The boy was still screaming.

She picked up a rock and smashed him on the head. He was semi-conscious as the noose was made, fitted round his neck, and flung across the tree branch.'

Simon cast a final dismissive look at Alex, whose mouth was bleeding more heavily than before, and then Innes became aware of her own nails cutting deeply into her hand. She looked at her palm. Inadvertently, she'd opened up the wine-glass scar. An abiding reminder of how this had all started. But, strangely, she felt nothing. Didn't even feel connected to her body. It was like she was looking down on herself. On them all. Head bent, speaking more to herself than anyone in the now silent room. 'And I missed all this. All because of some bloody cold that wasn't so bad after all. But . . . but surely if I'd been there I could've stopped it. Me and Abby together? But . . . but afterwards? How could I not have known? How? *In God's name, how?*'

51

Simon had moved forward into the light now and was looking directly at her. He was feeling tired. And ill. Ready to throw up. But time was running out. He looked at his watch before answering. 'Yes, well. That's fate, isn't it? A cold kept you away from that day's fateful events. And could you have changed anything? Impossible to answer. I don't hold you responsible. And you ask how you didn't know? Because you weren't looking. Why would you? You were not part of the individual and collective psychosis, no, *evil*, evil that inhabited this place all those years ago. Neither was Abby. She saw us all shortly after our abominations, and she seemed largely oblivious, merely, and understandably anxious to get back to the warmth and safety of the camp.

'And as for you, tonight? Now you know the truth. All of it. I'm sorry if it hurts you, alters your memories of this place. I don't know what your recollection of here is, but I doubt if it can compete with the nightmares that have haunted me and the others, deservedly so.'

She was barely aware of what she was doing, but the mixture of self-disgust, guilt, anger, had finished her. Simon was holding her tightly as she broke down, the sobs shaking her entire frame. And then he walked her over to the bed, sat her down and backed away again, hands outstretched in a gesture of appeasement.

'I'm afraid there's more. As you know, Danny told Abby about what happened in Argyll . . . well, at least *some* of what happened, when they were both on the ferry from

Stornoway. Up on deck they had a fight. She pushed him, and Danny fell overboard. Ask *her*. Isabella told every detail when she ran to *her* for help.'

Innes looked to Alex, who nodded. 'It's true.'

Innes shook her head at him. 'And what about you? You fell . . . from your garden?'

He offered her a bitter, triumphant smile. 'I called Alex. I wanted to have it out. Later, I went into the garden to get some air. I was upset . . . I'd been reading some of my journal . . . about when Abby died. I know now what happened to me. Alex must have arrived earlier than we'd arranged. Maybe even seen me go down the garden. Or perhaps she went into the house looking for me, saw I wasn't there and then went outside. The night was stormy, and I couldn't hear anything but the sea and the wind. She's a strong woman. I was leaning over the sea-wall at the end of the garden. Next thing I knew she had grabbed my ankles and toppled me on to the rocks below. But I managed to land on the sand. I was shaken but okay. I knew from that point onwards that we were into the end game. I laid low to make her think she was safe and that I was out of the way. By the time I'd climbed back up to the house, she was long gone, but she'd been in my house and found my journal with my innermost thoughts about all this. But I couldn't worry about that then. I took clothes and other things that I needed and went into hiding for a very short time in an out-of-the-way hotel far north, just outside Aberdeen. I made my plans. And here we are.'

He felt on the verge of exhaustion. He checked his watch. Not much time left. He looked at Innes. She'd just about had it. But he wanted her to know one final thing. 'I'm sorry for this but there is one thing else. Lydia.'

Innes frowned. 'She killed her entire family?'

He returned her shake of the head with his own. 'No, I have my suspicions.' Innes watched his gaze turn to Alex. 'I think you should ask *her* about that.'

He flung an acid glance at Alex.

Innes stood up again, spinning round, looking first at Alex, then back at him. 'Alex? Tell me? Did you?'

But Alex was screaming now. All control gone. 'She was an interfering little bitch!' Innes moved closer as Alex let out a sharp staccato laugh and wiped more blood from her mouth with the back of her chained hand. 'Do you think for one fucking minute that I was going to allow *her* to ruin my life? Sneaky cunt! Oh, yes, I went to see her. She tried it on. Her old tricks. Putting the pressure on. Trying to freak me out. Well, I sorted her, one way or another. Torched her life away!'

Innes could feel her chest tighten, but she was determined to rasp out the words. 'No, Alex. Not that. You didn't do that. The whole family!'

Then she felt herself uncontrollably flinging her entire weight at Alex, punches smashing into the already bloodied face, releasing what she knew were twenty-six years of pent-up fear and anger at the Alex of old. The intimidating, threatening and at times downright terrifying Alex of old. Only now, in her own act of involuntary but irresistible violence, was Innes able to make sense of the Alex she remembered from the Unit. The toxic atmospheres she had carried with her from room to room, situation to situation. The vicious threats and sneers. But most of all, and shamingly so, Innes knew she was lashing out through anger at herself. At her asinine inability to have read anything of the truth in the Unit. The punches she was raining down on Alex's face might well have been directed at her own wretched, useless self. And suddenly Innes stopped, staggering back a few steps, head bent forwards, staring at her bloody fists. The wine-glass scar had reopened fully now, trickling its red trail to meet the mess punched from Alex's face.

Next, she was aware of Simon standing behind her; she felt first his grip on her arm, and then a stronger embrace. 'That's enough. It's time now.' She stepped away to look at him, tears sliding down his cheeks. He stood in the middle of the floor, hands limply by his side now, the rangy frame sagging. 'I'm sorry.'

His hand was on Innes's arm again as he steered her to the door. She glanced over her shoulder and saw Alex pulling futilely at her bonds.

'*No! No, don't! Innes! Don't leave me! Come back. Please!*'

Innes felt his warm breath on her cheek as he bundled her out of the room. 'Don't let me have to use force again. Go on. There's nothing to worry about. It's going to be okay.'

'*No, Innes, no!*'

But he'd closed the door and was ushering her downstairs. 'Keep going please.'

She noticed again the matrix of scaffolding as he hurried her down the stairs. Once on the ground floor, she stopped at the entrance to the huge psychodrama room. She glanced at him and he gave her a single, knowing nod. It was too dark to see much, but she felt its space. Heard its echoes. Its memories. Its psychodramas. The Christmas party. The raffle. It all made sense now. A 'joke'. A macabre joke at Alex's expense.

'Please. Keep moving.'

He was at her heels, marching her along the final corridor, past the old study room, past the old Nurses' Office. For some reason she thought he was taking her to the kitchen. Why, she didn't know. Then, with a speed that took her by surprise, he grabbed her arms and pushed her through the main door into the cool, refreshing air of outdoors. The door slammed tight after them.

Standing outside in the orange glow of distant street lamps, she looked at his face. It was haggard, exhausted. 'What? Why are we out here again?'

In answer, he slipped a white envelope from his inside pocket. 'Abby sent me something before she died. I'm so glad I decided to see her . . . I . . . I wasn't going to . . . but look, she sent me this. It's for you. She'd apparently hung on to it, wanting to send it and then not. Here. Take it. Read it later. Take this too. It's the same as the package that I've sent to my colleague, Dr Sheena Logan. I made a spare to leave here. Just in case. But I know you'll know what to do with it. And now please, get away from this building immediately. You shouldn't come back. Forget about this place. For ever. I'm going to.'

He opened the door and let the Unit swallow him up again. The door slammed behind him and the lock scraped into place before she had a chance to question him any further. She looked down at the smaller envelope. It was blank and sealed. Stuffing it and the package into the front of her jacket, she moved round the side of the house and over the stone wall, looking for a way back in. Only now, out in the freshening air of the night, did she start to hear what had, in essence, been Simon's subtext, his secondary message. He was going to do something irrevocable. She had to get back in. Talk to him. Reason with him. Whatever he had planned for Alex, for himself, she needed to get him to think again.

She staggered up the incline of grass that led to the psychotherapy room bay windows. Entry was impossible:

all the windows along that side of the house were either barred or shuttered. She changed tack and sprinted back from where she'd come, passing the door she'd just exited, and made it to the adjoining single-storey annexe. Again, all seemed impenetrable. She jogged round the back of the building. There was a frosted window. A toilet. It didn't seem barred and was, maybe, big enough for her to get through. She foraged about at the edge of the garden. There were a couple of stones. One looked as if it might do it. She pulled her sleeve about her hand and then swung the stone. The window gave a crack but didn't shatter. Again. And one more time. If he heard, too bad. There was an actual hole in the glass now, and she kicked at it with her foot. It was the best she could do in the time. Carefully she eased herself through, catching her jacket and ripping it. Otherwise, she was okay. She jumped down into the toilet cubicle and then made her way through the wash area and found herself in the hallway of the annexe. The main Unit building was to her right. She could see the adjoining glass doors. What if they were locked? She'd just have to break them. But luck was with her. They pushed open. Then she found herself outside the old Nurses' Office. There was still no sound of the others. She started moving up the stairs, trying to look up through the stairwell to the top floor. But the scaffolding . . . what was it . . . yes, painters' scaffolding. Reaching all the way up to the ceiling. She quickened her pace. Floor one. Jog, jog, jog. Floor two, jog, jog, jog. And then she heard it. A steady creaking. As she reached the top landing, she saw them, clearly in view, the lamp-light from the bedroom flooding out to where they hung. Simon had, of course, gone last, his long body still penduluming, and the faintest of twitching still evident in the limbs. The face was in shadow, and she made no attempt to gauge its expression. Alex was almost still. Again, Innes shied away from looking at the face. Both nooses – made from climbing rope, she noticed – made a steady creaking noise as they stretched themselves against the scaffold poles.

She sighed, no longer confused, no longer afraid. The final executions had been carried out.

52

She'd arranged to meet Sarah Melville at the Unit at noon. Noon, November 8th. A deliberate choice, which both understood. The snow had made the garden beautiful and quiet.

'Will you walk with me to the swing?'

Sarah nodded. They made the two-minute journey in silence, the scrunching of their boots the only sound. Innes wiped the swing's seat clear and sat down, rocking gently as she watched an anxious and sad-looking Sarah. 'You okay?'

Sarah was trying a smile at her. 'Yeah, fine. Just a bit tired. But *you* look well. That's quite a tan for our winter.'

Innes smiled back. 'Yes, it is. I've been away for a few months. Sun and peace. I feel better for it.' She nodded up the hill towards the old house. 'What's the latest then, about that?'

She watched as Sarah made a cursory clean of a nearby bench with her mittened hand and sat down to face her. 'The hospital are in a bit of a pickle. Simon left the Unit building, which he'd bought outright, *and* a substantial amount of money to re-open the place as an adolescent unit. He wanted it to be named the Hamilton Memorial Unit. They're conferring with lawyers at the moment about what to do. But they're stuck. They'd love to open the place up but think of the PR disaster if, *when*, it all comes out. The police are looking into things, as you well know. That's never-ending as far as I can see. It's a bloody mess.'

Innes stopped her rocking. 'And?'

'And, he even suggested that he wanted me, *me* to have a senior role in the new unit. Unbelievable.'

Innes smiled at her. 'Is it? Seems to me he was just trying to make amends all round, as if that were possible. Though I reckon you'd be rather good at running a new unit.'

Sarah was shaking her head. 'No. No, never. I don't believe in those sort of therapeutic communities any more. They don't work. They're just too dangerous.'

'Oh, come on. Our intake was different. That's the whole point.'

But Sarah was giving her another emphatic shake of the head. 'I'm sorry. I'm just not convinced. Look, Innes, I've not got much time. I just wanted to see you and say hello. I've got to be getting on. It's been good to see you on and off these past months. I'll let you know how things pan out up here. I've got your contact details. I promise, I'll let you know.'

Innes could sense her urgency to be away. Sarah, the few times they'd met since it happened, had always seemed uncomfortable, uneasy, and she couldn't pin down why. Couldn't put her finger on it. Maybe Sarah felt somehow responsible, though she wasn't. How could she be?

'Okay, you'd better go. Oh, and *I'll* get in touch with you. I'm leaving London. I'm coming back to live in Scotland. Somewhere by the sea. Don't know about work, but I'll sort something out. I can't just go back to my other life. It's gone. Anyway, speak to you in a while. Goodbye, Sarah, and take care.'

Sarah's sobs filled the car. She'd scurried up the garden as fast as she could, terrified that Innes would notice the tears starting. That was the final nail: Innes, who had so obviously flourished these past months from having faced up to her demons from the Unit past. She looked well, happy even, and serene. She was going to have a new life. And what of her own? Since the hangings and the whole appalling story coming to light, she hadn't had one night's natural sleep.

She had confided in no one. Told the police lies. And this constant toing and froing of questions in her mind. Which had been the worse transgression? Having an affair with Alex? Or disbelieving and ignoring her story about the two children on the camping holiday? And why had she ignored it? Simple. She'd been more concerned about Alex's levels of distress *and* the worry about their relationship being exposed than listening, *really listening*, to what was behind Alex's story of a bit of sadism, frightening a couple of kids with a knife. And that was all that was admitted to, though it was surely bad enough. She knew she should have told the other staff about the story, whether she thought it true or not. She should have written it up in the daily report. She should have offered it up at the next case conference. Then they all could have looked into it more. But no, she chose to ignore it. And she knew the reason why. To save her own skin, to prevent any uncomfortable issues about she and Alex coming out. That last period with Alex in the Unit had been the worst. She'd taken weeks of sick leave to avoid her. Had herself been buried in depression and withdrawal. And then it was time for Alex to be discharged. The relief!

After that, what had she done? Blithely got on with her life. But now . . . how could she go merrily on? Oh, God . . . she would end up insane at this rate. Or finish up like Simon and Alex. Fitting perhaps.

She started the car and, with a backward glance at the Unit, drove off, guilt eating away at her heart, and her future.

Innes heard the sound of Sarah's car as it moved off and then leaned back on the swing, enjoying the silence again.

She tipped her head back as far as it would go, feet straight out in front. She remembered seeing Carrie doing this very same thing on this very same swing that first day. She smiled to herself. *So what?* And then the unsettling image of Lydia in the hospital grounds, also on a swing, washed across her previous memory. That one couldn't be shrugged off so easily. She had resolved to keep visiting Lydia, who sometimes did and sometimes didn't know her. But Innes had decided. She was going to buy somewhere to live along the coast near Lydia's clinic, so why shouldn't she see what she could do for her?

And who else had loved the swing? Of course.

She pulled off her gloves and reached inside her pocket. The envelope was more crumpled every time she looked at it. But then it had travelled a long way. From London to Scotland and into Simon's care. Back to her own home in London. On to her sun-soaked paradise. And back here again. A talisman? A mark of recompense? She pulled out the sheets again.

My Dearest Innes

It is highly unlikely that I will ever send this letter to you since it is over two weeks since I tried to get in touch with you and you have not returned my call. But I will write it anyway, as a form of catharsis if nothing else. But who knows? I might yet raise the courage to send you this.

I am sure that my call must have come as the severest shock. A ghost from your past. A past that maybe you have long buried. I know little of your life except that you live near me – how strange that feels. I wonder if we have passed in the street. Sat opposite each other in a café. Sat beside each other in the theatre. I have in recent weeks fantasized about you walking into my dental surgery!

To explain why I wanted – needed – to see you again after all these years is a tale too long and too painful for me to outline here. I suspect that, given time, the truth will out. You may one day hear from Simon, remember Simon Calder? If you do, listen to him. All you need to know at present is that something terrible came out of our time in the Unit. And something good was lost. My friendship with you was lost. I'm not quite sure how that happened. It was my fault and I think it was because I 'shut down' in the Unit. Wilfully became blind to others, including you, Innes.

Who knows, maybe if I'd acted differently maybe we would be friends today. Whatever might have been, I think it is significant that I turned to you recently when my Unit past came back to haunt me. I am sorry, though unsurprised, that you didn't respond.

I wish to remain oblique about why I felt the need to contact you just in case you remain untouched by the past, and the truth either does not emerge or does not reach you. However, I fear Simon will have pursued matters by now and nothing will be left to chance. Whatever he does I can never judge him. Nor should you. He will be judged by a higher authority, I feel.

I plan to take my own action because, essentially, I am a coward. The other Unit patients have or will find their own way. Alex, without doubt, can take care of herself. I met Alex recently. A deeply unpleasant experience. She has taken to keeping in touch and visiting me regularly. She has been scared, yes, scared, about me. That is why she has been so attentive. She should be scared. And for ever ashamed. I grieve for Lydia and her family. I pity Simon's children. This may all be meaningless to you. If it is, ignore it. If not, then take heed of what I say.

There is only one thing that I feel you must know, Innes. Perhaps the most important thing of all. Twenty-six years ago I fell in love with Danny Rintoul. A rapist. Twenty-six years on I fell in love with him again and pursued the desires I could never have then. I thought him a fine, loving man. I even thought mad thoughts of marriage, living with him in his idyllic home in the Hebrides.

And then he told me. Told me about the unspeakable act of evil he committed – and in which I now know the others were involved – that wretched day in 1977. Many, many things passed through my mind the moment after he told me. One of the lasting ones is my role in it. I should never have walked away. Maybe I could have stopped it. Maybe Danny would have if I had asked him. But I didn't try hard enough. Despite everything he did, I know he loved me then as he has loved me of late. My very presence could have stopped him, and he, in turn, would have stopped the others. That one, single act of omission makes me as guilty as the others. Perhaps more so.

We fought the day he told me. Fought on the ferry boat from Stornoway. I hit him. He told me how he'd begged for forgiveness. He'd been thinking of going to church, asking for redemption from a God he'd never before believed in. That seemed farcical, obscene to me. I felt fury. Rage. I hit him again and again. Pushed him. He fell into the sea. I killed him. Maybe that was right. Just. Apt. But I will for ever regret that the last words he heard from my lips were 'I hate you. I hate you.' I did not. Despite what he told me. That apart, I have only one other abiding and inconsolable regret.

That of ever having set foot inside THE UNIT.

Your friend,
Abby

It was time. Innes slowly made her way to the top of the garden. The wind was up now, sleet sheeting down in diagonal waves. She stood with her back to the Unit and took a deep breath. With cold trembling fingers, she tore the letter apart, letting the wind snatch the tiny white squares away, mingling them into invisibility with the falling snowflakes.